SULTAN ROAD

David Celley

BookLocker
St. Petersburg, Florida

ISBN: 978-1-64718-695-1

Published by BookLocker.com, Inc., St. Petersburg, Florida.

Printed on acid-free paper.

BookLocker.com, Inc.
2020

First Edition

Library of Congress Cataloging in Publication Data
Celley, David
Sultan Road by David Celley
Library of Congress Control Number: 2020911984

Dedication

James M. Woods
Jude Sharp
Bill Buller

Dedication

James M. Woods
Jude Sharp
Bill Buller

CHAPTER ONE

Sultan Road wandered through mostly empty, dusty fields in a hardscrabble portion of Los Angeles County that was left behind while the area's abundant real estate growth ventured elsewhere. But it provided the perfect scenario for the largest act of criminal conspiracy and cover-up in Southern California's history.

At the Paradise Cove nightclub, about midway down Sultan Road near Sepulveda Boulevard on the Thursday night before Memorial Day weekend, a slender Asian woman on her way to the ladies room accidentally brushed past a much larger Latina. The larger woman turned around quickly. A few words were exchanged, and then the Asian woman continued toward the ladies' room, only to be shoved from behind onto the floor by the larger woman. The Asian woman got back up and stared at the Latina. A few more words were exchanged, and then the larger woman grabbed her, punched her, and pushed her into a nearby table. The fight continued with another Latina joining in, grabbing the Asian woman and pinning her arms behind her.

Within seconds, all eyes in the nightclub were focused on the women as they slugged it out. Then the crowd surrounding the combatants spontaneously surged toward the side door exit that led to the parking lot. The lopsided fight continued with the hapless Asian woman beaten to the ground and kicked repeatedly. Suddenly, two men stepped into the middle of the fracas and pushed the assailants out of the way. One of the men announced that the victim was seriously hurt and needed to go to the hospital. In the middle of jeering and cursing by the two Latinas—along with some of the crowd—the two men carefully picked up the Asian woman and carried her to a pickup truck. They placed her gingerly in the truck's bay before driving off.

Just before eight o'clock the next morning, an office worker parked her car in the lot of the multi-story office building where she worked. She noticed a shoe protruding from underneath a branch of some bushes. As the shoe seemed out of place, she decided to take a closer look. When she reached down to pick it up, she let out a loud scream. The shoe was attached to the foot of a young Asian woman.

One of her office colleagues, who was on his way into the building, dashed over to see what had happened. She pointed to the shoe. Barely visible beyond the branch lay the mangled remains of a human body. Much of the female victim's torso had been smashed and crushed into a bloody mess. Only half of the victim's head appeared to be intact. The initial shock was unnerving to the woman. Even worse was the terrified look on the victim's face as if she had been abused or tortured before being bludgeoned to death. The colleague called 911, and the two remained at the scene until the police arrived.

The first responders cordoned off the area as a potential crime scene. A short while later, Detective Sergeant Carlos Aguilar of the LAPD Harbor Gateway Division arrived with his partner, Officer Harry Lee. Although standing only five feet ten inches tall, Aguilar had a rugged and sturdy build. An eighteen-year veteran of the police force, he had worked homicide for the last eleven years. Even all he encountered during that time (plus five years of boxing as a middleweight) couldn't prepare him for what he saw. As he stared at the victim's remains, his mind was actively churning.

"It doesn't appear that the victim put up much of a struggle," Aguilar said, while Officer Lee stood nearby.

The office building was six stories high and had a layer of bushes that surrounded the ground floor interrupted by an occasional palm tree. Officer Lee made a careful search of the immediate area for a purse, wallet, or some other item that might identify the victim. Afterward he said, "I don't see anything around here that could be helpful in identifying her."

"The question now is whether or not this is the crime scene," Aguilar said. "Or is this just where the body got dumped?"

Harry paused for a moment. At six feet, he was slightly taller than Aguilar. He was an immigrant from South Korea who had been in the LAPD for seven years. His given name was Lee Har-won which he changed to Harry Lee. He had been in apprentice mode for a year and a half, as Aguilar's job included mentoring him. "I don't see any blood other than the spot where the victim's body rests," Harry said.

"Look under that car," Aguilar said as he walked over to a parking spot a few feet away. Harry could see some red spots that were barely visible under the front bumper.

"Go inside the office building and find out whose car that is," Aguilar said. "If we can get it moved, we won't need to have traffic division come out and tow it."

As Harry went inside to look for the car's owner, Aguilar crawled back into the bushes and examined the corpse. The victim was fully clothed although her top was mangled along with her torso. Aguilar noticed that the zipper to her slacks was partially pulled down.

A short time later Harry returned with the car's owner, who promptly moved his car. Several spots of blood were revealed in the vacated parking space.

"We'll need to call CSI to get samples of that blood," Aguilar said. "They'll also remove the woman's remains without damaging any other forensic evidence. I want you to search the other side of this building to see if you can find anything that might be evidence as to who the victim was and how she got here. Whoever did this might have tossed her handbag into the trash or thrown it away somewhere."

While waiting for CSI, Aguilar took a statement from the woman who had discovered the body. After finishing his fruitless search, Harry used his cell phone to make a few pictures of the victim. When CSI arrived and began their work, the two detectives returned to their office at the Harbor Community Police Station in nearby San Pedro.

Logging in to his computer, Aguilar opened up the e-form that was used for filing a police report. A lot of routine details were required, and the two detectives filled most of them in. The exact location of the discovery of the body fell just outside of the LAPD's jurisdiction as the building and parking lot were actually just a few yards into the city of Torrance. To be sure about jurisdiction, Aguilar asked a colleague to verify if the spot was, in fact, outside of the neighborhood of Harbor Gateway.

"We found the body in a parking lot on the corner of Western and Carson streets," Aguilar said. "It was in the bushes, about one hundred feet west of the main entrance to an office building. Since the body was badly mauled and no sign of a struggle was visible, we believe that the crime was committed somewhere else and the body was just dumped there."

"Well it's definitely on the border with Torrance," the senior detective said as he looked at a computerized map of the area. "But if the crime scene was elsewhere and LAPD answered the call, you should mark it on the form that it's in our jurisdiction. By the way, you said the victim was female. Any pictures of what the remains look like?"

"Harry took some pictures, but he's not here right now," Aguilar said. "I can tell you that the victim was a female Asian. She was beaten into a bloody mess."

"The reason I asked is that we got a call about a big fight between two women last night at a bar called Paradise Cove down on Sepulveda. You should check with the bartender at that place. One of them might have been Asian."

Following up on the senior detective's tip, Aguilar and Lee visited the Paradise Cove nightclub just as it opened for the evening. Paradise Cove had its own building that was located in another large parking lot behind a much taller office building. The nightclub was set back from the street, making it less noticeable to passersby. The heavyset bartender with a short beard, who had placed the call to the police, explained that the fight started when an Asian girl walked past a couple of Mexican girls and brushed against one of them.

"It started out innocently enough," the bartender told them, "but words were exchanged and it escalated into pushing and shoving. I tried to get around from behind the bar to break it up. Before I could, some bystanders had pushed the whole mob out into the parking lot."

Harry furnished a picture of the murder victim. "Did one of the participants look like this?" he said. The picture showed barely enough of the victim's face intact to be recognizable.

The bartender looked at the picture and grimaced. Then he said, "I think so. I really didn't get that good a look at her. We have security cameras, and you can probably identify her from them."

Then Aguilar said, "What happened out in the parking lot?"

"I couldn't tell. Everyone moved outside so quickly. That's when I called the police. But our assistant manager might have gotten a look at what happened. I saw him go out the door following the mob."

The youthful assistant manager was available, and the two detectives interviewed him as well. "I got outside right behind the big group of patrons who followed the three women into the parking lot," he said. "They all stood around and watched these two Latina girls pummel the poor Asian girl senseless. I

started pushing my way through the crowd to try to break it up. Before I could get to the front, two other guys picked up the Asian girl off of the ground. They carried her away shouting to somebody in the crowd that they were going to take her to the hospital."

"Did you get a look at the two, ah, good Samaritans?" Aguilar said.

"I could only tell that they were two Latinos," the assistant manager said. "One was taller and had a ponytail."

"Did you get a look at the car they put her in?" Aguilar said.

"I couldn't tell. At that point, the crowd started to get rowdy. Some of the Asian and Mexican patrons were shouting, pushing, and shoving each other around. I had to devote my energy to restoring order until the police arrived."

At this point in the interview, a bar patron who overheard the conversation spoke up. "They beat the loving shit out of that little Asian girl," he said.

"Did you follow the fight outside?" Harry said.

"Sure did," the patron, a crusty looking white male of about age sixty, said. "Like I said, they pounded the Asian girl down to the ground and then started kicking her."

"Did you see the two men who took her away?" Aguilar said.

"One was a fairly tall Mexican, and the other one was shorter. The shorter guy didn't look like he was from around here. I mean, he didn't seem like your average, local Mexican."

Aguilar stopped for a moment to size up not only the speaker but also the comment. He didn't want to discuss being socially correct, but he did need a better description of one of the participants. "You mean he didn't look like a 'cholo'?" he finally said.

The bar patron looked back at Aguilar and then said, "Yeah, he didn't look like a cholo."

"Did you see where they took the woman?" Harry said.

"They put her in the back of a gray pickup truck and drove off."

"Where was the truck parked?" Harry said.

The bar patron looked at Harry as if he were dumb. "Down at the far end of the parking lot," he said.

Then Aguilar said, "When you were in the bar, did you hear anything said by any of the other bar patrons about what lead to the fight?"

"No. But when the shoving began somebody said, 'Watch out, Lisa'."

"One of them was named, Lisa," Aguilar said. "Do you know which one?"

"No."

While the two officers were talking to the bar patron, the assistant manager brought out a compact disk of the security video sequences. Harry then said, "Did either of you notice if anyone made a cell phone video of the fight?" He had realized that the security video wouldn't show what had happened in the parking lot.

The assistant manager shook his head.

The bar patron said, "No."

Both detectives then walked outside to take a look around the parking lot. "I wonder if there was any forensic evidence," Harry said. "This looks very cleaned up."

"I don't see anything," Aguilar said. "Somebody must have hosed the parking lot down afterward."

"I wonder why there were no cell phones anywhere making a video or taking pictures," Harry said.

"This place is on the border of some rival gangs—Mexican on one side and Asian on the other," Aguilar said. "If anybody had made a cell phone video of a gang-related fight, they might face retaliation."

"Do you think this was a gang-related fight?" Harry said.

"No, I don't," Aguilar said. "This doesn't have the characteristics of a gang fight. But if the bystanders thought that it was, they wouldn't have taken any pictures at all."

"This doesn't look like an ordinary bar fight," Harry said. "I mean, with the crowd pushing it so quickly out the door and into the parking lot where the security cameras won't see it. Two guys with a truck conveniently parked nearby step in and take the victim away. The crowd blocks the club assistant manager from getting a good view of events. All that seems like it was planned."

"Good point. But what you've just recapped is not what usually happens in a gang fight."

"If it wasn't gangs, then what was it?"

"I don't know yet. I'm concerned that maybe it was a professional hit."

"If it was a hit, then why did an apparently innocent young woman get beaten senseless?"

"To answer that, we need to first find out who the victim was," Aguilar said.

CHAPTER TWO

It was after the holiday weekend when the morgue called Sergeant Aguilar to tell him that the victim from the nightclub fight had been identified and the autopsy completed. There was little in the way of evidence to go on. But using fingerprints, blood type, dental records, and the portion of the face that was still intact, the medical examiner identified the victim as Lisa Nguyen. The breakthrough after a long weekend of work came when the victim's sister filed a missing person's report that included a recent picture. Aguilar picked up the missing person's report and called the sister, Rachel Nguyen Tran.

"Mrs. Tran," Aguilar said, after introducing himself, "I'm following up on the missing person's report you filed about your sister, Lisa Nguyen."

"Yes, please tell me. Have you found her?"

Aguilar always spoke in a low-key monotone despite the circumstances. Because he was often in deep thought, he rarely let himself get excited over what he knew or had discovered. For this communication, a deadpan approach better served its purpose. "There's no easy way to say this," he said, "but we believe your sister was killed as a result of some type of criminal activity."

"Oh! Oh no! This can't be true," Mrs. Tran said, and Aguilar heard her crying. After a moment, she gathered herself together and said, "Lisa would never do anything illegal."

"We don't believe that she did anything wrong," Aguilar said. "We don't know for sure how she died, either. But our lab technicians have a body in the morgue and they believe it matches up to your report."

"Oh, my God! Please don't let it be so." She continued sobbing.

After another pause, Aguilar said, "We will need you to meet us down at the morgue so you can confirm that it is your sister. And I want to say that I'm sorry for your loss."

Aguilar and Lee went to the morgue, that was located in downtown Los Angeles, to speak to the examiner.

"She has twelve broken bones and several internal injuries, including a portion of her lung that spilled out through her rib cage," the examiner said. "One side of the skull was partially crushed. She lost at least a quarter of her blood supply. Her ribs were crushed where her heart was located, and her heart and coronary arteries were mangled."

"Is it possible to determine which blow was the fatal one?" Aguilar said, as they looked at the cleaned-up body.

"You can take your pick," the examiner said.

"Her injuries are a lot worse than someone just beaten in a fist fight," Harry said. "Was a weapon used?"

"There's evidence of blunt force trauma especially to the head and torso," the examiner said. "Just what was used I couldn't be sure, but it was likely some kind of club."

"She was carried away after the fight," Aguilar said. "It looks like somebody tried to finish her off. Do you think that she was dead before she was carried away?"

"It's impossible to tell," the examiner said. "She might have received the fatal blow afterward. I just don't know."

"And you say she lost a quarter of her blood?" Harry said.

"At least that much," the examiner said.

"I wonder where all that blood went," Harry said. "We didn't see very much where we found the body, and there wasn't any at the nightclub parking lot."

During this interview, a reporter for the *Los Angeles Daily Journal* entered the morgue and introduced himself as Jason Phillips. At age thirty, he was young for a crime reporter. In physical appearance he was also quite a contrast to the two detectives—tall at six foot four, slim, blond, with a beach going tan. He was wearing cargo shorts, sandals, and a T-shirt with a large print of a surfboard across the front. His hair looked like someone had set off a tiny bomb in it and blew it up in all different directions. In contrast, the two detectives were neat and trim with business casual clothes and their badges hanging around their necks.

He was polite—just as Aguilar and Lee were polite—and he explained that it was his first assignment for a major crime story. He extended his hand to each officer saying, "You can call me Jay."

Aguilar was unimpressed with what he saw. But Harry looked Jay over more carefully as he didn't understand why the newspaper would assign such an inexperienced reporter to cover a grisly murder.

"Please tell me how the victim was killed," Jay said. He withdrew a notepad and pen from his backpack.

"We were just discussing that," Aguilar said. He gave Jay a summary of what had transpired thus far in the case as they waited for the victim's sister to show up.

"Can I have a look at the body?" Jay said.

"Be my guest," Aguilar said. He led Jay over to the examiner's table and pulled the shroud away.

"Oh my God!" Jay said. "That is just, like…awful." He stared for a few minutes and then started looking a little queasy. "Thanks. I've seen enough for now," he said.

Aguilar covered his mouth with his fist to stifle a laugh. Harry cracked a smile. "Are you…OK?" Aguilar finally said.

"Yeah, yeah, sure. I guess so," Jay said. "I mean, I was, like, getting a little weak at the knees. I sure hope all the dead bodies I see on this job won't look that bad."

"Some will be worse," Aguilar said with a small grin.

It was a short time later when Rachel Tran and her husband arrived. They were greeted first by the examiner, who led them over to the table where Rachel's sister lay.

"I must tell you that your sister was traumatized and badly mangled when she died," the examiner said. "It will not be a pretty sight."

Rachel looked at her husband and took a deep breath. "Okay, let's go ahead with it," she said.

The examiner pulled the shroud away. Rachel seized up when she saw her sister's body. She held her hands to her to her cheeks and staggered backwards. Her husband grabbed her shoulders and turned her away from the table. He pressed her body close to his. She gradually regained her composure and took another brief look. "Yes, that's Lisa," she finally said.

Rachel's husband led her over to a nearby bench to sit her down and help her recuperate. Aguilar went over to them and said, "I'm Sergeant Carlos Aguilar from the LAPD. I'm very sorry to meet you under these circumstances. But if you don't mind, I'd like to ask you a few questions about your sister."

Rachel looked at her husband. With his nodding approval, she then turned toward Aguilar and said, "OK."

Harry and Jay stood a few steps away but still within earshot. Aguilar began by explaining that Lisa was seen in a fight at the Paradise Cove nightclub.

"She was carried away by two unknown men from the parking lot, and her body was found in the bushes of an office building not far away," Aguilar said. "We are treating this as a homicide. But we wonder how she came to be in the nightclub, and why she would get into a fight in the parking lot there."

"I don't know," was Rachel's response. She held her head in her hands as she sat next to her husband. "Lisa would occasionally go out clubbing, but she almost never went alone. The last thing in the world she would do is get into a physical fight with somebody."

"Can we have her address?"

"Yes, of course." Rachel recited Lisa's address as Harry and Jay both took it down.

"Did she have any children or a husband?" Aguilar said.

"No. She was never married."

"How about her job?"

"She worked at Renaissance Estates on Sultan Road, north of the Harbor-UCLA Medical Center. She was the building's accountant."

"Did she have any problems such as angry or jealous boyfriends, drugs, gambling debts, large sums of money owed, or other similar issues?"

Rachel knew that the police were simply doing their job. But she became visibly upset by the idea that her sister might have been complicit in her own death. This pulled her out of her slump and she said, "Lisa was a kind, quiet, person who did not have a steady boyfriend. She was always careful with money, and certainly didn't gamble or do drugs. She kept to her job and to herself mostly."

"I see," Aguilar said. "Did she have a group of friends that she hung around with?"

"Yes," Rachel said. Her tired-looking eyes showed that she was worn out by the ordeal even though it was only late morning.

"I would like to get a list of her friends' names and phone numbers," Aguilar said. He gave her his business card. "You can email it to me when you have some time."

"OK, I can do that."

The examiner returned Lisa's body to the storage drawer. Then he took the sister and her husband to the office to complete the paperwork to claim it.

On their way back to the parking garage, Aguilar turned to Jay and said, "Well, Newsboy, now you know all that we know about this case."

"Thanks, Sergeant Aguilar. By the way, can I get one of those business cards of yours?"

Aguilar gave him one. "Now, don't forget to use this," he said. "Let me know anything you find out about this case no matter how trivial. Little things could turn out to be very important."

"Oh, totally. I'm good at staying in touch. I, ah, like, don't have my own business cards." Jay wrote down his cell phone number and email address onto his notepad. He tore off the page and handed it to Aguilar. "That's my cell number. You can reach me anytime—I always have it with me."

"It would help matters if you would tell one of us when your stories hit the papers," Harry said.

"Sure, I can do that."

When they walked through the door of the building that led to the parking garage, Aguilar said, "Uh, Newsboy, just one question."

"Yes?" Jay said as he turned back around.

"What is that thing sticking out of your backpack?" Aguilar said. He thought he already knew the answer.

Jay was momentarily puzzled. He had to figure out what it was that Aguilar saw. "Oh, you mean my skateboard," he finally said.

"Your…skateboard," Aguilar said.

"Hey, it's, like, the way I get around a lot," Jay said. "It's faster than walking, and easier than running. See you soon, guys." As they had entered the parking garage, he pulled the skateboard out and began skating down to the end of the level where his van was parked.

Aguilar and Lee watched as Jay skated away. "So, the *Daily Journal* has sent us a bright, young, kid with a skateboard who is working on his first crime story," Aguilar said.

"Do you think his youth will cause us some problems?" Harry said.

Aguilar thought for a moment and said, "No, we won't let that happen. Besides, it's his first time with reporting on a crime like this. He might dig up information about this ugly case that will be useful to us. People will sometimes say things to a reporter that they would never tell the police."

Harry continued to watch Jay skate away. "I hope you're right," he said.

CHAPTER THREE

With the information he had gathered at the morgue plus the police report, Jay returned to the newsroom. He sat down at his workstation and filed his first crime story. By pulling out the facts and laying them down in the order that they were revealed, he came up with what he considered to be an objective piece that would fit nicely with the other stories in the day's edition. He knew there would be no conclusion yet as the police were only in the early stages of their investigation. Unlike his sports reporting or surfing news, this story would be lengthy and would need to be delivered in multiple parts. He thought he had everything he needed, so he filed the story with his editor, Meredith Williamson. A short time later, Meredith called him into her office.

Meredith was a senior editor with the *LA Daily Journal*, having nearly thirty years' experience in writing, editing and publishing stories in daily periodicals. She was old enough to be Jay's mother and had the rigid demeanor of a schoolmarm. "Now, Jay," she began, "Do you expect what you've written here to be published?"

"Well, ah, yes, ah, I believe so, yes," Jay said. He felt that a chewing out was on its way.

"You don't seem too certain about that," Meredith said. "What you've got here is a good collection of facts about what happened to this murder victim, but it reads very much like a police report. We could just as easily print a copy of that instead."

Jay considered that point and then said, "Well, it's, like, there isn't that much that's known about the case yet by anybody. I mean, the police are working on it, but it's complicated and could take them a while to figure out."

"So, it takes the cops a while to figure it out. What are we supposed to do in the meantime? We have readers out there who are interested in stuff like this. This story is the kind of project that could land on the front pages at some point."

Jay was accustomed to being dressed down by Meredith as he was by every other middle-aged woman from his mother to his high school teachers. Even when it came to surfing news—where he was very much in step—he felt as though no editor would ever like what he sent in. "What's next then?" he said.

Meredith leaned back in her chair. Although she was in her mid-fifties, she still had a trim figure, distinguished looks, and a sharp intellect. She removed her glasses and let them rest on the chain that draped around her neck. She looked directly at Jay and said, "What do you think the police will be doing next on this case?"

Jay considered this. "Well, I suppose they'll be taking steps to find the killer or killers." He didn't know what else to say.

"And if they are doing that, what should *we* be doing?"

"I have the phone number for the detective sergeant who is in charge of the case. I can just keep on calling him and..."

"No! No! No! You won't get anywhere in a story like this if all you do is rely on the police. Journalists are usually looked down upon by the police as being a pain in the ass. Some cops make a habit of telling reporters as little as possible hoping they'll just go away. Other times they won't tell them anything at all."

"Well, what should I be doing next, then?"

"You said that the police would be looking for the killer or killers. Why don't you find out more about the victim? By researching the victim's background, you might find the heart of a terrific story. In fact, the story of the victim herself may do a lot to reveal why she was killed."

After a moment Jay said, "All I really know is her name and where she used to work."

"That's a good start. Go visit her boss." Jay was getting up to leave when Meredith said, "And by the way, don't take this too personally, but you should wear something besides cargo shorts, T-shirts, and sandals when you interview. I know the 'laid back' look is in, but you represent the newspaper, and should dress accordingly. You don't need to put on a coat and tie—business casual is what most of us wear."

Jay, who was wearing a T-shirt with a surfer riding on top of a huge wave, along with his usual shorts and sandals, took a look at himself. As she hadn't mentioned his shock of blond hair, he quipped, "The next thing you'll do is tell me to get a haircut."

"How did you know that, Jay?" Meredith said, clasping her hands together and beaming.

After a visit to the hairdresser's, Jay's hair was trimmed and combed straight back. It was still long enough to droop around his ears, but he carried a comb to keep it as neat as he could. He also invested in a pair of khakis to wear along with a golf shirt that matched them. He swapped out his sandals for his deck shoes. It occurred to him that he might still need to upgrade what he wore, but he didn't have the funds to do it all at once. With one arm of his sunglasses tucked into the V neck of his shirt and his backpack in hand, he climbed into his ten-year-old van and drove off to find Renaissance Estates.

He determined from a website that Renaissance Estates would be near the intersection of the 110 and 405 freeways. But it was surprisingly tricky to find it without using his cell phone app. Exiting the freeway, he noticed the large, empty spaces on both sides of Sultan Road and remarked to himself, *this area looks desolate—like the desert. It's like nobody cares about it.* As he turned the corner onto Sultan Road, he wondered how close he was to the Los Angeles Harbor.

Jay finally located Renaissance Estates. It didn't seem to fit into the industrial area north of the San Pedro Oil Refinery. It looked like a well-kept secret standing alone in an area that was nearly deserted. He noticed right away that the landscaping had a good design and appeared to be well maintained. The building's style was Spanish Colonial, with rounded tile roofs, archways, and a courtyard in the middle. Comparing it to his own mid-century apartment complex in Huntington Beach, he thought that Renaissance Estates couldn't have been built more than twenty years ago. There was nothing but vacant land surrounding it, as if development planned to move in next door, but hadn't started yet.

When he entered the office and stated his business to the receptionist, he was referred to Rudabeh Sirianni, the complex's assistant manager.

"Hi. I'm Rudi Sirianni," the short, attractive, young lady in her late twenties said as she extended her hand.

Jay straightened up and his eyes popped wide open. He shook her hand and said, "I'm Jay Phillips with the *Daily Journal*. I wonder if I could talk to you for a few minutes about Lisa Nguyen? I'm covering the story about her unfortunate death."

"Sure," Rudi said. "Let's go to my office where we can talk in private."

Rudi led Jay into her office and invited him to take a seat as she pulled the door shut. "What is it you would like to know about Lisa?" she said.

Jay found himself lost momentarily while looking deep into Rudi's big, brown, eyes. Her jet-black hair, that extended to her shoulders and created a "frame" for her friendly smile, was complemented by gold, teardrop earrings. Like the other office workers, she was casually dressed. But unlike the others, she wore a slightly shorter skirt.

"I, ah, well, I just was like, wanting to know more about her, what, ah, type of person she was, and, ah…this seemed like the best place to start," Jay said with a grin. What he felt like putting in his notes was, *Wow, this babe is hot!*

Rudi smiled. Jay was a contrast to most of the men that she knew in that he was tall, blond, tanned, and quite a good looker himself. "Lisa was the property's accountant," Rudi said. "She managed the books and paid the bills, among other things." Under her breath she said to herself, *This dude is really good looking!*

"I want to say first of all that I am sorry about her death, but I've been assigned to the story," Jay said. "Getting to know about her will help me write it."

"We all loved Lisa," Rudi said. "She was quiet and industrious. She often was a big help to the rest of us."

"I guess you know that she was killed at Paradise Cove—apparently in a fight of some kind. Is there anything you know about her that would lead her into a situation like that?"

"No, nothing at all," Rudi said. "I don't know that much about her personal life. In fact, I'm a little surprised that she even went to a nightclub. She was so quiet."

"Did she have a boyfriend or a group of friends that she hung out with?"

"Not that I know of. I mean, she must have had a group of friends somewhere and probably went out with some of them last Thursday."

"Did she have any enemies that you know about? Um, like, did she owe somebody some money she couldn't pay back, or something more sinister than that?"

Rudi smiled again. "No, she got along with everyone—both inside the office and with the tenants."

Jay was taking notes on his laptop. "Excuse me for just a moment. I think I better set up my digital recorder for this," he said.

Jay then continued by asking, "Were you Lisa's boss?"

"No, not directly. The management of Renaissance Estates has been going through some turmoil lately. I'm an employee of a property management company that is serving in the role of a consultant and managing the buildings by proxy. Lisa worked for the owner of the properties."

"And who would that be?"

"The properties are owned by the Harbor Gateway Community Housing Corporation. The owner of that company is Erica Knight."

"After we finish here, would I be able to speak to Ms. Knight?"

"She doesn't work on the premises anymore. She was forced to quit working here, and had to turn her managerial duties over to us."

"Wow, that's something. The lady that owns the place is not permitted to work in it. Can you tell me how that happened?"

"Well, it's a long story. I think it's a good idea that you got your recorder set up because it's complicated."

"I've got plenty of time as long as you do."

"The problems that led to Erica's dismissal came to a head when HUD came in to audit the books."

"And HUD is?"

"Sorry. That's the Department of Housing and Urban Development of the United States Government."

"Thanks for that," Jay said. He scribbled a note on his notepad.

Rudi smiled and continued to speak. "There were a number of troubling issues relating to the management of the properties, but the one that stuck out the most was that twenty thousand dollars of rent money was missing."

"Oh my God, that's a hell of a lot of money. Did Lisa have anything to do with it?"

"She was not a suspect, but I think she knew who took the money."

"How did the money go missing?"

"The auditors never found out how the money went missing. But owing to this and other management issues, HUD forced Erica out and required the consulting firm to take over the management of the apartments. There was some confusion here among the employees about who worked for whom. Lisa was never formally told that my boss, Brendon Millwood, would be the new manager."

"Then Mr. Millwood from the consulting company is the apartments' new manager?"

"That's right. And Lisa still worked for Erica. The other two people in the office also worked for the consulting firm. When Erica left, I think that Lisa didn't have anyone else she could turn to.

"It makes me think that the person who killed her may have been covering up the theft." Jay said.

"I have a lot of trouble understanding why anyone would kill Lisa Nguyen. She was so nice and pleasant a person," Rudi said looking down and shaking her head.

To broaden his understanding of the locale, Jay changed the subject. "What kind of tenant lives in a place like this?" he said. "I mean, it's, like, out here in the middle of nowhere."

"Many of the residents here are senior citizens who live here thanks to Section 8 Housing. The rest are mostly artists, although we do have a fairly large percentage of residents who still have jobs."

"Section 8 housing? What is that, or how is it different from just a plain old apartment complex?"

"Section 8 housing is sponsored by HUD. The government pays part of the rent of people who are poor enough to qualify for it. That way the apartment complex still receives the same amount of rent as it would otherwise. The difference is that only a part of it comes from the tenant. The rest of it comes from the government."

"Wow, I wish I could get some kind of help paying *my* rent."

Rudi laughed. "You should see what it takes to qualify. Some of the people here are really old and disabled. Others are just plain poor. Erica set it up in the beginning to provide housing for artists."

"At the time that Erica and her company built this place, did she know that some of her tenants would be Section 8 housing?" Jay said.

"Yes. In fact, she arranged it specifically that way. Artists are often poor, and struggle to make ends meet. Erica's idea was to provide good housing for them so that they would at least have an affordable place to live. To do that, she brought HUD in right away. They provided the capital to get the place built. But they also brought in lots of rules, regulations, and people looking over your shoulder."

"You mentioned that she's not working here anymore. But does she still get a paycheck of some kind since she's the owner?"

"She used to receive a dividend from the profits the complex made. Even that has stopped lately since the place no longer makes any money. Why doesn't it? Well, we have all these consultants like myself in here trying to figure that out."

The conversation continued on the topics of HUD and Section 8 housing until Rudi offered to take Jay on a tour of the premises. Their first stop was the art gallery, that was located behind the office in the same building. It contained a modest display of fourteen paintings. Although placed in an unused conference room, the gallery applied both subtle overhead lighting and more direct light to each of the paintings.

"Wow, look at this place!" Jay said. "Are all these paintings done by people who live here?"

"Yes, that's right," Rudi said. "That's why we have this space used for an exhibit."

As they walked over to view an apartment that was open, Jay admired the landscaping. The grass was neatly cut and all the shrubs and bushes that surrounded the buildings were trimmed. Maintenance workers were painting the interior of the apartment for its next tenant.

"Well, I can say that this looks better than some of the apartments where I have lived in Orange County," Jay said. When they returned to Jay's van, he made a point to take another deep look into Rudi's eyes.

At the risk of being forward, Jay decided to ask her a personal question. "If you'll pardon my asking, you don't look like any of the Latinas I know. Are you from way down south somewhere?"

Rudi chuckled. "That's because I'm not Latina," she said. "I'm from Mosul, Iraq. I've lived here with my aunt since I was teenager."

"I *knew* there was something exotic about you!" Jay said. "I just couldn't put my finger on it." He pulled his sunglasses from his shirt and put them on. "And, I want to thank you for your time and help with this project I'm working on."

Rudi smiled and said, "It was my pleasure." She again offered her hand for a handshake.

Jay again took her hand graciously with a warm smile. He felt more like giving her a peck on the cheek, but knew that he needed to keep himself in good graces with sources like this one.

CHAPTER FOUR

They didn't have much to go on, but at least Aguilar and Lee had the security CD from the Paradise Cove nightclub on the night of the fight. In an unused interrogation room that was equipped with video machines, they patiently watched the fight sequences over and over again trying to evaluate what had taken place. Aguilar's goal was to lay out in specific detail every step taken by all involved in the barroom fight. In addition to operating the viewing machine, Harry had his laptop open and was laying out everything they discovered in his notes.

"Let's see that one more time," Aguilar said. "Start with the victim walking past the bar." Harry started up the machine in slow motion.

Recounting what he could see, Aguilar said, "The victim walks between the bar and some tables. There are several people sitting on barstools, in chairs, or just standing around. She walks past a large woman and appears to brush against her by accident. The woman turns around quickly. Now, stop it there."

Harry stopped the machine. Aguilar studied the picture for a moment and then said, "Move it forward one frame at a time." The first frame gave way to the next, and then the next. "Stop it there," Aguilar said.

He looked at the next frame and then repeated the same steps for a few more frames. At another stopping point, he said, “It looks like the Latina backed into her.”

Harry repeated the frame sequence. “I see that,” he said. “It’s very slight, but a deliberate move.”

“And it looks like the victim was trying to apologize, as if she had bumped into her rather than the other way around,” Aguilar said.

Harry ran the last few frames through again. “How can you tell that?” he said.

“By the expression on her face,” Aguilar said.

Harry ran it by another time. “I don’t see it.”

Aguilar looked at it again and then said, “Continue one frame at a time.” The physical contact was followed by another woman stepping up and starting an argument.

“Now the victim is outnumbered two to one,” Harry said.

“And it looks to me like the victim may have known the second person who grabbed her arm,” Aguilar said.

Harry looked at Aguilar and then ran the sequence frame by frame again. “I see her grab the arm, but I can’t tell if the victim knew the second woman.”

“You’ll learn to see little things like that,” Aguilar said. “If the victim was accosted and never lifted a hand to defend herself, it could mean that she knew the person accosting her. That might mean there was a motive of some kind for the big Latina to start the fight. It doesn’t look like it was an accident after all.” Aguilar continued to study every aspect of what he was looking at. “The two Latinas may know each other as well,” he said.

Harry updated his notes and continued to roll the action sequence forward. It showed that the large woman appeared to shout something and then shoved the victim into the bar, where the victim fell below two men who were sitting on bar stools.

"Now, watch this part," Aguilar said. "The victim is shaken up by that shove. She does not retaliate. She gets back to her feet. She tries to continue past the big woman but gets pushed backward toward the smaller one. The smaller perpetrator then pins the victim's arms behind her back, letting the bigger one rough her up."

"That means that the smaller one might have set up the whole thing for some reason," Harry said.

"Or the bigger one might have done it," Aguilar said. "I don't think we have enough yet from this to tell which one was the instigator."

The next sequence of the video showed the crowd in the bar gathering around the fight and quickly moving the fighting women out through the door to the parking lot.

After analyzing the last segments of the video sequence, Aguilar said, "You can start contacting the people on the list of friends that the victim's sister sent us. Find out where they were that night, what they were doing, and how well they knew the victim. Since she was likely not alone, then someone on that list might have been at the club with her."

Aguilar continued to watch the security sequence, spending over an hour scrutinizing every face he could see. Since the nightclub was on the cusp of both Asian and Mexican gangs, he hoped that he could identify someone with whom he was familiar. Finally, one of the faces caught his eye. It was a Mexican gang member who had worked with him in the past. He set up a meeting for the weekend in a public park with Guillermo "Chilo" Jimenez to learn anything he knew about the barroom fight, and any of the participants.

That Sunday afternoon, with Harry keeping watch from the car, Aguilar walked through the public park past several Latino families who were enjoying picnics. Some young men were playing soccer, and a few children were playing on the swing sets and slides. He found Jimenez sitting alone at a picnic table under some shade trees out of the way of the activities.

"What can you tell me about the fight the other night at Paradise Cove—the one that started between some women near the bar and wound up outside in the parking lot," Aguilar asked him, dispensing with an exchange of greetings.

"All I can tell you about it is that our guys had nothing to do with it," Jimenez said. "We don't know any of those women."

"Were you there just to enjoy yourself, or was there another reason?" Aguilar said.

"I was out hitting up on a chick. She had nothing to do with them, either."

"You saw the start of it pretty good. What can you tell me about it?"

"The Asian chick was just walking along like she was going to take a piss. Then this *gorda grande* backs into her while she was walking and starts shoving and smacking her around. Another woman held her arms back while the fat woman laid into her."

"Did you follow them out into the parking lot?"

"No man, I wasn't interested. I left right after that out the other door."

"Why did you do that?"

"I didn't want to be at that place when the cops showed up."

Aguilar summed it up for him. "You and I both know that the fight was staged. The victim got her ass beat by those other two women for some specific reason. The club sits in gang territory right between the Asian Macau and the Mexican Dark Horsemen. Nobody there made a cell phone video of what happened in the parking lot. What do you think was behind the fight?"

"I just don't know, man," Jimenez said. "It ain't us, that's all I can tell you."

"You told me that already. Now just scratch your head and think. Who was behind it?"

Jimenez took a deep breath and let out a sigh. "There's a gang up around two hundred and tenth street that was in some trouble and asked us for help," he said.

"What kind of trouble?" Aguilar said.

"They had some drug deals gone bad. Then a couple of their aces turned up dead. It looked like they were killed by accident. But somebody in that gang said that there's a *pendejo* working the streets up around there. I mean the guy was pure evil, from what I heard."

"Just another Cholo?"

"No, man. I mean this bastard was from down south in Mexico—way south, maybe Zacatecas. Nobody ever heard of him around here. Nobody knows who he's working for. He's made a lot of people scared because he creeps up on you and strikes in silence when you least expect it. We've had to keep our shit extra cool on account of him."

"Has he got a name?"

"He's just known as 'El Puma'."

"I see. Do you think that's why there were no videos made in the parking lot?"

"Yeah, probably."

Aguilar thought for a minute. Although he had arrested this contact some time ago for drug possession, he had decided not to prosecute the case. The price Jimenez paid was to help Aguilar out in situations like this with information. Occasionally Aguilar provided other return favors, or sometimes even money. Aguilar had no evidence that this contact had ever lied to him. In return, he never put Jimenez into any kind of compromising position, and had even protected him once during a drug raid.

"Do you know anybody who saw the fight in the parking lot?" Aguilar said.

"No. I mean, none of our guys were there, and the chick I was hitting on left when I did."

At that moment, they were interrupted by two young women who came by to speak to Jimenez. Aguilar remained cool, but the gang member became visibly nervous.

"Hi Chilo," one of the young ladies said. "I want you to meet my friend Lolita." To her friend she said, "This is my boyfriend's cousin, Guillermo."

Greetings were exchanged. Then the first young woman said, "Who's your friend?" and looked at Aguilar.

"Ah, he's, ah, he works with my father."

"I thought your father was dead."

"Yeah, I mean, like, he used to work for my father."

The young woman looked perplexed. The gang member was starting to perspire. Ever smooth Aguilar stepped in. He looked directly at the young woman and said, "About twenty years ago I was in the ring, fighting as a middleweight. Guillermo's father was one of my trainers."

"You were a boxer?" the young woman said, her eyes as big as oranges.

"That's right," Aguilar said. "I went eleven and three before I quit."

"Wow, that's terrific. Chilo, you never told me you had a boxing connection."

Jimenez started to speak but not much came out, "Well, I, err, ah, yeah, I mean…"

Again, Aguilar stepped in. "If I'd beaten my last two opponents, I might have been in line to fight for the WBC middleweight championship," he said.

After some more small talk Jimenez appeared to be back in his comfort zone. Then Aguilar said, "Guillermo, ah, if you find out anything else about this problem I have, please call me as soon as you can." With that, he said goodbye, and casually returned to the car.

Obviously thinking that she had interrupted something important, the young woman said, “I’m sorry, it looks like I messed up your conversation.”

“Don’t worry about it. It’s just about some business, that’s all,” Jimenez said.

On the way back to the office, Aguilar said, “The guy says there’s a hit man working the area near here. Nobody knows who he works for—only that he creeps up on his victims and strikes in silence. He’s called ‘El Puma’.”

“Is there any idea what he looks like?” Harry said.

“Mexican, from way down south. There’s no other description.”

Back at the office, the two detectives returned to their respective desks when Aguilar got a phone call from Jay.

“Newsboy! Talk to me,” he said. It brought a smile to his face that his hunch about Jay had turned out to be correct.

“Sergeant Aguilar,” Jay said, “I just want to update you on what I found out today.”

“Let’s hear it,” Aguilar said.

“I visited the apartment complex where the victim worked and had a conversation with the assistant manager. She told me that Lisa Nguyen was the property’s accountant. She was a very nice person who was liked by all, but she did have one interesting thing happen to her. There was an audit of the books by HUD recently and twenty thousand dollars in rent money was missing. Lisa was not a suspect, but the assistant manager said that she thought Lisa knew who stole the money.”

“Did she give you any names?” Aguilar said.

"No. But I thought immediately that this might have been a motive for her murder."

"Stealing twenty thousand dollars under some circumstances could definitely be a motive for murder," Aguilar said. "We'll need to know more about this, though."

"Well, I thought I should tell you that part anyway," Jay said. "Do you have anything for me?" He sounded hopeful.

"No, nothing from us. But keep it up, Newsboy. You're doing great."

After the phone call, Aguilar put a message on the message board and sent an email blast to all officers that worked the precinct. He wanted to interview any Latina who was brought down to the Harbor Gateway office for any reason, no matter how slight.

Harry turned around from his desk and said to Aguilar, "I can't find 'Puma' anywhere in my Korean-English dictionary. I don't know if it can be translated to Korean."

"Think, ah, cougar," Aguilar said.

Harry looked up the word "cougar." After a moment he read out loud what his dictionary told him. "A large cat native to the Americas that is secretive and solitary by nature. It is an ambush predator that prefers dense underbrush or rocky areas for stalking its prey."

Aguilar sat back in his chair for a moment, looking at Harry. "Put that in your notes, too," he said.

CHAPTER FIVE

Jay wrote his article based mostly on what he had learned from Rudi. He had a lot of background information about Renaissance Estates, Section 8 housing, and the character of the murder victim. However, the only piece of news that likely provided information about the murder was the missing rent money. A short while after he'd filed the story, Meredith called him back into her office.

"Jay, your story is deviating from its main thesis. All this about Renaissance Estates is interesting. But what does it have to do with the murder? The missing rent money might have a tie-in, but you don't provide one. Remember, you're covering a murder, not writing a textbook. I can't print this."

Jay mulled over what she said. Having experience in being criticized didn't make the process any easier for him. "There isn't much else to write about for now," he said. "I'm, like, trying to get to the bottom of it. But there's very little out there at this point."

"You need to keep digging," Meredith said. "Explore the possibility about the missing rent money as being a motive, for example. The characterization of the victim is good and will be helpful over the course of this story. We need to fill in as much as possible about why and how she was murdered."

Jay sat in silence. He wasn't sure where to go or what to do next. He could see that his first shot at a front-page crime story was not going as well as he hoped.

Then Meredith pointed him in the right direction again. "This person who owns Renaissance Estates, Erica Knight, go interview her," she said. "You'll be able to corroborate every point that you're making from your one source, and maybe shed more light on the role of the missing money."

Jay rose from his chair and said, "Got it. I'm on it." He then left Meredith's neat, ornate, upper floor office with the large walnut desk and city skyline view, and returned to his stark, ground floor cubicle that faced out of the window toward the parking garage. He spent much of the morning researching Renaissance Estates through the newspaper's archives. After a while, he found the article about the HUD audit. Reading through it carefully he discovered that the missing rent money was an afterthought. The thrust of the article pointed to a host of management and administrative issues that had plagued the profitability of Renaissance Estates. To his mild surprise, the article was filed away with a copy of the HUD audit report, so he dug into that also. A few of HUD's issues concerned financial controls, but most of the other issues pertained to supervising maintenance and office staff. The HUD conclusions were more concrete than those provided by the article. Both the author of the newspaper article and the HUD audit report said that HUD placed most of the blame for the problems at the feet of Erica Knight.

At this point, Dylan Claremont, Jay's good friend and former colleague from the sports department, dropped by

Jay's workstation to say hello. He stood next to Jay's cube, with his arm resting on the divider as he overlooked it.

"How's it going, old buddy? How do you like writing about murders?" Dylan said.

"Hey dude! What's up?" Jay said.

Dylan was six feet tall and had dark brown hair trimmed neatly around his ears. He wore eyeglasses giving him a scholarly look. He was also the epitome of a business casual dresser with a neatly pressed, button-down shirt, and equally neat dress slacks. His lace-up shoes, that were always shined, gave him the appearance that Meredith wanted Jay to aspire to.

"I thought you might be out surfing on a day like today," Dylan said.

"I did for an hour this morning before coming in to work," Jay said. "If this weather holds up, I might get another chance later."

"I've often wondered what you'd do about surfing if the weather didn't hold up," Dylan said. "This is June gloom, and it's only sunny in the afternoon."

"Fortunately, it is not always the weather that matters—sometimes it's the lack of surf," Jay said. "In my sport, I can only participate if the conditions permit it."

"Well, I just heard some big news," Dylan said. "The NFL is trying really hard to locate a team here in LA. All we need to do is find a good place to build a new stadium."

"Oh really?" Jay said. His interest was immediately piqued. "What about the Rose Bowl and the Coliseum? I think either of them would work, if they just had an upgrade."

"There's not only those two in consideration but also a few others," Dylan said. "There's a plan to use an old rock quarry in Irwindale that the Raiders were interested in at one point. There's another possibility on an old ranch in the City of Industry, and also a downtown site near Staples Center."

"Which one do you think they're going to pick?" Jay said.

"There's something wrong with each of the plans as they're laid out. The Rose Bowl has issues with noise that would impact the surrounding locale, and the number of dates that the place would be available is limited. The Coliseum borders on a suspect neighborhood, and the NFL doesn't like the idea of games being played there at night. The rock quarry is probably dead on arrival since the Raiders couldn't work that out before they left for Oakland over twenty years ago. And the downtown site would cause monstrous parking and traffic issues beyond what the city's infrastructure could handle. Even the old ranch has some problems since the overall property is a little small to accommodate a giant football stadium as well as parking lots."

"Can't some of that be fixed?" Jay said. "Big money can take care of a lot of those problems."

"For sure, big money could fix some of these problems. The question is, how big is big. Bringing the Coliseum or Rose Bowl up to NFL standards might cost as much as building a new stadium from the ground up. I've heard a lot of numbers kicked around that run up to billions of dollars. Now that's a hell of a lot of money to build a place for a football team to play about ten games a year."

"Well, there's always the government."

"Yeah, there is, except the state and local governments are damn near broke. That leaves it up to rich investors, and any really rich person who wants to buy into this will also want a piece of the team's franchise in return. No NFL owner would want to move a team here under those conditions."

"It's sounding more and more like the NFL won't make it back here after all," Jay said, sounding somewhat downcast even though he was not a particularly avid football fan.

"There is one other location that is moving toward the top of the heap, though. Mayor McGinnis wants the new stadium to be located on some vacant land north of Harbor City. Sultan Road, I think."

"Oh my God! Get out! You can't be serious," Jay said. He was incredulous.

"It's not official yet, but a source that I've got in the mayor's office tells me that there's a large plot of land available in that area, and that there are few or no objections to its usage," Dylan said. "And it's fairly close to the 110 and 405 freeways."

"You're not going to believe this, but the story I'm working on is headquartered on Sultan Road north of Harbor City," Jay said.

"No shit!" Dylan said. It was his turn to be incredulous. "You mean to tell me that brutal murder took place down there?"

"More importantly the victim worked in an apartment complex located there. I'm finding out about complications with both her employment and the management of the place."

"Well, this is interesting," Dylan said. He took Jay's backpack out of his extra chair and placed it on his desk before taking a seat. "What kind of complications are we talking about?"

"The victim was the accountant, and there was some money stolen," Jay said. "Take a look at this article from six months ago."

Dylan turned Jay's desktop monitor toward him and read the article about the HUD audit. "Did the victim steal the money?" Dylan said. "The article doesn't answer that question."

"Unknown, but it's not likely. The victim probably knew about the theft, and might have tried to do something about it. Anyway, it's perfectly clear that she wasn't killed because of an argument of some kind that led to a parking lot fight."

"We could be sitting on a major gold mine here," Dylan said. "A murder takes place on Sultan Road just before the mayor announces that he favors that site for the new NFL stadium."

"Yeah, all that sounds exciting, but there's one thing about it that's peculiar," Jay said.

"Like what?"

"Like this apartment complex. It's in the exact middle of a large area of unused space. If you surveyed the place, you'd see that it would be impossible to put a football stadium in there. No matter how you designed the stadium, the apartments would end up being in the way."

"Well, we'll have to wait and see," Dylan said. "My source tells me that's what the mayor wants. And since the other suggested locations are disqualified for one reason or another, that should give Sultan Road the edge."

"I can't understand it," Jay said. "With all the money there is to be made in this world, why would somebody want to plunk it down on an expensive stadium for a football team that he doesn't even own?"

"When it comes to the profitability of an NFL stadium, there are other things to consider," Dylan said. "There's rent for the stadium itself with parking lot revenues, plus opportunities for bars, restaurants, hotels, retail stores, and even office buildings—all of which could be leased on a year-round basis. The stadium and the team would be what brings the commerce to the area. It could wind up being worth a never-ending fortune to whoever owns it."

Jay pondered this explanation and wondered if he should try to put something into his story about it. Before he could decide, his cell phone rang. The owner of the car shop told him his van was ready to be picked up and then told him how much the repairs were going to cost. Jay hit the ceiling.

"Oh my God, eight hundred and fifty bucks!" Settling down a bit, he asked the owner how long before the shop closed for the day. He ended the call with a different look on his face than when he started it.

"Damn! My van is going to cost me eight hundred and fifty dollars! I thought it was only going to be like two hundred."

"What did you have done to it?" Dylan said.

"He said I needed to change the timing belts. But after I agreed to that, he later said that I needed to get a new water pump. All this happened when I just wanted an oil change and the usual maintenance like tire rotation and filters replaced."

"They like to do those things when it's an older vehicle. It should benefit you in the long run, though."

"How in the hell am I going to come up with eight fifty," Jay said looking straight ahead into a blank spot on the wall above his cubicle.

"All right, I'll loan it to you until payday," Dylan said. "How's that?"

"Wow, that's cool. Thanks! No one has a chance in this town without a working vehicle."

Dylan was married with two young sons. He and his family lived in South Pasadena, a quiet suburb north and east of downtown LA. Dylan liked to tease Jay about his marital status whenever he could. "Now, if you were married, you could just call your wife and she'd come and get you, plus give you the money to get your van back," he said.

"You make that sound pretty easy," Jay said.

"Or you could call your mommy," Dylan said with a grin.

"You know my mother doesn't drive," Jay said. He knew that Dylan was pulling his leg.

"All the more reason to find the right female your age to settle down with," Dylan said. "What about that surfing girl you were telling me about the other day?"

"Oh, yeah, you mean the real golden surfer. I just helped her learn how to surf, that's all. I don't have any time for a romance with her, anyway." Jay chagrined as he spoke.

"Maybe you should *make* some time. How does she look in a bikini?"

"She's really hot. But believe it or not, she made the greatest impression on me when I saw her the other day fully dressed. We were both in a bar down at the Hyatt Regency. She was wearing this colorful, flowing dress and high heels. When she saw me, she walked up to me while staring directly into my eyes, like a lioness stalking her prey. I have to admit I melted right on the spot." Going out with her someday was his fondest dream.

"I guess she must be the right girl for you, then," Dylan said.

"She has lots of good qualities. But any woman that wants to be involved with me is going to have to love water sports."

"Then she qualifies, doesn't she?"

"Yeah, she does," Jay said with a sorrowful look on his face.

"In that case, you need to ask her out."

"I know. But before I can ever get anywhere with someone like her, I've got to make it as a crime reporter. The rate I'm going, I don't know."

"Hell, man, you're going to make it," Dylan said. "You just need to stick to it. I'm always here to help whenever you're in a jam."

This bantering went on for a while longer until Dylan finally said, "Come on, let's go get some lunch."

CHAPTER SIX

Although Jay was still in contact with Aguilar to get updates on the investigation, Jay's tie-in to the case gravitated towards looking into the mismanagement at Renaissance Estates. His next interview would be with Erica Knight, the owner of Harbor Gateway Community Housing Corporation, that owned Renaissance Estates. To meet with her, Jay traveled to Erica's high-rise condominium in Long Beach.

After the greetings, Jay took a moment to look out through the living room window. "Wow! Terrific view," he said.

"Thanks," Erica said. "We're on the eighth floor here. It's not the top but it's high enough to see the ocean."

"I bet you get good sunsets up here," Jay said. He gazed out the window at a group of yachts in a regatta, with their brightly colored spinnaker sails decorating the skyline.

"You bet right!" Erica said. "Won't you have a seat? I'm going to have a glass of wine. Would you like one, too?"

"No thanks," Jay said. He took another moment to admire the paintings and photos on display around Erica's living room before sitting down. "Did you paint any of these?" he said.

Erica returned with her glass of wine. "No, unfortunately I only support the arts. I was never a terrific painter myself," she said.

"This one here is awesome!" Jay said as he looked at a picture set in a box frame. It was the scene of a forest during autumn, with the leaves on the trees turning different colors.

"That one came from Vietnam," Erica said. "The artist created the picture on a piece of fabric that was silk screened. Then a seamstress methodically stitched the entire body of the picture with different colored threads. The fabric is in the box frame to protect it from dust."

"I'm impressed," Jay said.

"Are you an artist?" Erica said.

"No, just a surfer. And now a journalist for the *Daily Journal*. I do like to spend time admiring good artwork."

Jay took a seat in the living room across a coffee table from Erica. He set up his recorder and pulled out his notepad.

"I've been talking with Rudi Sirianni about Lisa Nguyen and also about Renaissance Estates," Jay said. "Rudi says that Lisa originally worked for you. I wonder if you would describe your working relationship with her."

Erica was an attractive, middle-aged African American woman who still possessed the style and grace of a modern dancer. She demonstrated her gracious manner in the way she spoke, walked, and acted. Tall and slim, she was dressed in brightly-colored, casual clothes that had an African design. Jay noticed that she had tired looking eyes probably, he thought, because of the stress of the ordeal she was currently going through.

"Lisa was our accountant," Erica said. "She was both a wonderful person to work with and an enormous help to me personally as a business advisor. Not only did she keep the books, but she also pointed out areas where we were spending too much money for what we were getting in return."

Jay already had a clue to the answer to his next question but wanted to get closer to the details. "I researched an article that the paper published about six months ago concerning the results of a HUD audit at Renaissance Estates," he said. "Without naming anybody, the article said that twenty thousand dollars in rent money had disappeared. This seems to be in Lisa's turf. Can you tell me what happened?"

"Lisa came into my office one day and explained to me that some cash was unaccounted for. She thought that it had to be from rent money that had been paid in cash. I told her to do her best to figure out how it could have happened and not to mention this to anyone else in the office as it might involve one of them."

"Was she able to find out anything?"

"As far as I know, she was still searching for answers when she was killed."

Jay had scribbled some notes in advance for this interview and now he referred to them briefly. What he just heard confirmed what he had been told before about Lisa from Rudi.

"I read that the HUD audit took place about that time," Jay said. "A question came up that I hope you can answer for me. Was the missing money discovered by the audit, or was it the reason for the audit?"

"Lisa called HUD and told them about the money. She was required by HUD regulations to inform them of any sizable loss of funds like that."

"I see. Then when HUD came in to audit, they couldn't find out what had happened either," Jay said.

"No. But the need for an audit got them in through the front door. Once they were inside, they starting snooping around in other areas. They found procedures, problems, and several other items that were not to their liking about the way Renaissance Estates was being run."

"Do you concur with all the things HUD found and put in their report to HUD's management?"

"Definitely not. They were nitpicking about little things that they didn't understand or that they thought were not in compliance with HUD regulations. For us to have lived by the letter of the rule, it would have cost us so much, we'd have gone bankrupt and closed up shop."

"Rudi mentioned that a consulting firm was brought in by HUD." Jay looked over his notes again. "I think the firm's name was the Millwood Group. Were they involved before the audit, too?"

"Yes, the company is called Millwood Property Management. Brendon Millwood was placed in Renaissance Estates by HUD before the audit took place. DeShawn Walker, who's the loan manager for HUD, brought Millwood in to find out how Renaissance Estates could be made to be more profitable. Since I was being paid a dividend out of the profits, I was interested in finding this out myself. But it turned out that the channel of information only went one way—from Millwood to Walker. Not long after Millwood started this gig, Renaissance Estates began to lose money. This ended my dividend and eventually put me on the sidelines. Whatever it was that Millwood told Walker about the way I was running things brought about all the problems that HUD discovered."

"Didn't Millwood tell you about it all since you were the owner?"

"All he did was keep bringing in more consultants to look at this 'problem' or that one and try to make a fix of some kind. Before too long we had about eight or nine consultants working in an office of only five regular employees."

"And did all this somehow mean that you had to quit managing the place that you had built from scratch?"

"Yes. But what really happened was that Millwood and all his consultants just stabbed me in the back over trivial things. And Walker sat back and believed every word of what they said without ever talking to me. Eventually, Millwood convinced Walker that I had to go, and HUD sued to have me removed as the managing agent of Renaissance Estates. The judge concurred pointing to a little-used clause in the HUD loan agreements that stated that the owner and the managing agent of the same HUD sponsored properties cannot be the same person. The result of this legal action was that Harbor Gateway Community Housing Corporation was still on the books as the owner of Renaissance Estates, but a new managing agent would need to be appointed. The next thing I knew, Walker had appointed Millwood Property Management as the new managing agent."

"It seems like Millwood and Walker were dancing pretty closely together to get you out of the way."

"That's exactly the way it felt to me. I think I was somehow 'framed' as a bad manager. The irony is that the place was operating smoothly and making money, until Walker decided to replace me with Millwood and his associates."

"Does this mean that you were limited to doing nothing there but watching what Millwood and his people were doing?"

"Not exactly. Right after Millwood was appointed as the property's managing agent, I started doing as much research as I could to see where the problems were really coming from. Millwood was not present all the time, and that gave me a chance to find out more about just what the complaints were. When the SOB found out about what I was doing, he got HUD to obtain a court order that prohibited me from being on the premises at all."

"Were you able to find out anything that proved what Millwood was telling Walker was untrue?"

"I was only partially successful. To keep some type of access to the front office, I recruited an old friend of mine, Ben Williams—who is also a resident there—to act as president of Harbor Gateway Community Housing Corporation. Everybody that worked for me liked Ben, and would do whatever they could to help me through him. He had access to the books and records if he needed, and could maintain Harbor Gateway's legal filings with the state of California to retain 501 (c) (3) non-profit status."

"What was it like to get Renaissance Estates established in the first place?" Jay said. He was so absorbed with the conversation that he scarcely noticed his pen was out of ink.

"Well, it sure was a lot of work. Sometimes I would work until eleven at night and also straight through the weekend. The people at HUD were very helpful, but there was just so very much red tape to deal with. There was an endless stream of forms to fill out about my background, financial resources, and so on. I had been a probation officer for Los Angeles County, and I had my own counseling practice when I began this project. It was over three years before Renaissance Estates opened up. When we finally went into business, I came into contact with virtually every politician in the region."

"I noticed all those pictures over there of you rubbing elbows with some pretty high-up politicians," he said, while she paused for a sip from her wine glass. "By the way, is that you dancing the Flamenco in that other picture?"

"Yes, that's me. That was back in my days with the New Orleans Dance Repertoire. But that was a long time ago."

"How long have you lived out here?"

"I moved out here when I was twenty-five years old, and that was nearly twenty-six years ago."

"I see," Jay said. He continued to admire the pictures and paintings that hung in Erica's living room. "This is my first assignment as a crime reporter. If I can make it in this genre, I think I might like to become an art collector."

"It's given me a large amount of pride and satisfaction," Erica said.

Jay thanked Erica for her time and returned to the office. He played his recording back to transcribe it into his notes. As her story had unfolded, he had developed an even deeper interest in it than he'd had at the outset. *How was it that this gracious lady could be railroaded by someone in a government bureaucracy and kicked out of a once prospering business that she had worked so hard to build?* he thought. It was sometime later that he realized the entire interview, however interesting, only added marginally to what he already knew about Lisa Nguyen.

CHAPTER SEVEN

Aguilar was sitting at his desk when two officers brought in a heavy-set Latina and took her up to the booking desk. While she was being booked, Aguilar flipped through the pictures he had obtained from the nightclub security CD. The match wasn't perfect, but it appeared as though one of the perpetrators in his murder investigation had just been brought through the front door. While the suspect was being booked on a shoplifting charge, Aguilar walked over to get a closer look at her. Being satisfied that she was indeed a match to one of his pictures, he asked the two officers to bring her over to an interrogation room after the charges were filed.

Just before entering the interrogation room, Aguilar received a copy of the shoplifting report from one of the arresting officers. He sat down at the table opposite the suspect, while Harry stood against the wall.

"Your name is Maria Maldonado," Aguilar began. His low-key monotone sometimes caused the suspects he interrogated not to take him seriously.

"That's right," Maldonado said with the look of apathy.

"You're charged with shoplifting from Macy's," Aguilar said. "You want to tell me about it?"

"Who the fuck, are you?"

"I'm a cop working on another case."

“I don’t have to tell you anything, then.”

“You don’t have to. But I think you should.”

Maldonado was wearing a sleeveless top that displayed various tattoos on her arms and neck. Aguilar carefully examined those markings for local gang connections while he made some small talk with her. “It looks like about a hundred bucks worth of cosmetics you nabbed,” he said.

“So?”

“It should get you about two to three in Chino Hills. It’ll really mess up your career as box lifter over in Santa Fe Springs,” Aguilar said, noticing from the report that Maldonado worked in a warehouse.

“I don’t need to listen to this. What the fuck do you want?”

Harry started up the computer that turned on a monitor mounted high on the wall. The security CD showing the fight from the nightclub was displayed.

“Did you go drinking the other night at Paradise Cove?” Aguilar said.

Maldonado started squirming noticeably in her chair. The look of apathy gave way to one of intensity. “What about it?” she said.

“You and your buddy got in a fight with an Asian woman much smaller than you.” Aguilar said. Harry froze the frame and zoomed in to enable Aguilar to confirm the woman’s tattoos with the ones on the security video.

“It was nothin’.”

“Who’s the person with you there?”

“I don’t have to tell you nothin’!”

At Aguilar's request Harry ran the sequence a few more times. "That little Asian woman is about half your size, and it still took two of you to beat her ass?" Aguilar said.

Maldonado sat silently in her chair. Her fear level was rapidly rising however, made clear by the beads of sweat on her forehead.

"You don't want to tell me who your buddy is," Aguilar said. "In that case you'll have to take the murder rap all by yourself."

Maldonado began to breathe harder. "What murder rap?" she said. Her eyes were wide open and focused directly on Aguilar.

"The one I'm going to lay on you in just a few minutes if you don't tell me what happened in the club…and out in the parking lot," Aguilar said.

"That little bitch kicked me when she walked past," Maldonado blurted out.

"Oh really? Just when did that happen?" Aguilar said.

Harry ran the sequence frame by frame, displaying the exact series of events that clearly showed Maldonado was not kicked.

"I don't see where she kicked you," Aguilar said.

"That doesn't mean shit. You fucked that up by altering it so it wouldn't show," she said. Her tone was just short of a growl.

"Then the whole group standing around pushed the three of you all the way out into the parking lot," Aguilar said. "What happened out there?"

"I'm not going to tell you any fucking thing at all. You're trying to fuck with me with that altered shit. *Mierda!*"

"The Asian woman's dead body was found a few blocks away, dumped in the bushes next to an office building. Who were the two men who carried her out of the parking lot?"

"I don't fucking know about any two men in the parking lot. And she was not dead, either."

Aguilar then displayed a picture of Lisa Nguyen's badly mangled body from the folder in front of him. "Did you do this?" he said.

Maldonado looked at the picture momentarily and said, "Fuck, no. I didn't do that. That little bitch had it coming anyway," she said with a snort.

"Why did she have it coming to her?"

"Listen *hijo de la gran puta*, I just told you why. Maybe you should clean the shit out of your ears."

Aguilar maintained his cool. "You killed her, didn't you?" he said.

"You're a goddamn liar. I need to smack your ass right here and now."

Aguilar was seated, but Maldonado had jumped out of her chair. Her fists were balled up as if she were ready to fight. She did not know that Aguilar was at one time a professional boxer and still did not have an ounce of fat on him anywhere. Harry slid around casually until he was directly behind Maldonado.

"You want to poke me in the mouth?" Aguilar said. "What's stopping you? You're not in jail yet."

Maldonado started to lose control. "You're nothing but a fucking punk, a *pendejo,* that's all," she said. Then she swung her right fist directly at Aguilar's face. With the swiftness of a jaguar, he parried the punch with his left hand and grabbed her right forearm all in one motion. Using only his left hand, he slammed her right arm down on the table, causing her to stumble against the front of it. After a moment, Aguilar released his grip. While dealing with this assault attempt, he showed her his teeth in a fierce grimace, startling her. Harry picked her up and promptly put the cuffs back on her. Then he pushed her back down into the chair.

Unruffled by the commotion, Aguilar calmly said, "I'm going to ask you again. Who were those two guys in the parking lot who carried the Asian girl out of there?"

Maldonado didn't answer. Instead, she just stared off into the corner of the room. She was still breathing hard, but slowly began to settle down.

"The Asian woman was murdered—beaten to death by you," Aguilar said. "Now, you've got a choice. You can help me out by telling me who your buddy was in the bar, and who the two men were that carried her away. Or you'll be going down for murder all by yourself while they sit back and laugh their asses off."

Maldonado continued to stare into the corner of the room.

After a while, Aguilar finally said, "All right. It's back to the booking desk for you."

Aguilar charged Maldonado with second-degree murder. Believing that the charge might be hard to prove, he explained what he knew to Captain Bill Kreider, his boss.

Kreider, a crusty veteran of thirty years, didn't think Aguilar had enough proof for second-degree murder. He sent the two detectives downtown to seek counsel from the district attorney.

The district attorney's headquarters was in the Hall of Justice located just north of city hall in downtown Los Angeles, across the Hollywood Freeway from Chinatown. Built in 1925, the elegant old structure had recently been retrofitted for better earthquake protection. With the file of evidence in hand, the two detectives were referred to Richard Frederick, the assistant district attorney who was assigned to prosecute the nightclub case. Frederick was relatively young, but had spent his entire professional career since graduating from law school working for the District Attorney of Los Angeles County. His recent experience was mostly in violent crimes such as murder. His conviction rate was over eighty percent, that put him on a par with most federal government prosecutors.

After a cursory review of the evidence, Frederick said, "How are you getting a murder charge out of this? All we really have here is a barroom fight. We don't know if the victim was actually killed by the fight, by the two guys who took her away, or someone else."

"I agree," Aguilar said. "But we've got to hold Maldonado. She's not connected to any local gangs. Some of the tattoos on her neck might mean she's tied to a gang across the border. I'm convinced that she's protecting somebody else in this case."

"Do any of the witness accounts support a murder charge based on her actions in the parking lot?" Frederick said.

"The witnesses just vouch that there was a huge fight and that the victim was beaten and kicked senseless while she lay on the pavement. They also vouch for the two guys, who acted as some kind of good Samaritans, carrying her out of there," Aguilar said.

Frederick considered the file's contents some more. "Do you believe that Maldonado killed the Asian woman? Or was it the two guys?"

"Even the medical examiner can't answer that," Aguilar said. "The victim received some punishing blows to the body and lost a massive amount of blood. At what exact point she died might never be determined."

Harry added, "The suspect claimed that the victim was still alive when she was carried away."

"Of course, she did," Frederick said. "She knows she can't get charged for murder if we believe that the victim was still alive when she was removed from the parking lot."

Frederick thumbed through the papers in the file. Then he said, "The simple fact that the medical examiner couldn't determine the exact time the victim died might make it impossible to convict this suspect on anything more than aggravated assault." He closed the file and said, "We're going to need more evidence to make the charges stick. But for now, based on her actions inside the bar, I'll go along with a manslaughter charge. From the CD, we can see that she was violent and aggressive toward the victim. That will hold her for a while. But the time will come when we'll need to take what you've got before a judge. We'll have enough trouble convicting her for manslaughter much less second-degree murder." He gave the evidence file back to Aguilar.

After they returned to the office, Aguilar asked Harry, "Did you contact all the names on the list of the victim's friends?"

"All but one—somebody named Randy Vo," Harry said. "We tried skip tracing, but it looks like he must have left town."

"What do the other friends have to say?"

"They all liked Lisa, and were sickened by what happened to her."

"Could they account for their whereabouts the night of the murder?"

"All except for Randy Vo."

"I see. Take the list over to missing persons and talk to Sergeant Simpson," Aguilar said. "Tell Simpson we're trying to find this Randy Vo guy as a material witness. He owes me a favor, so tell him I sent you."

Before leaving the office for the evening, Aguilar received a call at his desk. It was Jay Phillips, who was looking for a story.

"Well, Newsboy," he said. "You might have hit the jackpot. We made an arrest today in the nightclub murder case."

"Outstanding!" Jay said. "Let me have the whole story."

Aguilar was no rookie when it came to dealing with reporters. He only let out the exact amount of information that he would expect to read in the newspaper the next day.

As it turned out, it was enough for Jay to put together a good piece to publish.

CHAPTER EIGHT

In Erica's mind, the decision to remove her as the managing agent of Renaissance Estates was done underhandedly by DeShawn Walker. She was determined to find out why. While discussing the entire case with her pro bono attorney, Kamisha Franklin, she reached the conclusion that she needed to confront Walker and get some answers directly from him. She set up an appointment with him and went with Kamisha to his office on the ninth floor of the Federal Building in Westwood.

DeShawn Walker, an African American, stood six feet five inches tall. He had played basketball in college for the Cal State Fullerton Titans, and he still looked trim and fit thirty-two years later. He had worked for the federal government for twenty-seven years, becoming the director of loan management for Section 8 housing throughout the South Bay region of Los Angeles County. This distinguished accomplishment was something that he was highly proud of. He always looked the part of a corporate executive—dressed in a designer suit with a white dress shirt and paisley tie—even though he was only a mid-level bureaucrat. The meeting began with the customary pleasantries but soon slid into acrimony.

"I've got to be point blank about this," Erica said, as she and Kamisha sat directly across the desk from Walker. "I need to know why I am being blamed for the missing money from my housing project when I had nothing to do with it. There was no real evidence anywhere against me. Moreover, I'm being blamed for a whole litany of managerial problems that allegedly were happening at Renaissance Estates when all the people involved worked for Brendon Millwood. So here I am being held responsible by HUD for the actions of people who were not in fact hired by me, but were brought in by a property management consulting firm placed on the premises by HUD."

"Well, you are responsible," Walker said leaning back in his executive chair. "When you're the property manager of Section 8 housing, you are always responsible, whether you like it or not. The consulting firm was brought in as a response to evidence of mismanagement at Renaissance Estates. Their mission was to install procedures that were consistent with HUD requirements for housing complexes of that size."

Erica listened intently, but inside she was spoiling for a fight. "For the nine years that I managed Renaissance Estates before Millwood came into the picture, things ran very smoothly," she retorted. "Now that these other people have moved into my complex's operation, the 'problems' that you are referring to are just starting to occur."

"Don't you think that the problems showed up because somebody else from outside your organization came in, saw them, and reported them like I asked them to?" Walker said.

"You mean frame me for it," Erica said, still seated, but poised like a panther ready to strike.

"Nobody's trying to frame you," Walker said. "We're just trying to get and keep Renaissance Estates on the same track as other similar HUD properties."

"That includes getting a court order to kick me out of my own complex," Erica shot back. "And that's where we're at right now."

"If you remember from the court proceedings, the judge pointed to a clause in the loan agreement that prohibits Section 8 property owners from managing any property that they own. This clause is standard in all HUD supported housing."

"Well, that's nonsense," Erica said raising her voice. "I can name several other Section 8 properties that do not have separate owners and managing agents. In fact, it is common in California for complexes like Renaissance Estates to save money by having the owner run the property rather than pay for an outside manager."

Up to this point Walker had been courteous. But as Erica became aggressive, that courtesy started to fade. "Yes, HUD can waive the requirement if the owner/manager demonstrates sound management practices that conform to HUD standards," he said, with a noticeable rise in his voice.

"You wanted me out because I never applied for a waiver of this clause? And this is after nine years of doing so well that the place earned money unlike most other HUD properties."

Walker's anger started to become more apparent. "Are you forgetting what happened in court?" he said. "We were working with Mr. Millwood to straighten out what we considered to be serious managerial issues. This alone isn't what led to your ouster. Missing rent money is an act of malfeasance that HUD cannot overlook. And this is why you were removed."

Erica's own patience had worn thin. "In other words, the court's judgment against me was the result of my being somehow tried and convicted of embezzling funds without any evidence being presented. For this reason, I believe my rights have been violated," she said folding her arms in front and staring directly at Walker's eyes. Kamisha nodded in agreement without saying anything.

"You were not on trial," Walker said. "Your managerial practices were."

"And I was framed by Millwood. Or should I say 'my managerial practices' were framed by Millwood. The nonsense that he kept coming up with is something I would never have expected you to believe."

Walker was chagrined, but said, "The judge thought that there was enough evidence in the case to show that HUD was standing on solid ground."

"You mean there was enough manufactured evidence to keep you protected while still getting you what wanted," Erica shot back. "Isn't that true?"

Walker refrained from answering that last question. He looked at Erica with a scowl on his face.

Erica told him, “If the missing rent money is the reason for my removal, then I deserve to have my own representative audit the books and see exactly how the money went missing and who was responsible for it.”

“I just finished telling you that the property manager is always residually responsible,” Walker said. “And I don’t like having to repeat myself.”

“And I just finished telling you that I was framed by Brendon Millwood,” Erica said as she balled up her fists. “And I need to be given a reason why I can’t have my own books and records audited by my own professional representative.”

“Well I’m afraid that’s a moot point now, isn’t it?” Walker said.

“It’s never a moot point if the truth leads to a different outcome,” Erica said, pounding the edge of Walker’s desk with her fist. “Millwood never audited the books for the missing money. He never tried to find out what happened—he just wanted to lay the blame on me. The HUD audit didn’t turn up any evidence of what happened, either. Now, am I going to get my own auditor to search for that money, or are we going back to court?”

Walker remained silent for a moment. Letting out a sigh he relented. “All right,” he finally said. “You can bring in your own auditor to look for the missing money,”

“And to obtain evidence from the books and records to refute all that crap that Millwood is claiming,” Erica said.

Walker glared at Erica as if she had stolen his lunch. After a moment he said, “I’ll need to know the names of the people you hire for this and the dates they will be present in the office. I will also need to know the scope of what they will be doing while at Renaissance Estates."

"And I'm going to need a written letter signed by you to give to Millwood that authorizes this to take place, so he'll get out of my way," Erica said, beaming with satisfaction.

Up to this point Kamisha had been busy taking notes. "I'll transcribe a copy of these meeting minutes and forward it to you," she said to Walker.

"Yes, please do," Walker said. "I will also need a copy of the audit report when it is finished. Now, if there's nothing else, I have another meeting to attend to."

Erica looked first at Kamisha, then back at Walker. "We're done here for now," she said.

Erica was short of funds and unable to hire a professional auditing firm to perform the financial review that she needed. However, she knew a professional auditor, Arthur Garfield, who was also an artist. Two days later she was able to persuade him to take on the task pro bono.

Garfield reported to Rudi one morning at Renaissance Estates, and was shown where the books and records were kept in the filing cabinets behind the new accountant's workstation. Rudi also set him up at an empty desk in the office and offered to help Garfield in order to expedite the process, but he politely declined. She provided him with a "read only" log in to the computerized accounting system enabling him to view, but not alter, any transactions.

Garfield had settled in and begun his audit when Millwood suddenly showed up. Millwood was middle-aged, not tall, and had small flecks of graying hair mostly around his ears. Although not really obese, he was overweight, and sported a pot belly from imbibing his favorite alcoholic beverages. Before he went into the real estate consulting business, he spent twenty-five years in the navy, starting as an enlisted man and reaching the rank of master chief petty officer. This erstwhile environment of dealing with sailors led to his disagreeable disposition which he demonstrated frequently. The commotion he made wherever he went was more indicative of his bark than his bite. It was rare for him to dress down a male employee, who was physically bigger than he was, although he often did his smaller female employees.

Noticing Garfield working at a desk, Millwood went into Rudi's office interrupting her meeting with another employee. "There's a guy sitting out there at a desk," he said. "Just who in the hell is he, and why is he working in this office?"

"He's a financial auditor," Rudi said. "He was sent here by Erica Knight to get to the bottom of the missing rent money."

"He's what?" Millwood said just beneath shouting. "Just who in the hell told him he could come in here and do that?"

Rudi showed him a copy of the letter from DeShawn Walker that authorized Erica to bring an auditor into Renaissance Estates.

Millwood put the letter back on Rudi's desk and said, "I want to see you in my office right now."

Inside Millwood's office, Rudi was told to shut the door. "Just how in the flying fuck does Erica get to put an auditor in this office?" Millwood said in full "bark" mode. "Tell me, how in the hell does this happen? We're busting our asses around here trying to improve the profitability of this place, and we sure as hell don't need anybody from Erica's camp in here, nosing around through our financial affairs."

Rudi had been yelled at before by Millwood over events that were out of her control. Although she strongly resented being singled out, she hated even more the way he treated his other employees, who were mostly female. She remained calm, though, in face of Millwood's verbal assaults. "If you like, I can call DeShawn Walker and verify…," she started to say.

"Leave him out of this," Millwood said, still with the bad temperament. "The farther he is away from this place the more I like it." After a moment, Millwood calmed down and said, "Just find that guy a place to sit that's not in the office. I don't want him getting too comfortable here. I want him to get his job done and get the hell out."

"I could put him in the conference room."

"Damn it, I just told you that I want him out of the office! The conference room is still in the office."

"There's the art gallery. Is that off limits, too?"

Millwood thought for a moment. "Take him over to the maintenance shop," he said. "Set him up on one of the workbenches in there."

"The maintenance shop?" Rudi said.

"That's what I said, isn't it?"

Many times, Rudi had to do unpleasant tasks on Millwood's orders while Millwood sat in his office and puffed on a cigar. As she turned to leave, Millwood said, "I want to know every frigging thing this guy sees, hears, does, and asks about while he's in here. There's nothing that he gets to send out to either Erica or Walker that I haven't approved beforehand. Understood? You're going to have to spend some time with him and get inside his head to get a handle on everything he's doing."

Rudi nodded and started to leave again when Millwood added, "Don't be so glum about it. To be a manager in a place like this, you need to know what's going on all over—especially when you have enemies like Erica who are out to destroy you. You'll have to learn about that before you'll ever get to be a property manager anywhere."

Rudi apologized to Garfield for the move and then helped him carry his records over to the maintenance shop. She explained to Juan, the maintenance man, that there was no place else to put Garfield meaning he would have to work in the shop for a few days. Garfield's workspace was now cramped with tools, spare parts, paint, and chemicals used in repairs to the complex. The shop itself was smaller than the office. But being crowded with maintenance items, it seemed tiny. The lighting was bad. The floor and tabletops were dirty and cluttered with equipment and parts. Besides Juan, two other maintenance workers would come in and out during the day, getting different tools or equipment. To carry out his duties, Juan sometimes had to use machinery that made loud noises. There was, however, a small desk in the corner that was fairly well lighted for Garfield to work.

Garfield soldiered on with his audit occasionally visiting Rudi to ask questions about financial procedures and record keeping. Millwood tried several times to get Garfield to open up about what he had discovered, but Garfield put him off saying the job was not complete. A week later, when Millwood was absent, Garfield wrapped up his fieldwork. He thanked Rudi for her help and left Renaissance Estates.

When Millwood returned a day later, Rudi told him that Garfield had finished and left the premises.

"Did he give you a report of what he found?" Millwood said.

"No, he didn't," Rudi said. "He said he was going to finish his report from home."

"Did he *tell* you what he found?" Millwood said with a dose of vitriol.

"He didn't do that, either," Rudi responded.

"Goddamn it! This guy came in here and dug up a ton of shit for all we know. And now he's going to provide our main enemy with the goods on us. Just what in the hell did he learn while he was in here? I need to know!"

Rudi stood in front of his desk and calmly said, "He was looking to see who it might be that stole the money a few months ago."

"And what did he find?"

"He didn't find out who it was."

"He told you that?"

"Yes, that's right."

"What else did he discover?"

"I don't know. I wasn't looking over his shoulder."

"Goddamn it! I told you we needed to find out what that son of a bitch was doing!" Millwood said. He slammed the pencil he was holding down on his desk only to have it bounce off onto the floor.

Remaining calm, Rudi said, “I might have learned more about all that if you hadn’t moved him into the maintenance shop. If you had moved him into my office, then perhaps…”

“Now wait a minute! Don’t lay all this back on me,” Millwood said. “One of the reasons I’ve got you in here is so that you can get a grip on what’s going on when I’m not around. I’ve got four other apartment complexes to manage besides this one, and I need help from people like you when I’m not here.”

Rudi remained silent. Eventually the storm passed, and she returned to her office.

CHAPTER NINE

The real golden surfer was never far from Jay's mind, because he had an eleven by fourteen picture on the wall of his cubicle of a beautiful young woman with golden hair surfing a pipeline. It was not his true amour—just a picture of a model who was surfing. But it helped provide him the incentive he needed to make the grade as a front-page journalist. He had a long life ahead of him. Like most other young men, the idea of settling down was important to him. He knew that he would never achieve his goal if all he could do for a living was write about surfing news or other local interest stories from down at the beach. The challenge of becoming a front-page crime reporter was in his lap. He just didn't know for sure where it would take him.

He was lamenting this situation when Dylan dropped by. "What's up, man?" Dylan said.

"Nothing much, dude," Jay said. "I'm ready to go hang out somewhere—like the coffee shop."

"I read your story," Dylan said. "It's pretty good, but I've got a couple of recommendations for you if you're interested."

Jay had trusted Dylan's advice since he began his career in the sports department. "Well, what have you got, then?" he said.

"Bring it up on your laptop," Dylan said. He pulled an extra chair up to Jay's desk and plunked down in it. Dylan started out at the top of the page. "The first thing you need is to grab the reader's attention," he said.

"I thought I had that down," Jay said.

"The newspaper is in the business of selling the news, and we need to gain the attention of as many readers as we can," Dylan said. "It starts with the first paragraph."

"Uh huh. I guess I could, like, uh, use a little help in that area." Jay looked over at Dylan with concern as he spoke.

"You should make sure that you have every point you're trying to make in the entire piece inside the first paragraph. The first paragraph should tell the entire story at a big-picture level of what's to follow."

Jay looked at the first paragraph, but did not see what Dylan meant. "I don't see what's wrong with it." he said.

"Look at the second paragraph," Dylan said. "This item you mention here in the second sentence is an integral part of your story. But you don't mention it at all in the first paragraph."

"Hmmm," Jay said as he reread both paragraphs. "I don't see the difference."

"You can't assume that readers are going to continue reading your story past the intro. You want to put it all up front to capture their attention. In the ensuing paragraphs, you can drill down to the details. After readers read the first paragraph, they will decide about whether to continue reading the story or not. You don't want to lose them in the first paragraph by leaving out something that might catch their interest."

"I see," Jay said, although he was still concerned. "So then, it's like, we're drilling down to the details in the paragraphs to follow after a big-picture view paragraph. And the summary is at the beginning of the article instead of the end."

"Yeah, that's it," Dylan said. "Only the first paragraph does not draw any conclusions like a summary at the end should."

"That's funny," Jay said. "It's the opposite of writing an internet blog. In blogging, you're supposed to provide your summary at the end."

"Maybe," Dylan said. "But you're not blogging. In blogging, you use something else to catch the reader's attention such as a headline in a Facebook or a Twitter post. Then you provide a link to the blog page. Here, we have to keep readers tuned in from the moment they pick up the newspaper or log in to the website. And by providing a summary, you might be drawing a conclusion of some kind. This is not your goal. You're reporting the news, not commenting on it."

Jay looked gloomily at his screen. "Do you think I screwed this up?" he said philosophically.

"No, man, of course not. Besides, Meredith won't let the paper print something that's screwed up. Just keep it all in mind for the next time. By the way, what do you plan to do next with this story?"

"Right now, I don't really know," Jay said tilting back in his chair. His eyes were still focused on his screen.

"From what I read so far it seems as though there was more to the nightclub ruckus than just a fight. People aren't usually beaten to a pulp in a fight at a bar," Dylan said.

"Yeah, I know," Jay said. There's got to be something else behind it. I just don't know what."

"You remember the mayor's plans for a football stadium?" Dylan said.

"Yeah, but don't you think that's a long shot?" Jay said.

"Maybe. But we need to explore the possibility of some sort of conspiracy. The woman that was killed must have known something important that involved people other than the killer."

"She was the accountant. And, there's the missing money," Jay said.

"There's bound to be something more than just some stolen money," Dylan said.

Jay hesitated for a moment. "I appreciate any more ideas you might have on the subject," Jay said.

"Another suggestion. You mention here that this Erica person made somebody named Ben Williams president of the company since she was barred from working in the office herself. Have you talked to him yet?"

Jay turned toward Dylan and said, with a smile creeping across his face, "I should be back on my way down to Renaissance Estates pretty soon."

"Just a reminder that your interviews are a critical part of what you're doing. You need to listen well and protect your sources. But at the same time don't be afraid to ask tough questions. Just be philosophical and not argumentative. You're a journalist, not a prosecutor."

"Roger that!" Jay said. He wanted to end this little lesson on a light note.

Dylan glanced at his wristwatch. "You ready for some coffee?" he said.

"I've been ready. Let's go."

Jay made arrangements through Rudi to interview Ben Williams. Ben was a kindly, polite, elderly African American man who had been active in the Los Angeles artists' community for most of his life. He worked for thirty-five years at the Los Angeles County Museum of Art as a custodian and security guard. He had a collection of drawings by other artists hanging on the walls of his living room. His apartment, a small, single bedroom unit on the first floor, was not lavishly furnished, but it appeared comfortable to Jay. He especially liked some of Ben's tables that were made out of different pieces of scrap wood and given a highly polished finish. They were more works of art to him than pieces of junk.

After introductions were made, Jay took a seat at the end of the sofa and pulled out his recorder and notepad. "When did you first meet Erica Knight?" he asked Ben.

Ben wore glasses and had some graying around his ears. When he spoke, his voice was low and gravelly. "I met Erica years ago at a street art festival in Watts," he said. "It was called a 'chalk-in' by the promoter. It really was just a contest for residents of a housing community to make chalk drawings on the street corner for cash prizes. She got interested in how the apartment complex was built, and how it provided artists and other poor people with subsidized housing."

"I see," Jay said. "Do you think that this 'chalk-in' festival was what got her started in developing her own housing project?"

"Absolutely. She began sometime after that talking to people down at LACMA where I worked, and then over at city hall. Later, she found out that the federal government had a program that would help her put all the pieces together. She spent a lot of time visiting officials at different levels of government and also private charities. Finally, she met a man by the name of DeShawn Walker who worked at HUD. He made it all happen for her."

"What type of job does Walker do? I mean, like, what was it that he did for Erica that made her succeed?"

"Walker is the HUD loan chief for this area. He got her the financing she needed to build this place. There's a whole book of rules and regulations that comes with a project like this, and Walker helped her get a handle on it. He also knew the best places to find the land to put it on, and helped her get this land cheap."

"He was a good resource, then."

"That's right. And after this place opened up, he maintained contact to help her with some of the problems she had."

"Erica mentioned that she thought Walker was behind the effort to get rid of her here at Renaissance Estates," Jay said. "She said he is working with another guy named Brendon

Millwood. Do you know how it happened that she was dismissed?"

"Walker would get on Erica's case from time to time if things weren't working out the way he wanted. Most of the time, he was just trying to help the project make money. And that was a good thing for Erica, since she got paid as the owner out of the money the project made. I don't know exactly what made Walker bring in Millwood. His working relationship with Erica seemed to come to an end somehow."

Ben then said, "Erica and Walker had a romantic relationship going on while this place was being built. Maybe it had something to do with that."

"Well, *that's* interesting," Jay said. "How long did they date, and was it serious?"

"I don't know for sure how long it lasted. It was one of those things that just seemed to happen while they were working together. They spent a lot of time together when Renaissance Estates was being built, and that carried over into their personal lives."

"Why did the affair come to an end?"

"Erica broke it off suddenly when this place was finally built. I don't know why."

"It sounds like maybe she wasn't taking him that seriously after all."

"Maybe not, but he definitely was taking her seriously. I think he wanted to get married right before they broke up."

"Do you think Erica will end up selling Renaissance Estates?" Jay said. He thought he already knew the answer, but it was a question that had to be asked.

"No way!" Ben said. "This place is her baby. She spent lots of hours, long days, and many months working hard to get it built. She would never toss all that away over some consultant being brought in. It was her dream to open a low-income housing property that would cater to struggling artists. All the effort that it took brought her into contact with the mayor, city council members, county officials, and heads of civic development organizations. They all recognized her as being able to do good things and get out the vote in Harbor Gateway. For that reason, any politician who wants to see her shoved off of Renaissance Estates had better remember that and tread carefully."

"The story I'm working on began with the murder of Lisa Nguyen," Jay said. "My research is taking me through some of the problems that HUD has found that relate to the management of Renaissance Estates. I still wonder if any of those problems contributed to Lisa Nguyen's death. Can you think of anyone connected to this place in anyway who would have wanted to see the accountant killed?"

"Nobody that I know of," Ben said. "I can't imagine who would want to kill that woman. She was one of the politest, nicest people I've ever met."

Searching for a different angle, Jay said, "How about anybody from Millwood's Company? It seems like a stretch. What do you think?"

Ben paused for a moment. "Lisa would do anything for Erica when it came to overseeing the money and keeping down the cost of running the place. Then, when Millwood started up working here and brought in his people, it seemed like he wanted Lisa out of the way. It may be that he didn't like all the help she was giving Erica."

"How come he didn't just fire her?"

"He couldn't really fire Lisa because she worked for Erica. He tried to get her in trouble over the missing rent money. But there was no proof that she was the one who stole it. I really don't believe that she would take any money from this project anyway. As I understand it, she never touched the cash. The receptionist collected any cash that was paid for the rent and took it to the bank herself. I don't know that much about bookkeeping, but I believe that it was set up that way so that Lisa couldn't cook the books. She was pretty smart, though, and she might have figured out who it was that did steal the money."

"If she knew who it was, why didn't she go to the police?"

"That was explained to me by Rudi. When the money went missing, Lisa was obliged to tell HUD about it first. Then HUD came in here looking through the books to see if they could figure out who might have taken it. So far, nothing's happened."

"Can you think of any reason Lisa would have been killed other than knowing who it might have been that stole the money?"

Ben paused again. "Not really," he said.

"The reason I'm asking is I believe that there's someone behind Lisa's murder other than the people involved with the barroom fight," Jay said. "There could even be a conspiracy.

Since she worked here, it might mean that someone here was involved."

"I can't think of anyone," Ben said. "We have a small staff that works here."

"Erica said that you are her eyes and ears in the office," Jay said. "Does anyone else in the office, like Rudi for example, help Erica maintain control?"

"All the employees in the office now work for Millwood. None of them are very helpful except for Rudi. She and Erica have become very good friends in the year or so that Rudi has worked here. And in spite of working for Millwood, Rudi would probably do anything to help Erica. When Millwood's not here, Rudi is the one in charge. Then the office seems to run a little better. Rudi should watch her back, though. Millwood can be a mean motherfucker."

"How many office employees are there?"

"Let's see, there's Millwood, Rudi, Maria, Alysia, and Carmen—five."

"How about maintenance in the buildings? Who works on that?"

"There's Juan, Andreas, and Gonzalo."

"Do they also take care of the landscaping?"

"Gonzalo used to do it. But Millwood decided to have Gonzalo spend his time working only on building maintenance, so he brought in somebody else to take care of the landscaping."

"How was it that Millwood got picked to be the independent consultant and later became the managing agent?"

"Bringing in Millwood was Walker's idea. I don't know why Walker chose Millwood, except that Millwood manages other housing projects, and Walker must have known him from somewhere. I think Walker's idea was that Millwood was somehow going to save the project some money. Millwood's supposed to be an expert at making a project like this one run more efficiently. I can tell you for a fact that nothing's running any better since he's been here."

They talked for nearly another hour. But as the talk shifted away from the management of the project, Jay decided it was time to rein it in. He thanked Ben for his time and handed him a box of chocolates. As he walked back to his van, he walked directly past Millwood, who was walking from his car to the office. Millwood stopped and stared at him. He seemed to recognize that Jay was not a resident and walked back over to him as he was about to get into his van.

"Pardon me," Millwood said. "What is your business over here? I'm the project's manager."

"Oh, I'm glad to meet you, sir," Jay said politely. "My name is Jason Phillips, and I work for the *LA Daily Journal*. I was interviewing a resident about one of your office employees who was recently murdered, uh, Lisa Nguyen."

"Is this for a story for the *Daily Journal*? Is that why you're here?"

"Well, yes. I'm just..."

"Who was it that you interviewed?" Millwood said.

Jay was annoyed at Millwood's prying but thought perhaps he could use it to his favor. "I just interviewed Ben Williams," he said.

"And what did Ben Williams say?"

"Well, quite a lot," Jay said. "You can read about it in the *Daily Journal* tomorrow morning."

"As I said I'm the manager here," Millwood said, his voice rising. "Anything you want to print in the newspaper has to come though me first. Do you understand that?"

Jay was irked, but rather than give an angry response, he seized the opportunity. "I'd like to interview you too, sir, if you don't mind," he said. "Can we make an appointment to talk? Or, for that matter, I'm available right now."

Millwood was clearly caught off guard. Jay's ploy had worked, as Millwood hesitated for a moment and then said, "Not today. Just call the office, and I'll let you know."

"Thanks. I'd appreciate that," Jay said, and he got in his van and drove away.

Jay went home to finish and file his story. He played back what he had recorded and organized his thoughts into a document on his laptop. He took some time to compare what Ben had told him versus what Erica and Rudi had told him earlier. He concluded that at least he now had three independent sources who, although they knew each other, presented approximately the same story only with different aspects. He thought that his next move would be to expound upon the differences.

CHAPTER TEN

Aguilar was not a novice with a computer, but Harry was a whiz. Aguilar assigned him the task of going through Maria Maldonado's Facebook page and Twitter account to try to find a picture of suspect number two. Harry got to work on it at the precinct office early in the day. He scarcely looked up from the screen until late morning, when Aguilar checked in on what he was doing. Aguilar knew that he needed to help Harry with this task but wasn't sure how.

"Facebook can be complicated," Harry said, "but Twitter is easy. All you have to do is just click on the followers and also the people followed. You often get a pretty good picture of who the person is."

Aguilar had not worked with Twitter before, but he decided to give it a try. He watched Harry navigate around in it for a few minutes, and then sat down at the desk next to him to take a crack at it himself. Understanding how computer file systems worked, he eased his way around Maldonado's Twitter link and into her followers. Then he began to drill down through the followers checking the pictures to try to find the nightclub murder's other suspect.

"And what if I don't get a picture?" Aguilar said. He was looking at a Twitter page that did not have a picture of the owner.

“There’s a picture section at the upper right side of the page,” Harry said. “But just keep looking down the list of followers. There’s also a tab for the people she follows.”

Aguilar started checking Twitter as directed by Harry, while Harry made his way through Facebook. After a while, Aguilar said, “I think I’m lost.”

“That’s no problem,” Harry said. “Just start over with the original address.”

“Shit. That means I got to do all that clicking again to get back to where I was,” Aguilar muttered.

“It’s just a file system—like an upside-down tree,” Harry told him.

“I’ve got to get good at this very soon,” Aguilar said. He thought that the task was more difficult than it should be.

“I think it would help if you looked for gang connections,” Harry said.

“How do I do that?”

“Type the name of somebody who you know is in a gang in the search window. Then start checking who he follows and also the people following him. You should get a good look at a lot of gang members that way.”

“This could take a while,” Aguilar said.

“If you see a web address you need to remember, just write it down or copy and paste it onto a spreadsheet. You can go directly back to it using the search window,” Harry said.

Aguilar was indeed correct when he said this task could take a while. Taking only short breaks, they continued working after hours. Even after sunset when everyone else in the office except the night staff had gone, the two detectives were still poring over social media connections. It seemed like an endless journey to Aguilar. But at the same time, it aroused a huge amount of childlike curiosity in him. Finally, he interrupted Harry's concentration and said, "Let's call it a night. We can get back to this in the morning."

And they did get back to it the next morning, and the next, and the next, all the way to the end of the week. Aguilar had six pages of notes and addresses when he finally found a picture on Twitter of a woman who appeared to be the second perpetrator. To be sure, he checked it against the actual nightclub security compact disk. Then, feeling proud of this technical accomplishment, he called Harry over to see it.

"What do you think," Aguilar said. "Do we have the second perp here?"

Harry looked the picture over for a moment. "Let me see if I can find her on Facebook," he finally said.

After a while, he came up with the Facebook page of Anita Martinez, who bore a strong resemblance to the shorter Latina in the bar fight. He dug up some other pictures from Facebook that helped make a positive identification.

Aguilar watched over Harry's shoulder as he queried Facebook for more photos of Anita Martinez based from her friends' pages. Then they both saw what they'd been searching for.

"Take a look at that one," Harry said. The picture was a nearly perfect portrait of Martinez.

"Can you make some prints of this?" Aguilar said. "We'll need to show it to some of the witnesses from the nightclub."

While Harry went through his applications to recreate the picture in printable form, Aguilar returned to his Twitter connection and zeroed in on the tweets and followers of Anita Martinez. Time again went by without Aguilar discovering anything of real interest. He decided to compare the growing list of Martinez's followers with the LAPD's crime databases to see what matched. The most common connection that Martinez had with her followers was through the South Bay Neighborhood Association. Playing a hunch, Aguilar shifted his search to those matches from the crime databases that had the connection to South Bay. He wasn't ready to throw away his previous suspect list. He decided that every possible lead from South Bay needed to be pursued.

"Come look at this," he said to Harry. "See that ponytail?"

Harry's eyes lit up. "We could have one of the parking lot suspects here," he said.

"This guy's the boyfriend of suspect number two," Aguilar said.

Harry looked at Aguilar and said, "Is it time to get an arrest warrant?"

Aguilar looked at the pictures again, and said, "Let's take it to the nightclub first and see what our witnesses say."

Harry made some more prints of Anita Martinez and of her boyfriend, whose name was Fernando Suarez. Then they took the photos to Paradise Cove where the bartender and the assistant manager confirmed that Anita Martinez had participated in the fight. The assistant manager was unable to confirm that her boyfriend was one of the good Samaritans who had rescued Lisa Nguyen. He showed the picture to another parking lot witness who likewise wasn't sure.

"*Now* are we ready for the arrest warrant for perpetrator number two?" Harry said beaming confidently.

"No, our evidence is still weak," Aguilar said. "But let's take it to the captain anyway."

Aguilar and Harry brought their pictures and the evidence file into Captain Kreider's office. "We think this is our second perpetrator," Aguilar said.

Kreider spent a few minutes comparing the Facebook and Twitter pictures with the one made from the security disk.

"Do you remember the South Bay Neighborhood Association?" Aguilar said.

Kreider thought for a moment. "I think we broke up an insurance scam down there a few years ago," he said. "It was run out of the back door by some of the employees."

"This person," Aguilar said pointing to the picture of Anita Martinez, "is the girlfriend of this guy with the ponytail. He's one of the bosses over at South Bay Neighborhood Association. He was also a part of that insurance scam."

Kreider scrutinized the picture and then said, "What's up with the boyfriend?"

"His name is Fernando Suarez. Our witnesses say that one of the guys that carried the victim away was tall and had a ponytail."

"Can they identify him?"

"They aren't sure."

Kreider continued to look at the pictures. "Well, you can't do anything with Suarez until you get something we can hang our hats on."

"We can hold Martinez, though," Aguilar said.

"Yes, get an assault and battery warrant together for Anita Martinez," Kreider said.

"Assault and battery?" Aguilar said. "What about manslaughter?"

"No, assault and battery," Kreider said. "You'll need to see the DA if you want to charge her with anything more serious. You'll be lucky enough to make an assault and battery charge stick without solid witnesses."

"Bringing the South Bay Neighborhood Association into the case raises the stakes," Aguilar said. "If there's a connection there, we could have a conspiracy of some kind. Worst case scenario is that it could involve organized crime."

Kreider looked at Aguilar. "Quit dreaming about this," he said. "You don't convict killers with dreams—you need hard evidence. When you find enough evidence to go after South Bay Neighborhood Association, then you can move forward. But I want to know what's going on with them first."

The two detectives took their file of evidence including all the recently gathered pictures and went back to the DA's office to speak again with Richard Frederick. Frederick reviewed what the detectives showed him this time but balked at the idea of a manslaughter charge.

"What's different this time?" Aguilar said. "Why should Maria Maldonado get manslaughter and not Anita Martinez?"

"Maria Maldonado's aggression can be considered violent enough to commit homicide. There's nothing I've seen so far that would also apply to Martinez," Frederick said. "I told you before that Maldonado's manslaughter charge was weak. I only agreed to it so we could hold her like you requested."

"What about a conspiracy charge?" Aguilar said.

"I don't think that will work, either. The threshold of proof is lower for a conspiracy charge. But if we can't prove it on the first perpetrator, we could lose the second one as well."

"She works for an organization that's known for other criminal activity."

"What organization is that?"

"The South Bay Neighborhood Association."

Frederick furrowed his brow and seemed unable to recall the South Bay Neighborhood Association. "Where in South Bay are they located?" he finally said.

"Hawthorne Boulevard, in Torrance," Aguilar said.

Frederick typed something into his computer. When he saw the result he said, "Now, I remember them. They were running an auto insurance scam where they filed false claims and backed them up with fake police reports from the Torrance Police Department."

"I was in on breaking that up," Aguilar said.

"There was a guy in the Torrance Police Department that was working with them. Uh, I believe his name was Fernando Suarez."

"That's right, and Suarez is high on our radar in this case," Aguilar said.

On cue, Harry pulled out the picture of Suarez taken from Facebook and placed it on top of the other pictures on Frederick's desk.

"Notice the ponytail," Aguilar said. "The witnesses in the parking lot recognized it from the night of the fight."

"Will they come forward and recognize Suarez in court?" Frederick said. "There are a lot of ponytails out there on guys like this."

Aguilar looked back at Frederick in disappointment. Frederick knew what the answer to that question would be. As he turned back around and looked at a web page on his computer, he said, "Suarez was fired from the Torrance Police Department. He got eighteen months in jail for his part of the insurance scam. That makes him a criminal, but does not make him a killer."

Frederick shifted his computer pages around momentarily until he found what he was looking for. "You'll need to put him in the nightclub parking lot to charge him," Frederick said.

"His girlfriend is Anita Martinez," Aguilar said. "This is starting to smell like some kind of organized operation."

"Do you think that South Bay Neighborhood Association is using its resources to conduct some deadly deed, like murdering a young woman and trying to make it look like a bar fight?" Frederick said.

"I don't think it's a stretch to put South Bay into this case," Aguilar said. "My concern is what additional evidence do we need to move in on them?"

"Two of their employees are suspects in an event that was tied to a murder. They are boyfriend and girlfriend. That alone is not enough to get you even a search warrant."

"If it *was* a scheme, you think that the two of them might have thought it up all by themselves?" Aguilar said. He liked sparring over legal matters with a willing assistant district attorney as it could give him insight as to what course he and Harry should be taking. Discussions like this one were of greater value to him than anything Captain Kreider would come up with.

"Yes, and until you find more evidence, it leaves the rest of South Bay out of the case," Frederick said.

"What can we do with Anita Martinez?"

"We're stuck with assault and battery for now."

CHAPTER ELEVEN

Rudi was about to leave work for the day when the phone rang. She was heading for the door but turned and went back into her office to answer it. It was Erica.

"Hi. I hope I didn't catch you at a bad time," Erica said.

"No. But I was walking out the door. What's up?" Rudi said.

"I've got the report from Arthur Garfield on the results of his audit. I wonder if you would like to come over and review it with me."

"Sure. What about dinner? Should I pick up something?"

"That's not necessary. I've got dinner just about ready."

Rudi's first thought was that they finally had something concrete that they could use to go after Millwood. When she arrived at Erica's, dinner was all laid out on the table—beet salad, torn greens, and homegrown herbs.

"Erica," Rudi said, "I asked you if you wanted me to pick up something. Now it appears I'm about to eat your last meal."

"I simply can't invite you over without at least serving something to eat," Erica said.

"That damn Millwood is putting you in the poorhouse. I'm worried now that you can't even afford take-out food."

"I usually have plenty of rice and beans around. I'm not starving yet!" Erica opened a bottle of Chardonnay. Rudi had noticed on more than one occasion that Erica was drinking more heavily than she used to.

After dinner, they adjourned to the living room. Rudi made herself comfortable on the sofa while Erica refilled her glass of wine and sat across from her in the easy chair. Rudi kicked off her shoes. She lifted her right foot up onto the coffee table and raised the hemline of her pleated skirt up to her hips. With long, slow strokes she rubbed her right leg above and below the knee down to her ankle.

"Tell me something," Erica said out of the blue. "Do you ever have any feelings about that reporter, Jay—romantic feelings?"

"I've only seen him a few times, but he's just soooo beautiful to look at," she admitted. "A tall, good looking, blond guy with deep blue eyes is unheard of in Iraq."

"Have you ever thought about what it would be like to sleep with him?" Erica said.

"Oh no, I wouldn't dare," Rudi said. "I mean, I don't think…he's just not the right type…I don't know…"

"But those feelings don't go away after you finish seeing him, do they?"

"You're right. But that's where it ends—just a thought."

"Or a fantasy?"

"Oh, stop it now. That's enough. Yes, a fantasy."

"I'm just kidding," Erica said as she sipped from her wine glass.

The leg rub ended and Rudi curled her right leg up onto the sofa underneath her left leg and pulled her skirt over her right knee. Erica then picked up the file folder from the end table next to her.

"I've gone over this audit report several times, and although it's reasonably thorough, it doesn't come to any conclusions about the stolen money," Erica said. "I did see a lot about questionable accounting and financial practices, though. If you ask me, I'd say the door for corruption is wide open."

Erica handed the report over to Rudi who took a moment to review the highlights. "Arthur did spend a lot of time searching for the missing money," Rudi said, "but I wanted him to see much more than just that."

"You did really good with that, honey," Erica said. "Your MBA degree from USC taught you something about accounting principles. I guess we'll just have to give up on trying to find out what happened to the money. After two audits and no results we may never find the answer."

"Millwood has been messing up everything you did. It's no wonder the place is starting to lose money," Rudi said, as she gave the report back to Erica.

"Millwood has got to be in cahoots with Walker," Erica said. "I still believe that Walker is behind all of this. I was just hoping that Arthur would have discovered that there was a payment of some kind that Millwood made to Walker for bringing him into the management circle."

"The audit didn't *find* any evidence—but that does not mean that there isn't any," Rudi said as she leaned back against the cushions on the sofa. “It might be there but just carefully covered up.”

“Arthur found a lot of suspicious activities that the HUD audit didn’t find,” Erica said. “The HUD audit focused on putting the blame on me. Doesn’t that mean that HUD was deliberately trying to set me up?”

“Who knows?” Rudi said. “It might be hard to prove that HUD had driven their audit to a specific conclusion. Even HUD’s auditors have certain standards and regulations governing how they’re supposed to audit.”

“Do you think that Walker could have been paid a bribe, and Millwood had somehow covered it up so two different auditors couldn’t find it?” Erica said.

Rudi considered Erica’s point. “Well, what about the stolen money?” she said. “Couldn’t it have been arranged to use that money to pay off Walker?”

“Since we don’t know what happened, it would be hard to prove,” Erica said. “But I wouldn’t put it past him.”

“I’ve thought of another possibility,” Rudi said. “Arthur showed me a series of checks to the South Bay Neighborhood Association in the range of fourteen to fifteen thousand dollars each. He turned some of them over and showed me the markings on the back that indicate that the check was cashed instead of being deposited. He said when the bank cashes a huge check like that, the teller sometimes marks the number of bills of each denomination down on the back of the check.”

“Wow, I didn’t know that,” Erica said. “I thought businesses always put checks in the bank to keep the money safe. Since they were cashed, those very large payments could be a part of a bribe circulated back to Walker."

"Because it's all in cash, it might be hard to prove," Rudi said. "Somebody might have to go over to the South Bay Neighborhood Association and do an audit over there for the answer."

"Fat chance of that happening," Erica said. "We certainly can't count on the cops to do it unless it ties into Lisa's murder. And there's no way in hell I'd ever get Arthur to go over there for any type of audit."

"This is a brainstorming exercise," Rudi said. "The more thoughts we generate between us, the more likely we are of coming up with an angle to pursue."

"Walker can be pretty shifty," Erica said. "Somehow, he always seemed to know a lot about the problems at Renaissance Estates before he even asked me about them. He must have had somebody inside the office who was feeding him information. That points to Millwood."

"Millwood's not always there," Rudi said. "And when he is there, he spends a lot of time grilling people like me to find out what's been going on."

"But he does find out eventually, doesn't he?" Erica said.

"Yes, he does," Rudi said. "There must be one or more other persons involved with Millwood. There must be a conspiracy of some kind."

"No matter how it's sliced and diced, I believe that Walker placed Millwood in Renaissance Estates specifically to spy on me," Erica said. "He wants to get info on me so that he can take me out of the picture."

The bottle of wine was half full. Rudi still had the one glass she started with, and that was nearly half full. The more they talked about Walker, the more sips Erica took from her glass.

Rudi then said, "I think that Walker must be getting bribed. Why else would he be acting the way he does?" She folded her arms in front of her, as if this conclusion was final.

"I hadn't told you this before," Erica said, "but a number of years ago, Walker and I dated."

"Oh really!" Rudi said. She looked at Erica with wide open eyes.

"Yes, over a period of about six months or so."

"What was he like away from the business?"

"Just the same as at the business. He was often difficult and occasionally physically or mentally rough when we were together. I reached the point where I had to break it off. He was just too intense."

Rudi was quiet for a moment. "Was he…abusive?" she finally said.

"Usually only mentally so. But once or twice he physically jerked me around."

"Why did you keep seeing him?" Rudi said. "If he was physically rough with you, why didn't you break up with him right then and there?"

"I'm an old romantic," Erica said. "He was good to me most of the time. He even was quick to apologize when he lost his temper. Besides, he was so much help to me when Renaissance Estates was built, I don't think I could have finished the project without him."

"Isn't that behavior a sign that he might be bipolar?" Rudi said.

"I don't think so," Erica said. "Bipolar is hard to diagnose, but usually you can spot the depressive side of it. In all that time, he never seemed to be depressed to me. He just would lose his temper and then later regret it when he calmed down."

In an admission of her own observations, Rudi said, "He does seem to be in really good physical condition."

"He was a basketball player in college. He still plays in the YMCA over-forty league."

"Was he interested in keeping the relationship going with you?"

"For sure. He called and called and visited and bothered me for another three or four months after the relationship was over."

"He must have a jealous hangover, then. If he can't go out with you, he'll just ruin you financially."

"Hmm...," Erica said. "I never thought of it that way, but you may be right."

"It's very low behavior for someone to try to ruin another person's life over a failed romance," Rudi said. "I think you should go after him and defend your rights."

"I was hoping this audit would give me the ammunition I needed to do that," Erica said. "It breaks my heart that it doesn't."

"I think you're giving up too soon," Rudi said. "The audit might be just enough to get the authorities to act. If an official investigation is opened, the real truth has got to come out eventually."

Erica thought about that for a moment. "Well, there is this person in the FBI that I met once who might be able to do something."

"Then send that person the audit file," Rudi said. She was driving this point harder than Erica. "Let me take it to the office and copy everything first so that it doesn't get lost."

The conversation continued until 10PM, when Rudi decided it was time to go home. She put her shoes back on and stood up from the sofa.

Erica stopped talking for a moment and just looked at her. "Are you leaving?" she said. "I was hoping you'd like to hang out here tonight."

Rudi smiled. Then she said, "I can't tonight. I'm just too tired. Millwood will be in the office tomorrow, and I need to get in there early to get ready for him."

Erica appeared to be dejected with that statement until Rudi followed it up by saying, "But there's always tomorrow night. And this time I'm bringing something over for dinner."

Erica then rose from her chair and the two embraced before Rudi left.

A few days later, Rudi returned the file to Erica plus one extra copy. She retained another copy for herself for safekeeping. Erica then called Marsha Jackson of the FBI, whom she'd met a few years previously at an art opening in Silver Lake. To her delight and amazement, Jackson told her that she had some experience working on cases that involved

Section 8 housing. She made an appointment to meet with Jackson and show her the audit results.

Erica went for her appointment with Jackson at the FBI's West Los Angeles office, located ironically in the federal building just a few floors above HUD. After greeting Jackson, she said, "I want to thank you for taking the time to see me over this problem that I have."

"I'm happy to talk to you," Jackson said, "and I hope the Bureau can be of some help." She was a tall, rawboned, country girl from Modesto, California, with short, brunette hair tucked behind her ears. She said that she remembered meeting Erica a few years before. "I know I haven't seen you in a while," she said, "but I've read up on how you've put together a Section 8 housing project literally from scratch. I want to say that I'm really impressed."

Erica gracefully accepted the compliment. Then she said, "The reason I'm here is I am having some difficulty with Renaissance Estates that may involve HUD's loan officer, DeShawn Walker. I was falsely accused of mishandling money, and without any proof of this misconduct I was removed from the role as manager of the project I had built from scratch. Mr. Walker then appointed a friend of his as the new manager. There was no evidence to support the claim that I mishandled rent money, so I sent in my own auditor to see if the real facts could be determined. I brought with me the results of that audit."

Jackson sat quietly and listened. She had attended Southwestern Law School and was educated as an attorney before undergoing FBI training.

Erica handed her the audit folder. “Let me say from the beginning that everything this audit turned up is circumstantial in nature,” she said. “I just believe that the great weight of the findings might be enough for the FBI to investigate Walker for malfeasance. The treatment I’m getting from the Department of Housing and Urban Development is completely unfair. Of course, you’ll make your own conclusion. I believe that Mr. Walker is doing all that he can to get rid of me to protect a kickback he’s getting from the consultant now running Renaissance Estates, Brendon Millwood. And I want to point out that I ran those properties for over nine years and had no complaints from anyone at HUD. And what’s more, I ran them at a profit. Thanks to the ‘new management’, Renaissance Estates is now losing money.”

“I see,” Jackson said. “The Bureau takes matters such as this very seriously. The bribing of a federal official connected with Section 8 housing is a felony with possible eight to ten years in a federal penitentiary. Bribery and kickbacks are often very hard to prove, since the perpetrators usually go to great lengths to cover them up.”

Erica went on describing events at Renaissance Estates, beginning with Millwood’s entry as a consultant and ending at the current time. Jackson took it all in, asking a few questions from time to time for clarity. When Erica reached the end of her spiel, Jackson said, “I would like to review this file. I’ll return it to you in a few days and let you know if we intend to pursue this.”

"I want to thank you for your time," Erica said as she stood up and shook Jackson's hand.

CHAPTER TWELVE

Because of the long commute on the freeway from Huntington Beach to downtown Los Angeles, Jay would not arrive at the newsroom at the same time each morning. On one particular day, Dylan was sitting at Jay's desk waiting for him.

"What's going on, dude," Jay said.

"Hey, Jay," Dylan said. "How was the surf this morning?" Dylan said, as they fist bumped. Before Jay answered, Dylan moved over to the extra chair so Jay could sit down.

"Today it was great," Jay said. "We're having some south sea swells that are giving us better than usual waves."

"I just noticed that you haven't published anything yet this week," Dylan said. "How's your story coming along?"

Jay didn't mind Dylan's interest in his story. He was growing accustomed to the mentoring he was receiving from Dylan, and was actually glad he had somebody he could turn to for help. He set his backpack down in its place under the desk and logged into his workstation. "I'm still trying to figure out what might have happened to the twenty grand that went missing," he said.

"Have you got a tie-in to the murder?" Dylan said.

"It would be a motive if the killer were the thief, wouldn't it?" Jay said. "Corruption is another possibility. The police don't have a motive yet, either."

"What did you find out so far about the corruption angle?" Dylan said.

"The lady that owns the place has been pushed out," Jay said. "In addition to owning it she used to manage it. But HUD went to court to have her removed as manager."

"Well OK. But it sounds like that could happen anywhere," Dylan said. "The person who killed the accountant seems to be some kind of wild animal, according to the police report."

"Oh, totally, he has to be a wild animal. You should have seen the body at the morgue. It was sickening to the max."

"Do you think anybody at those apartments could qualify as a wild animal?" Dylan said.

"Well, none I've met so far, anyway," Jay said.

"Have you got a plan for using the material you've been gathering?" Dylan said.

"I was going to wait until I found a connection between the money and the murder," Jay said. "There are plenty of circumstantial things to write about. But I'd look awfully stupid if it turned out that none of them related to the murder."

"Actually, you wouldn't," Dylan said. "The reason I say so is that if you have enough material, you should publish the story within the story. If it sounds interesting enough and has a noteworthy conclusion of its own, the readers will like it.

And if it does tie to the murder, you could win the Pulitzer Prize!"

"Oh, dude! Don't talk that crap with me!" Jay said. "I'm just trying to make it as an investigative journalist, that's all. Besides, I got chewed out more than once for not having a tie-in to the murder for what I wanted to publish."

"Stories like this need to be rolled out in serial format—like a soap opera or a miniseries," Dylan said. "Readers will buy the paper each day to continue reading about what's going on with that place, uh…"

"Renaissance Estates," Jay said.

"You'll make them come back for more," Dylan said.

"But doesn't that just amount to hype?" Jay said. "I mean, it's like all the noise you get before the Super Bowl. It sometimes makes the game itself a real let down."

"Maybe," Dylan said. "But it's the best way to keep readers' interest in a long running story. Criminal cases like this might go on for several weeks or even months before they are resolved. Then there's the courtroom drama afterward and so on."

Jay took a moment to listen to his phone messages. One of them was from Rudi. "Pardon me, but I've got to call this person back. She's my main source from Renaissance Estates," he said.

"Oh, no problem," Dylan said, leaning back in his chair.

Jay called Rudi, and his jaw dropped as he listened to her. "You're shittin' me!" he said. "Wow, that's awesome."

Dylan's interest was piqued, as Jay went on exclaiming about what he was hearing. Then he ended the call.

"Well, I just got some cool news for you," Jay told Dylan. "The HUD official for Renaissance Estates, DeShawn Walker, is under investigation by the FBI for bribery."

"No shit!" Dylan said. His eyes lit up, and he and Jay popped a high five. "You see what I was just talking about? Here's a perfect piece to write that will extend the soap opera until more is known about the killer."

Jay explained that the FBI was investigating Walker for bribery based on the audit done by Erica's auditor. Jay mentioned some of the more inspiring findings about the financial workings at Renaissance Estates that had been uncovered by the audit.

"What you do next is call the FBI agent and confirm it," Dylan said. "Then we can add this piece to today's edition."

"I can do that," Jay said. "By the way, I appreciate all the help you're giving me, but don't you have other work to do?"

"The Lakers' season is over," Dylan said. "I won't have anything to cover for them until free agency in July. Fall camp doesn't begin until September. And next season won't begin until mid-October this year."

"Then you are unofficially here as my personal tutor?" Jay said. He tried to just look curious, but inside he was hopeful.

Dylan took a deep breath and let out a sigh. "I wasn't supposed to tell you this, but I *am* officially your mentor. Meredith asked me to do it. During the summer months, I pick up different projects, and this year the project is you!"

“Wow! “Meredith did it, huh?” Jay said. He hadn’t realized that what he was doing, was that important to the paper’s success.

“The newspaper has a declining readership,” Dylan said. “It’s like that all over—many daily papers are struggling to stay in publication. News on television and news blips on cell phones are replacing the morning newspaper.”

“Are you saying that we’re going down the shitter, or something desperate like that?” Jay said.

“No, not yet, anyway,” Dylan said. “It becomes more important that we develop younger writers like yourself who can write stories that will appeal to younger readers. We’ve got to find ways to get them hooked on what we’re printing.”

“I definitely want to do my part.”

“Good. By the way, have you gotten an interview with that Millwood guy yet?”

“No. I was going to try again this morning.”

“Keep after him,” Dylan said. “He could be a very important part of this puzzle. Now, that brings up an interesting point. From what I gather, this Millwood guy is going to be a tough, negative interview. But you can’t walk away from him without asking the hard questions. You see, by not answering a question, he could be telling you that he has something to hide. We don’t need another person to corroborate what we already know from the three people you’ve talked to. What we need is to get Millwood to give up something new.”

“I’ve got a list of questions all lined up for him,” Jay said, with a sardonic grin.

"Good," a still serious Dylan said. "But don't start out with the hardest ones first. You need to set the tone with some easy questions and then build up to the hard-hitting ones."

Then Dylan said, "And don't forget to confirm the investigation with the FBI agent!"

"Yes, sir!" Jay said with a fake salute and another grin.

Grinning also, Dylan gave Jay a pat on the back and then left for his own workstation.

For several weeks, Millwood had been putting Jay off for an interview or cancelling after promising to meet with him. This was the day that Millwood apparently realized that Jay would not go away, because he agreed to talk to Jay at Renaissance Estates. It would be for a "limited time only," and they must stick to the subject of Lisa Nguyen's murder.

Jay traveled out to Renaissance Estates to interview Millwood. After introductions, Jay presented Millwood with a box of cheroots at Rudi's recommendation. Millwood was impressed and lit one up, as Jay set up his recorder and pulled out his notepad.

"Let's start with what Lisa's duties were here at Renaissance Estates," Jay said.

"She did the bookkeeping and accounting for the property," Millwood said.

"And what activities did this include?"

"I don't know much about bookkeeping except that it involves collecting the rent money and paying the bills."

Jay showed Millwood the article from the *Daily Journal* about the HUD audit that had uncovered the missing rent money. "Do you think that Lisa might have known who was responsible for what happened to this money?" he said.

"Well, she had to know something about it," Millwood said. "It comes right out of her territory."

"Do you believe that she was the culprit?"

Millwood hesitated for a moment, as if an instinct told him that Jay was violating a security zone. Then he said, "No, I don't think she was the culprit. She was the type of woman who would never have done anything wrong like that. And if she knew who did it and how it had all happened, she would have told me about it."

"Then she didn't tell you what she did know?" Jay said.

"No, and I don't know why not. Rather than speculate about it, she just kept quiet. She was a very industrious person who was particularly careful with details. I've known other accountants who were like that—they have to be exact in what they do or say."

Jay thought that the door might have just opened to include some of the tough questioning that Dylan had talked about. He thought he'd lay a trap for Millwood to see if he would start bad mouthing Lisa. "My research has shown that some payments were made from here that actually pertained to other properties and not this one," he said. "Did Lisa ever say anything to you about that?"

Millwood reacted swiftly. He set his cigar in the ashtray and leaned forward in his chair. "She never paid any bill that didn't belong to this property," he said. "She would never do anything improper, as I just finished saying."

Jay decided that Millwood was blocking that route, so he tried another one. "There appears to be an arrangement of some kind where two landscapers get paid five thousand dollars a month each and also receive an apartment to live in for free. Can you comment on that?"

"Erica Knight, the former manager here, was the one who signed that contract. We are only honoring it. You'll have to talk to her if you want more information on that."

"It seems an exorbitant salary," Jay said. "I mean, that's a lot of money to pay someone just to cut the grass."

"Talk to Erica," Millwood said. "By the way, she meddled in a lot of other things that cost us a bunch of money, too. Most of it was out of bounds for her in the first place."

"Such as, what?" Jay said.

Millwood was now clearly annoyed at the mention of Erica. "Like meddling with the maintenance man's work by interfering with his duties to fix what she wanted, when she wanted it. It forced me to hire outside contractors just to keep the place up."

Jay decided to pull out all stops. "There are apparently some very large payments made on a regular basis to the South Bay Neighborhood Association for security," he said.

Millwood hesitated for a moment. "What's so unusual about that?" he said. "Every apartment complex in this area has a security service."

"What's unusual is that these checks were not deposited in the bank by South Bay Neighborhood Association. Instead, they were turned into a large pile of cash."

"Well, that's the association's business. If you think it's important enough for your story, why don't you go over there and ask *them* about it?"

"The amounts are as high as fourteen to fifteen thousand dollars, and it gets paid twice per month. It seems like for that amount of money, you would have guards all over the place. I didn't notice any security this morning or any of the other times I've been here."

Jay saw that he was pushing Millwood over the edge. He could hear the rise in Millwood's voice as he said, "Apartment security costs a lot of money. The South Bay Neighborhood Association patrols the area all night long, and they have a 24-hour monitoring service. We're being watched by them right now." Millwood pointed to the cameras in his office and hallway.

"My sources say that you sign the checks," Jay said. "It seems you should know what it is you're signing."

Millwood raised his voice again and spoke slowly and deliberately. "I sign all the checks over two thousand dollars because they require two signatures," he said. "Rudi Sirianni uses the check signing machine for the other signature. Now, just who in the hell are your 'sources' who are telling you all this?"

"I'm sorry, Mr. Millwood, but I can't reveal who my sources are."

"I demand to know who's been telling you about this bullshit you're asking me!" Millwood roared. "We were supposed to be talking about Lisa Nguyen. Interview concluded."

Jay had more to ask Millwood, but decided not to push any further. He thanked Millwood for his time. The he quickly packed up his gear and left. Millwood watched as Jay walked out the front door, then he summoned Rudi into his office.

"I just had that newspaper guy in here asking a lot of questions about how we run this business," he began. "Do you want to tell me how he knew all about the inner workings of our accounting system?"

Rudi was standing at attention in front of Millwood's desk. "Jay came in and talked to me about an article in the paper several months ago that pointed to the HUD audit over some missing rent money. He was very polite, and of course since he's from the *LA Daily Journal*, I co-operated as much as I could."

"And told him every fucking thing that goes in this place."

"I just tried to be helpful."

"Goddamn it! We don't need anybody from the newspapers nosing around in here and finding out about all our problems. He can publish it for everybody in the world to see."

"He asked me about Lisa Nguyen, who—as you know—was murdered. It also happens that she was the property's accountant and knew a lot about the financial activities around here."

Millwood cleared his throat. "And what do payments to the South Bay Neighborhood Association have to do with Lisa's death? He said that the checks were cashed, and asked me why that would be. What difference could it possibly make to us if South Bay Neighborhood Association either cashes the checks we send them, or deposits them in the bank? It's their money."

"It could make a lot of difference—we don't know." Rudi said. "Lisa's killer is still out there somewhere, and the reason she was murdered is not known."

"Lisa was killed accidentally in a brawl that took place at a bar."

"You and I both know that Lisa would never get caught up in brawl at a bar," Rudi said, without letting down her guard.

Millwood backed off a little bit. In a controlled manner he said, "If anybody else from the press, the authorities, or any other interested persons ask you questions about how things are being managed here, talk to me before answering. I don't want to answer to any more critics about our problems than I have to."

Rudi who was still standing at attention in front of his desk, said, "I will do that." She then turned around and walked out of his office.

CHAPTER THIRTEEN

Harry was tracing Maria Maldonado's car through the DMV and local police databases to see if it was either stolen or used in another crime. After a while he found a police report that indicated that the car was recently involved in an accident. He showed the findings to Aguilar.

"Our first suspect's car was in an accident a few months ago," Harry said. "It was banged up pretty bad. Take a look." He showed Aguilar a photograph of the car after the accident.

"What happened?" Aguilar said.

"The report says that she was turning left in the middle of a city block through a traffic break created by two pickup trucks. When she turned left in front of the trucks, another car came around from the right and slammed into her," Harry said.

"There's lots of damage," Aguilar said, still looking at the picture.

"The report says she did not have insurance," Harry said.

"I wonder how much it cost her to get all that fixed," Aguilar said. He looked at the picture for another moment. Then he picked up the phone and called a friend he had in Traffic Division. He was told that the car had to be towed to a repair facility. He placed a call to the repair facility and found out that the repairs cost almost five thousand dollars, and that the owner reclaimed the car by paying in cash.

"It cost her nearly five thousand to get the car fixed," Aguilar told Harry. "Where do you think she got that much money from?"

"Well, wasn't it the other driver's fault?" Harry said. "I mean, the other car hit her. It seems to me that she should have collected from the other driver's insurance."

"It doesn't always work that way," Aguilar said. "My brother-in-law did the same thing once and he was responsible for the accident."

"Oh, I guess I better quit doing it myself then," Harry said.

"The biggest question I have is, how did she get the money if she had no insurance and didn't collect from the other driver?" Aguilar said.

"I don't think it was from savings," Harry said. "If she had that much money saved, it seems she would have had bought insurance to begin with."

At that moment Aguilar's phone rang. After a brief conversation, he said to Harry, "We might be finding out the answers to these questions very soon. The warrant for Anita Martinez is ready. Let's go pick her up."

With a photo, a warrant, and the address of the second suspect in the nightclub murder in hand, Aguilar and Lee located Anita Martinez's place of residence and staked it out. Early in the afternoon, she drove up and parked her car on the street in front of her apartment building. She was alone. As she walked toward the front entrance, she was intercepted and arrested without fanfare. Instead of taking her to their office, the two detectives took her to downtown Los Angeles, where Maria Maldonado was in jail.

In an interrogation room with a see-through mirror, they began questioning Anita Martinez. To their surprise, she waived her rights to an attorney. It soon became apparent, however, that she would not cooperate. She sat calmly in her chair as Aguilar fired question after question at her about her activities at the nightclub on the night of the fight. Harry showed her the fight sequence from the security disk, that put her there and displayed her involvement. She seemed unfazed by it all and sat quietly with her arms folded in front of her. After a time, Aguilar exited the room and turned the interrogation over to Harry.

Playing tough cop/nice cop with his partner, Harry switched the conversation to the subject of immigration. He still hit a brick wall, but at least she changed her facial expressions.

"I'll never forget when I first came to America," Harry said. "I lived near Koreatown but had the worst time trying to find a good restaurant. I just could not get used to eating hamburgers and burritos."

Martinez managed a wry smile.

"The language was very hard for me to learn," Harry said. "The letters in the alphabet—Korean is altogether different, like Chinese and Japanese. Did you know English before you came here?"

"I was born here," Martinez told him, nodding her head up and down.

"I sure wished I knew some English when I arrived. If it weren't for my friends, I could have starved," he said. With a subtle move of his hand, he pulled a picture of Maria Maldonado out of an open file and placed it on the corner of the table to his side. "You've been working for the South Bay Neighborhood Association. What does the association do?" he said.

"They do security for apartment complexes."

"Are they all in South Bay?"

"Yes, they are," Martinez said, once again nodding affirmative.

"Are there any Koreans working there for you?"

"No," she said at first. Then she said, "Oh yes, we do have a Korean lady working there. Her name is Angela Kim."

"I wonder how much they pay her. Probably more than I make as a cop," Harry said.

Martinez's eyes lit up and she nodded her head up and down again. What she didn't know was that this seemingly innocent interview, with Harry's deliberate sidetracks, was being viewed through the see-through mirror by both Maria Maldonado and Sergeant Aguilar. Aguilar had stepped out to bring her there from a different interrogation room when Harry began his one on one with Martinez.

"Your friend is in there fingering you for the Asian woman's murder," Aguilar said.

Maldonado observed her picture on the corner of the table and Martinez's head nodding up and down, apparently confirming what Aguilar had just explained. "She's not my fucking friend," she said.

"But she was with you at the nightclub and was in the fight, correct?" Aguilar said.

Maldonado let out a sigh and said, "Yes."

Then Aguilar led Maldonado back to the other interrogation room to have a different conversation.

"Your car was in a wreck recently," Aguilar said. "It cost almost five thousand dollars to get it fixed."

"There's nothing wrong with my car," Maldonado said.

"What I need to know is, who gave you the money to get your car fixed?" Aguilar said.

"I told you, there's nothing wrong with my car," Maldonado said. Her voice quivered.

Aguilar showed her pictures of her car before and after the repair work was done. He also showed her the police report. "Do you see that?" he asked her, pointing to the photographs.

Maldonado started to perspire. "That's not my car," she snapped.

Calmly, Aguilar showed her the license plate, that was clearly visible in both pictures. "That's your license plate right there," he said.

Maldonado began to breathe more quickly. Aguilar then said, "Have you been sued by the other driver? You don't have any insurance to pay for the damage. And you didn't get this car fixed with your good looks. You need to tell me, who gave you the money to get this fixed?"

Maldonado was silent for a moment. Then she said, "The fucking cop at the scene set me up. He said it was my fault for turning left, the son of a bitch."

"You shouldn't feel too bad about that. It happens to a lot of people—my brother-in-law included," Aguilar said. Then, with a smirk on his face, he added, "We know you didn't have the money to get this fixed. All we want is the name of the person who gave the money to you."

Maldonado dropped her head and said, "A friend loaned me the money."

"And what is your friend's name?"

She looked back at Aguilar. "He told me not to tell anyone that he loaned me the money."

"But he still has a name."

"He didn't tell me his name."

"But he's your friend, isn't he? How are you going to pay the money back to him if you don't know his name?"

"I don't know. I guess he'll come look me up."

"In jail?"

"Damn it, I told you I don't know his name."

At that point having finished his conversation with Anita Martinez, Harry entered the interrogation room.

"What's up, Harry Lee?" Aguilar said.

Harry leaned against the wall with his arms folded in front of him. "I just finished talking to your accomplice," he said, looking at Maldonado. "She says you're the one who started the barroom fight the other night."

"That's a damn lie!" Maldonado said.

"That's not what she said," Harry said, while shrugging his shoulders.

"I tell you she's a fucking liar!"

Aguilar said, "What you're saying is that *she's* the one who started the barroom fight. Isn't that true?"

Maldonado turned around and faced Aguilar. "That little bitch caused all the fucking trouble that night. She put me up to it. When we got out to the parking lot, she started kicking the woman. Then those two guys came up and carried the woman away."

"Did *Martinez* loan you the money to fix your car?" Aguilar said raising his voice.

Maldonado looked back at him and after a moment said, "Fuck, no. I wouldn't trust that *puta* with anything, including her money."

"Then tell me who the hell it was that gave you the money," Aguilar said.

"I told you I don't know his name. Somebody mentioned the words 'El Puma' when he gave me the money. That's all I know."

"No, it's not all you know," Aguilar said. "He gave you the money to kill that woman, didn't he?"

"Hell no!"

"That's murder for hire," Harry said. "You could get life imprisonment."

Maldonado looked at Harry and said, "He paid me to start the fight, that's all. I was just supposed to shove the woman around in the bar. I didn't know it was going to end up outside in the parking lot, and I didn't know that the woman was going to get killed."

"Who were the two guys who carried the victim away?" Aguilar said.

"I don't know. No one told me they were going to be there."

"Was the victim still alive when they picked her up?"

"Yeah. She was beat up, but still alive."

"Did you kick her when she was on the ground?"

"Hell no. I wasn't paid to kick nobody. The little bitch did all the kicking."

"You seem to know her pretty well," Harry said. "Is she a former friend?"

"I don't know her at all. I was told she would be there to assist me in the fight. I didn't know that she was there to set me up."

"The other woman is willing to sign an affidavit saying that it was you who kicked and punched the victim in the parking lot," Harry said. He looked at her with the same stern expression as if he were a judge that had just handed her a guilty verdict.

"Well, she's a whore, and I don't care what she says."

"We're going to charge you with murder one if you don't feel like telling us the name of the person who paid you," Aguilar told her.

Maldonado breathed hard and grimaced without saying anything. She started to stare off into the corner of the room.

"But if you want to cooperate, maybe we'll give you a break," Aguilar said.

Maldonado quickly snapped back to attention. "What kind of break?" she said.

"It depends on how much you tell us," Aguilar said.

She hesitated again and then said, "Well, what do you want to know?"

Aguilar relaxed and leaned back in his chair. It appeared that he was achieving the results he wanted, and that Maldonado was starting to turn her thinking in his direction. "We're going to take you to an artist," he said. "He's going to create a computer image of this guy, 'El Puma' based on what you tell him. And if what you tell him turns out to be bullshit, you'll go down for murdering that woman."

The two detectives still had Anita Martinez waiting in the other room. As they walked back to her, Aguilar said, "I'm going to let you break the news to her since she seemed to open up to you."

"OK," Harry said. Once in the room he sat down behind the table across from Martinez. Aguilar stood in the corner.

"We have some news for you," Harry began, recognizing that Martinez was still in stonewall mode. "Your accomplice has decided to blame you for killing the victim. She's willing to sign an affidavit that will put you away for murder one."

At last the stone face turned red. "*Eso es una mierda*," she said. "*Tu policia no sabe nada*."

Harry didn't understand, but he said, "She told us the whole thing. Now it's time to hear what you have to say about it."

Martinez stood up and got in Harry's face, "*Puedes ir a la mierda, tu estupido chino mono!*" she said. "*Chino mono*!" she repeated and swung her fist to punch him in the face. But with quickness seen only in a martial arts contest, Harry left his seat, easily parried the movement with his left hand, and simultaneously drew his pistol with his right hand pointing it directly at her face inches away from her nose. Martinez froze.

Aguilar then stepped in and pushed her back into her seat. "Actions speak louder than words," he said. "You've just got yourself into a murder charge."

Believing that they could upgrade the charges later, Aguilar decided to file the only charges they could prove at the time—aggravated assault. He went to talk to Captain Kreider about upgrading the charges to murder.

"We've got both perpetrators in the nightclub murder behind bars," Aguilar told him. "We think the second one is the instigator of the fight. We want to charge her with second-degree murder."

Kreider was looking into the computer screen on his desk. He looked at Aguilar and said, "You're nuts! You want to charge the smaller woman with murder when the bigger one did all the punching and kicking? I thought you were smarter than that."

Aguilar was used to disrespectful remarks from his boss. He had less and less respect for Kreider who spent most of his day in the office dealing with his other officers or the LAPD top brass. He rarely ventured into the field.

"It's no coincidence why the second woman was there," Aguilar said. "You can see from the security disk that she was there specifically to make sure that the first woman started the fight. Then she helped her out…"

"You don't have anything, sergeant—just assault and battery like I said before."

"The first woman was paid to start the fight," Aguilar said. "She told us so."

"Who paid her?"

"She doesn't know the person's name. She's willing to work with the composite artist to create a sketch…"

"She got paid to start a fight, and she doesn't know who paid her? How much was she paid?"

Aguilar took a deep breath before answering. "Five thousand," he said.

Kreider sat in silence, considering what Aguilar just told him. "I'm sorry, I just don't believe you," he finally said. "It sounds too flaky to me."

"I don't think you're looking closely enough at the evidence," Aguilar said.

"That's because you don't have any!" Kreider told him. "Charge the second person with assault and battery. That's it."

Aguilar knew that Kreider had left him a loophole when he arrested Maldonado, giving him the opportunity to show the evidence he had to the DA. He left Kreider's office and went to visit Richard Frederick again.

"This sounds like the last time you were in here," Frederick said.

"The difference," Aguilar said, "is we got the first suspect to confirm that somebody else paid her to start the fight. She also said that she didn't know that the fight would wind up in the parking lot or that two guys would carry the victim away. Because she was paid, this tells us that those two guys were planted there also and are a part of this scheme. She also said that she never saw suspect number two before that night."

"What you've got is too thin for murder two," Frederick said. "This witness can't confirm that the murder took place while the victim was in the custody of the two 'saviors.' The first suspect was more violent and agitated—hence, the manslaughter charge. But the second one can only get charged with assault and battery."

"What about conspiracy to commit murder?" Aguilar said. "We've got to hold this person. I'm starting to believe that the first suspect isn't lying. She described the whole thing as setting her up to take the fall for the crime."

"To charge either perpetrator with conspiracy, we've got to connect the two killers with the two women who started the fight. Since we can't confirm who the killers actually were, we can't make this connection. I'm sorry, but assault and battery is the best we can do for the second suspect for now."

"What about the first suspect? Aren't you going to change what she's charged with, based on what we've just said?"

Frederick thought about it for a moment. Then he said, "I can drop manslaughter and charge her with conspiracy to commit murder based upon her being paid to start the fight. But you've got to come up with the person who paid her."

"Then she's going to make bail and be out of here as soon as that happens." Aguilar said, concerned that whatever work they'd done so far would then disappear.

"I don't think so," Frederick said. "If she were to have a resource post bail in this case, it would have happened by now."

CHAPTER FOURTEEN

Jay was at work reviewing his notes to see if there was anything besides the stolen money that might provide a motive for someone to kill Lisa. The phone on his desk rang.

"Funny thing that you should be hearing from me, huh Newsboy?" Aguilar said. "It's usually the other way around."

"I *am* surprised, Sergeant Aguilar," Jay said. "But also delighted! You must have something for me."

"I do. We made another arrest in the nightclub case—we got the other Latina who was involved in the fight. She's being held on an assault and battery charges, pending further investigation. There might be more charges in her case."

"Cool! What further charges are we talking about?"

"That's where you come in, Newsboy. The Renaissance Estates connection is all we have so far. Who have you been talking to over there lately?"

"My main source is the assistant manager. Her name is Rudi Sirianni," he said, and then realized that in the excitement of the news of a second arrest he'd neglected to protect his source. "By the way, I almost forgot," he said, regardless. "Did you know that the owner sent her own auditor over there to go over the books?"

"Tell me about it," Aguilar said.

"Well, as we know, the victim was the accountant. The Federal Department of Housing and Urban Development audited to try to find out what happened with the stolen money, but they didn't find anything. I just found out that the owner sent in her own auditor to try to figure out what happened."

"And what did happen?" Aguilar said.

"Erica's auditor didn't find out who took the money, or how it went missing. But he did find out a lot of other things."

"Such as…"

"They've been paying the security service tens of thousands each month for security, and the checks are being cashed instead of deposited in the bank," Jay said. "The security service doesn't seem to be providing that much security over there, according to what I have heard as well as what I can see for myself."

"What's the security service's name?"

"South Bay Neighborhood Association."

Bells and whistles went off in Aguilar's head. "I need to see the results of this audit—the one ordered by the owner," he said. "How can I do that?"

"Call Rudi Sirianni. She can help you with that."

"Did you see anything else in the audit that might be helpful?"

"No. Rudi explained that there's a lot of waste going on there that didn't happen before. People being overpaid for simple jobs, contractors being brought in to do what employees were already paid to do, stuff like that. She made it sound like a campaign was being conducted to run the place into the ground and then blame the former manager."

"Is there anything else we should know about?" Aguilar said.

"I was just thinking," Jay said. "If somebody was wasting money and doing shady things, sooner or later the accountant would find out about it. Maybe somehow Lisa knew too much, and that's why she was killed."

"My exact thoughts, Newsboy! Good work. Keep it up, and keep us informed."

After he hung up the phone, Jay remembered that he had just dropped the name of his major source in the story to the police. *Damn, I shouldn't have done that*, he thought. Then he picked up the phone again and called Rudi. "You might be getting a call from the police working on the Lisa Nguyen case," he said.

"Whoa! What would they be calling me about?" Rudi said.

"The detective in charge of the investigation wants to see the audit that Erica had done."

"I'm glad you told me ahead of time," Rudi said. "I don't like getting surprised by the police."

"Could you make a copy of the audit results for him? His name is Sergeant Carlos Aguilar of the LAPD."

"I can't do that. I'll have to send him to Erica."

"Damn, I guess I should have thought of that," Jay said. He was deeply regretting his faux pas about exposing his sources.

"Oh, no worries," Rudi said. "I'll handle it. I just hope he comes over here on a day that Millwood is not around."

"I believe he'll call you ahead of time and give you a chance to arrange the meeting."

When he got off the phone he turned around and saw Dylan standing right next to him. "What's happening, man?" Dylan said.

"There's been another arrest in the nightclub murder case—the other woman involved in the barroom fight," Jay told him.

"Cool. You can see that the chances of a big conspiracy are improving," Dylan said.

"Well, I'm trying, man. I'm trying."

"Yes, you are. But before you go anywhere, I need you to check your emails."

Jay turned around and read through his messages. He quickly saw one from Meredith that said she needed to see him right away in her office. As he read the email with Dylan looking over his shoulder, he said, "Oh shit. I must be in trouble again."

"She just wants an update on the story and a recap of what you've been doing," Dylan said.

Jay noticed that Dylan was copied in on the email. "Are you coming, too?"

"Yeah, I'm afraid so."

The two reporters sat down in their editor's office. Jay had brought his notes with him since he thought he might need to pull out some details.

Meredith began by saying, "Jay, we need to take a long, hard look at what you've written here about the nightclub murder."

"What about my piece about all the corruption and malfeasance at Renaissance Estates?" Jay said, thinking that his best defense might be a good offense.

"Are you able to back up everything you say in that?" Meredith said. "You seem to be accusing the powers that run Renaissance Estates of fraud of some kind."

"Oh, I can totally back it up. I've got the assistant manager who works there right now and I've got the former manager who's still the owner of the complex. And I also talked to the current manager who wouldn't confirm or deny any of the issues when I confronted him. And I've got the stand-in president of the holding company who corroborates everything."

"OK, OK. Let's say you can back it up. Tell me how all this ties into the murder."

"The motive to get rid of the accountant might be to protect whomever it was that took the missing money. This person might still be working there, I don't know. Also, my sources swear that there's a campaign going on to push the owner out by discrediting her."

"That's pretty flimsy," Meredith said. "What else can you tell me about this 'corruption campaign'?"

"HUD did an audit when the money—about twenty thousand--went missing. They didn't find out what happened to the money. But they did find out a lot about what they called 'managerial malfeasance.' The HUD loan manager blamed the owner for it all, and that's why she got removed as manager."

"This information doesn't sound like it's taking us anywhere. What else?"

"The owner hired a different auditor to check on the missing money and also on the managerial problems. The second auditor discovered that sums of money were being systematically removed from the premises in the way of overcharging for security services." Jay paused to see if Meredith was buying in to what he was telling her.

"Go on," Meredith said.

"I just found out that the FBI is investigating the loan manager at HUD who provided the funds to build the place. My sources believe he's being bribed with the money that's been pilfered."

Meredith paused then said, "Who would stand to gain by bribing the HUD loan manager?"

"Well, it's got to be whoever wants the owner out of the way," Jay said.

"I thought you just said the HUD loan manager wanted the owner out of the way."

"I don't think he's orchestrating all this." Jay said. "I think he's being bribed by someone else. For sure he's heaping all the blame on the owner. He's also probably in a position to take the property away from the her, if he can prove managerial failure of some kind."

"But you don't know who's behind it all. You're suggesting that whoever is bribing the HUD loan manager, if that's the case, could be the one driving this effort to get rid of the owner—including murder."

"You've got it.," Jay said, with a grin.

"No, I don't. You haven't found out who that person is yet. Before we pursue this any further, you need to tell me how this fraud and malfeasance came to light."

Jay took a deep breath and let it out slowly. He knew he had a story, but he also knew that it could get killed right then and there by Meredith. "Let's start with the missing money," Jay said. "Then came the HUD audit. This was not conclusive but pointed out managerial issues. The issues got the owner, who was also the manager, fired. This person is still the owner and managed to get another audit with someone she hired to review the case. The second audit was also not conclusive, but it turned up financial irregularities that had not been discovered before. The irregularities revealed lots of misappropriated money that could be used to bribe the HUD official, who might in turn be able to force the owner to sell."

"And the accountant knew about it and that's why she was murdered," Meredith said.

"Totally."

Meredith mulled that explanation over for a moment. "Well, it's plausible, but it's still weak. We still need something more concrete to be able to point to a murderer."

"So do the police," Jay said. "By the way the detective sergeant who is investigating the case stays in close contact with me. It's almost like we're working together."

"Oh, he does, huh," Meredith said. "You'd better remember that he has police procedures and protocols to adhere to. He won't make any accusations without evidence. You're trying to do that with your story. It's turning into a sideshow."

"Maybe. But the sideshow might be every bit as good as the main event," Jay said. When backed up against a wall, he still had the wherewithal to push back. "There's got to be some kind of connection. The victim was not killed in a barroom fight. She was carried off by two guys acting as rescuers, and then she turned up dead. That means there was a plot behind it."

"The end result of your story is only that the owner of Renaissance Estates was removed as manager. It doesn't point to a murder," Meredith said.

Dylan spoke up. "Excuse me, if I may just add something here," he said.

"Go ahead," Meredith said, shifting her attention to Dylan.

"The mayor has expressed that the land along Sultan Road in Harbor/Gateway is his favorite for a new NFL football stadium. Jay and I were talking about this just the other day, as there is a concerted effort to bring an NFL team here. This Renaissance Estates apartment complex is dead center in the middle of the land that the mayor wants. It would be impossible to build a football stadium without removing it."

Again, Meredith contemplated what she just heard. "Now you're saying the mayor wants the land for a football stadium," she said. "And to get it, he first needs to get his hands on Renaissance Estates. To do this, he has to shake up the ownership of the place therefore the corruption. Somewhere along the way, the accountant discovered that money was being pilfered and used for nefarious purposes—like bribing a HUD official."

Both Jay and Dylan looked at her with smiles on their faces.

"I don't know guys. I don't know," Meredith said. She did not have a smile on her face. It was apparent, though, that she understood that all the pieces of the puzzle that Jay had been putting together were likely very important. "We sure as hell can't publish anything suggestive like that without proof." She contemplated some more, looking out her window. Then she returned her focus to Dylan. "But if it were true, it might be so big a story that it would even put Watergate to shame," she said.

Meredith scrolled though her computer for a moment, perusing the files that Jay had sent her. "All right," she finally said. "You guys are both on the story. But major investigative work is needed here. You can't mess it up with accusations or innuendos that aren't corroborated and that could offend the mayor, the HUD official, or anyone else. Take out the bribery charge for now, and write up what you found out based upon the two audits. You can claim that the victim probably knew about the missing money, and so on. Get something ready for me—I need it by three this afternoon."

"Oh, one more thing I forgot to tell you," Jay said.

"Yes?" Meredith said.

"The police made another arrest. They've got the second person who was in the barroom fight."

"All right, get that to me first. And get them both by three. Let's get moving, guys."

Jay and Dylan left Meredith's office acting calm. Once they were outside, Jay turned around, did a hop, skip, and a jump, and high fived Dylan.

"Man, we've got a blockbuster!" Dylan said. He started rubbing his hands together.

"Totally!" Jay said. "Beginning with a gruesome murder that could include a cover up that leads to city hall. I love it, I love it, I love it."

Soon after Jay and Dylan had left, Meredith received a phone call from the *Daily Journal's* publisher, Albert Hudgins. "I thought you had some sort of murder mystery story about a housing project being worked up," he said.

"I do," Meredith said. "But it's still in its infancy. The nasty nightclub fight in Harbor/Gateway that lead to a woman's death might be part of a plot."

"Who have you got on it?" Hudgins said.

"Phillips."

"Phillips? Wasn't he writing surfing pieces for us a few months ago?"

"Yes, it's the same guy."

"Well, you better think about putting one our aces on this instead," Hudgins said. "If there is a plot, I want it covered on the front-page. We *need* a good story like this. A good serial story with a plot of some kind can do a hell of a lot for us."

"I'm sticking with Phillips, but I've got Claremont helping him."

"Why do you like Phillips so much?"

"His delivery is smooth, and his articles make a great read for our readers. Further, he relates with the younger set as well as older, more established readers. He's hungry and working his ass off because he's trying to succeed. His research is turning out to be thorough. All he needs to do is to learn not to waste words."

"And you said Claremont is helping him?"

"That's right."

"Claremont's just a sports writer."

"He dug up something vital to the story. It appears that Mayor McGinnis has indicated that the land that this housing project is sitting on where the murder victim worked, should be used for a new NFL football stadium."

"Someone wants the land for a football stadium badly enough to kill for it?" Hudgins said, without being sarcastic. "If this turns out to be true, it could be sensational for us."

"That's my exact thought."

Hudgins was silent for a moment then said, "All right, but if this story gets botched, some heads will roll."

"I'm watching it like a hawk," Meredith said.

CHAPTER FIFTEEN

Millwood had his own office in Torrance complete with a small staff. Although the office was located on the corner of two major boulevards, it was tucked away on the bottom floor around the back of a recently built two-story building. But much of the time, he would work at one or another of the five Section 8 housing complexes that his firm managed. He was in the Millwood Property Management offices one morning, preparing to go to Renaissance Estates, when the phone rang. It was DeShawn Walker, who sounded upset.

"I have got a huge problem on my hands thanks to Renaissance Estates," Walker said. "I need to talk to you here in my office as soon as you can get over here."

"Well, I was just on my way out, and I do have a lot of appointments today," Millwood told him. "Any chance we can handle this problem over the phone?"

"Goddamn it, that bitch has convinced the FBI to investigate whether or not I received a bribe! Can you believe that? A motherfucking BRIBE!"

Millwood sat back down in his chair. "The FBI? A bribe? Just what in the hell happened?" he said.

"The FBI has subpoenaed my banking and tax records, and they were over at my house yesterday, doing an inventory of my possessions including my wife's jewelry! I'm so goddamned mad that I would kill that bitch if she was anywhere near me right now."

"I guess you mean Erica Knight," Millwood said.

"Get your ass over here right away. Cancel your damn meetings. My entire career is on the line."

Millwood told his assistant to reschedule his meetings and then got in the car for the long drive through late morning traffic to Walker's office in Westwood. He wasn't sure what he could do about Walker's dire straits. But he knew he needed to keep Walker on his side. Walker was responsible for much of his success with government housing, and he didn't want to be standoffish at a time like this.

The drive took an hour and a half from door to door. When he finally arrived, Millwood sat down in front of Walker's desk and heard the details of the problem. Walker had calmed down somewhat by then.

"I've had my house searched, my financial records subpoenaed, my laptop taken, and even my cell phone has been confiscated by the FBI!" Walker said. His voice rang out with anxiety. "They've gone around to the neighbors, asking questions. Hell, they even went to my country club and talked to some of the members. And it all got started by that bitch."

Millwood knew that to put a plan together, he needed to find out more information—even at the risk of aggravating Walker further. "First off, I'm sorry for what happened," he said. "Erica had no right to do anything like this. And further, I know that she didn't have any evidence to give to the FBI. What was it they told you when they came calling?"

"Nothing," Walker said, after finishing a sip of water. "They just handed me the warrant and started snooping around."

"If Erica tipped them off, it had to be about something specific. It might have been written down in the warrant. Can I see it?"

In a much calmer tone of voice Walker said, "I gave it to my personal attorney."

"If we just knew what it was that triggered…"

"She had that goddamn auditor over there!" Walker yelled. "Something he found out about the finances of the place translated into a bribe that I was supposed to be getting."

"Well, that's ridiculous. I know for a fact that her auditor didn't find a damn thing. And we both know that nothing in the way of a bribe came up in the HUD audit six months ago."

"The FBI thinks that the accounting practices are so bad that money is being pilfered and falling into the wrong hands."

"What, exactly, about the accounting practices? After the one bookkeeper died, we brought in another one who seems to me to be doing the job just fine."

"Have you ever heard of the South Bay Neighborhood Association?"

"Well yes, and that's the second time this week somebody asked me that question."

"Who the hell else wants to know about me 'supposedly being bribed'?"

"Oh, there was the young reporter from the *Daily Journal*. He was asking about some checks that we paid to South Bay Neighborhood Association..."

"A reporter for the *Daily Journal*!" Walker said, his voice was near a shriek. He shot to his feet and put his balled-up fists on his hips. His jaw dropped as he looked at Millwood.

"Yeah, he was young guy, just a kid," Millwood said. His tone also rose slightly in response to Walker's outbursts.

"And now my problems with the FBI are being published in the newspaper so that three million readers in the Los Angeles area can read about it?"

"No, no, no. This guy just asked me about the South Bay Neighborhood Association and the checks we have sent them. That's all. He wanted to know why they had cashed the checks instead of depositing them into their bank account. I told him he should ask them, because I sure as hell didn't know."

Walker looked at Millwood as if he'd expected an ice cream cone but had gotten a turnip instead. "Those checks that are being cashed—the FBI thinks they are the source of the money that's bribing people, including me. They also think that the money that was stolen might have landed into my lap as well."

"Huh. That's amazing," Millwood said. "Nobody seems to know what happened to the stolen money. And I can tell you that I really don't give a shit what South Bay Neighborhood Association does with the checks we send them. I can guarantee you that nobody over in the

Renaissance Estates offices is getting kickbacks from anyone."

"Then why the hell am I on the motherfucking grill over this? Tell me that. Even if they clear me of any wrongdoing, my career will still get a black eye over it." Walker sat back down at his desk. It didn't appear to Millwood that Walker would ever calm down as long as they continued talking about bribes and kickbacks.

"Well, let's see what we can do about damage control," Millwood said, trying to steer the discussion onto a less volatile topic. He could empathize with Walker being in a hot seat, since his own seat was getting a little warm.

"I just wish I hadn't let her talk me into having her own auditor." Walker said, lamenting his circumstances. "All I had to do was say 'no', and none of this shit would have happened."

Millwood's mind began to turn and a few thoughts occurred to him. "What you need to do is go on the offensive," he said.

"How am I going to do that?" Walker said. "It's the FBI we're talking about. I don't have much of a chance going on the offensive against the feds, do I?"

"Your real problem is Erica and not the feds," Millwood said. He was already on an offensive of his own and was now trying to get Walker on board. "The FBI is going to come up with nothing at Renaissance Estates exactly like I just finished telling you. It's squeaky clean over there."

Walker gave Millwood that same look of disgust and despair. "And just what do you think I should do about

Erica?" he said. "I've already removed her as manager of Renaissance Estates. I can't get her to give up being the owner unless there's some criminal activity on her part. Trying to fuck me over is not considered criminal activity."

"She slandered you," Millwood said with a look of conviction. "In fact, I think it amounts to libel. You should try to sue her."

"I don't want to sue her," Walker said. "I can't collect anything. She's got an unpaid-for condominium in Long Beach, and she's got Renaissance Estates. And the value of her stake in Renaissance Estates isn't worth very much as long as HUD has a large mortgage on the place."

Millwood continued to think hard as if his future depended upon coming up with the right answer. "You can have her arrested for illegal trespassing."

"Look, damn it, I need some real ideas here. I can't get her arrested for illegal trespassing—I gave her permission to send someone in there."

"How about if you deny that you ever gave permission?"

"I can't. I signed a paper authorizing her to send in her own auditor to look at the books and records."

Millwood started to perspire. He thought he might be running out of time to turn Walker around and aim him at Erica. "Suppose you and the federal government were to file a civil lawsuit against Erica that required her to divest herself of Renaissance Estates? In fact, you should be able to get her prohibited from doing business with any branch of the federal government for a period of, say, twenty years to life."

Walker pondered that for a moment as if he recognized that this idea might actually be something useful. "On what grounds does the federal government sue?" he finally said.

"Bad accounting practices, missing money, wasteful management, lack of institutional control. And, if we keep expounding upon it, the list can get longer and longer."

"I've already kicked her ass around for all that."

"Not for irresponsible financial practices. The HUD audit did not include that, but her audit did. You should just turn the tables and blame the entire thing on her. The great weight of a lawsuit of divestiture filed by the federal government could bring her to her knees. And further, it might go a long way toward proving to the government that you were being shit on and slandered by her."

Walker leaned back in his chair. "I get her to divest herself of the property by intimidating her with a lawsuit," he said, rubbing his chin.

"It would not only intimidate her, but it would also serve to clear your name."

Walker had finally calmed down. With his elbows on his desk and his nearly bald head in his hands, he went into thinking mode. After a moment, he looked up and said only, "Hmm."

"We could design it so that her current debarment would be extended to include all persons employed by her company," Millwood said. "That would include anybody she put in as president of her company, cutting her off from all aspects of management."

Walker stared at the floor. Millwood could tell that Walker liked what he had just heard enough to give it careful consideration.

"If the suit is successful," Millwood added, "her ownership stake would be reduced to only a name on a piece of paper somewhere in HUD's archives. She would have no other alternative but to rid herself of the property."

Walker smiled. "There might even be a federal law that gives HUD the right to take the property away from her and then sell it to the highest bidder," he said. "I think I'll look into that."

"The remedy put forth in the lawsuit could be simply that her company must sell the property and not assign it to somebody else. This cuts out anybody who could somehow sit in the leadership role as her proxy."

"I'm starting to like this," Walker said. "But I don't know about its chances for success. She's a stubborn woman and she won't give up easily."

"That's why you're going to heap on the pressure," Millwood said. "During the course of settling, we can make it crystal clear that if she sells, the debarment will end or perhaps be reduced to a period of, say, five years."

"And if she doesn't sell?"

"You will have effectively cut her off at every turn. There won't be anything left for her to do—no more Section 8 housing, no more government sponsored programs for the needy, no more nothing. She'll be finished."

"It sounds good. In fact, I think it's worth taking a shot at," Walker said. "I knew you'd come up with something. I owe you a lot."

Millwood felt that at least he'd turned Walker's focus away from the FBI. Now he decided to pursue a hidden agenda of his own. "What do you think will happen to Renaissance Estates if she does finally divest herself of it?"

"If she's going to sell it, HUD would need to approve the sale. But don't worry. Your role as managing agent would stay the same. I don't want anybody else to come in until all the dirty linen has been cleaned up. That's what you're there for."

"Do you think that the court would conduct a sheriff's auction of some kind if she decided to fight it out?" Millwood said.

"That's stepping into legal areas that I don't know that much about," Walker said. "I'll find out soon. I'm going to talk to HUD's attorneys and see what they have to say."

"I'd like to be there, if you don't mind."

"Thanks, but you've done enough to help. I appreciate your advice. I might have a way out of this trap after all."

CHAPTER SIXTEEN

When Jay got the next edition of his story back from Meredith, he was shell-shocked. The comments were virtually after every paragraph—often after each sentence. The overall comments were short and to the point—cut out a third of the story to get it printed. He read through all the comments carefully trying to understand everything that Meredith was looking for. It frustrated him to find out that what he had worked so hard to write was so unacceptable that he would have to rewrite it. Doubt replaced the confidence he had felt recently that he could make it as a journalist. He couldn't help the feeling that failure was looming. With the "Golden Surfer" staring straight at him from the picture in his cubicle, he decided he needed Dylan's help. He went upstairs to find him.

"I got to show you this, dude," Jay said. "You won't believe the edit on my last piece." He logged into Dylan's workstation with his own login ID that enabled Dylan read the comments firsthand.

Dylan spent a few minutes reading through it, and then he went to the end to see the terse comments. "Well, I get where she's coming from," he said. "The story's content is not the problem. It's the delivery. It really needs to be cut down."

"How do we do that?" Jay said.

"The overall gist of what you are saying should not require this many words," Dylan said. "I can see right away a few sentences that can be trimmed out."

"Why can't they just add more pages to the paper?" Jay said, not really joking.

"Remember what I told you about holding the readers' interest?" Dylan said. "All adding more pages will do is increase the cost of printing and distribution. The name of the game is holding the readers' attention."

"If the content is good, why does the length matter?" Jay said. "If it's a good story, the reader should keep on reading."

"Most readers don't pick up a newspaper article to sit down to a good story," Dylan said. "If a good story is what they want, they'll get a novel, or a biography, or something. They're usually just looking for a quick information fix. They're often busy and need to be doing something else, so they can't kick back and read something that's really long. Also think of the alternatives. Radio and TV spit the news out at you while you are driving, or at home eating dinner, or doing something else at the same time. Reading requires more attention. Further, the average person's attention span is getting shorter with each generation. People our age are usually satisfied with getting their news requirements from a cell phone rather than a newspaper."

"I know, man, but you can't trust everything you see on the web," Jay said. "I'm more likely to believe what I read in a newspaper or magazine than with cell phone or computer news."

"Sure, but that's you," Dylan said. "Daily newspapers are a dying breed. We need more readers—especially younger ones."

"I can't stand watching the network news," Jay said. "They fire it at you like you're a deer and they're the hunters."

"Network news uses a lot fewer words for the same amount of content," Dylan told him. "That's what people are looking for. You can probably fit the network news' entire half hour's content onto half a page of our newspaper."

"Maybe so. But what about the debates they have where they pit people on different sides of an issue against each other?" Jay said. "What do the networks gain from that?"

"Their concept is that both sides to the issue are represented. The presentation will give the viewers more information to help them make good decisions."

Jay didn't agree. "You should listen to some of it," he said. "It degenerates into talking between bullshit artists, spin doctors, and professional propagandists. The 'winner' is usually just the person who talks the loudest and interrupts the opposition the most."

"Maybe. But people watch it."

"And the networks fire advertising at you the same way."

"All this complaining still isn't helping you get your story out."

"I know. But sometimes I just wonder if I'm in the wrong business."

"Would you rather be writing news copy for the network news?"

"Not really. And I'm not wild about social media either."

"We've got social media beat," Dylan said. "It's popular, but people are beginning to realize that it's not good journalism. Further, it's often actually untrue. The growing amount of disinformation is slowly pushing people back to credible news sources like us."

"I understand," Jay said, as he took it all in. In the final analysis, he was merely venting his frustrations. "But what am I going to do about this edit?" he said.

"I need to show you how not to waste words," Dylan said. "That's all."

It took about an hour, but Dylan showed Jay how to cut down his story by one third without eliminating vital content. Jay was impressed as he saw firsthand what he had overlooked when he first reviewed his own writing. Much of what could go was now obvious, and he felt a little foolish. As he incorporated Dylan's changes and sent the story back to Meredith for publication, Jay asked Dylan about the next steps in his investigation.

"You've told me that Sultan Road is largely vacant land," Dylan said as he leaned back in his chair. "Have you found out anything about how it got to be that way?"

"No. Hell, I wouldn't know where to start," Jay said.

"One thing you could do is take a trip to Norwalk," Dylan said.

Jay thought Dylan was pulling his leg. "Norwalk?" he said. "Now, just what is it in dumpy Norwalk that I need to go see?"

Dylan looked him straight in the eye. "Ever heard of the Los Angeles County Hall of Records?" he said.

"Well, no. What is it?" Jay said.

"You can look up property transactions there. With a little research you could come up with the complete history of all the title transactions of the vacant land around Renaissance Estates."

Jay pondered that for a moment. "That sounds pretty good," he admitted. "How do I get started?"

"You'll need to get your hands on as many specific street addresses as you can in the area along Sultan Road and its cross streets," Dylan said. "You'll need those addresses to be able to look up title transactions on the hall of records' system. If you locate a some of them, you can start guessing at the ones next to or between those you found."

Jay hesitated, then gave Dylan that "lost" look that had served him well in the past. "Any chance you could come with me just to get me started?" he said.

"Naw, man, you're a big boy," Dylan said. "You can do it. It's on Imperial Highway in Norwalk. You can't miss it."

Jay spent the afternoon digging through some of the newspaper's reference materials and putting together a list of as many addresses in and around Sultan Road as he could find. Armed with this list, he made his first trip to the hall of records the next morning.

At first glance, the Los Angeles County Hall of Records appeared to be an ordinary office building with large glass windows on each of its four stories and a large parking lot in front. As he walked from his van to the front entrance, he noticed reflections of white, puffy clouds and the blue sky on the building's glass windows. Once inside, he saw that the interior of the building more resembled that of any other county or city office building—stark walls, direction signs with arrows, and people waiting in line to get to the records they wanted. There were no luxuries such as carpets or modern furniture that the typical corporate office building might have.

Jay began to dig through microfiche files searching for the details of transactions for the properties on Sultan Road and the surrounding area. He had brought an extract of a map of the area to help him. It was tedious at first, but he began to notice two names that kept turning up in the documentation. Many of the transactions transferred ownership of the land from Jefferson Square to Regal Management Associates. Most transactions took place between 1996 and 1999. Then he found a title transaction that really caught his attention—in March, 1999, a large tract of land was sold by the Jefferson Square Company to the Harbor Gateway Community Housing Corporation. He was so completely engrossed in his work that he forgot to take a lunch break. He kept grinding away at his research until the security guard came around and told him he had to leave since the hall of records was closing for the day. He went back the next day, and the day after that to complete his research. By that time, he had acquired so much material to peruse that he decided to go back to the newsroom and sort out what it all meant.

Using a larger map fastened to the wall of his cubicle, Jay pinpointed the location of some of the transactions he had discovered. Then he sat down to mull them over with Dylan.

"Wow, you did quite a lot while you were over there," Dylan said. "I'm impressed!"

"I found a lot," Jay said. "I'm just not sure yet what it all means."

Dylan looked at Jay's map and then at the summary he'd made. "Well, it looks like the Jefferson Square Company sold a lot of the land in that area to another company named Regal Management Associates."

"Take a look at this sale in particular," Jay said. "It's from the Jefferson Square Company to the Harbor Gateway Community Housing Corporation."

"That's a big plot of land, and it's near the middle of the overall area," Dylan said, as he continued to examine what Jay had turned up.

"The dates…look at the dates of these transactions," Dylan said. They're all after June of 1996, and they run up to 1999. Did you find any transactions that were outside of this date range?"

"Yeah, I think so," Jay said. He looked through his notes just to be sure.

"Here's what I see happening with all this," Dylan said. "The dates begin about six months after both the Rams and the Raiders moved away from LA"

"Yeah," Jay said. He looked at the map as though the answers to the questions he still had must be staring back at him.

"And the single biggest transaction is the Harbor Gateway plot, that is right smack dab in the middle of it all," Dylan said.

"Ah huh," Jay said slowly. He didn't see what Dylan was getting at.

"The mayor wants a new football stadium to be built there."

"I'm with you," Jay said, even though in truth he was still lost.

"The Regal Management Associates have been busy acquiring the land in that area as if they knew there would be a football stadium there one day."

It started to come together for Jay. "The mayor must somehow be connected to Regal Management Associates," he said.

"Maybe," Dylan said. "But somebody knew that a big development would be coming to this area, as the land has just been sitting there mostly unoccupied for nearly twenty years."

"All true. But there's one more thing," Jay said. "The Harbor Gateway Community Housing Corporation is the owner of Renaissance Estates."

"Wow!" Dylan said snapping his head around to look at Jay. "You're not shitting me, are you?"

"Nope."

"That means that all this stuff you've been finding out about the owner of Renaissance Estates being pushed to sell must be because it's sitting in the way of the new football stadium," Dylan said, as if his prophecy of the week before were about to come true.

"Do you think that this means that the mayor might be behind it all?" Jay said. "I mean, even Lisa's murder?"

Dylan still looked incredulous. He kept his eyes on the map as if he, too, expected the answers to jump out at him. "I don't know," he finally said. "I really don't know." He paused for a moment. Then he said, "But we're going to have to find out. If it's true, we've hit the bullseye."

At Dylan's request, Jay began to dig through the newspaper's files to see if there were any stories about the Jefferson Square Company. Jay's research led him to an article in the *Daily Journal* from nearly thirty years before about the Jefferson Square Company. They pioneered the move of a large tract of housing from the Westchester area, next to Los Angeles International Airport, to the Sultan Road area in order to make way for an airport expansion. The company acquired these houses, before they were to be condemned by the county under eminent domain. They then relocated them in and around Sultan Road, that was at that time a rundown industrial area. The plan for Jefferson Square was to lease the houses with an option to buy to mostly working-class tenants, who could not afford the down payment necessary to purchase a house in the usual manner. The tenants were promised ownership of their homes after a period of twenty years of paying rent. Jay read further that the Jefferson Square Company was badly mismanaged. Faced with bankruptcy, the company sought a buyer to bail them out. Enter Regal Management Associates.

In further research, Jay found another article about tenants of Jefferson Square being evicted by Regal Management without receiving any of the equity of their houses as had been promised. Still another article revealed that arguably illegal means on the part of Regal Management Associates were used to take possession of some of these properties. A few of the tenants had even attempted to get a court order to block eviction until it could be ascertained as to what equity was owed to them.

A while later, Dylan and Jay had another meeting to discuss this new research.

"The pattern that's emerging here," Dylan said, "is that those people who leased their homes from Jefferson Square wound up being pushed out into the street and screwed out of the title to the property by Regal Management Associates."

"And it's still going on at Renaissance Estates," Jay said.

"Exactly," Dylan said.

Jay and Dylan went to Meredith's office with Jay's notes and map.

After reviewing Jay's notes drafted in outline form Meredith said, "This looks interesting, but how does it all come together?"

Dylan took the lead by making series of summarizing statements. "Beginning after the Rams and the Raiders moved from LA, this Jefferson Square Company began to unload their properties in the Sultan Road area to ward off bankruptcy. The major buyer was Regal Management Associates. The people who lived in those relocated homes—who all had leases with the option to buy—were systematically kicked out. The homes were then leveled, and the land was left unoccupied. The only major structure remaining is Renaissance Estates. Jay's research has discovered that they're still trying to kick the owner of Renaissance Estates off that large piece of land with audits, court actions, and so on."

"I still don't see the tie-in to the Nguyen case," Meredith said.

"Lisa Nguyen was murdered because she knew that some people were trying to get ahold of Renaissance Estates illegally," Dylan said. "Renaissance Estates is the only thing left on Sultan Road that could block a major development."

"What is it that she knew that was important enough to get her killed?" Meredith said.

"The mayor wants the land for the new NFL football stadium," Dylan told her.

"And you think the accountant knew about that?" Meredith said.

"We don't know for sure," Dylan said. "No one knows, but we're working on it."

Meredith mulled that statement over. "That's a little outrageous, wouldn't you say?" she said. "If we published something like that accusing people in high places of murder to protect a major business deal, the whole story could come crashing down around us. There's nothing in the world like having members of the local government crying and screaming about all the 'fake news' we're generating that points directly at them. We could end up in court if this turns out to be incorrect. I know that Jay's been busy with research, but have you been checking the facts?"

"We're working on that, too," Dylan said. "Do you see the theory we're developing?"

Meredith didn't answer right away. "What about Regal Management Associates, what do you know about them?" she asked instead.

"I had a hard time finding out anything concrete about them, since they did not disclose individual owners on their business license," Jay said. "Getting those names will take some more digging. I think they might be a group of silent investors who want to keep their names private. In the cases that I read about, just about all those tenants had their leases voided and were shoved out of their homes when Regal Management bought the land."

Meredith thought some more, and then said, "We still don't have a solid tie-in to the murder."

"There might be one, and there might not be one," Dylan said. "Even if the murder turns out to be unrelated, the corruption story would still be huge."

"Perhaps. In any case I see two stories here, the murder, and the corruption. They are not related at the moment. And the most important story is still the murder."

She removed her glasses and let them hang on their chain. "Jay, the murder is supposed to be your territory. We're getting dribs and drabs about this but no meat and potatoes. I know you're putting forth the energy, I just think it's going in the wrong direction. Get me something else on the murder. If the story of the killing turns out to involve a conspiracy of some kind, we should be in a position to cover it."

After Jay and Dylan left her office to get back to work, Meredith received a call from Albert Hudgins.

"What are we doing today with the Harbor City murder?" Hudgins said.

"Great timing," Meredith said. "I just got an update from the guys on that. Their theory is that the story that began with a murder near Harbor City might leave a trail that ends at the feet of the mayor of Los Angeles."

"Oh, really?" Hudgins said. "I'm intrigued, tell me more."

"It's complicated, but it could be connected to illegally gaining control of the vacant land along Sultan Road for a football stadium," Meredith said.

"Fabulous!" Hudgins said. "Is it on the front-page?"

"Not yet, but it will be soon, I hope. The guys still have some more work to do."

"Listen, I need you to do everything you can to help them. This is the kind of story we need on the front-page. We have an interest payment due in a couple of months, and better ratings and an increased circulation just might help us make it."

Hudgins didn't have to mention that without making the timely interest payment, the *LA Daily Journal* would have to seek bankruptcy protection. Meredith already knew that.

CHAPTER SEVENTEEN

Following Jay's tip, Aguilar decided to review the results of Erica's audit to see what accounting defalcations, if any, might be pertinent in the nightclub murder. He contacted Rudi first and then sought permission from Erica, since the audit was originated by her and she owned the results. Based on what he saw, it appeared that a fraud investigation could be opened. Aguilar stayed focused on what he was after. He wanted to know if any of the money that was missing or misappropriated had been used to hire the killer or killers in his case. Then he discovered the copies of the checks that had been made payable to the South Bay Neighborhood Association. He made copies of them before returning the audit work file to Erica.

The checks themselves were not conclusive evidence. But with their hefty amounts made payable to the South Bay Neighborhood Association, they might prove to be the key to this case. His familiarity with the South Bay Neighborhood Association made him believe that he had just stumbled upon how the criminal activities in his case had been financed.

Aguilar found Harry and showed him the check copies that he had made.

"That's a lot of money," Harry said. "And you say that it all came out in cash?"

"That's what we're going to find out right away," Aguilar said. "Put these in the file and bring the file along with you."

Their first stop was not the South Bay Neighborhood Association, however—it was the bank located in Harbor City where Renaissance Estates kept their account. The back of the checks showed a bank stamp that belonged to the same bank. The detectives spoke to the branch manager first.

"We need to know who came in here and cashed this check," Aguilar said.

The bank manager looked the signature over and said, "I can't make it out other than the W and the N."

"What about the tellers?" Aguilar said. "These checks are brought in here about every other week or so. They all are for large amounts of money. Somebody should remember something about the person who brings them in."

The bank manager went behind the teller windows to the first available teller as the detectives came up just outside that teller's window.

"These officers need to know who it was that cashed this check," the manager said. "They say it happens here often. Do you remember who cashed it?"

The teller, a young woman in her twenties, looked at the check for a moment and said, "I don't think so." Then she took a look at the endorsement on the reverse side and said, "No, I don't remember this. I'm sorry."

The bank manager then went to the next teller and asked her the same question. When she also said she didn't remember, Aguilar asked, "Don't you always ask for an ID?"

"Yes, I do sometimes," the teller said. "The customer usually sticks a debit card into that machine in front of you and enters a PIN number. The name on the account pops up on the screen in front of me. If he or she does that, I usually don't need to ask for a driver's license."

"Certain people come in and cash checks all the time and are easy to recognize," the bank manager told the detectives. "The tellers don't always remember names, and if it's a company account, different people can use the same card and pin number."

"Have all the tellers worked here for a long time?" Aguilar said.

"Well, there is some turnover," the branch manager said. "Sonya has been here for five years. Let's talk to her."

The first teller on the far end of the cage was Sonya. She looked at the check and recognized it immediately. "These checks are usually cashed by a man named Napier," she told them.

Harry then showed her the picture of Suarez with Anita Martinez. "No, that's not him. But that guy has also been in here cashing checks from this company. His name is Suarez, I think. And that woman has been in here with him, too."

"Could you tell us what Napier looks like?" Aguilar said.

"Sure. He's fairly tall," she said. "He's black, and he's very polite. He always wears a hat—I think it's called a fedora or something like that."

"Does he always come to you to cash these checks?" Aguilar said.

"Ever since I started managing the business window."

"I see," Aguilar said. "Uh, one last question, if I may. Are you the one who writes down the breakdown of the checks on the back like this?" He showed her the back of the check, where it was marked how many bills of each denomination were rendered.

"Of course. I break it down like that to help me balance my cash at the end of the day."

Aguilar hesitated for a moment, not quite understanding why writing the breakdown was necessary. "I see. Thanks a lot," he said, being satisfied that somewhere there was a good reason. At least he knew it was the teller that did that.

Back in the car, Aguilar looked at the backs of the checks side by side and he noticed that one was very different from the other.

"The cash breakdowns on these checks are quite different," he said to Harry. "One has a lot of smaller bills, while the other is almost all hundreds. Why do you think they would have different breakdowns of the bills?"

Harry pondered that question for a moment as he drove down the freeway toward Torrance. "For some reason, the needs of the people who were paid changed from one check to the next," he said. "Maybe they had to pay off a group of people with one of the checks, but the other one went primarily to one or two persons."

"Good thinking," Aguilar said. "It makes me certain that a slush fund exists."

Their next stop was the South Bay Neighborhood Association. The association's two-story office building in Torrance was located back from the street behind a large parking lot that had trees dotted around and through it. The office building itself, with its entrance guarded by palm trees, appeared to date back to the art deco era. Once inside, Aguilar went up to the receptionist and asked to speak to Fernando Suarez. Harry stood next to the front door to watch his partner's back.

"Mr. Suarez is not here at the moment. Can somebody else help you?" the woman said. She noticed Aguilar's badge hanging on a neck chain.

"Can we speak to the head person who manages the business's finances?"

"Let me get you Mr. O'Donnell," she said.

A few minutes later, a man came out front and greeted Aguilar. "I'm Edward O'Donnell, the accounting department manager," he said.

Aguilar identified himself. Then he showed O'Donnell one of the check copies, and said, "Could you tell me why this check was cashed and not deposited in the bank?"

O'Donnell looked at the check copy, both front and back, and then said, "How do you know that this check was cashed?"

"We asked the teller at the bank," Aguilar said. "Look on the backside. Those markings are the numbers of each bill denomination that she gave to the customer who cashed this check. Can you tell me who it was in your organization that cashed this check?"

O'Donnell hesitated. "It's usually Willis Napier. He's a vice president."

"Is Mr. Napier here? Can we talk to him?"

"No, I'm sorry. He's not here."

"You still haven't told me why this company would cash checks from its customers instead of depositing them into its bank account," Aguilar said.

O'Donnell hesitated again before answering. He appeared to be nervous and searching for what to say. "We have employees that work here who are poor and don't have a checking account," he finally said. "We pay them in cash so that they don't have to go to one of those check cashing places and pay a fee."

"How does the company pay all its other bills?" Aguilar said. "Does it use cash for that, too?"

"No. We pay our other bills by check like most other companies."

Harry moved up to join the conversation and said, "Why aren't the Renaissance Estates checks deposited in the bank and then the payroll withdrawn at the same time, thereby leaving a record of the transaction?"

"It takes more than one check cashed to cover the payroll," O'Donnell said. "We keep a separate record of the payroll so we can keep control over the transaction."

"Does the sum total of the checks that are cashed equal the amount of the payroll each payday?" Aguilar said.

"No, there's always more cash."

"What happens to the leftover cash?"

"We keep a cash fund for such items as office supplies, coffee, or anything else that doesn't require a check."

"How much is in the cash fund?" Aguilar said.

O'Donnell paused and appeared to be thinking. "It varies. But it's about a thousand dollars," he finally said.

"Are the checks all cashed for the same breakdown of bills each time? I mean, the payroll should be about the same each payday, shouldn't it?" Aguilar said, as Harry showed O'Donnell the group of check copies.

O'Donnell looked at the checks again and said, "The bill denominations are not always the same because the need for petty cash is different from the need for payroll cash."

"I thought you just said that it all goes to the same place," Aguilar said.

"It does all go to the same place," O'Donnell said. He was perspiring noticeably and his hands began to shake.

Changing the line of questioning, Harry showed him the artist's drawing of "El Puma" and said, "Do you recognize this person?"

O'Donnell looked at the drawing and simply said, "No."

"Does anybody who works here go by the nickname of 'El Puma'?" Harry said.

"No, there's nobody here by that name."

"When do you expect Fernando Suarez to come here?" Aguilar said.

"I don't know. He doesn't keep regular office hours."

As they walked back out to their car, Harry said, "These 'poor' people that work here don't look like they're doing all that bad. I can see three Mercedes Benzes, about five BMWs, two Audi's, and a Lexus in this parking lot."

"Not only are they not poor, but I bet you they're paid with a paycheck like everyone else," Aguilar said. "Besides, paying workers in cash is going to get this company in trouble with the IRS if they don't report it."

"What happens to all that cash they keep getting?" Harry said.

"I guarantee you it goes into a slush fund," Aguilar said.

"How are we going to prove that? Harry said.

"No matter what, there's a disconnect between how much cash they get, and how much is needed for the payroll," Aguilar said.

"There must be some way we can find out how much extra money they have each payday," Harry said.

They got inside the car and Aguilar said, "We would need a court order to get somebody over there to audit the books. I don't know if anybody from our department could do it, and I doubt they'd bring in auditors from the city auditors' office unless we made an arrest first."

"It seems like it's the perfect slush fund," Harry said.

"It's money laundering," Aguilar said. "It puts the case in a whole new perspective. That excess cash could be used to bribe officials or to pay off people like Maria Maldonado. And, of course, to pay for a hit man."

"Then it might have been used to hire the two guys who killed Lisa Nguyen after the nightclub fight," Harry said.

"That's right," Aguilar said. "She must have figured out that a slush fund was operating at South Bay Neighborhood Association. She probably saw that the checks they wrote didn't add up to the amount of money that was due to South Bay's employees. She must have said something to the wrong person about it."

“Then, there’s also a cover-up taking place,” Harry said.

“The South Bay Neighborhood Association has had trouble with the law before,” Aguilar said. “They could be some kind of an organized crime outfit. This clever, out-of-town, killer could not have operated without support and direction. This requires other people to be involved and plenty of cash to keep him moving. We know where the cash is coming from, and we might know one of the other people involved—Fernando Suarez.”

“I still don’t think we have a motive,” Harry said.

“Just keep reading the newspapers,” Aguilar said. “Newsboy is going to dig that up for us.”

CHAPTER EIGHTEEN

From his research, Jay discovered the name of a potential source who rented a house through the Jefferson Square Company that was ultimately acquired by Regal Management Associates. He located him in a seniors' apartment complex in Temecula and got an interview. Jay didn't often drive to the inland empire as his surfing and sports stories were usually centered around the beach. As he drove inland, he noticed a number of retirement communities that had proliferated out in the area that bordered on the desert to the east of the urban areas of Orange County. He finally found the place he was looking for. He went inside the building's lobby that also served as a recreation area for the residents. There waiting for him, was his source.

Jay marveled at the inside of the lobby, that resembled a hunting lodge replete with a fireplace and comfortable easy chairs. Jay noticed magazines and newspapers strewn about on tabletops. The room had mellow lighting from lamps that helped create a friendlier ambiance than bright, overhead lighting. Mounted above the fireplace was a moose head trophy, and along the walls he could see pictures of California's mountains. Other than an attendant at the front desk, all the persons in the building that Jay could see were septuagenarians or even older.

"Hi. I'm Jason Phillips of the *Daily Journal*," he said extending his hand to the man.

"I'm Roger Le Moyne." Jay's source took his hand and shook it firmly. Then they then found a quiet space in an alcove and sat down for a chat.

"It appears that you were once living on Sultan Road," Jay said, "but you were evicted by new owners who wanted the land."

"That's right," Le Moyne said.

"What were the terms of your possession of the property?" Jay said.

"It was a lease to buy arrangement. If we stayed in the home for twenty years, we would own it."

"Did you manage to live there for twenty years?"

"We tried. But another company came in and changed the rules of the agreement. We lived in that house for nearly fourteen years and wound up with nothing."

"And that company would be Regal Management Associates?"

"Yes, that's correct."

"What rules were changed?"

"The original agreement we had was with Jefferson Square who went belly up. We knew something was wrong because they wouldn't fix any of the plumbing problems we had. We had to do all that ourselves. Then they sold just about all the properties in the area to Regal Management Associates. Regal Management wouldn't honor the lease for our house that they acquired from Jefferson Square. They came by and told us that if we wanted to stay in the house, we would have to pay nearly three times as much rent."

"Were you offered a chance to buy the place?"

"No. And I don't think we could have afforded to buy it, anyway."

"What happened next?"

"They gave us thirty days to come up with two month's rent, plus a security deposit of five thousand dollars."

"Whoa! Plus a security deposit of five grand?"

"That's right. Five thousand dollars plus all that rent. It came to something like twelve thousand, I believe."

"Were you able to pay that?"

"No. And we told them that it was outrageous. There was no chance for us or for any of our neighbors to manage living there at that cost. On top of that, I still think it was illegal to do that to us."

"Did you consider taking any legal action along with any of your neighbors?"

"We did talk to a lawyer. But he said the case was not strong. Plus, he wanted twenty thousand dollars up front to represent us."

"Did you have anywhere to move to, like family for instance?"

"Not with just thirty days' notice. We have two children who are grown up and have families. One lives in New Jersey and the other in Seattle. Neither could really put us up, even though they both said they would send money to help us get relocated. I told them that sending money should not be necessary."

"When thirty days were up, what happened?"

"Exactly thirty days after the notice, a representative from Regal Management Associates came pounding on our door. He told us he was repossessing the property and that we had to be out that very day. We had begun packing, but didn't have a truck or any help to move the furniture."

"Where did you wind up going?" Jay said. He was fascinated by what he was hearing.

"We had just found an apartment in Long Beach the day before. After we argued with that man, he finally agreed to provide us with a truck and some movers. When they arrived later that day, they slammed and banged the furniture around, damaging some of it. They carelessly piled the boxes we had packed up on top of it. When we arrived at our new location, we saw the damage that had been done to a few of our antiques and old curios. One old family picture was so badly damaged we had to throw it away."

"Were any of your neighbors treated the same way when their time was up?"

"Several. One of our closest friends woke up one morning to find a bulldozer revving up to demolish their home while they were still inside. The man was a heart patient, and his wife had Alzheimer's Disease. He went out in front to plead with the construction crew not to crush the place until he could at least get his wife dressed and out. The crew was willing to wait until the same man who had thrown us out showed up. He gave them thirty minutes. After exactly thirty minutes, the bulldozer rammed through the front of the house. We called the police, because we thought that they didn't make it out. But it turned out they had a backdoor exit. My friend later told me that they had made it out through the backdoor just as the building began to crumble in the front."

"Oh my God! They could have been killed!"

"That's what we thought, but they survived. All they had left was the clothes on their backs and a few personal possessions."

"Did Regal Management Associates give you any credit at all for the rent you had paid under the terms provided by Jefferson Square?"

"No. Not one dime."

"I see," Jay said. He knew he was onto something here. "What about the money you had to pay out of your own pocket for maintenance? Did you get any of that back?"

"From Jefferson Square, no. As I was saying they were in such bad shape financially that the money they got from Regal Management might still not have gotten them out of bankruptcy. We told Regal Management Associates maintenance people about the plumbing problems, but they weren't sympathetic. They said because we worked on the plumbing ourselves we now owned the problems."

"Were there any other legal options available?"

"Oh, they offered all of us arbitration. But to my knowledge, nobody took them up on it because it was all to be arranged by Regal Management Associates. Why should we bother talking to another group of lawyers who were just planning to kick us out anyway?"

Jay's next move was a bold one. He hesitated for a moment and then pressed forward. "I would like to take your picture and include it with my story," he said, at the risk of scaring off his source. To his surprise, the man agreed and further stated that he would be happy for Jay to quote him on anything he just said.

Jay thanked Mr. Le Moyne, but as he was ready to leave, the elderly gentleman had another pleasant surprise for him. He told Jay that there were four other people who lived in that retirement community who had similar or worse problems with Regal Management Associates. With Le Moyne's assistance, Jay went to interview them all as well. Each one told Jay a story similar to the one Le Moyne had said. One person even mentioned that he knew of several people who were forcibly removed from their homes by private security people who acted without a court order. In yet another case, the crew tasked with clearing the land started knocking down an elderly person's house with nearly one hundred thousand dollars' worth of antiques and art left inside. A fire broke out and destroyed most of it. One of these other sources said that he did apply for arbitration, and that he planned to go to present his case himself. But an attorney friend of his told him that the deck was stacked against him and that his chances of winning were nil.

The next morning in the newsroom, Jay worked up a precis of what he had learned from his sources in Temecula and showed it to Dylan.

"Apparently these people were screwed royally by Regal Management Associates," Dylan said. "They were pushed out of their homes without any consideration for what they had paid in." Looking at Jay, he said, "We've got to find out who was behind all this."

"How do we do that?"

"Central Library has a lot of information about business structures. You need to look for the names of the owners of Regal Management Associates, the president, or the chairman, or whoever it is that runs the company. Maybe even a senior partner."

"Can't I write this article based on these facts that I've already gathered?"

"Sure," Dylan said. "But we can't let it start and end with this. Finding out the principals of Regal Management to fix responsibility is paramount at this point."

"Le Moyne's opinion was that he was screwed by them," Jay said. "If I say it like that, won't I be slanting the news?"

"Don't write it like that—just say that he was forced out of his home for the reasons he stated. Let the readers draw their own conclusions. If somebody from Regal Management Associates wants to dispute Le Moyne's story, you can interview them for their counterpoint."

"Take a look at this." Jay pulled out a copy of a magazine with an exciting storyline and showed it to Dylan. "Whoever wrote it had to be slanting the news."

Dylan read the story. "Well, technically speaking, this guy may have slanted the news," he said. "Remember, he's writing for an audience that he believes cares more about law and order than about a criminal's rights. I do this all the time when I write about the Lakers. I have to report what happened in the game. But I know that my readers are more interested in reading about the local team than about the teams from New York, or Boston, or somewhere else. I don't distort anything, and I don't lie about anything, either. I try to put the best face on the Lakers whether they win or lose. Most journalists do the same thing. It's about knowing what your readers want to read."

"Then I've got to figure out who my readers are and what they want to read about," Jay said.

"That's the idea."

"How am I going to do that?"

"It's a part of your growing up as a reporter, good buddy!" Dylan said. "It takes some effort on your part, but you'll get the hang of it over time. Meredith will help with this, too, since she won't publish any story that appears to be radically different from what our readers are expecting."

Jay put the magazine away. "There's so much to think about when I'm writing. I'm just trying not to forget something vital," he said.

"You're worrying too much," Dylan said. "You're going to be writing front-page crime stories. You've got the talent. You just have to develop it, and then you have to deliver it."

"I hope my luck doesn't run out in finding these great sources," Jay said.

"You need to take care of your sources for sure. Otherwise people won't want to talk to you. But they should know that what they are saying will go straight into the newspaper. And the readers will get to the conclusion of your story when you get to the conclusion of your research and give it to them."

Jay got to work, and crafted his story. He painted a picture that somebody mysterious who worked behind a corporate veil was very busy shoving people out of their homes by highly questionable or even illegal means. When he had finished, he emailed it to Dylan.

After a while, Dylan dropped by Jay's workstation. "I just sent you my article to Meredith for tonight's print run," he told Jay. Dylan had written a piece that pointed to Sultan Road as being the mayor's choice for location of the new NFL stadium.

Jay opened it up and read it. After a few minutes he looked at Dylan and simply said, "Cool!"

"You like that, huh?"

"Totally. It's great from top to bottom."

"Our stories cover each other since I'm referring to what you found out about Regal Management Associates."

"Are you sure that the mayor favors Sultan Road?"

"I've got a source inside the mayor's office."

"Wow! That's awesome!"

"Notice that I had to make him anonymous, but I quoted him anyway."

"I noticed that. I am so ready to see what the mayor has to say about the NFL stadium and Sultan Road," Jay said.

They didn't have to wait long for Mayor Andrew McGinnis to respond. He held a press conference the morning after Dylan's story broke. Dylan attended and brought Jay along.

When McGinnis appeared in front of the microphones, he started the press conference the same way as he usually did—by reading from a prepared statement.

"I just want to set the record straight after the *Daily Journal* published a story yesterday about the NFL's return to Los Angeles," he began. "The NFL has stated that they want to place a team Los Angeles that has the second largest television market in the country. This naturally has caused a lot of speculation as to where the new team will play. Sites such as the Los Angeles Memorial Coliseum and Pasadena's Rose Bowl Stadium already have tenants, and would require much in the way of modernization to be brought up to NFL's standards. Other sites, such as downtown near the convention center, or out in the City of Industry are a possibility, but would need to be built up from scratch.

"I want to categorically deny that I ever endorsed any particular location in the Los Angeles area for a new football stadium. In some discussions I've had with my staff members, the Sultan Road location has come up from time to time since it provides easier freeway access than any of the other choices. These discussions do not in any way constitute a preference for the Sultan Road location. My office remains neutral and will support any bona fide location in the Los Angeles area as long as it brings us a team."

With that, McGinnis opened up the conference for questions and nearly a dozen hands went up. Dylan and Jay were in the front row of the audience, and Dylan was chosen first.

"Mr. Mayor," Dylan said, "Are you aware of the activities of a company named Regal Management Associates that pushed people out of their homes in the area around Sultan Road?"

"I don't know anything about either Regal Management Associates or whatever happened to those people," McGinnis said.

Without hesitation Dylan said, "The people who were forced out their homes had originally moved there with the promise that they would own their homes after paying rent for twenty years. Can you comment on this?"

"I think it's awful that anyone should lose their home as a result of an honest plan gone awry, but this appears to be the case. I remember when the Jefferson Square Company moved those houses from Westchester to Sultan Road. I don't know why the deal collapsed. Being familiar with real estate in Los Angeles, I can tell you that these things sometimes happen."

As McGinnis got ready to call on a different reporter, Dylan jumped right back in with another question. "Are you aware of the low-income housing tract known as Renaissance Estates, and that this property sits directly in the middle of a large area of undeveloped land on Sultan Road?"

"I've heard of them, yes," McGinnis said.

Keeping the heat on the mayor, Dylan said, "Isn't it true that the owner of Renaissance Estates has been placed under extreme pressure by unnamed persons to sell the property, thereby making that remaining space on Sultan Road finally available for an NFL stadium?"

"I'm sure that the right offer could be made to acquire any outstanding land if the NFL chose to come to Sultan Road," McGinnis said.

"What if the owner does not want to sell?" Dylan said.

McGinnis looked at Dylan with dismay. "My experience tells me that when the right offer is made, any owner will be willing to sell."

"Have any of your associates been involved in pressuring the Renaissance Estates owner to sell?" Dylan said, without giving McGinnis a chance to recognize a different reporter.

McGinnis then said, "I'm sorry, but I need to recognize some of these other reporters." With that, he picked another reporter. To the mayor's dismay, this reporter also asked him about the Sultan Road location, virtually picking up where Dylan had left off. Again, McGinnis had to make his denials and try to find a different reporter who would ask him about something else. McGinnis battled back and forth with a few other reporters over the Sultan Road location until he finally gave up and ended the press conference.

After the mayor's press conference, Jay and Dylan went to lunch. Jay complimented Dylan on the way he had kept after the mayor about Sultan Road.

"Notice that I didn't mention any names," Dylan said. "My hope was that he would drop some names, but he didn't."

"You got the ball rolling and then the other reporters kept it in motion," Jay said.

"That's how we get what we want out of a press conference like that. The mayor started out stating what he wanted and he expected to answer questions based on that. We crossed him up with the drill down to Renaissance Estates."

"I wonder how so many other reporters knew about the problems going on over there," Jay said.

"Jay," Dylan said, "these reporters read your articles. They're locked onto what you've discovered. And they're not the only ones. I've seen this story on local TV, and I've also read about it from some syndicated columnists. Pretty soon periodicals like *The New Yorker*, and *TIME* Magazine will pick it up."

Jay's jaw dropped. He was surprised to hear that what he was writing was actually being relied upon by other reporters and editors. He was not in this work for the fame, or so he thought. This sudden surge of readership meant that he had to redouble his efforts to prevent himself from letting his new readers down.

CHAPTER NINETEEN

Erica was not surprised when she was served with Walker's lawsuit. As she read through the documents, it occurred to her that there was virtually nothing new in this latest legal action to get her to divest herself of Renaissance Estates. It was disconcerting to find out that Walker was seeking not only to require her to sell the property, but also to prohibit her from doing business with the federal government for a period of at least twenty years. A few days later, she received another letter from a HUD attorney that requested her to be present in Walker's office for a deposition as part of the legal process. She could visualize Walker coming at her on a steamroller trying to squash her once and for all. In dark moments like these, a small, weak part of her told her to give up. But the stronger side of her decided that she still had some fight left.

Erica's former attorney had gotten a job with a big law firm and therefore would not be able to represent her in this case. After some searching, she found Joyce Mitchell, who worked for a law firm that took on charitable cases. Along with Ben Williams, the three of them kept the appointment to meet with Walker and the HUD attorney for a deposition at Walker's Westwood office. To their mild surprise Brendon

Millwood was also there to provide information as a "friend of the court."

To open the deposition, Walker first read a condensed version of the lawsuit, pointing out both the problems that existed and the solutions that the government was expecting. He closed this portion of the proceedings by saying that the government was interested in "getting all matters settled" at Renaissance Estates. The only way that he believed that this could be accomplished would be for Erica to sell her interest in it.

"If you choose to sell Renaissance Estates," he said, "this lawsuit and all other complications related to violations of federal housing regulations will be dropped. There will be no further actions on the part of the federal government in this case of the United States Department of Housing and Urban Development versus Harbor Gateway Community Housing Corporation or Erica Knight as a private citizen. However," he continued, "if you choose not to settle the suit in this manner and decide to fight the charges in a court of law, separate criminal charges regarding willful violation of the Section 8 housing code would also be filed. These charges, if proven in court, could bring a penalty of up to ten years in prison."

The threat of a prison sentence did not faze Erica. Although this was the first time that criminal charges were discussed, she was fully prepared to defend her actions as well as her ownership of Renaissance Estates.

"Mr. Walker," she began using her own prepared remarks. "There is nothing in this lawsuit that brings new light to this case. It's simply the same old stuff that's been thrown at me before now being thrown at me again. We both know that there is nothing in either the HUD audit or any other investigation into the management of Renaissance Estates that would require me to sell the property as a remedy for wrongdoing or mismanagement. I've already been dragged into court and had my role as manager of the properties that I own removed over these same tired, old charges that you keep dredging up over and over again. If you can't supply anything new to this process, you leave me with no choice but to request a dismissal of all charges and complaints represented by this lawsuit. And furthermore, I would like to add that I resent the constant harassment from you and your associates that have led us to the point where we are today. I believe it is an attempt on your part to retaliate for my calling the attention of the FBI to the potential of bribery of government officials connected with Renaissance Estates."

Hearing this terse response to his opening remarks, Walker exploded in anger. He shot to his feet and leaned forward on his desk. He stared down Erica as if the two were about to grapple in a wrestling ring. "The FBI investigation that you started is nothing more than a witch hunt designed to embarrass me!" he said. "You are attempting to disgrace me not only in the eyes of my colleagues and superiors in the federal government but also in the business community of public-assisted housing." Pointing his finger at Erica's nose, he told her, "I want you to get it straight, right here and right now, that this lawsuit is being brought by the federal government and not DeShawn Walker. There are real issues contained in it as well as numerous problems that still do not have a solution. For this reason, it's the *federal government* that wants you to divest yourself of Renaissance Estates." Taking a deep breath, he said, "And, if I find out that whatever it was that you told the FBI about me was untrue, then I, as a private individual, will bring a separate lawsuit against you for slander. I have NEVER taken a bribe in return for any special consideration from anyone. And I never, ever will. Just the idea of what it's going to cost me to clear my name because of you makes me sick." He was so visibly agitated by Erica's assertion and his forceful reply that he wouldn't sit back down.

"I'm sorry, Mr. Walker, if being investigated makes you sick," Erica replied. "It seems like a dozen times that I myself have been investigated, and I sure don't like it either. But somebody is being paid to run me off the project that I built from scratch. There is clear evidence of that. And that is why the FBI was called in."

Walker finally eased his way back down into his chair and said, "We are present here today, Ms. Knight, to obtain a deposition to shed light on the charges in this lawsuit. We are not here to discuss whether or not the FBI has sufficient evidence to charge anyone with bribery. Do we have that point straight? Can we proceed?"

"Since you've threatened me with not only ten years in prison but also with taking away my livelihood until I'm over seventy years old, what alternative do I have?" she said. "Your problem is being told when you are wrong, isn't it?

Throughout our entire relationship, you have always had to be right about everything—even when you're proven wrong."

Walker sprang to his feet again. "What in the holy hell does our personal relationship of fourteen years ago have to do with you being here in a deposition? Huh? Tell me that!"

The door of opportunity for Erica to have her say had just swung wide open. "When I left you, I told you the reason," she said. "And it's the same reason that I just finished saying. You can't listen to anyone. What you say has to be right simply because you're the one who said it. You don't see what other people are doing with their lives because you're too narrow-minded. That was the reason then and it's the same reason now."

"Well, thank you very much, Ms. Knight, for that lecture," Walker said. "I haven't had a good talking-to like that since my momma caught me cutting a day of high school. Now, if you don't mind, I'd like to proceed…."

"The root cause of this legal wrangling is that you just can't get over being called out for being wrong," Erica said. "It is your personal feelings that are driving this lawsuit. And they should be left outside the door."

At this point, Joyce intervened. "Mr. Walker," she said, "I think it's best in these circumstances that we take a short break to cool off before we try to begin this deposition."

Walker looked at the HUD attorney who nodded his head in agreement. "All right," he said in a more civil tone. "We'll take a break of about fifteen minutes or so. You can use the conference room through that door on my left."

Joyce, Erica, and Ben huddled together in the vacant conference room next to Walker's office to discuss handling the suit's defense. Joyce made it clear what the stakes in this deposition were, and asked Erica to please focus on the "nuts and bolts" of it rather than to start discussing other matters. Erica acknowledged that she had already had her say and would do her best to cooperate from this point forward. After a short while, they all reconvened in Walker's office.

The HUD attorney started the deposition by calling Millwood to testify. Before being sworn in, Millwood asked to place an addendum to the lawsuit on the table in the form of a claim for past due charges not paid to Millwood Property Management by Renaissance Estates. The claim detailed a long list of charges that totaled almost a quarter of a million dollars. Millwood asked that this claim be attached to the remedy portion of the lawsuit so that it could be paid from the proceeds of any sale of Renaissance Estates that might take place.

Erica, Ben, and Joyce had not seen the list of charges before. "I will need to review this list with my client before I can agree to have this entered in as a part of the lawsuit," Joyce said.

Walker was clearly taken by surprise. He conferred with the HUD attorney, who told him that this should be managed separately since it was not a part of the lawsuit. He decided to work through it before the deposition began rather than wait until after the lawsuit was settled.

"All right," Walker said. "Let's get a couple copies of this made. I also want to see it."

Erica, Joyce, and Ben all reviewed a copy of the list. Then Erica said, “All the charges on this list have already been paid by Renaissance Estates. There’s nothing here that’s still outstanding.”

Ben Williams added, “At the time of the transfer of management from Harbor Gateway Community Housing Corporation to Millwood Property Management, I was assured by Lisa Nguyen, our accountant, that there were no outstanding invoices and that all accounts had been settled.”

Millwood responded, “No, these charges all have unpaid invoices and all are still outstanding. I’ve done a careful job of keeping track of these. As you can see, some of them are well over six months past due.”

Walker put his copy of the list aside and said, “We’ll need to subpoena the accountant from Renaissance Estates to see if these charges are indeed still owed.”

“The accountant, Lisa Nguyen, is dead,” Erica said.

“What?” Walker said with a start. He hadn’t been told about this.

“Lisa Nguyen is dead,” Erica said again. “The police are treating her death as a homicide.”

“Well, that definitely complicates this matter,” Walker said. “There’s nothing we can do about this without another audit.”

“Not so fast,” Millwood said. “These charges are certified by me as being owed. What’s especially crippling is the amount of my fees that are still not paid.”

"There was nothing in the audit that HUD performed that indicated that any accounts were past due," Walker said. "I'm not going to put this into this lawsuit."

"May I say something here?" Erica said. When Millwood and Walker stopped arguing, she said, "The fees here are for the wrong amount. The correct amount was paid when it was supposed to be paid."

"That's impossible!" Millwood said jumping to his feet. "I will guarantee you that the monies owed here have been properly calculated, and that I need to be paid." He looked at Erica with a fearsome expression.

"The management fee was supposed to be paid only on the amount of rent collected from the tenants and was not supposed to include the government's supplement," Erica said. "These charges are based on the government supplement portion of the rent, that is not a part of the management agreement to bring Millwood Property Management onto the premises."

"Well, you are absolutely *wrong* about that, Ms. Knight." Millwood protested. Now it was his turn to be upset. "My management fees include all rents paid to the property from all sources not just what's collected from the tenants. If this money is not paid to me, I will sue and sue and sue until I get every damn penny of it including interest!"

"All right, all right, enough of this," Walker said. He then asked the HUD attorney which side was correct about the amount of Millwood's management fee. He was told that the matter would need to be researched.

Joyce Mitchell then stood up and said, “We’re not here to debate the merits of these additional charges. We came for a deposition. I’m beginning to wonder if we are going to have this deposition today or not.”

Before Walker could answer, Millwood raised his voice and said, “This money is owed to me and *must* be a part of this lawsuit. I will not stand to lose nearly a quarter of a million dollars because somebody thinks that I don’t know what my fees are based on.”

Ben Williams said, “These charges are not fair, and I won’t agree to pay them. Our accountant took care of everything back when it was supposed to be done, God rest her soul. I know that none of this is bona fide.”

“If you want to put this in the lawsuit,” Erica said to Walker, “it’s up to you. But we’re not paying it. The only way we’ll ever pay anything like this is after another audit.”

“I want it understood here and now,” Millwood yelled, “I will sue to block any sale of Renaissance Estates if these charges aren’t paid or aren’t agreed to be paid out of escrow. I am owed this money!”

“All right, that’s enough!” Walker said, throwing his hands up in disgust. “This deposition is postponed.” He got up from behind his desk and walked out of his office, leaving the door wide open.

As they weaved in and out of the freeway traffic driving back to Long Beach, Joyce reminded Erica of her precarious position in this case. “The judge is the same one that ordered you to step down as manager of the properties,” she said. “He will be pressing you to settle with the government on these matters. You should also remember that if you do decide to sell, you will still be in a position to pick up on other Section 8 housing opportunities. If you don't sell, you risk losing everything including your freedom. You could go to prison."

"Yes, I understand that," Erica said. "But who will ever understand the tremendous amount of effort it took me to build Renaissance Estates from scratch? Until recently, I had made a damn good living out of it. It's been the driving force of my entire life. I'm not about to toss it all away over what's happening to me—especially since I believe I'm in the right. I'm being framed!"

"That's right," Ben added. "You should never sell it because of what they are trying to do to you."

"I'm just acting as your counselor," Joyce said.

"Believe me, I appreciate it," Erica said. "There's something else, though, that both of you should be aware of. The *LA Daily Journal* is publishing reports that the land along Sultan Road is being looked at as a potential site for a new NFL football stadium. Now, do you still think I should just give up and let go of my baby without finding out how much Renaissance Estates is actually worth?"

CHAPTER TWENTY

Early one morning, equipped with the artist's drawing of "El Puma," Aguilar and Lee staked out the South Bay Neighborhood Association to watch all the employees as they came to work. Strategically parked, they waited for the employees to walk up to the front door so that they could identify the one that matched the description in the picture. At seven thirty, the first employee showed up and unlocked the office door. She was a short Latina whom they had not seen on their previous trip. Shortly after eight, the majority of the employees began to trickle in. They came in all different shapes and sizes. None fit the description in either the drawing of "El Puma" or the picture of Fernando Suarez. Nine o'clock came and went, with still no sight of their persons of interest.

"I think we've seen just about everybody that's coming to work today," Harry said.

"Maybe," Aguilar said. "But the two we're after don't keep regular hours. I hope you didn't have any big plans for today."

"I never have any big plans," Harry said. "That way I don't have to disappoint the wife by breaking them."

Aguilar took a look at his partner and smiled. "You're pretty smart, my good man," he said.

A short time went by, then a tall African American man wearing a fedora walked up toward the front door.

"That looks like him," Aguilar said. "He might be armed."

The two officers exited the car and quickly intercepted the suspect before he got inside the office. Harry frisked him, finding no weapons. Then the trio moved over to the side of the building out of the way of the entrance.

The tall suspect looked down at the shorter Aguilar and said, "What do you want, man? I've done nothing illegal. I'm just going to work."

With Harry standing a few steps behind the suspect, Aguilar showed the man the artist's drawing. "Do you recognize the person in this drawing?" he said.

The man took a look at Aguilar's drawing. "No," he said. "That's nobody I know."

"You should look in the mirror more often," Aguilar said. "Let me see your ID, please."

Again, the suspect looked down at Aguilar. Slowly, he reached into his pocket for his wallet. He retrieved his driver's license and handed it to Aguilar.

"You are Willis Napier?"

"That's right."

"Mr. Napier, what are your duties here at this company?"

"I'm a vice-president."

"Do you ever cash large checks at the bank like this one?" Aguilar held up a copy of one of the large checks from Renaissance Estates and showed him his own signature on the back.

Napier thought for a moment and then said, “Yeah, that’s part of being in the management. I sometimes have to cash checks like that.”

“What happens to the money once you’ve left the bank?”

“The money comes back here, where I check it in with the secretary.”

“What does she do with the money?”

“I don’t know for sure. You’ll need to ask her.”

“Why are these checks cashed? Why aren’t they deposited in the company’s bank account?”

Napier hesitated for a moment. “I don’t know,” he finally said.

“But you’re a part of the management,” Aguilar said. “You should know what happens to company funds, shouldn’t you?”

Napier didn’t respond to Aguilar’s question.

“Do you know a woman by the name of Maria Maldonado?” Aguilar said. Harry handed Aguilar her picture.

Napier looked at the picture and then looked back at Aguilar “I, I’ve got nothing else to say.”

“Mr. Napier, you’re a person of interest in an investigation we’re working on,” Aguilar said. “We’ll need you to come with us for some more questioning.”

Without any sign of resistance, Napier accompanied Aguilar and Lee to the detectives’ car. Once there, Aguilar looked back at the office and said, “It’s police procedure—we need to put on the cuffs. We’ll do it behind this tree, where people in the office won’t see us.”

Harry cuffed Napier while the trio stood behind the tree. Then he helped him into the back seat of the car. They drove him downtown for more questioning.

Aguilar took Napier to an interrogation room. Napier requested that his attorney be present, so they made some small talk about what type of business the South Bay Neighborhood Association was in while they waited.

In the meantime, Harry brought Maria Maldonado around to view Napier through the see-through mirror.

"Is this the man who paid you the money to start the fight?" Harry said.

"Yeah, that's him."

"Is he called 'El Puma'?"

Maldonado thought for a moment. "I don't know," she said. "I mean, I don't know this guy's name, either."

"How come you called him 'El Puma'?"

"When we made the deal and he paid me the money, somebody else there said 'This is 'El Puma's' opportunity,' or something like that. I thought they were talking about this guy, but maybe they weren't."

"Can you describe the guy who said that?"

"He was another Mexican."

"Does he look like this?" Harry showed her a picture of Fernando Suarez.

"Yeah, that's him."

"Now, please think for a moment. Is this man 'El Puma'?"

"I'm sorry. I don't know who the hell he is either."

"But he was there when you agreed to start the fight, and he did say the words 'El Puma'?"

"Yeah, that's right."

"Was anybody else present when this happened?"

"No."

"One last question," Harry said, while still showing her the picture of Suarez. "Was this man one of the two guys who took the woman away from the parking lot after the fight?"

Maldonado took another good look at the picture. "Yeah, that's one of them," she said.

"Thanks. You've helped a lot."

Napier's attorney arrived, and after talking with his client he advised Napier not to say anything more to the police. Before the interview broke up, Harry returned to the room and whispered into Aguilar's ear what he had been told by Maria Maldonado.

"Mr. Napier, before you go anywhere, I need to inform you that you are under arrest," Aguilar said.

"What charges?" Napier's attorney said.

"Your client paid a person five thousand dollars to start a fight in a nightclub," Aguilar said. "The victim in the fight was killed. We believe that she was murdered by a hired killer, and that your client orchestrated the whole thing."

"That's preposterous!" the attorney said.

"Your client is charged with conspiracy to commit murder. Now, are you sure you don't want to tell me more about Maria Maldonado?" Aguilar said while looking directly at Napier.

"Absolutely not. We'll save whatever we want to say for court," Napier's attorney said.

After filing conspiracy charges and completing the paperwork, Aguilar and Lee got a search warrant for Napier's apartment. The search turned up nothing of substance. But based on Maria Maldonado's identification, Napier was charged and arraigned for conspiracy in Lisa Nguyen's murder. He was held in lieu of one million dollars bail.

Back at the station, Aguilar was called into Kreider's office to update the captain on what had just happened. "We arrested the moneyman in the nightclub case," he said.

"Who is it, and how do you know he's the moneyman?" Kreider said.

"His name is Willis Napier. Our first perpetrator ID'd him as the man who paid her to start the fight. We're holding him on a conspiracy to commit murder charge."

"What has he told you?"

"Nothing. He's not cooperating. But since he's the moneyman, he can lead us to who put up the money for the hit. He's the key to a much bigger case."

"A much bigger case, as in what?" Kreider said.

Aguilar took a breath and let it out slowly. Then he said, "A hit man was brought in from deep in Mexico to kill a young woman who turns out to be the accountant of a federally funded housing project. I'm certain that the victim was killed to silence her about something. Napier might tell us what it was that she knew."

"You're still dreaming about a big conspiracy going on here, aren't you," Kreider said. "I can't see it that way with what you've discovered so far. You need to stick to finding the actual killers. This guy and his conspiracy charge are not likely to help you out with that."

"Captain Kreider," Aguilar said. "The fact that this man paid at least one of the perpetrators to start the fight is evidence of a wider plot. Yes, we're trying to find the killers. But sooner or later your thinking needs to come around that a bigger game is being played here."

"What bigger game?" Kreider said. "If the killer isn't Suarez, you don't even have the him identified. And now you want to go off building a big conspiracy case of some kind?"

"We're deeper than scratching the surface here," Aguilar said. "There's a lot of solid, circumstantial…"

"One more thing," Kreider said, interrupting him. "Before you go shouting out to the press that a 'big conspiracy' of some kind is going on, you better talk to me about it first. Is that clear?"

Aguilar sat quietly for a moment, with a look of disgust on his face. "Our first suspect also identified Fernando Suarez as one of the two men that carried the victim away from the parking lot," he finally said, holding back a large head of steam. "That should bring in the South Bay Neighborhood Association, where he is a high-ranking employee."

"Is Suarez the *killer*?" Kreider said raising his voice.

Aguilar sat in his chair and seethed. He was processing what Kreider had said in response to what he had told him. Then, without saying a word, he got up and walked to Kreider's door. He turned around and said, "Is that all, Captain?"

"Leave the door open on your way out," Kreider said.

The next day Aguilar and Lee went to visit the district attorney. Richard Frederick faced the same dilemma that he had with the other arrests that were made in this case—the evidence was very thin. It relied on the testimony of Maria Maldonado, who was cooperating, but facing felony charges herself. After discussing the evidence, he agreed to the conspiracy charges as long as Aguilar could tie Napier to the actual killer or killers.

Then Aguilar asked him, "What can we do about Suarez?"

"If Maldonado places him in the parking lot and carrying off the victim, he has a connection to the murder. It's a little thin, but you have justifiable cause for a search warrant."

CHAPTER TWENTY-ONE

Two days later, Napier quietly made bail and was released. Although his passport had been confiscated, he had a friend take him to his apartment so that he could pack some things and get out of town. In less than an hour, Napier had a suitcase filled with as much clothing and personal items as it would hold. He put some cash and personal papers in his briefcase. He handed the keys to the apartment to his friend to clear it out for him later. Then he got into the friend's car for the trip to the airport.

With the friend driving, they started down the street toward the boulevard that would take them to the freeway. When they made a left turn onto a cross street, they needed to go just two more blocks to get to Crenshaw Boulevard. At that moment, a gray pickup truck pulled up alongside the driver, and a man on the passenger side with a pistol motioned him to pull over.

"Who the hell's this motherfucker with a gun?" the friend said to Napier.

Napier took a look over at the truck. "Pull over to the side but don't get blocked in," he said. "Leave the engine running. When the truck pulls in behind us, be ready to hit the gas and get the fuck out of here."

Napier's friend's eyes got wide. "That sonofabitch looks like he's going shoot us!" he said, looking back at the truck, that was now directly behind them.

"He wants me, not you," Napier said. "Now do like I said."

The friend complied. The gray pickup pulled in behind them, and a thin Latino with a shock of black hair and droopy eyes got out carrying a pistol in his hand. He walked toward Napier's passenger's side window. Napier watched each step in the side view mirror while slumped down in the seat. When the man with the gun was just a few feet away, Napier said, "Hit it, now!" His friend stepped on the gas pedal and drove off with tires squealing. The gunman took quick aim and squeezed off a shot at Napier. Napier was still down in the seat, and the bullet smashed into the passenger side mirror.

"Keep moving!" Napier said. His friend sped the car out into traffic on Crenshaw Boulevard, heading toward the 105 freeway.

The gunman raced back to the pickup, and he and the driver gave chase. They were able to catch up to Napier's friend's car and follow it onto the 105 freeway toward the airport.

Los Angeles International Airport had several separate terminals that were located very close together, with two loops running between them—one on top for departures and one underneath for arrivals. Inside the loops across from the terminal buildings were parking structures.

"What are we gonna do now?" the friend asked as they arrived at the beginning of the departure side level. Perspiration was dripping down his forehead.

Napier carefully checked outside the rear windshield to track the pickup. "Head onto the departure level and follow it around," he said.

Once inside the airport departure loop, the traffic slowed to a crawl.

"We're going all the way to Terminal Four," Napier said, while still ducking down in his seat. "Stay in the middle lane until I tell you to change lanes to the right."

"What if that motherfucker starts shooting at us while we're stuck here in this traffic?"

"He won't," Napier said. He turned around to check how far the truck was behind them. But he hadn't counted on the stop light at the crosswalk for Terminal One changing to red. "Run that red light!" he said. It was too late. His friend had already stopped the car to let people cross in front of them.

The gray pickup pulled up in the lane next to them on the driver's side. Napier's friend began to panic when he saw the gunman in the passenger's seat lift his pistol barely above the edge of the window. The gun was covered with a cloth of some kind. Napier's friend reflexively pushed himself back into the driver's seat, inadvertently making Napier a better target.

Passengers continued to walk across the crosswalk in both directions in front of the car. No police were in sight. The crosswalk traffic slowed down to a trickle, then it stopped altogether. It would be just a second or two more and the light would finally change back to green.

Suddenly, one more passenger pulling a suitcase started running across the crosswalk just as the light changed. He was passing directly in front of the gray pickup when he dropped a package that he was carrying. As he stopped to pick it up, he blocked the pickup from moving, and that gave Napier's friend a split-second chance to get away.

"Hit it now!" Napier yelled. His friend did, and the car sped away, mixing into the traffic in front of Terminal Two.

Slowly but steadily, they moved past Terminal Two, Terminal Three, and the International Terminal, until they finally made it to Terminal Four.

"Now pull over to the side in front of that cop car," Napier said.

The friend pulled the car over to the curb in front of a parked police car, where other passengers were disembarking their rides to enter Terminal Four. Then Napier noticed that the police car was empty, and no officers were in the vicinity.

"Damn!" he said. "No cops around. Park it, anyway."

They sat inside the car for a moment, only to watch the pickup make its way through the traffic and pull to the curb fifty feet in front of them.

"OK listen up," Napier told his friend. "I don't know if they can see that the police car is empty. I've got a plane to catch. Just get out of the car, open the trunk, and put my luggage on the sidewalk. Leave the trunk open, and get back in the car. After I get out, stay here until the pickup leaves."

His friend did what he was told, and Napier got ready to make a break for the terminal. He took one more look at the pickup to see if anyone was taking aim at him, but at that moment, providence intervened. Another car pulled in between Napier's friend's car and the pickup and parked next to the curb. A family of four got out and started unloading their luggage. As they walked toward Napier's friend's car on their way to the terminal door, Napier got out and walked in front of them, picking up his luggage along the way. This gave him a human shield that, along with the open trunk, allowed him to get inside the terminal safely.

The friend then shut the trunk of the car and sat back down in the driver's seat. He waited a few minutes for the pickup to leave. He continued to wait as five minutes became ten, and still the gray pickup did not move. His impatience gave way to anxiety. He started the car and slowly began to pull away from the curb out into the traffic. But when he came close to passing the pickup, the driver lurched the truck forward in front of him and stopped, causing him to bump into the driver's side rear.

At the same time, the policeman returned to his empty squad car and immediately noticed the accident ahead. He pulled the car up behind the accident and put on his flashing lights. When he asked Napier's friend for his ID, the friend said, "One of those guys in that truck pointed a gun at me."

"Which one?" the policeman said, without looking up from the friend's driver's license.

"On the passenger's side."

"Stay here for a minute. Don't get out of your car."

The officer went back over to his squad car and made a call on his radio, apparently to check the license plate number of the gray pickup. Then he walked over to the truck and observed from the driver's window that no gun was visible. He checked the license of the pony-tailed driver and registration of the truck, and then asked the driver where he was going.

"We came to pick his sister up," the driver said, nodding toward the passenger. "She's arriving from El Salvador."

"You're leaving. Why didn't you pick her up?" the officer said.

"We went to the wrong building. I think it's the one behind us, over there."

"The car behind you has dented your fender. It's small and not serious. Do you want me to fill out an accident report?"

"No, we'll fix it ourselves."

"All right," the officer said as he handed the license and registration back to the driver.

As the officer walked back toward his squad car, he noticed a few spent pistol shell casings in the bay of the truck.

"Hold it!" the officer shouted, as the pickup began to pull away. He drew his pistol. At that same moment the passenger fired a shot through the rear window. The shot hit the officer just below the collarbone, near his left shoulder. Then the pickup drove off.

Napier's friend hurried to the aid of the officer helping him back to his squad car, where the officer called for backup. In a few minutes, additional airport police arrived on the scene followed by an ambulance. But by that time, the gray pickup was long gone.

CHAPTER TWENTY-TWO

Millwood was extremely upset that both Erica and Ben were refusing to pay him the two hundred and twenty-five thousand dollars he claimed was due him. He was also miffed that Walker would not add the claim to the government's lawsuit against Erica. He decided that he would need to bring his own legal action against her. He was wary of the possibility that the opportunity to get paid this amount might slip through his fingers. He understood that the government's pending litigation against Renaissance Estates was in the way.

Late one afternoon he called Rudi into his office. "I need you to do a little project for me," he said. "It takes precedence over whatever else you are doing right now."

Rudi stood in front of his desk like always—standing at attention in front of her commanding officer.

"I'm having some difficulty getting reimbursed for charges and fees that pertain to our work here," Millwood said. "I need you to prepare a spreadsheet with all the bills, charges, and amounts owed to me that are in this folder. On the spreadsheet, show the date of the charge, the invoice or reference number, the amount of the charge, and a brief explanation of what the charge was for. When you're done with that, print it out and make a Xerox copy of all this documentation that backs it up. I apologize for giving this to you with such short notice. But my attorney needs to have it as soon as possible. So, it needs to be done before you leave today."

Rudi opened the folder and looked at the stack of paperwork inside. She checked her watch—it was 4:15 p.m. Then, without saying a word, she walked back to her office and began this new task. She spread the contents of the folder out over her desk and began looking through each item. On the top were some electric bills that dated back from over two years before. A closer look at the bills showed that the service address was different from the Renaissance Estates address on Sultan Road. She went over to the new accountant's workstation and browsed the paid bills drawers in the nearby filing cabinet until she found the electric bill folder. Comparing one of the bills from Millwood's folder with one from the paid bills' drawer, she noticed that the paid bill from the drawer had the correct service address for Renaissance Estates. Further examining the bill, she made a baffling discovery. Both the bill from the paid bills' drawer and the one in Millwood's file had the same account number supplied by the vendor. But the one from Millwood's folder had a different service address. This meant that the power company had two different service addresses for the same account. She spent a few minutes trying to decide if she knew what business was at the service address on Millwood's bill. She had no idea what might be the reason for having one account number for two different service addresses. She made Xerox copies of both invoices before returning the original to the file drawer.

When she returned to her office, she decided to start a file of her own with this problem and any others that might turn up. She knew that it would be fraud if Millwood wanted Renaissance Estates to pay a power bill for a different location.

Rudi continued to work on Millwood's spreadsheet when she came across an invoice for fixing door locks. The invoice was from a vendor named Bernard Locksmiths in San Pedro, and the charge was for eighteen standard door locks plus a separate charge for installing them. Again, the address was incorrect. Further, it was different from the suspicious address on the electric bill. She went back to the accounts payable drawer and looked for the folder for Bernard Locksmiths, but didn't find one. Maria Hernandez, the new accountant, had gone for the day, so Rudi was unable to find out who it was that had installed door locks at Renaissance Estates. She already knew that only Juan Delgado, the head maintenance man, ever installed a new door lock, and that was not a common occurrence. She further saw that the invoice was not signed by anybody to prove that the locks actually were received and installed. A copy of that invoice went into Rudi's new file also.

The next suspicious item in Millwood's folder was one of the invoices for unpaid consulting fees claimed by Millwood Property Management. The only explanation given on the invoice for the charges was "consulting fees" along with the time period claimed. There were several of these invoices that covered nearly two years. She pulled them all out and included the fees on the spreadsheet. They added up to one hundred and ninety-six thousand five hundred dollars. Since Millwood had told her he wanted a "brief explanation" added to the spreadsheet, she took these invoices into his office to get the explanation from him.

"There's no indication of any kind as to what these invoices are for," she said, as she showed the bills to Millwood.

Millwood took a look at them and said, "They're for consulting fees just like the invoice says."

"The consulting fees have already been paid," Rudi said. She showed him copies of the statements for fees paid to Millwood Property Management for the corresponding time periods.

"Oh, those statements are incorrect," Millwood said. "You see, those bills were computed only on the amount of rent paid by the tenants here. The consulting fee is supposed to be computed based not only on the tenant's rent but also on the government's supplement. What you have in those invoices is the amount of the difference."

Rudi thought about that explanation for a moment. "What should I put on the spreadsheet?" she finally said.

"Consulting fees will be good enough."

"Does Erica know about this?"

Millwood looked up at her. "What difference does that make? The consulting fee for Millwood Property Management is based on the rent per the contract. I'm sure that Erica knows about the contract. And if she doesn't, she will when I get finished suing her for it."

"What are these electric bills for?"

"Those bills are a good example of this place's negligence. I had to pay those bills in my office from my company's money, since the incompetent person who managed the books wouldn't pay them. Now, they're going to pay me back for it."

With that, Millwood's phone rang, so Rudi packed up the invoices and left for her office. She decided to make an additional copy of everything and discreetly give it to Erica. Even though she thought she'd seen it all when it came to vendor invoices, the fraudulent power bills were a first for her. She didn't think Erica knew about the consulting fees, either. But this quantum leap in expenses owed to Millwood Property Management would swamp the budget for Renaissance Estates. It would be such a shock that it might even push Harbor Gateway Community Housing Corporation into bankruptcy.

A while later, she completely finished the project and printed it all out. She put it into a large manila envelope for Millwood, and tucked Erica's copy into her hand bag. Then, with Millwood again on the phone, she shut her office door and called Erica.

"I need to see you as soon as possible," Rudi said. "Millwood's planning to sue Renaissance Estates for unpaid consulting fees. He had me assemble a package of unpaid invoices with a spreadsheet. I made an extra copy of everything for you."

"Thank God you did that," Erica said. "When we were in Walker's office, he tried to get a large sum of money added to Walker's lawsuit for unpaid consulting fees."

"I can bring this by tonight if you're around."

"Great, thanks. I'll see you when you get here."

Since it was nearly six-thirty, Rudi wanted to wrap the project up with Millwood and leave. With the parcel in hand, she opened her office door and went toward Millwood's office. When she was almost inside his office, she froze in her tracks. Millwood was obviously exercised about the money he felt was owed to him and was in a very animated conversation with whomever it was on the phone. He was in his chair, that was swiveled around and facing out the window behind his desk. He didn't notice Rudi standing there just outside his office door.

Rudi could hear what Millwood was saying but couldn't tell who it was he was talking to. She heard Millwood say, "Fuck that bitch. If she doesn't pay me my money, I'll sue her in every courtroom in the state." This startled her, and she decided to quickly duck back into the hallway out of sight. She could hear more anger and foul language coming from Millwood. She continued to listen but couldn't hear quite as clearly from farther away. Millwood was silent for a moment and then said, "I'm telling you, KB, that son of a bitch Williams is just plain worthless. He kept saying that all monies owed to me were paid, and that the woman who was killed had confirmed that to him." Rudi crept a little closer to hear better when Millwood suddenly swiveled around in his chair and said, "Kill the useless bastard." Rudi quickly ducked back out of view. She had been unable to hear the latest sentence in its entirety and did not know what so-called bastard Millwood was talking about. Quietly, she slipped back into her own office. A few minutes later, she walked back in front of his office. But he was still talking, so she waited outside.

When Millwood finally got off the phone, Rudi took a deep breath and walked into his office with the envelope. Millwood took the package and told her to shut his office door, even though all the other employees had left for the day. He also shut the blinds to the window behind him. The only light was from the lamp on his desk. He opened up the envelope and placed the spreadsheet on his desk, setting the copies of the backup documentation aside and putting away the originals. He reached into his desk drawer and pulled out a bottle of Scotch along with a drinking glass. He then poured himself a drink and went over the spreadsheet with Rudi standing there, as usual, in front of his desk.

After a short time, Rudi interrupted Millwood's concentration by saying, "It's past six-thirty and I need to leave now."

Millwood ignored what she said and kept perusing the spreadsheet. "Something's wrong here," he finally said. "The amount for the consulting fees is too low. You're showing only one hundred and ninety-six thousand five hundred dollars."

"That's what your invoices added up to."

Millwood looked up at Rudi and said, "That can't be right. I know it's not right. You must have added them up wrong. It's supposed to be two hundred and twenty-five thousand dollars."

"The spreadsheet software added it up, not me."

"Well you need to double-check it, because it's wrong." Millwood took a sip of his drink and said, "Come over here. I want you to look at this."

Rudi let out a quiet sigh and then walked behind Millwood's desk. She passed behind his chair and stood between him and the desk's L unit, as he continued to look at the spreadsheet.

Millwood asked a few simple questions about the work she had done and then leaned back in his swivel chair partially blocking her avenue of escape.

He sipped his Scotch again and then said, "You know, you have a lot of talent. But there are times when you just don't deliver what I'm after. I'm putting together information that will result in claiming that almost a quarter of a million dollars is due to my firm from this place. That's money that I need to pay your salary, among other things. You don't seem to care if I'm able to collect this money or not. In fact, I don't think you're taking this whole thing seriously."

Rudi leaned back against the L unit portion of his desk and listened as Millwood continued with another of his lectures.

"To do this job," Millwood said, "I need somebody I can completely trust—somebody who'll deliver what I need, when I need it. I thought this person was you, but now I'm not so sure." He observed that Rudi was uncomfortable with her position behind his desk, so he moved his chair back and blocked her in.

"I think it would be tough for you if you lost your job," he said before taking a sip of his drink. "I know that you send money each month to your parents in Iraq. I think it's to keep them out of trouble with the terrorists over there. I hear that if Christians don't pay a tax to the terrorists they can be crucified. It would be an awful thing if this happened to your parents just because you lost your job here and couldn't send them any money."

Now Rudi appeared to be truly fearful. She started to fidget like a child who needed to go to the bathroom. Millwood had found the right buttons to push to get what he wanted.

"Mr. Millwood," she said, her voice quavering. "If there's anything wrong with this spreadsheet, I will stay here and fix it. Just show me exactly what it is that's wrong."

Millwood slid his swivel chair closer to her, virtually pinning her to the L unit. "You know, you really weren't qualified for this job in the first place," he said. "I put you in it because I believed in you. I can see that you're in over your head. I'm sorry."

Rudi began to perspire at the brow, and her trembling prevented her from making a sensible reply.

Millwood reached over and slowly stroked her arm. "Don't worry, you'll always have me to take care of you," he said. He slid forward in the seat of his chair and parted his legs, fitting her body between them.

"It takes a lot of money to pay off the terrorists in Iraq. A lot of money," he said. Then he placed both hands on her bare knees, casually stroking her legs down to her ankles.

"You can stop doing that, please!" Rudi said. Her voice sounded a little bit emphatic, but she was still trembling. She squirmed, but she was trapped behind his desk with little room in which to maneuver.

"Being crucified—what an awful fate. It's barbaric. Worse than being beheaded," Millwood said. He then brought his stroking motion up beneath her skirt to her buttocks.

"Stop it!" she said. She continued an agitated squirming motion.

Millwood lifted her skirt up around her waist as he continued to stroke her upper legs. "I know that you're sweet on Erica. I knew that after you'd been here for a month or two. I think it's time that you prove to me that you like men as well as liking women."

Millwood's own sexual pleasure began to rise. He felt that he reached the moment when he would score with Rudi, who always turned him on the way she dressed. He reached again underneath her skirt up to her waist until he felt the top of her panties. He grasped them near the elastic band slipping his fingers inside. Then he began to pull them down.

"Stop it! Please," she said with as authoritarian a voice as she could muster. She appeared as if she might pass out. She started to sob gently.

At that moment, the phone rang, diverting Millwood's attention. He pulled the chair up to his desk to answer the phone, creating enough space for Rudi to escape. She ran out from behind Millwood's desk and went into her office. She quickly fixed her underwear and straightened her skirt out. Grabbing her handbag with the envelope for Erica inside, she raced out the front door.

CHAPTER TWENTY-THREE

It had been several days since Jay last talked to Erica. He wanted to ask her about the big meeting that he heard had taken place involving her and HUD. But he decided to call Rudi first to find out what she knew about it.

"The last time I talked to Erica, she wouldn't tell me anything," Jay said. "She didn't sound too happy, either. I also called her lawyer, and she said only that they were in a major meeting with HUD over Renaissance Estates. I tried to press for details, but she wouldn't budge. Do you know what's up?"

Rudi closed the door to her office and sat back down at her desk. "HUD wants to sue Renaissance Estates."

"HUD wants to sue! What the hell for?" Jay said.

"They're trying to force Erica out. They dreamed up a whole bunch of nonsense they say is against regulations, and then they concluded that the only thing for her to do was sell Renaissance Estates."

"Oh my God! Well, this adds another twist to the story."

"On top of that, they want to prohibit her from ever doing business with the federal government again. In other words, they're trying to ruin her for all time."

"I see. Listen, this is getting really gnarly. I've got to get it into the story. It would help if we could meet somewhere, instead of trying to talk about it over the phone. How about I meet you for dinner?"

Rudi hesitated for a moment. "I don't feel good about what's going on. Today might not be a good day," she said.

"I'll try to keep it as brief as possible," Jay said.

Rudi hesitated again, then she finally said. "What did you have in mind?"

"How about someplace close to you?"

"I live in Cypress."

Jay gave her the address of an Italian restaurant in Cypress. He thought that would provide enough privacy for them to discuss this turn of events and shield her from being spotted with him by anyone she knew.

When Jay arrived at the restaurant, he found Rudi sitting near the front door having an emotional breakdown. She appeared to be in mourning. It took a couple of drinks, but Rudi loosened up enough to explain everything she knew about Erica's lawsuit. They were in a quiet corner of the restaurant, and Jay had his recorder running. He could tell that Rudi was very upset.

After Rudi told him about Erica's situation, Jay said, "Was there anything else that came out of the meeting besides HUD trying to get rid of Erica?"

Rudi looked up and said, "There definitely was. Millwood tried to tack on another two hundred and twenty-five thousand dollars worth of consulting fees and expenses that he claimed were never paid to him."

"I knew that guy was an asshole the minute I saw him," Jay said.

"The consulting fees he claimed were to be based on a different formula than what was used."

"Was that true? I mean, did he, like, deserve the money?"

"I don't know for sure. He had me detail out the invoices that he said were owed. First of all, they didn't add up to what he said they would. Then, there was nothing on the invoice that indicated why the money was owed. He said it came from his contract with Renaissance Estates, that I've never seen."

"Sounds like the whole thing could just be another way to suck her blood?" Jay said.

"Exactly. Lisa told me several times that all accounts between Renaissance Estates and Millwood Property Management had been paid. I think Millwood wanted to use HUD to somehow provide leverage to help collect this undue amount, and the lawsuit would be the best way to do it."

Rudi appeared to have perked up a bit, so they ordered something to eat. While they waited, the conversation continued.

"I noticed something else very peculiar about Millwood's claims," Rudi said. "He was claiming reimbursement for some power bills that he said were paid by his firm on behalf of Renaissance Estates. He wanted me to make copies for him. Since I knew that Lisa had paid all the power bills, I decided to investigate. The bills he wanted reimbursement for had the same account number as the power bills that Renaissance Estates paid each month. But the service address was different—it was for some other place, not Renaissance Estates."

"Holy shit! He's trying to get the power bills from one of his other clients paid by Renaissance Estates. That's fraud, isn't it?" Jay said.

"I would definitely think so. There was also a locksmith bill for buying and installing eighteen door locks. Now, I can tell you definitely that Juan, the maintenance man, is the only person who ever installed any door locks. He might do only a few each year, and he hasn't done one in months."

"More fraud. Does Erica know about this?"

"While I was busy building the spreadsheet with all this information on it, I made an extra copy of everything and gave it to her."

"Cool. What did she say about it?"

"She was not surprised. Nothing surprises her about HUD or Millwood anymore."

"I don't blame her for that," Jay said.

"The worst thing is that Millwood's mismanagement has already taken away her dividend," Rudi said. "This leaves her without any source of income. And if this bullshit two hundred and twenty-five thousand dollars ever goes through, Renaissance Estates will likely go bankrupt, and she will be wiped out."

Rudi appeared exhausted. It seemed that her misery over the struggles, past and present, that her best female friend was enduring had brought her to tears. She settled down a short while later when dinner was served.

After dinner, Rudi invited Jay up to her apartment. While Jay perused the artwork in her living room, she went into the kitchen and made them both a cup of tea.

"You're quite an artist," Jay said without knowing exactly which paintings she had done herself.

"Thanks," she said. "I didn't do everything you see here. But I did paint those on the wall behind the sofa. I also took those photographs in the corner behind the television."

"I'm impressed!" Jay said. To his delight, she took him around the apartment and explained everything she knew about each work of art, regardless of its origin. Jay used his cell phone to capture pictures of the ones he liked the best.

When they sat down to have their tea, Rudi said, "There's something I have to tell you. I don't know if you can publish it, but somebody needs to know about this."

Jay hesitated and then said, "Wait a second while I set up." He pulled out his recorder, notepad, and pen.

"I was in the office late one day working on that spreadsheet project. I overheard a phone conversation that Millwood had with somebody who was apparently very important. I was walking into his office with the completed project, but I stopped at his doorway. I don't think he saw me since his chair was swiveled around facing out the window. He was talking about Erica at first and how he was going to 'sue the bitch.' What bothered me the most was what he said next. He was putting down Ben Williams by saying that Ben was useless since he wouldn't back up Millwood's claim about the money. There was some more conversation, and then he suddenly swiveled the chair around and said, 'Kill the bastard!'"

"Whoa! You heard him say that he wanted someone to kill Ben?" Jay said.

"That's the problem. I didn't hear the first part of what he was saying since he had turned his chair around. Then I had to duck out of sight because I didn't want him to know that I might have heard anything."

"Do you think it was Ben that he was talking about?"

"He was just finished bad-mouthing him. It had to be Ben that he wanted killed."

"Have you told the police anything?"

"Not yet. I mean, I didn't hear Ben's name specifically, but I just *know* he was talking about him."

"What about Ben? Did you talk to him?"

"I told both Ben and Erica about it. They both said that it was nothing new. Millwood has threatened both of them before, but nothing came out of it."

"Do you have any idea who it was that he might have been talking to?"

"No, not really," Rudi said. Then she thought for a moment. "Wait a minute! I remember that it was somebody named KB, whoever that might be."

"KB," Jay repeated. "Doesn't sound familiar."

"I just can't think of who it is," Rudi said.

"I'm connected to the police detectives working this case. I can at least tell them about all this," Jay said.

"What can they do? Nothing has actually happened. It would be great if they could catch Millwood before he did anything to Ben. But what if they can't?"

"Maybe a peace bond of some kind would work."

"I doubt it. No peace bond will ever keep Millwood out of Renaissance Estates."

"Are you sure that Millwood didn't see you standing there while he said that?"

Rudi hesitated. "No, I'm not sure," she said. "I don't think he did, but I'm not positive."

"That makes me worried about your safety. If Millwood was behind Lisa's murder, he might be willing to kill whoever he thinks might blow his cover."

"Don't worry about me. I'll be all right," she said, "There is a favor you can do for me, though."

"Sure, anything. Just name it. I owe you more than one."

Rudi sat back in her chair. "I want you to print a story naming Millwood as being responsible for the mismanagement at Renaissance Estates," she said. "I can give you a copy of all the documentation I have including what's in HUD's lawsuit to help prove it. I need you to do that to help Erica. She's too good a person to be treated like this. Any decent person would tell you that this world needs more people who are willing to go to great lengths to help the poor. And I can't think of anything more valuable to a poor person than a safe, affordable place to live."

"As I'm sure you know, I was assigned to this story to pursue Lisa's murder," Jay said. "It's a crime story. The information you've given me has helped tremendously. But what I need to do to get this part published is to find a tie-in to Lisa's murder. Let me ask you, why do you think Lisa was killed?"

"I don't know," Rudi said with a look of chagrin. "I've thought about it many times. But I just can't come up with the reason."

"To my mind, she knew something," Jay said. "And it probably was something financial, since she was the accountant. What do you think that could have been?"

Rudi pondered for a moment. "There was the stolen money…"

"Do you think that could have gotten her killed?"

"There were also accounting problems like those that the audit discovered."

"But isn't that the kind of stuff you get fired over and not killed for?"

Rudi paused and then said, "She must have known and confronted somebody about the money that was being systematically pilfered."

"That could do it. Who would that be? Millwood?"

"Maybe." She thought some more and said, "Yes, it might have been Millwood. He has plenty of financial mischief to hide, and she was in a position to expose it."

"Is there anybody else that works there who might be of help? I mean, is there anybody else I can talk to in confidence about this?"

"No, absolutely not. Nobody that works there can be trusted since they all work for Millwood. And please, don't ever let anybody know that I'm telling you all this."

"Oh, I won't do that. I promise." Then he went on to say, "I want to publish what we've talked about. But I can't do that unless I have some evidence to back it up or unless someone else can corroborate it."

"What about Erica?"

Jay hesitated. "I don't know," he said. "I think it would be hard to use the victim as a corroborator—the story might be viewed as too one-sided. I would have just Erica's statements, with an anonymous person as the corroboration. I think my editor would consider that as too much of a stretch."

Jay packed up his recorder and other materials. "Find me some evidence. More invoices, emails, and more financial problems. Especially something about money," he said. "Lisa was killed because she knew something financial was wrong. I've got no one but you to help me with this."

"I'll see what I can do," Rudi said. She seemed as though she wanted to say more, but didn't.

When Jay got back to his van, he picked up his cell phone and called Aguilar to tell him about the threat to Ben Williams. Aguilar was off duty and at home with his family, but listened for a few minutes as Jay went over the details.

"I can't do anything with this information, Newsboy, until something actually happens," he said. "It's department policy not to get involved with threats like this. Even if Ben Williams were to come in and complain about it, the most we could do would be to get a peace bond. Millwood would be able to fight it in court, and we would need your sources to come forward and tell what they heard. I don't know if you really want to do that."

"There's got to be a connection somewhere," Jay said.

"Then help us get the evidence," Aguilar said. And with that, the call concluded.

CHAPTER TWENTY-FOUR

In the latter part of any afternoon, Ben Williams would often make the short drive to see his daughter, who lived a few miles away. He usually stayed for dinner and sometimes took some laundry with him, since she had a washing machine and dryer in her garage. On this particular day, he got into his car and started up the engine. As he turned around to back out of his parking space, he saw a man standing directly behind his car smoking a cigarette. Ben waited for a moment to see if the man would move and then made a motion for him to stand aside. When nothing happened, he turned back around to get out and see what this person's problem was. To his great surprise, another man was standing right outside the car door blocking him.

"Whoa!" he said, through the rolled down window. "You scared the shit out of me, man. Say, what's going on here? I'm trying to…"

Before he could finish that sentence, the man next to him brandished a pistol and aimed it directly at his belly. He then fired two quick shots that struck Ben in the upper stomach and chest. Ben slumped forward, banging his head on the steering wheel. He died instantly.

The man at the car window carefully tucked his pistol into the front of his trousers underneath his shirt. He then quickly walked toward the back of the car. When he joined the other man, they both started running toward a gray pickup truck parked nearby.

While driving back to the precinct after answering another homicide call, Aguilar and Lee got a call that a murder had taken place at Renaissance Estates. Harry, who was driving, immediately exited the freeway and changed directions back toward Renaissance Estates. There they found out that Ben Williams had been shot to death in the driver's seat of his car. The first responders on the scene had cordoned off the parking lot where Ben's car was parked. After Aguilar and Lee examined Ben's position, the medical team moved the body from the front seat of the car to the ground a few feet away. The police officer on the scene showed the detectives a witness. Aguilar had Harry take the witness's information while he surveyed the crime scene further.

The witness, a Mrs. Alma Robinson, was a tenant at Renaissance Estates. She had been walking toward her building when the murder occurred.

"Mrs. Robinson," Harry said, "would you please tell me what you saw and heard."

"I was walking from the bus stop over there back to my apartment, which is over here," she said, pointing to the two locations. "Then I heard two pops, like firecrackers, or something, that came from over in this direction." Again, she pointed to where the shots had come from.

"Did you see anybody over there?" Harry said.

"I stopped and turned around to look as I thought it might be gunshots. There was two Mexicans standing next to that car. One was behind it, and the other one was next to the window. Then they both ran away."

"Did you see where they went?"

"They got into a pickup truck that was parked down there further near the street corner. Then they drove off somewhere."

"Can you tell me what they looked like?"

"Well, they was both Mexican. One was taller than the other. They was walking. But then they started running really fast to get outta here."

"Was the tall one standing next to the car or behind it?"

"Behind it."

"Can you tell me what kind of clothes they were wearing?"

"One of them was wearing khakis. That's all I remember."

Harry then showed her the photo of Suarez. "Did the tall one look like this?"

Mrs. Robinson looked at the picture and said, "I didn't see his face, but he had a ponytail just like that."

"Did you notice anything else? Even something small can be important," Harry said.

Mrs. Robinson thought for a moment and then said, "The one standing behind the car was smoking a cigarette and he threw it away when they left."

Harry's eyes lit up. "Thank you very much for your help," he said. He then gave her his card and asked her to call him if she remembered anything else.

While Harry was talking to the witness, Aguilar was examining the crime scene. He noticed the bullet holes in the driver's seat. He further noticed that they did not exit the back of the seat and therefore were likely still inside the upholstery. With a thin bladed knife, he carefully pulled out the spent bullets from where they had lodged. He also found two spent shell casings and placed them all in evidence. Then he called LAPD central to tell them to relay to CSI that he had removed two bullets from the crime scene for the lab to examine.

With the tip from Mrs. Robinson, Harry walked behind the car and started searching for a cigarette butt. He checked the surrounding parking spaces on both sides. He checked underneath Ben's car in the back and the front but was unable to find it. He stood for a moment behind the car and faced the driver's side window. Then, as if he were attempting to reenact the killer's movements, he imagined how he would toss out a cigarette if he suddenly had to leave. He turned directly to his right and walked across a vacant parking space to the car in the next space over. Checking underneath near the rear tires, he found what he was looking for. Carefully, he picked it up with tweezers and put it into an evidence bag. He then walked back over to the driver's side of Ben's car, where Aguilar was still searching inside.

"What's that you've got?" Aguilar said, as Harry held out the plastic evidence bag.

"A cigarette butt," Harry said. "That witness said she saw a guy with a ponytail standing behind the car smoking a cigarette."

"Outstanding!" Aguilar said. "If we can get a sample of Suarez's DNA, we can place him at this murder site."

A short time later, the two detectives wrapped up their investigation and sent the evidence they had to the lab. During the drive to the lab, Harry said, "Didn't you tell me just the other day that Newsboy said this man's life had been threatened?"

"That's right," Aguilar said. "Newsboy said that his source heard Brendon Millwood tell somebody in a phone call to kill Ben Williams."

"Doesn't that mean that we have our guy? A threat come true is no coincidence."

"We can't arrest him over that. But we sure can have nice, long talk with him."

After sending their evidence to the lab, the two detectives drove directly to Millwood Property Management and intercepted Brendon Millwood as he was wrapping up business for the day. They dispensed with formalities by only presenting their identification. Then they crowded Millwood in his office standing in front of him as he sat at his desk.

"Mr. Millwood," Aguilar said. "We'd like to have a little talk with you. Another person connected with Renaissance Estates was murdered this afternoon."

Millwood appeared to be caught off guard. "Oh, Really? Who was that?" he said.

"Ben Williams," Aguilar said, after a slight hesitation.

Millwood also hesitated before posing another question. "So, what do you want me to do about it?" he finally said.

Aguilar took Millwood's response to be flippant. He motioned to Harry to shut the door to Millwood's office. "Ben Williams was president of the Harbor Gateway Community Housing Corporation," Aguilar said, still in his trademark, low key-monotone. "That's the company that owns Renaissance Estates. He was shot while sitting in his car in the project's parking lot."

"Well, I'm sorry to hear that," Millwood said blandly. He started to pack up his briefcase.

"That's the second person connected to Renaissance Estates who was killed in the last thirty days," Aguilar said. "The other one was Lisa Nguyen, the accountant. Do you not see a pattern of some kind going on here? The accountant is killed, and then, a few weeks later, the president of the holding company is killed. Seems like more than a coincidence, don't you think?"

"I had nothing to do with either of those killings. I just manage…"

"But you do have plenty to do with Renaissance Estates, don't you?" Aguilar said, both interrupting Millwood and raising his voice.

Millwood stared at Aguilar. "I'm the managing agent of Renaissance Estates," he finally said. "I run the place, not Ben Williams or anybody else affiliated with the Harbor Gateway Community Housing Corporation. Yes, as a matter of fact, I do have plenty to do there."

"Then you can tell me why payments made by Renaissance Estates to the South Bay Neighborhood Association were greater than the amounts that had been invoiced," Aguilar said. His voice was now almost a shout. "And you can tell me why the checks for these payments were cashed by the bank, can't you? After all, you do run the place and, therefore, you should know the answer."

"Look, I don't know anything about payments being made," Millwood said, his voice trembling. "That was Lisa's job, not mine."

"There has been a lot of cash flowing over to the South Bay Neighborhood Association from Renaissance Estates," Aguilar said. "The kind of money that can't be tracked in an accounting system. Does that mean that they have a slush fund?"

"You're asking the wrong guy," Millwood said, bobbing and weaving around Aguilar's verbal thrusts. "You should be asking *them* if they have a slush fund."

Harry then brandished a copy of a check for over fourteen thousand dollars from Renaissance Estates that was made payable to the South Bay Neighborhood Association. At the bottom was Millwood's signature.

"Isn't that your signature?" Aguilar said.

Millwood looked at it. "So, I signed a check," he responded. "What does that mean?"

"It should mean that you know what that check was for, shouldn't it?" Aguilar said.

"The bookkeeper hands me checks to sign that are over two thousand dollars. That's in the bylaws."

"And you sign them without knowing what they are for?"

Millwood's was fidgeting with a pen and perspiring profusely. "All right," he said. "That's it. That's enough. I want to talk to my attorney."

Aguilar picked up the telephone receiver from Millwood's desk and handed it to him. "Call him," he said.

Millwood's attorney met them at the precinct and advised his client to say nothing at all. The detectives continued to badger Millwood about the murders, the checks, and what he knew about a slush fund at the South Bay Neighborhood Association. After a while of giving no answers, Millwood was released.

Later that evening, the lab report was posted to the LAPD's confidential database. The report showed that the markings of the bullets matched those retrieved from two other unsolved murder cases. Both those cases had ties to the South Bay Neighborhood Association and involved the same gun.

"Now we know where the gang's headquarters is," Harry said.

"Ben Williams was shot at about four in the afternoon," Aguilar said. "South Bay Neighborhood Association closes up for the day at about five. Maybe the killers haven't been paid yet."

"I think that means we're heading over to South Bay early in the morning," Harry said.

"I think you're right," Aguilar said.

On the chance that Ben Williams's killers would turn up at the offices of the South Bay Neighborhood Association to get paid, Aguilar and Lee drove to Torrance at six thirty in the morning and staked the place out. Again, they parked strategically in order to observe who walked through the office door, as well as minimize their own presence.

Time passed, and they watched as the employees walked through the front door one at a time. Then Harry said, "Wasn't Napier the money man of this operation?"

"That's right," Aguilar said, his eyes firmly fixed on the building's entrance.

"Well, since he's been arrested, why would the killers come back here to get paid? I mean, there must be somebody else filling that job."

"That's a good point. Somebody else has to pay them—either here or someplace else."

"How do we know that the new moneyman even works here?"

"We don't. But we do know that the money is in there. It's our only lead right now."

Then around eleven thirty, a woman walked out of the front entrance with a briefcase.

"Does that woman look familiar?" Aguilar said.

"Yes, but I don't remember from where," Harry said.

"She's the lady who controls the money in the safe."

"And she's carrying a briefcase full of it somewhere," Harry said as he started the car.

The woman got into her car and drove toward the parking lot exit. Casually, the two detectives followed her car, being careful not to crowd her, but keeping her in plain view. She led them to a public park that was quiet on this workday morning. She got out of her car with the briefcase and sat at a nearby picnic table. She started reading a magazine, apparently waiting for someone to show up.

Harry parked their unmarked police car on a side street near the park's entrance. Aguilar could view the woman with the briefcase through binoculars. Harry was poised to photograph the transaction using a digital camera with a powerful telephoto lens. A short time passed, and then a gray pickup truck came down the street and turned into the parking lot. It parked in an angled space next to the walkway that went around the park. Out jumped two Latinos, one thin and of medium height, and the other taller with a ponytail. They walked over to the woman sitting at the picnic table. After a short conversation, they received the briefcase. Suarez, the one with the ponytail, opened it, and Aguilar could plainly see stacks of bills packed neatly inside. Harry clicked a dozen or more photos while this took place.

Aguilar quietly said. "Start the car and move up slowly. Don't catch anybody's attention."

Harry put his camera onto the back seat and drove into the parking lot. At just the same time, the conversation at the picnic table came to an end, and the two suspects started back toward the pickup truck. Harry then pulled the car a few feet behind the truck and blocked it in its parking space. Both detectives got out of the car with their pistols drawn while Aguilar shouted, "Police!" The man with the briefcase stopped a few feet in front of the truck. He looked directly at Aguilar, providing him with a clear view of the mysterious man he'd been after. The shock of black hair and droopy eyes made an immediate imprint on Aguilar's mind.

Ignoring the shout, Suarez continued to the truck and slid into the driver's side seat. The man Aguilar now knew to be "El Puma" was carrying the briefcase with the money.

"*Baja el malentin!*" Aguilar told him. *Put the case down!* "El Puma" slowly bent down and placed the case upright on the ground.

Suarez had not closed the truck driver's side door yet when Harry shouted, "Get out of truck, now!"

Suddenly, Suarez slammed the door shut making a loud, distracting noise. Instinctively Aguilar turned his head toward the sound. "El Puma" quickly pulled a pistol out of his waistband and aimed it at Aguilar, who was caught out in the open. "El Puma" opened fire, sending two bullets directly into the car door behind Aguilar. Just as Harry opened fire at Suarez, Aguilar immediately dashed behind the trunk of the car for cover. "El Puma" fired again at Aguilar while he was running, hitting the closed rear door. From behind the car Aguilar starting shooting at his assailant, nicking him in the leg, and the two men continued to exchange gunfire.

While Harry continued to shoot at the driver, Suarez started the truck and put it into reverse. He raced backward, slamming into the detectives' car and knocking Aguilar on his backside. "El Puma" reacted quickly to this distraction and pitched the briefcase inside the truck's bay. He dove head first into the bay, as Suarez switched gears to go forward. Aguilar got back to his feet and shot at him several more times. Bullets zinged back and forth, hitting the car, the pickup, the park's public toilet building, and a nearby palm tree.

Harry also fired again several times trying to hit Suarez, who had ducked down as he drove away. Suarez drove over the curb and onto the park's walkway to get around the detectives' parked car. He bounced back into the parking lot directly into the line of fire of both detectives. Aguilar loaded another magazine and fired eight more times, and Harry fired another five shots. Again, bullets ripped into the driver side door, through the open window, and into the siding that went around the truck's bay. Remarkably, none hit either of the suspects. The pickup raced down the parking lot to the street and turned right.

The detectives got back into their car to give chase. As they turned to go back toward the exit to the street, the woman who had brought the briefcase backed out of her parking spot and blocked their way. Harry pounded on the horn, and Aguilar shouted out of the passenger window at her to get out of the way. She slowly pulled her car forward down to the exit stopping there momentarily. Right behind her Harry blasted on the horn again, and Aguilar shouted until she finally turned right and pulled out into the street.

Once on the street Harry sped the car out from behind her and they raced past her to chase the pickup, that by now was approaching the entrance to the 405 freeway. Aguilar picked up the radio handset and called for backup trying to get a helicopter to join the pursuit. Within a few moments the freeway traffic had slowed the pickup down, enabling the detectives to gain on it. When Harry pulled behind the truck,

"El Puma," lifted one arm above the bay's back gate and fired a shot, bouncing off the detective's windshield.

"Ease up!" Aguilar said. "We can't have a gun battle out here on the freeway." Harry slowed down and let the pickup gain more distance. Then they both saw that it was heading down the transition road to the eastbound lanes of the 105 freeway. They followed it but lost it momentarily in the freeway traffic on the 105.

"This is where we need a helicopter," Aguilar said. He tried again to get a helicopter to join the pursuit. At that point, they'd spotted the pickup again. It had gone off the freeway onto Prairie Avenue and disappeared into the Inglewood-Crenshaw District. They exited and continued after them combing the area searching for the gray pickup truck. They checked the area north of the freeway to no avail. Then Harry said that they might have gone south after exiting the freeway. With the helicopter and other police cars now involved in the search, the two detectives turned south toward Hawthorne and Gardena. But after a thorough street by street search of that area, they found no trace of the gray pickup truck or either of its occupants.

The helicopter and other police cars continued searching the area south of the freeway. But the two detectives started making their way northward to expand the search zone. As they cruised up Crenshaw Boulevard for another look, suddenly Aguilar shouted, "There they are, going the other way!"

In that area, Crenshaw Boulevard was a divided parkway. They were in the middle of a block when Aguilar saw the pickup. They were also seen by Suarez and his partner as the pickup began to speed up in the opposite direction.

"Cut across the middle!" Aguilar said.

With many car horns honking, Harry drove up onto Crenshaw Boulevard's parkway and down onto the other side. They were now half a city block behind the pickup, that was turning right onto Century Boulevard.

Aguilar radioed in the new location of the assailants as they gave chase by going westbound on Century. Within minutes they became bogged down in traffic since Century Boulevard was undergoing construction. When they reached an intersection with a traffic light, Aguilar spotted the truck on the other side of Century as it pulled into the parking lot of a Target Store.

"They went into the Target parking lot," Aguilar said. "Pull through the intersection and turn left in front of those cars!"

"With his emergency lights flashing and horn honking, Harry cut in front of the cross traffic, causing several cars to slam on their brakes to avoid a crash. A few curse words were uttered, but luckily there was no collision.

Thinking they might be able to trap the fugitives in the busy parking lot, the detectives turned into the fire lane next to the store. A moment later, they saw the pickup traveling away from them on the far end of the parking lot.

"Down through the parking lot and then to the left!" Aguilar said, as he saw the gray pickup turn the corner around the end of the building. Harry turned down the parking lot lane, but they immediately got halted when a car pulled out of its parking spot and another one waited to claim it. Showing his badge, Aguilar shouted out of his window trying to get the car to move out of the way. It took a couple of precious minutes, but they were finally able to pass by. Carefully, Harry managed to squeeze the car out of the parking lot avoiding the jam. By the time they reached the end of the building, the gray pickup was gone.

"Damn it!" Harry said as he banged his fist against the steering wheel. "Where in the hell are the helicopters?"

"They have to fly back around downtown to avoid the flight path of the airport," Aguilar said.

They both looked right and left to be sure that the truck was not still in the lot somewhere. "Back over this way!" Aguilar said pointing to the left.

Harry drove down the fire lane, but he had to slow down to avoid hitting shoppers who were walking to and from the store's entrance. The detectives got to the end of the building but did not see the pickup anywhere.

"All the way down to that street!" Aguilar said.

They drove down to the end of the parking lot to get a view of the street in both directions. There was still no sight of the gray pickup.

"Check it row by row," Aguilar said.

A thorough search of each aisle of the parking lot took them twenty minutes and turned up nothing. Aguilar again reported his status and the last sighting of the gray pickup to the support command. Then they sat and waited. An hour later, the helicopter reported that it had made no sighting of the truck and was returning to its base.

Seeing that the chase was over, Aguilar said, "All right, back to the precinct." He let out a deep sigh as he spoke.

When they made their way back to the freeway, Harry said, "We must be the first cops in history to lose two serial killers in a Target Store parking lot."

CHAPTER TWENTY-FIVE

The stress on Erica to sell Renaissance Estates was taking its toll on her. The nightly drinking had become as routine as taking prescription medicine. Since she spent much of her time in her condominium by herself, loneliness often set in. Even though she still had a number of contacts in the art world and in city hall, she only occasionally got as much as a phone call from any of them. Sometimes she would stare out of the window at the ocean feeling crushed by the conclusion that all she had accomplished in her life would soon be taken away from her. Owing to her pending legal dispute and her age, she felt that she would never be able to even get a job in a housing complex much less own or manage one. Her decision to try to escape the poverty she grew up in as a child in New Orleans was now haunting her. Her loneliness had brought her to tears more than once.

It proved to be a mild shock when Brendon Millwood finally got ahold of her and invited her out to a lavish dinner. In a fit of insanity, she accepted thinking that she had nothing to lose.

Millwood picked an upscale Mediterranean restaurant in Beverly Hills that featured Greek and Italian dishes. The two met there early one evening and began with a bottle of fine, red Italian wine. To Erica's further astonishment, Millwood put on as much "nice guy" charm as he possessed. After some casual niceties, the conversation gravitated over to HUD's lawsuit.

"I just want you to know that you have my sympathy over this lawsuit," Millwood said. "I think the whole thing is unnecessary. I'm dismayed that Walker has to stoop this low."

"I'm glad we can agree on that," Erica said. Her skepticism of Millwood's intentions was still at the forefront of her mind.

"I've seen this sort of thing happen before with other properties that I've managed," Millwood said. "The property owner has only limited control because of Section 8 regulations, and this enables HUD to come in and flex their muscles whenever they don't like what's going on. The threat of legal action generally speaks for itself. But when the threat is made to property owners who are heavily mortgaged by HUD and don't have a lot of resources, it can be intimidating."

Erica sipped her wine and listened intently. For the first time in her experience with Millwood, he seemed to be making some sense. She wondered what he was setting her up for, though.

"In my opinion," Millwood said, "the suit is baseless. The accusations aren't anything specific or concrete—just a lot of generalizations that are vague but well worded enough to be believed by a judge. Then the suit could get dragged out while each generalization becomes more specific and each detail must be verified. It's not that difficult for the government to do. What about small landowners? Like small businessmen, they can get wiped out just trying to defend against a senseless suit like this one."

So far, this guy is right on, Erica thought while Millwood continued his speech. In her mind, she was ever aware that Millwood still was attempting to collect two hundred twenty-five thousand dollars for himself that might come out of her pocket. She continued to listen intently while waiting for the other shoe to drop.

The waiter took their dinner orders, making Millwood lose some momentum. He took a swig from his wine glass and continued the conversation from a different angle.

"With Ben Williams's murder, I'm becoming very concerned for your personal safety," he said. His voice was lowered to avoid drawing attention from anyone else in the restaurant.

"I'd like to thank you for that," Erica said, also lowering her voice. "But I don't feel in any more danger now than I did before."

"What concerns me is that what happened to Ben might have been the work of professional killers," Millwood said. "It appeared to be a street crime such as a carjacking. But nothing was stolen, and the act took place in broad daylight with witnesses. In my opinion, street thugs would do a real carjacking at night when nobody else would be around. Professional killers would be slick enough to do it and get away with it—even if they were spotted by somebody."

"Nobody has any proof of that yet," Erica said.

"That's correct. Nobody has any proof. But if you give this some thought, I think you will agree with me that it appears that somebody wanted Ben out of the way. It could mean that this same person or persons would be willing to commit murder to achieve their goals. They might want you out of the way, also."

"Ben did not own Renaissance Estates. He only stood in for me since Walker and HUD pushed me out of my management role," Erica said. Her voice was slightly raised.

"That's all the more reason for you to be concerned about your own personal safety."

"I'm just not afraid anymore," Erica said. "I feel so bad for Ben. He was an amazing friend in my life helping me out when I needed it the most."

"And to add to that, I think he served you admirably in his capacity," Millwood said. "I'm going to miss working with Ben. He was truly a gentleman."

Erica kept her cool, but felt like scoffing at that last remark. She recalled what Rudi had told her about Millwood's phone conversation when he said he wanted somebody to "kill the bastard." She thought the better of throwing that at Millwood, since he might trace it back to Rudi thereby placing her in jeopardy.

The waiter served dinner, slowing Millwood's momentum again. After a time, he brought himself around to what seemed like his real purpose for their meeting.

"I know that there are powerful people out there who are very interested in Renaissance Estates," he said. "I know that you've been offered good money for it in the past, but this time it seems to me to be different."

"How so?"

"I can't tell you exactly who might be behind the effort to displace you. It's not clear to me, either, although I've been hounded by all sorts of different business types who want information about the availability of the land."

"What do you usually tell them?"

"I always tell them that the property is HUD Section 8 housing that's owned by a private entity. Any sale would be complicated by the need for HUD approval."

There was a silence between them, then Erica finally said, "Are any of these interested parties wanting to take over Section 8 housing and run it themselves?"

"I can't answer for all them, but I know for a fact that a few of them are just interested in the land. Once it was obtained, they would probably move the tenants out of the way and demolish Renaissance Estates for some other, bigger purpose."

"Just how would you and your company figure into any sale of Renaissance Estates?" Erica said. "Wouldn't you lose out if the buyer did want to tear it down?"

"Of course," Millwood said in a rush, as if he had rehearsed the answer. "I think you know by now that I'm not at all interested in owning Renaissance Estates. In fact, the government would be all over me if I tried to own it and still manage it at the same time. I'm in the business of managing properties especially Section 8 housing. That makes HUD an important resource of mine. As for Renaissance Estates, I think that you and I could get along nicely if the government would just leave us alone."

Erica thought there had to be more coming from him, and she was correct.

"I wanted to take this time to talk to you in a civil manner and try to share with you what I see happening around Renaissance Estates," he said. "In the final analysis, I think it would be better for you if you did sell. Somebody wants that place very badly—enough to kill for it. I would not feel right if I didn't at least talk with you about it."

After a pregnant pause, Erica said, "I'd like to thank you again." But inside, she knew that Millwood was hiding something. It was so unlike him to come forward like this.

After dinner while driving back home, she called Rudi and told her about the meeting.

"He's up to something," Rudi said.

"That's just what I thought," Erica said. "Why don't you meet me over at my place in an hour? I'm driving back now."

When Erica arrived at her home, Rudi was already there having let herself in with the extra key that Erica had given her.

"Well, I've had an interesting day," Erica said.

Rudi poured two glasses of wine. They sat down in the living room to chat. "I still can't believe that you actually went to see that man," she said. "With everything that's been going on lately, just what is it that he wants now?"

"I don't know for sure," Erica said before sipping the wine. "He bent over backward to be nice. There's got to be something behind it all—something that's motivating him that's not apparent to me."

"Did he explain why he brought you all the way to Beverly Hills just to wine and dine you?"

"He said he wants me to sell for safety's sake. He thinks that something could happen to me just like it did Ben."

"But the final word was 'sell,' wasn't it? You see, that's how he plans to get paid that big chunk of money he thinks he's owed"

"He did raise some interesting points. He believes that Ben was the victim of a professional hit. And he thinks that some powerful people are behind the effort to oust me from my property."

"Did he include himself?" Rudi said.

"Oh, he swears he doesn't want to own Renaissance Estates. He just wants to manage it."

"I don't trust that guy. He's got hidden motives behind most of what he says and does."

Erica took another large swig of her wine. "What if he's right about Ben?" she said.

"You mean, that Ben was killed by a hit man as a part of a conspiracy?" Rudi said.

"Maybe somebody very rich and powerful is trying to get the land that is underneath Renaissance Estates."

"I could accept a conspiracy theory from Millwood only if he were a major part of it," Rudi said, reaching for her own wine glass.

"I'm wondering if he isn't a pawn in a much bigger game," Erica said. "A lot of what he said had to do with HUD and the government. This would point to DeShawn Walker."

"DeShawn Walker?" Rudi said. Her interest was piqued since she had never considered a large plot being concocted by him. "A conspiracy started by Walker. I just don't see it. He's too comfortable where he is. Most bureaucrats like him are just looking forward to a government retirement."

"You haven't seen the way his wife spends money," Erica said. "This is why I think he is on the take somehow."

"But I mean a conspiracy? And one that includes killing people?"

"You don't know Walker like I do. He has a superhot temper and gets angry about little things that seem to be wrong to him. I can't picture him killing someone himself. But I could see him sending somebody else to do it. I also believe he could be the kingpin of some kind of crime organization—maybe one that specializes in screwing people out of their property."

"By the way, now that we're talking about Walker, how did the FBI investigation we got started against him turn out?" Rudi said.

"I found out yesterday that he was exonerated. The FBI dropped the investigation without charging him with any crime." Erica said.

"Damn!" Rudi said, with a look of disgust on her face.

"If it's not Millwood and not Walker, who else could it be that wants Renaissance Estates badly enough to kill people over it?" Erica said.

"If there is some sort of organized crime effort to get the land, what do the police say about it?" Rudi said.

"Up to now, nothing. I'm sure they aren't going to tell us what's going on during their investigation. If it is organized crime, it might be many months or years before they get it all sorted out."

Rudi finished her glass of wine. "You seem to be concerned about the idea of a conspiracy," she said. "Are you afraid that you might be next?"

"Not entirely, but who knows?" Erica said. "Ben Williams's murder was the most senseless thing that ever happened to someone I knew. I could say the same for Lisa. They were both kind, wise, people who would do anything for somebody like me. If I ever find out who it was that killed them, I might rip him apart myself."

There was a short pause in the conversation, and then Rudi said, "I didn't want to tell you this, but given the circumstances, I think you need to know."

"Go ahead, Babe. Don't hold anything back."

Rudi took a deep breath and let it out slowly. "Please, don't ever trust Millwood for any reason."

Erica put down her empty glass and gave Rudi her full attention.

"I know you don't trust doing business with him," Rudi said. "But you can't trust anything he tells you, either. I know what I heard when he said, 'Kill the bastard.' I know that he was talking about Ben. And I know that he's trying to sue you for practically all that Renaissance Estates is worth. He really wants to destroy you completely."

"Something else is bothering you," Erica said. "Go ahead and tell me."

Rudi took another deep breath and let it out with a sigh. Then she said, "The day I put together that spreadsheet with the unpaid bills, I worked late in the office after everyone else had gone home. As he was looking it over, he got me to walk behind his desk by pointing to the spreadsheet and challenging the results. Then he changed the conversation to my job security. I think he was threatening to fire me."

"Fire you? Honey, if he did that, he would have just screwed himself to the wall at Renaissance Estates," Erica said, in disbelief.

Rudi looked down as she prepared to speak again. It became obvious to Erica that Rudi was deeply troubled about something.

"The conversation shifted to what would happen to my parents and sister in Mosul if I lost my job," Rudi continued. "He kept telling me that the terrorists would crucify them if I didn't send them enough money. Then…then he started talking about how I needed to be loyal to him." Rudi paused and looked up at Erica, who saw that she had starting crying.

"Well, he's an asshole," Erica said. "And don't worry, he's never going to get rid of you."

"There's more," Rudi said. "I was cornered behind his desk. He backed the chair up so that I was blocked in and couldn't get away. Then he started touching my legs. He said he wanted to know if I like men as well as women. A few moments later he started stroking my legs underneath my skirt. He reached all the way up to the top of my legs… and then the phone rang and interrupted him… and I ran away." Rudi placed her head in her hands and started sobbing.

"He did what?" Erica shrieked. She jumped up from her seat appalled at what she just heard. Rudi's tears were uncontrollable.

"Honey" Erica said. "That son of a bitch needs to be taught a lesson. He just sexually assaulted you, and he's gonna go to jail for it."

"I'm so ashamed," Rudi said, her voice trembling. "I was just standing there, afraid of what he would do next. I think I would rather die…"

"Honey! We are going to do something about this and right away. We're not going to stand for this—not for one minute!" Erica sat down on the sofa next to Rudi.

"Last night I woke up at about two AM in a deep sweat," Rudi said, her voice still quavering. "My heart was pounding out of control. It felt like I had been running for my life. What woke me was that I had dreamed of my mother and sister being raped and having their heads cut off by terrorists. And my father being nailed to a cross upside down."

"Babe, it was all a bad dream. It's gone. It's never, ever going to be like that. I promise you," Erica said, as she put her arm on Rudi's back and gently rubbed it.

"I didn't want to make any trouble with Millwood," Rudi said as the teardrops started to subside.

"Oh, Sweetie, you did nothing wrong." Erica put her arms around Rudi and gave her a loving hug the way a mother would hug her child. Then she kissed Rudi on the lips. Rudi wrapped her arms around Erica, and they consoled each other with hugs and kisses.

After a while, the hugging let up and Erica gently pushed Rudi's hair away from her face. Then she said, "Honey, you and I have been together for nearly a year. I don't care what my circumstances are, I am never going to let someone like Millwood ever do anything like that to you again."

Rudi reached out for her with both arms, and Erica continued to hug and caress her. It was over an hour later when they got up from the sofa and went arm and arm back to the bedroom.

CHAPTER TWENTY-SIX

Before leaving the newsroom for the day, Jay got a call from Rudi, who sounded anxious.

"I need to see you right away. Tonight. As soon as possible," Rudi said.

"Sure," Jay said. "Is everything OK? I mean, you sound like you're in a big hurry."

"I have what you need for your story. We can talk more about it when you get here."

"I'm on my way. Traffic's really gnarly, so it'll probably take an hour or more."

"No problem, just get here."

Jay looked up at Dylan, who had been standing next to him when Jay got the phone call. "She sounds like she wants my body," Jay said, joking.

"Is that your Renaissance Estates source?" Dylan said.

"It sure is. And she's hot to see me!" Jay said, grinning in jest.

"You sound like you're hot to see her, too. Do we have some kind of budding relationship here?"

"Only on a professional basis," Jay said, as he packed his laptop into his backpack.

"Too bad," Dylan said. "I forgot that you're committed to staying single."

"Oh, she's good looking," Jay said. "In fact, she's beautiful. But you know how it is with me. I'm hung up on blond babes."

"Yeah, I know how it is with you," Dylan said, as he took a glance at the "Golden Surfer" picture. Then he said, "It's just as well, though. Your credibility would take a hit if you were carrying on with her while you're using her as a source. What has she got for you this time?"

"I don't know, but she said she has the information I need for my story." He hoisted his backpack, skateboard inside sticking out, onto his shoulder and headed out the door.

The late afternoon, downtown Los Angeles traffic made for a slow crawl down the Harbor Freeway toward Renaissance Estates. On the way, Jay mulled over all the material he had for the next installment of his story. After a while, his cell phone rang. Caller ID showed that it was Rudi again.

"Traffic's really slow," he said to Rudi. "It may take at least another half an hour or so."

"Meet me at the same restaurant where we met before," Rudi said.

"That's over in Cypress," Jay said knowing that he would have to reroute himself in the middle of this traffic. "Are you sure everything's all right?"

"Yes, I'm sure."

Rudi was waiting for him inside the front door of the Italian place where they had met previously. When Jay walked in, she got up and greeted him.

"I'm sorry for all the secrecy, but I need to talk to you in total privacy," she said.

"Oh, no problem," Jay said. "Let's try to get that same table we had before."

"I don't want to stay here. We need a place that's even more secluded than this," Rudi said.

Jay thought for a moment. Then he said, "There's always my place."

"Erica's apartment is closer. Let's go there."

"But…what about Erica?"

"She's at a political engagement. But I have a key, and you're driving."

"Didn't you bring your car?"

"No, I Ubered."

Once they were inside his van, he said, "I'm finishing up the next installment of the story we talked about. It's an awesome piece, but I'm going to need that backup support to get it published."

"No problem. I've got the documents with me," Rudi said.

Jay needed some gas, so he stopped to fill up. He pulled up to a pump and went into the mini market to prepay. When he came back to the pump, he noticed a car pulling up to the pump across from his. The young woman who got out seemed familiar. As he started to pump his gas, the young woman also went into the mini market. A moment later, he looked into the passenger seat of his van and was surprised not to see Rudi there. He looked over at the mini market, and then looked around the front of the station. There was no sign of Rudi anywhere. Jay was confused. She had been sitting in the passenger seat when he had walked into the mini mart. But suddenly she was gone.

He finished pumping, and then took another look around for her. *Maybe she just went to the bathroom,* he thought. He waited a moment as the other woman came back to pump her gas. Then he walked around to the front of his van and saw Rudi lying down flat, behind the seats out of sight. She held her index finger in front of her lips. Jay continued around the front of the van and got in on the driver's side. Without looking at or speaking to Rudi, he started the engine and drove away.

"You had me scared there for a moment," he finally said, as he pulled out of the gas station. "I thought I lost you somehow."

Rudi crawled back into the passenger seat. "Sorry," she said. "I had to duck out of sight when that car pulled up next to us. The woman in that car works at Renaissance Estates and has a big mouth. I can't let anyone from work see us together."

"I see," Jay said. He felt considerably better that she hadn't actually disappeared. "I can understand the need for super secrecy."

"Everybody who works in the office is scared after what's happened," Rudi said. "Even the new people who did not know Lisa know what happened to her. Now that Ben is also dead, the fear is mounting."

When they arrived at Erica's condominium, Rudi seemed to relax. They sat down at the dinner table where Jay pulled out his recorder and notepad.

"A lot of this fear concerns Millwood," Rudi said. "You and I talked about the threat to Ben before, and now that he's dead, I think that Millwood might be heading off a cliff. He's forgetting things and leaving things out of place. And for a control freak like him, that is totally unusual. It's like somebody is getting to him. Somebody's got him on the run."

"Do you think it's the police?" Jay said.

"I don't know, but something's going on," Rudi said. She thought for a moment and then said, "Maybe the police did shake him up. He's really changed—I think he's running scared."

"With Ben's tragic murder, that makes two people connected to Renaissance Estates who have been killed," Jay said. "I know there's got to be a conspiracy of some kind. Do you think that Millwood crossed somebody?"

Rudi paused and pondered that for a moment. "If so, I can't imagine who," she said.

"It's seems more and more like some dangerous people are involved in things that are going on around there," Jay said.

"Now you know why all these privacy concerns," Rudi said. "I just can't trust anybody at Renaissance Estates anymore. Everyone except Juan and his maintenance helpers works for Millwood. Even rumors about somebody not being loyal might set Millwood off."

"Are you concerned about your own safety?" Jay said. "I mean, if things are that tough, maybe you should just find a different job."

"I can't quit for two reasons. First, I need the money. And second, quitting would not stop that bastard from coming after me. I know he's somehow connected with both Lisa's and Ben's death."

Jay then said. "This is the heart of the story. Let's have it all."

"When Lisa and I were both working late one night, she came into my office and confided in me. Her workstation was directly in front of Millwood's office. She said she was walking back from the restroom after hours one day and saw a big wad of money change hands from somebody over at South Bay Neighborhood Association to Millwood. She figured that South Bay had to be running a slush fund of some kind and was using the money that Renaissance Estates paid for security above and beyond what was owed."

"Wow, a slush fund? They could use that to hire killers. Sergeant Aguilar is going to want to know about this," Jay said.

"And that's probably why Lisa herself was killed. She had discovered what was happening."

"Did she write anything down about it or talk to anyone else?"

"I don't think she talked to anybody else. She couldn't trust most of the people that worked there, either. And I know that she hated Millwood for the way he treated her. I can recall specifically that he tried to replace her with someone from his office, but Walker wouldn't let him."

"I think we should tell this to Sergeant Aguilar," Jay said.

"When you do, please leave me out of it," Rudi said. "I have to watch every step over there from now on."

"You don't know what I'd give to have Lisa sitting here, swearing to me it was all true," Jay said.

"All I know is what I just told you. I'm sorry that's the best I can do."

"I owe you a lot of thanks."

"I'm concerned about Erica's safety, too," Rudi said. "I just don't know what Millwood will try next. All these killings might be his way of closing in on her."

"Well, at least she lives in a secure building," Jay said as he looked around the confines. "This would be a hard place for a killer to get into. I've been over to your building. Is it a secure building, too?"

"All we have is a locked gate."

"By the way," Jay said, "I'm wrapping up a story about some other people being pushed out of their homes along Sultan Road."

"I bet Millwood's behind that, too," Rudi said. "He probably figured out a way to hide his involvement. Some of the correspondence I encountered refers to a few different companies that have shadowy origins. He might be using them to hide his own illicit actions in the area."

"Do you know the names of any of these shadow companies?" Jay said.

"I don't have a list. But if I think for a moment, I might be able to come up with a few."

Rudi spent a minute trying to remember the names of the shadow companies that she knew about. She stared at the wall seeming to draw a blank. Then she did manage to recall one of them.

"One of them was named the Long Beach…Property Connection." In a reassuring manner she said, "Yes, that's it—the Long Beach Property Connection."

"Cool," Jay said. "That gives me something specific to work with. I can start digging into their business records and find out who the owners are."

"There's another one…" She propped her elbow on the table and held her hand to her forehead. After a pause, she said, "I just can't…remember for some reason."

"It's all right. When you do think of it, just give me a call."

Then she blurted out, "Harbor City!"

Jay paused for a moment and said, "OK, Harbor City…" He added a little inflection into his voice to try to draw more out of her.

"Harbor City *something*," she said. "Damn, I must be losing my mind. All this stress, I think I'm getting a headache."

"How about a glass of wine, or beer, or something?" Jay said.

"Good idea. Would you like one, also?"

"I'll pass, thanks.

In the refrigerator, Rudi found a bottle of wine that was already open. She poured herself a full glass and set it down on the table in front of her.

They continued the discussion for a while longer. When they reached a stopping point, Jay said, "We haven't had any dinner. Aren't you hungry?"

"I'll just fix something here," she said.

"Don't you want me to at least take you home?"

"No, thanks. I'm going to wait for Erica. She should be back in a little while."

Shortly before eight thirty, Jay wrapped up the interview and drove back to Huntington Beach. He was starving, so he pulled into his favorite burrito place and picked up an order to go. When he got back home, he realized that he did not have the corroborating evidence that Rudi said she had with her. He called her but had to leave a message on Erica's answering machine when she didn't answer.

"Hi. I'm sorry to mention this, but I forgot to get that documentation you said you brought with you today," he said in his message. "If it's not too late, just call me back, and I'll run back over there. Talk to you soon."

After Jay had left, Rudi decided to take a shower before Erica returned from the political engagement that she was attending. She went into the bathroom and began to remove her clothes, unbuttoning her blouse first. She folded it neatly and put it on the bathroom armoire. Next, she kicked off he shoes and set them to the side of the toilet. She unzipped and removed her slacks folding them up and placing them on top of the blouse. She checked herself in the mirror. Her makeup had partially worn off revealing a face that showed signs of severe stress. Dark circles had formed under her eyes. She noticed some small wrinkles developing in her face that was uncommon for someone her age—only thirty. Then she noticed something even more troubling. She saw a tiny streak of gray running through her black hair. Next, she removed her underwear. As she reached over to turn on the shower, she noticed a slight movement in the mirror behind her and turned around with a start. She immediately grabbed a bath towel from the rack and wrapped it around her nude body.

"What are you doing here?" she cried out. When there was no answer, she shouted, "Why are you in here? What are you doing?"

Without responding the intruder got close to Rudi. "Get away from me!" she screamed. "Get out of here!"

The intruder stood in front of Rudi for a moment, looking straight into her face and saying nothing. Rudi's eyes were as big as saucers, and she was trembling.

Still silent, the stranger snatched away her towel and shoved her naked body backward into the bathtub, knocking her over. She screamed as loudly as she could and tried to flail at her assailant, but it was of little use. The intruder reached down and grabbed her by the shoulders. He shook her upper body crashing her head against the bathtub spigot. She let out a groan and lost consciousness. He then removed a cord from a pocket and used it to strangle Rudi as she lay on the bottom of the bathtub. Within minutes, she was dead. The killer turned the shower on to wash away any evidence that might have clung to Rudi's body. Satisfied that the job was finished, the killer took a different towel from the rack and used it to clean up the water that had spilled out. Then he carefully exited the scene using the wet towel to wipe up any footprints. As he departed, he left the towel near the front door.

CHAPTER TWENTY-SEVEN

Early the next morning when Aguilar got to the precinct headquarters, he was greeted by grisly news. The watch commander brought him the report of another murder that took place the night before that was related to the case he was working on. Without even sitting down he summoned Harry Lee, and the two detectives went to Erica Knight's condominium.

Police from Long Beach, along with their CSI department, had already been there analyzing the crime scene putting together what evidence they could find. When Aguilar didn't see any officers present, he assumed that their work was finished and asked Erica if they could look at the crime scene. She took them back to see the bathroom. Except for Rudi's body being removed and some slight damage to the shower curtain, there was little out of the ordinary. There was no sign of blood, no footprints on the floor, nothing was wet, and there was no obvious forensic evidence anywhere. Rudi's clothes were still folded and resting where she left them.

"It doesn't appear that there was a struggle in here," Harry said.

Aguilar took a close look at the bathtub and shower. "Has this area been cleaned up yet?" he asked Erica.

"No, the police asked me to leave it until later this afternoon.," Erica said.

With an eagle eye, Aguilar checked every inch of the bathroom for anything that might have been overlooked. "Apparently, the victim either knew her killer, or didn't suspect that person of anything unusual," he said. "Was there any sign of forced entry?"

"Not that I could see," Erica said. "The front door was locked when I came home, and there isn't any way somebody could have gotten in here without a key."

"She could have let the killer in though," Aguilar said.

"Yes, she could have," Erica.

"Where was the body when you discovered it?" Harry said.

"Lying in the bathtub on her back," Erica said.

"Had the body been washed clean?" Aguilar said.

"I don't know. It was still a little wet when I found her."

Erica looked glassy-eyed. Aguilar suspected that she had taken something to quell her anxiety.

The detectives finished searching the crime scene. "The preliminary report we saw earlier this morning said that she was strangled," Aguilar said. "Was there anything like a rope, sash, cord, or some other item like that missing from your apartment?"

"I didn't see anything missing like that," Erica said.

"Was there anything of value taken?" Harry said.

"No. "I don't have very much here that's valuable to begin with, and nothing is missing."

They left the bathroom and returned to the living room.

"Did the victim have any other visitors last night?" Aguilar said.

"Only Jay Phillips from the *Daily Journal.* Rudi sent me a text saying that she was trying to get him to publish a story about all the crap that's been going on over at Renaissance Estates."

"Do you know if anything was going on between them?" Aguilar said. "Anything that could have led to a lover's quarrel of some kind?"

"They were not lovers," Erica said. "Rudi was…lesbian." It took a moment for Erica to get that word out as it was a secret kept by most people that knew Rudi. "She liked Jay as a friend," Erica said. "She mostly needed him for his access to getting the story of my problems at Renaissance Estates published."

"Yes, I've already read some of his stories in the *Daily Journal,*" Aguilar said. His scrutinizing eyes checked out every inch of the apartment, high and low.

"Was there anyone else you know of that might have come over here last night?" Harry said.

"No. I usually don't get visitors unless they call first."

"Were there any phone messages when you came home?" Aguilar said.

"Just one from Jay. He was hoping to find some kind of documentation that Rudi was supposed to have given him. He said that he'd left here without it."

"Did you find documentation of any kind that might be what Jay was looking for?" Aguilar said.

"No. I haven't seen anything like that."

After a few more questions, the officers thanked Erica and left.

Jay was awakened by a loud rapping at his front door. He looked at the clock and saw that he had slept much later than usual since he had stayed up very late to work on the next installment of his story. He got up and answered the door. There he found Sergeant Aguilar and Officer Lee.

"Good morning, Newsboy," Aguilar said. "Did we wake you up?"

"Hi Sergeant Aguilar," Jay said. "Yes, I just woke up." That much was obvious to Aguilar and Lee, since Jay was dressed only in his pajama bottoms. He opened the door and invited both officers in.

"You must have been very busy last night," Aguilar said as he walked into Jay's living room. He thought that Jay might not know about Rudi having been killed. He was trying to test Jay to see if he *did* know that a murder had occurred. Ever observant, his scrutinizing eyes checked every corner of Jay's messy studio apartment.

"Oh, totally!" Jay said. "I'm working on the next piece of the story. Here I can show you."

"We'll skip it for now," Aguilar said. "We're here on official business."

"OK," Jay said slowly, not certain why this encounter with Aguilar and Lee would be any different from any other. "Can I get you some coffee? I sure need some."

"Newsboy, where did you go last night?" Aguilar said.

Jay walked around the corner into the kitchen and started to make coffee. "I was working on my story, and I got a call from my source at Renaissance Estates. She needed to see me right away. I went and picked her up at a restaurant, and then we went to Erica Knight's place in Long Beach."

"Why did you go there?" Aguilar said.

"She had the key and wanted to go somewhere that was completely private where we could talk."

"And what did your source tell you?"

"A lot of things. Why don't you guys sit down while I get my cup of coffee?"

Neither detective sat down. Harry's eyes were also busy scrutinizing Jay's apartment. As he looked around from corner to corner of the living room, he counted four surfboards of different sizes, and one apparatus standing up that appeared to be a mast with a sail wrapped up in it. Across from that was a wet suit hanging on a hanger that was suspended from the ceiling. Below the wet suit, he could see flippers and several face masks. On the wall next to the wet suit, was a life-sized poster of Duke Kahanamoku, the famous Hawaiian pioneer of surfing. A few other pictures of surfers were mounted on other parts of the wall. Harry did not find what he was looking for—any firearms or other weapon that could endanger the two officers.

Aguilar fixed his eyes on Jay. Finally, he said, "A lot of things? Start telling us what they were about."

Jay detected Aguilar's police-like tone but didn't know yet what was actually going on. "The most important thing I heard," he said, "was that Lisa Nguyen said in absolute confidence that she knew about a slush fund involving Millwood and the South Bay Neighborhood Association. It came from the exorbitant amounts of money that were overpaid for the security services that they were allegedly performing. I think I already told you about that possibility."

"How did Lisa know it was slush fund?" Aguilar said.

Jay got his coffee and sat down at a table outside of the kitchen. Suddenly, it occurred to him that he was being interrogated. He trusted Aguilar so he carried on. "She told my source that one evening, when she was working late, she saw some big shot from South Bay hand a large wad of money over to Millwood. Lisa, I guess, put two and two together and figured that the excess money was flowing back and forth."

"What else did your source tell you last night?" Aguilar said.

Jay looked at him for a moment and then said, "I was promised that I would be provided some documentation that would support my story about how numerous homeowners were pushed off the land near Renaissance Estates. The story is almost finished, but I still needed to see the documentation to confirm what I am writing about."

"Do you have the documentation?"

"I got back here and realized that I had forgotten it. I even called to ask my source about it. There was no answer. I had to leave a message."

Then Aguilar changed the subject. "Tell me about your personal relationship with your source?"

"I don't really have a personal relationship with her," Jay said. "She was just helping me with my story. Look, why don't I just give her a call and we can straighten this …"

"You can't call her, Newsboy," Aguilar said. He had the deadpan look of a tough detective about to drop a bombshell on a suspect. "She's dead."

"What!" Jay shot up out of his chair. "No! You can't be serious!" There was a moment's silence with nothing said by anyone. Then Jay said, "Don't tell me, you are serious."

"She was murdered last night, sometime after you were there," Aguilar said.

"Oh my God! She's dead? Rudi…Rudi's dead?" He slumped back down into his chair and held his head in his hands.

"That's right," Aguilar said.

It took a few minutes for Jay to get a grip on himself. "Can you tell me what happened?" he finally said.

"We were wondering if *you* could tell *us* what happened," Aguilar said.

"Wait a minute, guys," Jay said, quickly snapping out of his slump. "I left there at about eight thirty, and she was just fine. I was only there for the story." Jay looked around for his recorder and found it under the chair in front of his work station. "Let me play back this conversation, and you can hear everything that went on while I was there."

For an hour and a half Aguilar and Lee listened to the recording of the interview Jay had at Erica's place with Rudi.

"And you don't know where that documentation is?" Aguilar said.

"I forgot the damn stuff. She must have had it in her handbag."

Harry said, "The Long Beach Police Department didn't find anything on her in the way of documents, folders, or computer files."

"Maybe Erica found it when she got home," Jay said.

"We visited her earlier, and she said she didn't," Aguilar said. "Now, you need to listen to me carefully. The Long Beach Police Department is investigating this crime. They will be calling on you very soon, since you were at the crime scene around the time of the murder. We don't have jurisdiction in this case. But we are a party to the investigation since it involves an employee of Renaissance Estates."

Jay swallowed hard and looked Aguilar in the eye. His sorrow gave way to deep concern. "Do *you* think I did it?" he said. "Is that why you're here, grilling me, because you think I did it?"

Aguilar hesitated for a moment. "No," he finally said abruptly. "But as I said, we don't have jurisdiction in this case."

"You still haven't told me what happened," Jay said. "I've got to get the details from you so that I can get it onto the paper's website immediately. It goes on the front-page tomorrow morning."

"It's under investigation. There isn't much we can tell you."

"Aw, come on. There's got to be something. I thought we had a great working relationship."

Aguilar looked at Jay for a moment saying nothing. Finally, he said, "We saw the crime report from the Long

Beach Police Department. She was strangled…when she was about to take a shower. All we know is that the killer had access to the apartment. The crime scene was very clean when we got there. There won't be much forensic evidence. It's just like the other two murders. It's a safe bet that all three killings are related."

"I see," Jay said.

"Well, we've got to get going," Aguilar said. "Be sure to watch your back for a while until we can find this killer." With that the two detectives departed.

Once back in their car, Aguilar asked Harry if he'd seen anything unusual in Jay's apartment.

"There were no oil wells in there," Harry said in jest, referring to the oil wells across the street.

"Weapons?" Aguilar said.

"Not unless you think a surfboard is a weapon." Shifting to a more serious tone he said, "After listening to that recorded conversation do you think that the evidence points to Millwood?"

"I don't know," Aguilar said. "But, as I said, I think it's a safe bet that all three murders are somehow related. It's not a coincidence that these people were killed in what's made to look like random killings."

"Then if they're all three related, doesn't that mean that somebody else is directing the killers and picking out who gets killed next?"

"It definitely should. We know that several people were involved in the first one. Somebody set Ben Williams up in the second one. And somebody let the killer into Erica

Knight's condominium in the third one. There's got to be someone directing all of this.

"Who do you have in mind as the boss of all these killings?" Harry said.

"I don't know for sure," Aguilar said. "But our best lead might start with Millwood."

"Wasn't the woman who just got murdered Newsboy's source?" Harry said.

"Yes, he said she was. It's too bad she didn't survive. She could have been a key witness for us, too."

"The apartment was owned by Erica Knight," Harry pointed out. "How did the killer know that this other woman would be in there alone?"

Aguilar looked at Harry. "You're really on the ball this morning! They might have hit the wrong person."

"Now we have a cover-up. What do we do next?" Harry said.

"You unravel a cover-up from the outside in," Aguilar said. "You start with the soldiers—the people who have actually committed a crime. If you get them to talk, they'll lead you to who was calling the shots. It's usually hard to get evidence on Mr. Big without it coming from a witness who works for him. And when you do take a shot at the top guy, you can't afford to miss. But it all starts with the first person that got arrested. In our case, that's Maria Maldonado. She pointed to Anita Martinez and Willis Napier. Anita Martinez pointed to Fernando Suarez. Suarez and Napier have pointed to South Bay Neighborhood Association. The recording we heard has confirmed what we thought. There must be a slush fund that exists over there that is paying for professional hits. And there's some complication with it all involving Millwood."

"Then we should bring Millwood in," Harry said.

"And if the victim were still with us and could finger him, we could grill him about that slush fund—but she isn't," Aguilar said. "We need something new and fresh to bring him in. That recording alone won't do it."

Harry looked like a light bulb had gone off in his mind. "How about that woman who brought them the money to the park? She should know about the slush fund, right?" he said.

Aguilar again turned and looked at Harry, who was driving. "That's what you're getting paid for, coming up with thoughts like that," he said with a smile on his face. "Even if she didn't know much about it, we can arrest her for obstructing justice when she pulled her car out and blocked us in the parking lot. It might take some squeezing, but she could tell us about the slush fund and could give us some names. Somebody told her to take that briefcase full of money out there to meet the killers."

"Then let's go pick her up," Harry said.

"That's on our list," Aguilar said. "First, we need to do more checking about this murder."

Their next stop was the security office of Erica's apartment building. Since they did not have a warrant, the security officer called the Long Beach Police Department. After confirming their identity, they granted them permission to review the security recordings. Painstakingly slow and thorough, both Aguilar and Lee slugged their way through eighteen different cameras that covered nearly all the hallways, stairwells, elevators, and parking areas in the building complex. All the views seemed to be routine to them until they noticed a man riding the service elevator up to the same floor as Erica's apartment at 8:40 p.m. He wore a uniform that indicated he was a service repairman of some sort. He had a baseball cap on that shielded his face from the camera that was mounted near the ceiling of the elevator car. Aguilar asked the security officer if there were any emergency calls for service that evening, and he said that he would need to check the logbook. The two detectives continued looking at this short sequence over and over again. The subject seemed to be familiar. The security guard returned and said that no service calls had been logged in from the previous night. Then the two detectives found what they were searching for. The camera on the eighth floor showed a very brief glimpse of a maintenance worker turning a corner and walking in the direction of Erica's condo. They looked at it over and over again, and both men agreed who the person in the maintenance uniform was. He had a shock of black hair and droopy eyes. It was "El Puma."

CHAPTER TWENTY-EIGHT

It didn't take long for the Long Beach Police Department to get in touch with Jay. A short time after his visit with Aguilar and Lee, he was down at LBPD headquarters talking to the investigating officers. Fearing nothing, Jay waived his rights to an attorney and tried to cooperate.

"You left the victim at 8:22 p.m. last night," the lead officer said. "The coroner puts the time of death between eight and nine. Do you want to tell me what you were doing over there?"

"I'm a reporter for the *LA Daily Journal*. Rudi was a source of information for my stories. Since she worked as assistant manager at Renaissance Estates, she had access to a lot of information about problems…" Jay started to say.

"That not what I asked you," the lead officer said. "I asked you what the fuck you were doing over there."

Jay straightened up and looked directly at the officer. "I was talking to her about some information that she had for my story," he said. He quickly realized that talking to these two cops would not be like talking to Sergeant Aguilar and Officer Lee.

"And what information was that?"

"I'm sorry I can't tell you that," Jay said in a slow and deliberate manner. He decided to rethink whether he would cooperate.

"You can't? Listen, asshole, we don't like hearing that from a suspect like you. We don't like that worth a shit. Now, goddamn it! What were you talking about with her?"

Jay dug in his heels. "I told you already. That's all I'm going to say about that."

"How'd you get over there?"

"I picked Rudi up at a restaurant where she had told me to meet her, and we drove over to Erica's condominium where we could talk."

Then the second officer took a turn. "You mean you went over to a friend's place where you could fuck the victim. Don't you?"

Jay took a deep breath, wanting to fire a broadside of words at his interrogators. He restrained himself and simply said, "It was Rudi's idea to go to Erica's place."

"You got there and she wouldn't fuck," the lead officer said. "What did you do next?"

"I told you already why I was there."

"You took her there to fuck her. And she wouldn't do it. Then she told you that she had been fucking her boss."

Again, Jay felt like ripping a fusillade right back at them but thought the better of it. It took a moment for him to gain his composure. "We did not have sex," he said, speaking slowly and emphatically.

"Listen, you dumb shit, we already know that," the second officer said. "You didn't fuck her because she wouldn't let you. Then she laughed at you and told you how much she loved to fuck her boss, somebody named Millwood. That pissed you off to no end, and you decided that if she wouldn't fuck you right then and there, you were going to see to it that she never fucked anybody else ever again, didn't you?"

Jay remained silent. The juices were still pumping through his body and particularly his brain. He gave the look of apathy to the two officers. It took an extra effort to control his internal turmoil.

"What did you do with the rope you killed her with?" the first officer said.

"I did not have sex with her, and I did not kill her," Jay said, wondering how long his patience would last.

"That's bullshit. Do you hear me? BULLSHIT! You went on a jealous frenzy and tried to rape her. You ripped her clothes off and cornered her in the bathroom. When she resisted, you took a piece of rope and strangled her. Now, goddamn it, where's the fucking piece of rope?"

The probing finally hit its target. Jay loaded up and opened both barrels at the cops showing a tough streak of his own. "I don't know anything about a piece of rope!" he blurted out. "I liked Rudi. She was a big help to me. I'm sickened to know that something brutal like this happened to her. I'm also pissed off about it."

"Well good, asshole, because we're pissed off about it, too," the second officer said.

Jay was ready to fire another round when the interview was interrupted by another plainclothes policeman. The two officers left Jay in the interrogation room. It was nearly three hours later when a uniformed policeman came down to the interrogation room and told Jay he could leave.

As he walked out of the police station Jay shuddered to think about what had happened to Rudi. The hints he had picked up from the LBPD did not correlate to what he had learned from his two LAPD sources. When he reached his van, he called Aguilar to relay what else he had learned.

"I told you to watch your step down there, didn't I?" Aguilar said.

"Oh, totally. But those guys said that Rudi was sleeping with Millwood," Jay said.

"Do you think she was sleeping with Millwood?" Aguilar said.

"No, I don't. In fact, I would be stunned if it were true," Jay said.

"Yes, you would—and you don't know the real reason why," Aguilar said.

Jay hesitated for a moment. He was caught slightly off guard but knew he should press forward. "No, I don't know the real reason, Sergeant Aguilar. But I believe that you're going to tell me."

"She was a lesbian," Aguilar said.

"Wow, I didn't… know that," Jay said. With this news, his mind came up with many questions. "That explains why she came to this country when she was still a teenager. If she'd stayed in Iraq, things could have been seriously tough for her."

"Did you say much to the Long Beach police?" Aguilar said.

"No. Those butthole cops didn't get anything out of me."

"Well, no worries. We called them and told them that you didn't do it."

"Oh, geez. Thanks. I was getting ready to blow up in there at those two fucksticks."

"We saw evidence from the security videos that another person was in the condo just after you left."

"Can you tell me more about it? I've got a story to file."

"No can do, Newsboy. Not now anyway."

"Well, thanks for your help."

"Just keep me posted on Renaissance Estates," Aguilar said.

Jay went to the newsroom to polish his story before submitting it. He knew that he needed some more details about Rudi's murder to get that story out. The information she had given him about Lisa's account of the slush fund made the perfect piece to add.

Dylan dropped by his workstation to see what he was doing. "What's going on, man?" he said.

"Dude, I had a busy night last night and an even busier morning today," Jay told him. "There's good news and bad news."

"We can use some good news. Start with that."

"I found out from my source that Lisa did know about a slush fund at the South Bay Neighborhood Association. The police have been theorizing that this was the case.

"Are you inputting that into your piece?"

"I am. But there's a problem."

"Well you better tell me about it before you show this to Meredith."

"My source was murdered last night."

"Whoa! You mean that woman who works at Renaissance Estates?"

"Yeah, I'm afraid so. I've got a recording of everything that she said while I was with her. What does this do to my story?"

"Damn. We had two sources. Now we only have the woman who owns the place."

"She'll vouch for everything I'm saying."

"Yes, but if she didn't hear it from Lisa, then it becomes secondhand information." Dylan said.

Jay looked at him and grimaced. "I can't help it," he said. "I'm doing the best I can. Rudi's death kicked me straight in the mouth. She was a great resource for me at a time when I needed it. I wasn't in love with her, but I can tell you that I'm going to miss looking into those deep, beautiful, brown eyes."

"We're all going to miss her," Dylan said. "She was crucial to our story."

Dylan read what Jay had written. He paged back over it a few times, as if he might have a question. When he had finished, he said, "It's good, my man, it's really good. But we'll have to come up with some creative ways to substantiate it."

"Rudi had a stack of documentation that backed what she was saying," Jay told him.

"Great. Where is it?"

"That's the other problem I'm having."

"Don't tell me you lost it!" Dylan said, astonished.

"She never gave it to me," Jay said. "When I got back home, I realized I didn't have it, so I called but had to leave her a message."

Then Dylan's cell phone rang. "That was Meredith," he said after the call. "She wants your story right away."

Meredith read Jay's story on her computer while Jay and Dylan sat across the desk in front of her. "How much of this comes from the woman that was killed last night?" she said after she had finished reading.

Jay let out a sigh. "Almost all," he said.

Just as Dylan had done earlier, Meredith scrolled through Jay's story looking for loose ends. "Then how are we going to substantiate this? You've got one source that was discredited, and now the other one is dead."

"Rudi said she had documentation for me," Jay said.

"Let me see it," Meredith said.

Jay dropped his head. "I don't know where it is."

"You don't know?" Meredith said. Her glasses fell onto their chain.

"She must have forgotten to give it to me."

Meredith sat in her chair with a blank expression on her face. Then she said, "Jay, this story is a no-go if you can't back it up. If you've got some documentation from your source, even if she's dead, I need to see it. This sits on the shelf until you come up with it."

Jay felt as if he had just lost the World Series for his team.

"Dylan, help him find it," she said. "We might have something big here, but we need to back it up before it can go out."

Then she threw another punch at Jay's gut. "What have you got on the woman's murder?"

"I was grilled this morning by the Long Beach Police Department since I saw the victim before she was killed," Jay said. "Then my LAPD source apparently called somebody over there and vouched for me, saying they saw the security video that showed another person arriving at the condo right after I left," Jay said.

Meredith knew to be patient with Jay since he often beat around the bush. However, it was doubly difficult at a time like this. "Do you have a story written about the *murder*?" Meredith said.

"Well, not yet. I mean I've just got back here and…," Jay started to say.

"Jay, you've been scooped!" Meredith said. She pulled up the Long Beach Dispatch morning edition on her computer and swung it around for Jay and Dylan to see. There on the front-page was a story about Rudi's murder.

"Oh shit!" Dylan said.

Jay's jaw dropped as he looked on in disbelief.

"Have you got *anything* on this?" Meredith said. "We're getting schooled by another paper, and we need to get a story of our own out really soon. What can your LAPD source tell us?"

"Nothing," Jay said. "I talked to him a while ago, and he said he couldn't give us any details at this time other than what was in the police report."

"All right, listen up," Meredith said. "Jay, find the corroboration we need for the story about the slush fund. Dylan, you're on last night's murder. You suckers really left your shit all over the floor today. I don't know how in the hell this paper is ever going to survive with journalism like this." She shook her head as she spoke, and then emphatically said, "Now, get moving."

Back at Jay's workstation, Dylan pulled up a chair and the two sat down to brainstorm what could have happened to Rudi's documentation.

"Here's what we've got to do," Dylan said. "We're going to retrace your steps yesterday from the time you left here to the time you got home and realized that you didn't have the documentation."

Jay took a deep breath and began by saying, "It started when she called and wanted to see me. I picked her up at the same restaurant where we met the previous time. She didn't want to stay there since she was concerned about privacy. I suggested my place, but she said we should go to Erica's condo instead because it was closer. I asked her about the evidence that she had mentioned before. She said she had it with her. When we got to Erica's, I started recording and asking her about the slush fund. I forgot all about asking her for the documentation."

"It sounds like she forgot to give it to you," Dylan said. "Now, we've got to figure out *why* she forgot because it might tell us where she left it."

"Wow, how are we going to do that?" Jay said. "I'm no mind reader."

"Did she bring anything with her? Any folders, files, a laptop, a box, a backpack?"

"No, just a handbag."

"Was it a large handbag?"

"It was just a handbag. I don't know if it was, like, big or small."

"A large handbag might have had a folder or an envelope inside it."

"It didn't seem very large to me."

"What about computers?" Dylan said. "Did she put all the information on her computer?"

"Maybe. I don't think she has a laptop. I've never seen her with one, anyway. She might have kept a copy on her computer at work."

"Well, that's out," Dylan said. He leaned back in his chair and crossed his arms. "We'll never get into her workplace without a court order. Either Millwood or somebody else is bound to have wiped her computer clean by now, anyway."

Jay put his elbows on his desk and grabbed his head with both hands. He stared directly at his keyboard as if it should begin typing by itself.

Dylan hesitated for a moment and then said, "Do you think it's possible that the killer would have taken it?"

"How the hell is the killer supposed to know what it is?" Jay said.

Dylan kept wracking his brain. "Did you go directly to Erica's place?" he finally said.

Jay turned around and looked at Dylan. "Yes, I already told you," he said. "We went to Erica's from the restaurant."

"Did you stop along the way?"

"Just to get gas."

Dylan perked up at that answer. "Where?" he said.

"It was just down the street from where I picked her up. Wait a minute!" Jay said. "I went to pay for the gas, and when I came back I couldn't find her. I mean, the van looked empty. Then I saw her laying down behind the seats. She said she was hiding from a woman who works in her office that had pulled up to the next pump."

"Did you check your van? She might have left it in there somewhere."

"Let's go look."

They both jumped out of their seats and went to the parking garage to check Jay's messy van. They pulled out his surfing and seafaring paraphernalia searching for some clue that would lead them to the missing documents. After some time looking with no results, Dylan looked under the passenger seat and found a flash drive. "What's this?" he said, holding it up for Jay to see.

"Wow! Look at that! That's got to be it," Jay said.

"It's not yours?"

"Nope"

They hurried back up to Jay's workstation. When they opened the flash drive on Jay's computer, they discovered a bonanza of information. Dylan immediately copied it onto his laptop so that the two could peruse what they saw independently. There were dozens perhaps even hundreds of emails mainly to or from Millwood. Further, Rudi had supplied copies of the invoices she had assembled for Millwood that proved overpayments and outright fraud. Then they stumbled across an email from Lisa Nguyen to Rudi that indicated Lisa's concern about the existence of a slush fund at the South Bay Neighborhood Association. Jay and Dylan continued the search until Jay came upon a partnership agreement that was familiar to him. He remembered it from the hall of records when he discovered that a shell company named Harbor City Partners was on the title of a large part of the land that surrounded Renaissance Estates. They got to the end of the document and noticed one of the partner's signatures—Andrew McGinnis.

"Holy Jesus, this is a gold mine!" Dylan said.

Jay made two copies of the flash drive—one for safekeeping, and the other for Sergeant Aguilar.

"Get your story written," Dylan said. "Give me what you have on Rudi's murder. I'll meet you back here with it mocked up in…in," Dylan looked at his watch, "thirty minutes."

Jay made some changes to his story and inserted Andrew McGinnis's name as one of the partners of the silent partnership that owned a substantial amount of land surrounding Renaissance Estates. Then he remembered that it was Regal Management Associates that had acquired the land from Jefferson Square. What he didn't yet know was how Harbor City Partners got the land from Regal Management Associates. He thought he should put the connection into his story then decided against it until he knew for sure what had happened.

He made a few more changes to the article he had already filed with Meredith and sent it back to her. She immediately called him. "Jay," she began, "we were just talking about backing up this slush fund business. Are you able to support this?"

"Check your emails," Jay replied. "We found Rudi's documentation stash."

With Jay still on the phone, Meredith checked her emails and opened the one from Jay. He had forwarded Lisa Nguyen's email to Rudi about the slush fund. Meredith read the email and said, "All right Jay, we're going with this."

"Hold on a second," Jay said. "I want to change the title."

"Hurry up! We're holding up production already."

Since Aguilar had told him that all three Renaissance Estates murders were connected, Jay changed the title of the article to, "Serial Killer Stalks Harbor City Area."

When he told Meredith this, she simply said, "All right, we can do that. Now, get deep into what else you've got. You're going onto the front-page day after next."

Jay hung up the phone as Dylan arrived at his workstation with his piece on the murder. Jay looked up at Dylan with disbelief.

"What's wrong now?" Dylan said.

"It's going onto the front-page in two days," he said.

"Yesss!" Dylan said. "You see? I told you that you could do it if you just stuck to it and bore down." He gave Jay a slap on the back.

"I just don't believe it," Jay said, laughing in wonderment.

"You better get used to it. And don't let up! You're in the big leagues now," Dylan said.

In her office, Meredith had hardly put the phone down when she got a call from Albert Hudgins. "How's the Renaissance Estates murder story coming?"

"Another great piece is coming out tonight," Meredith said. "After that, it's going onto the front-page."

"Terrific," Hudgins said. "Now maybe I can get a good night's sleep. Thanks."

CHAPTER TWENTY-NINE

Jay pulled into the parking lot of the Del Amo Fashion Center. He drove around for a few minutes until he found the car he was searching for. Inside were Sergeant Aguilar and Officer Lee who had arranged to meet him there. He parked his van and then skated over to them on his skateboard.

"Good morning, Newsboy," Aguilar said. "Why don't you jump in the back?"

"Good morning, gentlemen," Jay said, as he slid into the back seat. Then he handed the flash drive to Aguilar. "You're gonna love the contents of this."

Aguilar looked at the flash drive and said, "What's on it?"

"Just about everything you can think of," Jay said beaming with pride.

"How'd you find it?"

"She left it under the seat in my van."

"Any evidence we can use?" Aguilar said. He dropped the flash drive into his shirt pocket.

"The one you really need to see the most is the email from Lisa Nguyen to Rudi confirming the slush fund at South Bay Neighborhood Association. Put that together with what she told Rudi about seeing a large sum of cash paid back to Millwood from one of the big shots at South Bay, and it ought to confirm the existence of the slush fund you were wondering about."

"Anything else?"

"Lots. Lisa also complained to Millwood that a temporary worker filling in for the receptionist was the one who stole the money that went missing."

"Any names?" Aguilar said.

"I didn't notice one on the email," Jay said. "Lisa's emails were not always thoroughly written. That might be because English was a second language for her. It should be easy enough to find out, though."

"What do you think it all means?" Aguilar said.

"It tells me that Millwood either performed the hit on Lisa, or set it up," Jay said.

"Millwood has an alibi for the night she was killed," Aguilar said. "Plus, he doesn't fit the description of the killer that was provided by the witnesses."

"He's in it somehow," Jay said. "There's too much in here that points to him as being either the driving force or a willing participant."

"Anything else about the South Bay Neighborhood Association?" Aguilar said.

"A lot of vague invoices. Lots of money was sent to them without anything in writing as to what it was for," Jay said.

"What about Ben Williams?" Aguilar said.

"There's some activity concerning his refusal to approve different payments that Millwood was trying to make," Jay said. "I didn't see anything that looked like a smoking gun there."

Aguilar's questions went on for a while longer. Then he got out and opened the car door for Jay to exit—not out of courtesy but out of necessity, since the back doors did not open from the inside of his undercover car. Jay then pulled out his skateboard and skated back to where his van was parked.

"How much evidence do you think we got?" Harry said. "Jay was not too specific."

"We won't know until we look at it, page by page and line by line," Aguilar said.

Aguilar tossed the flash drive over to Harry, who put it in his shirt pocket. "Your job now is to go through every piece of it and sort out what you think can help us," he said.

Back at the precinct Harry copied the contents of Jay's flash drive onto his computer. He made another backup copy of the flash drive and returned the original to Aguilar. He then painstakingly read through every item word for word. He categorized and sorted all the files by subject matter, and then set up a list in chronological order of all the documents on each topic. After several days of this work, he told Aguilar that he was finished.

Sitting at Harry's computer, Aguilar looked at the outline that Harry had created. He noted that the documents were placed in order in the computer's file system.

"Nice work—I'm impressed," Aguilar said. "What do you think we have here?"

"There appears to be a lot of circumstantial evidence that we might be able to use," Harry said. "It should allow us to get a search warrant for Millwood's office, and bring him in for more questioning."

Aguilar continued to peruse the computer files scrolling down Harry's categorical breakdown and spot-checking a few of the documents.

"There are a lot of documents pointing to Millwood as being involved in the murders," Harry said. "He may have an alibi, but I think he knew about the killings before they occurred."

"Do you think the pattern puts Millwood in charge of the killing spree?" Aguilar said.

"He definitely has a connection to them," Harry said. "But there's nothing that says he's the one who's in charge."

Aguilar leaned back from the computer and faced Harry. "Maybe it's time we paid Mr. Millwood another visit," he said. "Before we do that, I want you to go through these again and pull out all the documents that link Millwood directly to the murders. I want to review them myself."

It took Harry some more time to organize a computer file with just the documents that directly connected Millwood to the murders. While Aguilar was waiting, he got a phone call from CSI telling him that some long-awaited evidence was now available from the nightclub killing. He was told that either he could pick it up, or they could send it down to the precinct. Aguilar asked them to send it to the precinct.

Harry finally finished organizing a separate folder with only those documents that linked Millwood to the murders. Aguilar reviewed that collection trying to determine how Millwood fit into the puzzle. Was he the leader? A willing operative? A silent beneficiary? It took him the entire next day to answer those questions, and then another day to review the remainder of the documents. When he felt that he had a handle on all of it, he took what he now knew into Captain Kreider's office.

"We have three people killed who are all connected, in one way or another, to Renaissance Estates," Aguilar began. "The first one was the project's accountant who was killed in the parking lot of a local nightclub. The second one was a resident who acted as the proxy to the owner of the property after the actual owner was forced out by HUD. The third one was the assistant manager of Renaissance Estates. There was practically no forensic evidence found at any of the crime scenes—only the bullets that killed the second victim. They were traceable to the same weapon used in two other unsolved crimes that were connected to the South Bay Neighborhood Association."

"The same bunch that we've talked about before," Kreider said.

"The most important thing," Aguilar added, "is that all three murders are connected and were definitely committed by the same person or persons."

"But we don't have any names for these suspects, do we?" Kreider said.

"Yeah, we do. One is Fernando Suarez, an employee of South Bay Neighborhood Association. We don't know the true name of the other one. We only know his street name which is 'El Puma'."

"And you're sure you can identify Suarez and place him at the murder scenes?"

"There were witnesses at the nightclub, who saw Suarez in the parking lot. An eyewitness from Ben Williams's murder saw them both. Officer Lee and I encountered both suspects at a park when they were being paid off, and got a good look at them both. Here's a picture of them receiving a case full of money. We can confirm that 'El Puma' was present at the place and time the third victim was killed from the security videos at the victim's Long Beach condo complex.

"The MO's are all different. Have you considered that?"

"That's because of this guy—'El Puma'. He is doing the killings in a manner that makes each one look like a random act. He goes to great pains to prevent us from finding any forensic evidence."

"What have you got on 'El Puma'?"

"As far as we can tell, he's not your basic psychopath. He's probably a professional who has worked for Mexican drug gangs. He covers his tracks very well and disguises his crimes to attempt to throw us off. Suarez might only be his handler. We don't have any proof that Suarez actually committed any of the crimes, but he has been spotted with 'El Puma' at two of the three crime scenes."

"Why haven't you brought in Suarez?"

"We want to catch them both. It might be all but impossible to find 'El Puma' unless we can get Suarez to lead us to him."

"Do you have a plan for that?" Kreider said.

“Not yet,” Aguilar said. “Putting Suarez under close surveillance is an option that we’ll probably go to.”

“Don’t count on any extra resources for that,” Kreider said. “If you think they are professionals, who do you think is paying them?”

“Suarez works for South Bay Neighborhood Association. We believe that this organization is either extorting or fraudulently extracting money from Renaissance Estates. We don’t know exactly how the money changes hands, but we know that Willis Napier was facilitating the transfer. In any case, it appears that money laundering should be added to the list of charges against these two.”

“Proving money laundering could be hard to do unless some of these suspects start to talk. Is Napier cooperating?”

“He made bail and slipped out on us. We have a warrant that we sent to the FBI. We’ll have to wait until he surfaces to find out more about the transfer of the money.”

“He’s not the only one making bail,” Kreider said, changing the subject. “Anita Martinez is due to be released the day after tomorrow.”

“I see,” Aguilar said. “She might lead us to Suarez. Anita Martinez is seen in a lot of social media pictures with him. They look like boyfriend and girlfriend.”

“We need to start putting some of these people away for those murders,” Kreider said. “We’re already getting heat from the chief’s office as well as the newspapers.” He pulled out a copy of the *Daily Journal*, featuring Jay’s story on the front-page with the headline, “Serial Killer Stalks Harbor City Area.”

Aguilar took a look at the headline, but did not read any further. He had already read Jay's article.

"One more thing," Aguilar said, "Thanks to the writer of that story we have a ton of documentation concerning the victims and other people who they worked with. There's a long trail of circumstantial evidence that leads to city hall. It shows the mayor as being connected to an effort that's under way to get ahold of that government backed property."

"You have a ton of documentation?" Kreider asked in disbelief, looking directly at Aguilar. "I want to see it—all of it. And right away."

Believing that this was coming, Aguilar had prepared an extra copy of the flash drive. He pulled it out of his shirt pocket and handed it to Kreider, who looked at Aguilar as if he had just admitted to stealing his wallet.

"Sergeant Aguilar, your job is to find the killer," Kreider said. "Don't waste any time trying to build a conspiracy that leads to city hall. Whatever you find in the way of a 'ton of documentation' like this comes to me first. Understand?"

"Are you saying that we should ignore any evidence that could lead us to the person behind all this killing?" Aguilar said.

"I'm saying *find the killers*," Kreider said. "Don't waste time with circumstantial evidence like all this you've been telling me. It doesn't count for anything! You got that? Or do I have to spell it out for you."

Careful not to overreact, Aguilar knew that he had to make a rebuttal, or the chance to apprehend the person who was behind the killings might be lost altogether. "Captain

Kreider," he finally said. "We all know that these killings are the work of organized crime…"

"Yes! Yes! The South Bay Neighborhood Association, you've shown me that. But until you get me some solid evidence, you need to stick to apprehending the killers. Do you understand that? *The killers*."

"And when we have the killers, will you suddenly change your mind about the wider plot?"

Kreider was incensed. "Just what in the hell do you mean by that remark?"

"It sounds to me like you want us to find the killers and then make it end right there. That would just mean ignoring who's behind it all."

"Do you think that I'm obstructing justice?"

"I didn't say that, you did."

"Then you do at least think I'm standing in the way of your investigation?"

"Not that either, but perhaps you're shielding somebody."

"Goddamn it!! I have been on this police force for nearly three decades. If you're not up for this job, Sergeant, then I'll just have to take you off it and give it to somebody else. Somebody who's more qualified and experienced than you are. Do I make myself clear?"

Aguilar sat in his chair and gave his trademark deadpan look at Kreider, who looked back at him as if he were just an idiot. After an uncomfortable moment, Aguilar got up and walked out of Kreider's office.

Aguilar mulled over his meeting with Kreider afterward, wondering if his hands were being tied on this case. He recalled a similar investigation few years earlier into the murder of the wife of a city councilman. The wife, who owned an oil fortune, was allegedly planning to seek a divorce because the councilman had been cheating with other women. The murder had the earmarks of a professional hit, but was carefully made to look like an accident. When the detective involved went to the press with what he believed had happened in the case, he wound up being transferred far away. Further, he received a permanent black mark on his career. The killer was never apprehended. With this in mind, Aguilar decided to present a copy of his file and Rudi's flash drive to the FBI. But first, he thought he should talk the situation over with his wife, Claudia.

At home that evening it was getting late, and the children had already gone to bed. As Aguilar and Claudia were also getting ready for bed, Aguilar said, "Claudia, I need to talk about something with you. It won't take long, but it's important."

Claudia was brushing her hair at her dressing table. She stopped and turned toward her husband, who was sitting on the bed. "What's wrong, my love?" she said.

"This investigation I'm working on might involve some powerful people—people in high places. Since it now includes three killings, the stakes are high and the pressure is on."

Claudia continued to listen, but she starting brushing her hair again. "You've had situations like this before. You've investigated some bad criminals with big connections, and it all worked out all right. What's bothering you this time?"

"Kreider is steering me away from the direction I need to be going. It isn't like him to do this. It makes me wonder if he's protecting somebody."

"And if he is, what can happen?"

"He's my boss. I could have a difficult time proving this case if he turns out to be a willful accomplice. He threatened to take me off the case today."

"But he can't fire you, can he?"

"Not very easily. What might happen is that I could get transferred to San Fernando or someplace else far away. I might also be assigned to a different and more dangerous unit, like drug enforcement."

Claudia put down her brush and went to sit next to her husband on the bed. "We are always behind you, you know that. You're a good husband and a good father, and we love you very much. Do not be afraid to do what is right."

"I don't want us to have to move somewhere far away. This is where the kids have grown up. Bad things could happen to me if I pursue the case in a way that Kreider doesn't like. And if he *is* involved and I don't go after him, I'm just as guilty."

"Do what you must. But always do the right thing. If I ever lose respect for you, it would be because you did something dirty at work."

"That will never happen," he said, and embraced his wife.

Calling Marsha Jackson from a public phone, Aguilar arranged to meet her at a bar in Harbor City. Aguilar arrived first and waited at the bar. A short time later, Jackson arrived wearing a summer print dress that was a far cry from normal FBI work clothes. She sat down at the bar next to Aguilar.

"You look a little different from what I expected," Aguilar said. He had never met Jackson before and was surprised by how nicely she was dressed.

Jackson took a brief look around the nearly empty lounge, and then casually opened her oversize handbag to allow Aguilar to see her FBI badge. "You told me that you didn't want anyone else to know about this meeting," she said. "This is the way I dress when I'm undercover." Having said that, she suggested they order drinks and then adjourn to a booth in the rear of the lounge.

"When I called you earlier," Aguilar said, "you told me that you had some exposure to the fraud and mismanagement problems at Renaissance Estates."

"That's right," Jackson replied.

"We know that the killings that took place over there were the work of a professional hit man. We are closing in on him, but I'm concerned that we'll never be able to apprehend who is paying for his work. Our investigation recently uncovered some evidence that was captured by an employee of Renaissance Estates who herself became one of the murder victims. This evidence leads to city hall."

"I see," Jackson said, continuing to listen.

"My problem is this—the evidence is largely circumstantial and does not implicate any specific person. But patterns have emerged that clearly point out the need for further investigation in some high-up places. My boss at the LAPD has told me not to pursue it and to stick with finding the killer. This leads me to believe that no further investigation will ever be made by the LAPD, and we'll never catch the person who is responsible for arranging these murders."

"Do you have this documentation with you?" Jackson said.

Aguilar pulled a flash drive out of his shirt pocket and handed it to her along with an envelope of other information.

"Ordinarily, the Bureau does not get involved with local crimes, as you probably already know. However, we've observed the possibility of financial misgivings at Renaissance Estates that is federal Section 8 housing. We want to stay close to your case without being in the way. And besides, cover ups are often messy and difficult to unravel. I will take a look at what you have here and see if anything can help either of us."

"Thank you," Aguilar said. "By the way, there is one person you can help us find. We arrested the moneyman who facilitated the hits, but he made bail and skipped town. If you can get him back here, he would be a wealth of information."

"What's his name?"

"Willis Napier."

"Oh yes, our friend Mr. Napier."

"You're already familiar with him?"

"Yes, we are. He's a suspect in a scam to loot a government run property in Illinois. I'll try to find him for you."

"Thanks again," Aguilar said.

Jackson put the flash drive in her handbag. She then got up and walked out the front door, looking not like an FBI agent but more like an ordinary woman going shopping.

Aguilar and Lee still needed to make another journey to the South Bay Neighborhood Association to visit with the woman who had blocked them in the parking lot. Early one morning they waited outside in their strategically placed car and again watched while all the employees filed into the building. Not seeing their suspect walk through the door, they decided at nine thirty to go inside and look for her.

"Good morning," Aguilar said to the receptionist as he identified himself. "We need to speak with this person," he said as Harry showed her a photo of the woman sitting at the picnic table in the park. "Could you ask if she would come out here for a moment?"

"Sure," the receptionist said as she dialed the woman's phone extension. A few minutes later she said, "No one's answering. Would you like to leave a message?"

"No, we need to speak directly to her on an important matter," Aguilar said. "Do you have her home address and phone number?"

Without hesitation, the receptionist looked up the employee's home address and phone number. She then wrote the woman's name and contact information onto a sticky note and handed it to Aguilar.

"Thanks," Aguilar said. He and Harry then went back to the car.

"Her name's Nancy DiCarlo," Aguilar said. "The address is in Lakewood."

"I wonder if she knows we're after her," Harry said. "That receptionist might call her at home and tip her off."

"What do you think her next move is?" Aguilar said.

Harry pondered that for a moment. "I bet she's talking it over with a lawyer," he said. "She's in a jam. She knows that we know where she works. She either has to quit her job and move away or face us and obstruction charges."

"And also accessory to murder," Aguilar said.

They staked out the residence, a modest home on a quiet street. They had to wait until nearly seven o'clock that evening until their suspect finally walked up to the front door. Aguilar and Lee walked directly up behind her and took her into custody without any difficulty.

In the precinct interrogation room, she waived her rights to an attorney but would not truthfully answer any of Aguilar's questions.

"How come you didn't go to work today?" Aguilar said.

"I didn't feel good," DiCarlo said.

"You were observed with two of your colleagues in a public park last Friday," Aguilar said.

"I didn't go to any park on Friday. I was at work," DiCarlo said.

Harry then placed a photograph of her sitting at the picnic table across from Suarez and "El Puma" with the briefcase open and the money on display. When she saw the picture, she appeared to be startled by it.

"You're sitting across the picnic table from Fernando Suarez and another guy who we don't know," Aguilar said. "Can you tell us who that other person is?"

DiCarlo clearly still didn't want to cooperate. "I don't know who he is," she said.

"You handed him a briefcase full of money," Aguilar said.

Harry then placed another photograph in front of her that showed her handing the briefcase to "El Puma," followed by yet another photo of Suarez holding up a bundle of large denomination bills.

After a pause, while DiCarlo was looking at the picture, Aguilar said, "How much money was in the briefcase?"

Still looking at the picture, DiCarlo said, "I don't know."

"Didn't you count it before you left the office?" Aguilar said.

"I don't know how much was in there," DiCarlo said.

"Well, I have some news for you," Aguilar said. "The other guy sitting next to Suarez is a murderer. He's killed at least three people recently. The money you handed to him is to pay him off for at least one of those killings."

"That makes you guilty of accessory to murder," Harry said, shaking his head slightly from side to side as he spoke.

"The thing that pisses me off the most was how you blocked us in the parking lot when we were trying to catch him," Aguilar said.

"That makes you guilty of obstruction of justice," Harry said, again shaking his head.

DiCarlo sat quietly and continued to stare at the pictures. She appeared as though she thought that there had to be a way out for her. She kept nervously staring at the picture, but the detectives could tell that her mind was in a dilemma.

"We need you to tell us who gave you the money and how the money got into the office," Aguilar said. "If you can tell us that, things might get a little easier for you."

"OK, OK," DiCarlo said. "I…I want to see my lawyer."

After an hour's wait, DiCarlo's attorney arrived and spent another hour or so with her privately. Then he asked Aguilar what she would be charged with.

"We need to know the name of her contact who tells her when and how much to pay the killers," Aguilar said.

"And what does that do for her?" the attorney said.

"We also need to know just how the slush fund that she managed at South Bay Neighborhood Association operated."

"What slush fund is that?" the attorney said.

"Your client keeps a large amount of cash in a safe where she works," Aguilar said. "She checks the cash in when a company exec brings it to her from the bank, and she takes out what she needs to pay a murderer for the jobs he does."

The attorney huddled with DiCarlo again for her explanation on that subject. A short time later the attorney said, "All right, you get both things. But I need to know beforehand what she gets charged with."

"We have to charge her with accessory to murder and obstruction of justice just to get her into court. When you talk to the DA on the case and he hears what you have to say, he will decide whether to throw either of those charges out."

"Obstruction of justice? What is that about?" the attorney said.

"You better ask your client about that," Aguilar said.

After another short conversation with his client, the attorney said, "All right, we're all in."

"And the name of your contact?" Aguilar said to DiCarlo.

"Karl Brazelton," she said.

"And who is Brazelton?" Aguilar said.

"He's the owner of South Bay Neighborhood Association."

Then Harry stepped in. "Karl Brazelton is a silent partner in another company called 'Regal Management Associates'. Have you ever heard of that company?"

After a pause DiCarlo replied, "No."

"How long have you worked at South Bay Neighborhood Association?" Aguilar said.

"Eleven years," DiCarlo said.

"What are your duties in addition to managing the slush fund?"

DiCarlo looked again at her attorney who nodded approval. "I'm an administrative assistant," she said.

"Do you work directly for Brazelton?"

"Yes."

"I need you to think back over the past eleven years," Aguilar said. "Do you mean to tell me that you never typed a letter, a memo, or an email in all that time that mentioned Regal Management Associates? If you don't' feel like answering that question, that means we'll have to go check it out for ourselves. And in case you're challenged in court, I'm going to expect to have access to those emails."

"OK, OK, I did send letters and emails for Karl concerning Regal Management Associates," she said.

"Can you tell us the primary recipient of those letters and emails?" Aguilar said.

DiCarlo dropped her head and seemed to mutter something to herself.

"I'm sorry, I didn't hear that," Aguilar said.

She looked again at her attorney as if to plead with him not to make her answer that question, but he nodded approval. She turned and faced Aguilar. "Andrew McGinnis," she finally said.

CHAPTER THIRTY

Millwood was alone after hours in his office at Renaissance Estates checking a draft of his planned lawsuit against Erica when the phone rang.

"You need to give me an update on what's going on over at Renaissance," the caller said. "Our mutual benefactor is running out of time. He has to move on the property right away."

"We're no closer to the goal today than we have been in weeks," Millwood said.

"No closer to a deal? Goddamn it! Do I have to come over there with a fucking bulldozer? Is that what it's going to take? You've got a job to do, Millwood, and you're not getting it done. Just when in the hell will we get what we want?"

Millwood was taken aback. "We've had two employees and one resident murdered, KB. People are on edge. The person who owns the place has no recourse but to stay put. And I'm not sure how much my friend at HUD will cooperate. He seems like he's ready to punch her out one moment and let her go the next."

"I've had to use my resources to clean up a lot of your problems lately. I don't like having to do that. But I'm going to keep doing whatever I think I need to in order to finish what's been started. And finish it very soon."

"I'm doing what I can, but it doesn't help having outside muscle screwing things up. You need to tell them to watch out who they go after."

"My resources do their work from the information you gave me. If a problem comes up, it's because you didn't do a thorough enough job of giving us the logistics. Now, when in the hell are we going to be done with this exercise?"

"We're close. We're just not there yet."

"Did you fucking hear me? Time is running out. I'm going to have to settle this thing my way if you can't give me some results."

"Even the newspapers are causing problems. There's a reporter from the *Daily Journal* who's been all over this story wanting to expose and upset the plans."

"Then you better fucking do something about him, too!"

"How in the hell am I going to do that?" Millwood said.

"Well, you'll just have to figure out a way, won't you? When our benefactor brought you into this project, he thought your expertise and experience would be perfect for our purposes. Do you want me to tell him that this isn't the case? Do you want me to come to the conclusion that I was wrong by letting him put you where you are? Do you?"

"You just don't understand," said Millwood in a pleading voice. "We're are on the right track. We just need a little more time."

"No, no, no, it's YOU that doesn't understand! The caller yelled. "We are running out of time altogether."

Millwood hesitated for a moment and then said, "All right. I'll play every card in my hand if necessary."

"It IS necessary, do you get that?"

"Yes, yes, yes, I get that. I get that."

This phone conversation lasted for no more than a few minutes. It served its purpose as it rattled Millwood. After he put the phone down, he pulled out his bottle of scotch and drinking glass.

A few more minutes went by before he made an alarming discovery. The security camera in his office was focused on his desktop instead of in front of his desk, as it usually was. He stared at it for a moment not believing what he was seeing. Then he got up from his desk and put a chair underneath the camera. He stood on the chair to reposition the camera to where it was supposed to be focused. That done, he looked through and behind the cabinets, the lamp on his desk, and any other place where a tiny microphone could be hidden. He took a look at the phone on his desk. Then he disconnected the set from the line and opened the handset using a screwdriver. There he found a bug in the mouthpiece. He carefully removed the electronic device and replaced the cover on the handset.

He collapsed back into his chair. He did not wonder who was bugging his phone—he knew that already. His only remaining question was how long had this been going on. How long had everything that he had said or done been seen and heard by these other people. A cold fear gripped him as he recalled several phone conversations, like the one he'd just finished, that preceded someone's murder. He realized that his logistical information about the victims might make him just as guilty as the actual killer. He didn't picture himself as being a part of the victim's demise. But the information he rendered was, whether he knew it or not.

He left and returned to his firm's office in Torrance. To his shock, he discovered that the security system there had also been tampered with. Again, he stood on a chair and repositioned the cameras that had been moved. He checked his desk phone and discovered yet another bug. He removed that one also and thought *All right, goddamn it. That's enough!*

Millwood checked his security system at his home in Cerritos next. Nothing appeared to have been tampered with there. He checked his landline telephone to verify that no device had been planted to eavesdrop on his calls. With his wife and daughters out of town, he sat in his living room to assess the damages and risks he was now facing.

That son of a bitch has really done it now, he thought as he stared out the living room window. *For years I've worked my ass off to help him rip people's property away from them, and this is what I get in return. I'm sorry that I ever decided to help that bastard with anything.*

On the coffee table was a recent edition of the *LA Daily Journal.* On the front-page was a story about Renaissance Estates by Jason Phillips. He had already read the story, and now he thought he should get his point of view across to the paper in an attempt to try to get the focus off of him. He decided to call Jason Phillips from his home phone and ask to meet him in a public place so that he could give him "his side of the story."

The next day, Millwood met Jay in a quiet bar in Seal Beach. They sat down at a table in a corner far from the entrance. Millwood ordered a glass of single-malt scotch straight up. Jay just had a glass of water.

"By the way, please call me 'Jay,' the young reporter said.

"Now, I want to be perfectly clear up front," Millwood began. "I'm granting this interview to set the record straight. There's been a lot of false information floating around in the media. I'm not blaming anyone—I just want to clear it all up."

"I'm cool with that," Jay said. "Do you want me to begin with a question, or would you rather start with a statement?"

Millwood had already prepared a statement. "There are five issues I want to talk about," he said. "The first one is that Renaissance Estates is not putting any money into a slush fund by overpaying its bills. Somebody has put it into your mind that by overpaying the South Bay Neighborhood Association, Renaissance Estates was adding to a slush fund that could be used for illegal purposes. This is not correct."

"The people who put it into my mind were the police," Jay said.

"Well, even if they think there is a slush fund, they don't have any proof of it. There can't be any proof if it doesn't exist."

"Did Lisa Nguyen ever ask you about a slush fund?" Jay said. "Or about people from the South Bay Neighborhood Association exchanging large sums of cash while at Renaissance Estates?"

"Nothing like that ever happened. I don't know where you are hearing all these bullshit stories, but I can tell you that it's just not true," Millwood said.

"Would you be willing to submit to an independent audit of the books to see if any defalcation took place?" Jay said.

"We've already had two audits and neither one uncovered anything that pointed to the problems that have been reported in the press. I can't see the need for any more audits."

Backing off on that point Jay said, "Let's go on to issue number two."

"The blame for any and all accounting irregularities should be placed at the feet of the previous accountant, Lisa Nguyen, who is now deceased," Millwood said. "We have a new accountant who is handling the books, and there hasn't been any problems or issues since. I don't want to disrespect the dead, but all this strange activity took place when Lisa was working at Renaissance Estates."

"Are you familiar with an email sent from Lisa Nguyen to Rudi Sirianni that said that a temporary worker who was filling in for the receptionist might have been the one that stole $20,000 in rent money?"

"Where's the proof?" Millwood said. "Did she witness the temp take the money? Or did she perform her own investigation to reach that conclusion?"

"Apparently, the temporary worker was collecting the rent money while the receptionist was on vacation," Jay said. "The email said that a large portion of the monthly rent was paid in cash because not all the tenants had checkbooks."

"If she's accusing the temporary person, she better have some proof," Millwood said. "Just an email doesn't prove anything."

"Were you aware that the temporary person came from the South Bay Neighborhood Association. That is the same company that allegedly received the large cash payments from Renaissance Estates? It's also the group that allegedly has a slush fund."

"I just finish telling you there is no slush fund! I wish you'd just accept that fact and print it in the newspaper."

"How long have you worked with people from the South Bay Neighborhood Association?"

"For years. Look, we're getting nowhere with this," Millwood said. "Issue number three is that Ben Williams being appointed as Erica Knight's proxy only caused more problems. He didn't understand much about Section 8 housing and asked us to do things that were impossible"

"Things such as…what?"

"Such as hiring only tenants to work in the office and in the maintenance area. The tenants at the place are mostly elderly, retired people. Even if they had worked in an office in the past, they wouldn't necessarily know the ins and outs of Section 8 housing."

"Was Ben Williams's death connected in any way to his refusal to sign certain legal documents?"

"Ben Williams was never obliged to sign any legal documents. He objected to many of the plans and business activities that were carried on at Renaissance Estates. But neither he nor Erica Knight were in a position to do anything about them."

"The police believe that Ben Williams's murder is connected to Lisa Nguyen's murder. Do you know anything about that?"

"How should I know? I had nothing to do with either one."

"As property manager did you see or hear anything that would lead you to believe that there might be a connection between the two murders?"

"Ben Williams was murdered in an obvious street crime—somebody trying to carjack him. He resisted and was shot. That sort of thing can happen in the area around Renaissance Estates. Lisa Nguyen was beaten to death in a nightclub parking lot—another street crime. I'd like to see the neighborhood be safer, but I don't see how the crimes are connected."

"Rudi Sirianni told me that she overheard a telephone conversation where you referred to Ben Williams as 'totally useless.' She further heard you say, 'kill the bastard'. Would you please comment on this?"

"In a flick of anger, I did say that 'Sometimes I wish somebody would help me out and kill the bastard.' I was being facetious at the time. I didn't like Ben Williams, but I never suggested to anyone that he should be killed. I hope you understand that and don't print anything to the contrary."

"Next issue," Jay said. They were interrupted when a waitress came by asked if they wanted anything else. Millwood ordered a double of the same.

"Issue number four concerns Rudi Sirianni," said Millwood. "I know she was a source for your articles, but you really should check your sources more carefully before you start printing what they say. Rudi often stretched the truth whenever I confronted her about her misconduct."

"Are you aware that the police in Long Beach believe that you were having an affair with her before she was killed?" Jay said.

"That's nonsense! Total nonsense!" Millwood said with contempt. "I'm married with two young adult children, and I never ever touched that woman. She was marginal in the job she was doing, and whenever I reprimanded her, she would come on to me in an effort to protect her job. I always resisted knowing that it would only lead to trouble."

"And the Fifth Issue?"

"I know of no effort on anyone's part to try to get Erica Knight to sell Renaissance Estates," Millwood said, after downing the drink he was served.

"What about HUD's lawsuit to try to force her out?"

"HUD's lawsuit was designed to push her further away from running the properties. HUD cannot terminate any Section 8 housing ownership unless there is clear evidence of criminal wrongdoing or serious violation of HUD regulations."

"Are you aware of any criminal wrongdoing on Erica's part?" Jay said.

"No," Millwood said. "But I can definitely attest to a whole host of managerial problems and violations of HUD regulations."

"Can you name a few for me?"

"There are way too many for you to publish unless you're writing a book," Millwood said.

Throughout the interview, Jay observed that Millwood was clearly under some significant duress. At times, he talked in circles. At other times, he would ramble about Erica and her mismanagement. Near the end of the interview, Jay could see an abnormal amount of perspiration forming on Millwood's forehead, then he was served another drink.

Jay thought that Millwood might quit talking at any moment. But he decided anyway to ask him about the shell companies that were formed to buy up the land along Sultan Road. To his amazement, Millwood opened up like an internet website.

"My research on the ownership of the land along Sultan Road has turned up two major real estate companies and at least three partnerships," Jay said. "Are you familiar with either the Jefferson Square Company or Regal Management Associates?"

"The Jefferson Square Company moved a number of mid-century houses away from Westchester a few years ago to avoid having them knocked down for an airport expansion," Millwood said. "They relocated the houses to Sultan Road. There were lots of problems with the company, and eventually it folded. When Jefferson Square went bankrupt, Regal Management Associates bought most of those houses."

"Looking at the titles of some of that land, I found that most of it is owned by one of three partnerships: Harbor City Partners, Sultan Road Group, or Long Beach Connections,"

Jay said. "Have you ever heard of any of these three partnerships?"

"Yes, in fact, I've worked with some of those people in the past," Millwood said.

"How did they get ahold of the land from Regal Management Associates?"

"I think they're actually one and the same. I don't know, though, and don't quote me on it."

"Is Mayor McGinnis a part of any of these partnerships?"

"He's a partner in all of them."

"Can you tell me who the other partners are?"

"I'm not sure if I know them all, but I can give you three names: Roger Blackstone, Gary Smithfield, and Karl Brazelton."

"What about their addresses and phone numbers?"

"Sure," Millwood said. He pulled a small notebook out of his pocket. Without hesitation, he gave Jay the address of all three. Apologetically, he said that he did not know any of the phone numbers.

Jay was astonished by his willingness to share this information. He observed that after trying to play hardball, Millwood had provided the most important details of Jay's investigation to date. Jay didn't know why except maybe the amount of scotch Millwood drank had covered over his inhibitions. Millwood then ordered yet another drink. Jay decided to push his luck.

"If Mayor McGinnis is a partner in each of these groups, and these partnerships own most of the land along Sultan

Road, isn't it safe to assume that the mayor wants to take over all the land in that area?"

"Well, sure. Wouldn't you?" Millwood said. "I can tell you that if you're developing land for any purpose, it is much easier to work with too much land than too little. This is Southern California. There's just not enough good land to go around. Therefore, the value of what's there keeps going up."

"Do you know what the mayor has in mind for the area, since he basically owns it?"

"Not really. But I can tell you that it has a host of commercial and industrial possibilities."

"Like a new NFL football stadium?" Jay said.

"That, too," Millwood said.

"If he wanted the land for a big project like that, wouldn't he also want Renaissance Estates?" Jay said.

"It would be impossible to build a football stadium there around it, that's for sure," Millwood said.

"To get that land, he would need the owner of Renaissance Estates to sell, wouldn't he?"

"Of course. However, the de facto owner is the federal government. It isn't clear that they would be willing to authorize a sale."

"What would keep the government from authorizing a sale?"

"The loan officer at HUD. His signature is required before any transfer of assets can take place."

"The loan officer would be DeShawn Walker, correct?"

"That's right."

"Has the mayor brought any pressure on Erica Knight, the owner, to force a sale?" Jay said.

"The mayor isn't doing anything like that. It's his partners who are actively pushing it forward," Millwood said. Then he suddenly stopped himself, but it was too late. With that disclosure, Millwood excused himself to use the men's room. When he didn't return after nearly thirty minutes, Jay went looking for him. He did not find him anywhere on the premises.

The next day, Millwood sat down in his living room with the *Daily Journal* and read Jay's story. Although the article did cover the subjects that they had talked about, for some reason it just didn't serve the purpose that Millwood had hoped it would. He had been hoping for a public vindication of his tenure of managing Renaissance Estates that happened to coincide with the murders of three people. Instead, he got the idea that his disclosures had provided too much additional detail for Jay's story and might be getting him into worse trouble. In a panic, he called his attorney and told him what happened. His attorney advised him to go to either the California Attorney General's office or the FBI with whatever evidence he had. The attorney further stated that he needed to be with Millwood when he did this.

Millwood didn't show up for any of his appointments that day. He sat alone at home and contemplated what he should do next. He concluded that his best course of action would be to call Marsha Jackson of the FBI. When he did call, she invited him to her office But Millwood told her he thought he was being monitored and that they needed a private space. At his request, Jackson agreed to meet him the next day at the same bar where he had met Jay.

When the next morning arrived, Millwood got into his car, that was parked in his driveway. He started the engine. Before he could put the car into gear, he was hit on the head with a metal club by someone hiding in the backseat. He lost consciousness immediately, and another person hiding behind the corner of the house came around to open the driver's side door. Millwood was then pushed over into the passenger's side and buckled in. The second person took over the driver's seat and started driving. Millwood was then driven to a remote place in the desert, and his car was followed there by a gray pickup truck. While still unconscious, he was then buckled back into the driver's seat. He was doused with an ample amount of gasoline and set on fire.

It was a few days later when Jackson read the report from the La Mirada sheriff's office and discovered why Millwood never showed up for their meeting. Then she talked to her supervisor about Renaissance Estates, Millwood, the newspaper articles by Jay, and the large amount of mostly circumstantial evidence that she had received from Aguilar. She said that her contact didn't think that the LAPD would be conducting an impartial investigation of the information contained in the documentation since the results could lead to the mayor's office. After reviewing a select portion of the evidence, her supervisor told her that even though Renaissance Estates was a HUD sponsored property, no federal laws appeared to have been broken. Therefore, the Bureau had to leave the investigation up to either the local authorities or the state. Heeding this mandate, Jackson packed up the flash drive and the file that Aguilar had given her and shipped them to the office of the California Attorney General in Sacramento.

CHAPTER THIRTY-ONE

In the next installment of his story, Jay sought to expose Mayor McGinnis as being connected to Regal Management Associates by way of partnerships filled with silent partners. What Millwood told him had confirmed what Jay had thought all along—that the silent partnerships were set up to try to disassociate the real owners from what had taken place with the people who were pushed out of their homes. Jay was careful to back up everything he wrote with his transcribed recordings, notes, and Rudi's documentation. The story hit the mayor hard, causing a major furor in the local television news media. McGinnis decided to call another press conference to try to rectify his position.

As he usually did, McGinnis began the press conference with a statement. "I would like to repudiate a specific story in the *Daily Journal* about my supposed involvement with a large amount of property along Sultan Road, north of Harbor Gateway. Under no circumstances did I ever have any professional connection with Regal Management Associates, the Jefferson Square Company, or any other entity that sought to acquire property in the Sultan Road area with the intent to build an NFL stadium there. The story in the *Daily Journal* is categorically false on all points that relate to my alleged involvement."

Jay and Dylan were among the reporters and media staff covering the press conference. While the mayor continued with his opening statement, Dylan whispered to Jay that Jay's credibility was on the line, and that he needed to stand up and defend it.

When McGinnis's opening remarks were finished, a group of reporters including Jay shot their hands up to ask questions. McGinnis picked a reporter he knew to be from the Associated Press.

"Isn't it true that you favor the Sultan Road location over all the other possibilities for the new football stadium?" the reporter said.

"It's true that I favor that location," McGinnis said, "but that's because it has great freeway access and the land is already mostly vacant. It's large enough to accommodate a new stadium plus sufficient parking for up to 75,000 fans in attendance."

"Who would build the stadium, and how much would the taxpayer have to pay?" the same reporter interjected, not giving McGinnis a chance to select someone else.

"It would not cost the taxpayer a penny," McGinnis said. "As to who would build it, there are many possibilities, since we have over three hundred construction companies in this state with the right experience that could be hired as general contractors."

"Once it was built, who would own it?" the reporter said, continuing his hold on the floor of the press conference.

"Well, I would assume that a developer would step in, buy the land, co-ordinate the construction, and then either finish it for another owner, or own the place himself," McGinnis said appearing to provide a philosophical answer.

"Do you or anyone in your family have any monetary interest in any of the land along Sultan Road that would be subject to a possible stadium development?" the reporter said.

"Absolutely not." With that, the mayor decided to recognize another reporter. He unwittingly called on Jay, since Jay had an unfamiliar face.

"Mr. Mayor," Jay began. "I'm Jason Phillips from the *Daily Journal*. Isn't it true that you belong to a partnership that has a major interest in Regal Management Associates—the company that owns a majority of the vacant land along Sultan Road north of Harbor Gateway?"

"That's absolutely not true. I do not have any partners…" McGinnis started to say.

Jay cut the mayor off. "Do you know Roger Blackstone, Gary Smithfield, or Karl Brazelton?" he said.

The question clearly threw McGinnis off balance. As he paused, he appeared to realize that he was talking to the reporter who had caused him so much trouble. "No, I don't know any of those people," he said, stammering a little on the word "people."

"Well, sir, they all signed on to a partnership with you that owns Regal Management Associates," Jay fired right back.

"That is absolutely false. I don't like repeating myself so let's not ask that question again," McGinnis said.

"Do you know Brendon Millwood?" Jay said.

Again, McGinnis hesitated before answering. "No, I don't know him either. What do these people have to do with an NFL football stadium?" he said.

"Brendon Millwood was the property manager at Renaissance Estates, and he said that you, sir, are a party to a plan to acquire Renaissance Estates," Jay said. That statement caused an audible stir among the reporters, and many hands started writing or typing onto cell phones or tablets.

"I still don't know what that has to do with an NFL stadium. This conference was called to deal with that issue, not…"

"Isn't it true that Renaissance Estates sits on the last piece of land along Sultan Road that is not available for development?" Jay said, all guns blazing.

"I have no idea where Renaissance Estates is located. In fact, I've never even heard of it before," McGinnis said, apparently forgetting that he had admitted to knowing about the place in a previous press conference. In spite of Jay's being ready with another question, McGinnis decided to call on a different reporter. Unfortunately for him, he called on Dylan.

"Mr. Mayor," Dylan said, "it has been reported in the *Daily Journal* that the owner of Renaissance Estates, Erica Knight, had been pressured by Mr. Millwood and others to sell the property. Was this pressure directed by you or your office?"

"Absolutely not! I have no idea who Erica Knight is, and I've never heard of Renaissance Estates."

"In your last press conference a few weeks ago, you confirmed to this reporter that you *had* heard of Renaissance Estates. Isn't it true that you *do* know about Renaissance Estates as well as the actions of Mr. Millwood to pressure the owner to sell?"

"I have nothing to do with any sale of a place I've never heard of," McGinnis said, reiterating his denial of knowledge of Renaissance Estates.

"You've stated that you didn't know the late Brendon Millwood. But didn't you hire Millwood Property Management to manage two of your apartment complexes—Urban Meadows and Kalifa Gardens?"

McGinnis faltered yet again. "I think that was a different person than the one mentioned earlier. I don't know Brendon Millwood," he said.

"Brendon Millwood was the sole proprietor of Millwood Property Management. If you hired the management company, didn't you meet the proprietor at some point?" Dylan said, keeping the pressure on.

"I'm sorry, *I don't know this person.*" McGinnis then picked another reporter, clearly hoping to get off the subject. Instead the next reporter picked up right where Dylan and Jay had left off.

"Mr. Mayor," the reporter said, "you have placed a lot of emphasis on the Sultan Road location as being the right one for the NFL stadium. In light of the *Daily Journal's* story saying that you and some of your partners are in control of most of that land, what future development are you considering for the area?"

"I can't speak about any details of the development of land that I do not own," McGinnis said. "Maybe somebody else is planning to build an NFL stadium there—I don't know. All I can say is that I believe it would be the perfect area for something of that size and purpose. And we don't have that much free land available in this city anymore."

"Do you believe that Brendon Millwood's involvement with Renaissance Estates, was what got him killed?" the reporter asked next.

"Once again—and for the last time—I do not know who Brendon Millwood was or what happened to him."

McGinnis continued his denials, but he simply could not shake his relationship with the late Brendon Millwood, or with what was happening at Renaissance Estates. Finally, he turned around from the speaker stand and walked away in disgust throwing his notes onto the floor for an aide to retrieve.

After the press conference had ended, Dylan congratulated Jay on his performance. "Wow, you did really good, man," he said. "You unleashed the dogs that drove McGinnis away from the podium."

"I wish I had another shot at him," Jay said. "I've got a list of other questions to ask him. And I know that the SOB is lying about Renaissance Estates."

"Yeah he is, for sure," Dylan said. "And seeing the way he was rattled today makes me think that he's starting to come apart. Let's get back to the newsroom. I've got something to show you."

Once back at his workstation, Dylan showed Jay an article he was releasing that day for the next morning's paper. In it, Dylan wrote that the owner of the St. Louis Rams was the frontrunner to get the nod to move his NFL franchise to Los Angeles. Further, he pointed out that the same man owned a large tract of land in Inglewood where the now closed Hollywood Park Racetrack stood. It was on this land that he planned to build his own stadium including retail shopping, restaurants, corporate offices, parking garages, and some housing, should he be selected by the owners to make the move.

That same afternoon, Jay called Aguilar to see if there were any updates on the criminal investigation.

"Sergeant Aguilar," Jay said, greeting the detective the same way he always did. "Any news for our readers?"

"Good timing, Newsboy," Aguilar said. "We've arrested the administrative assistant to Karl Brazelton, the owner of the South Bay Neighborhood Association. She's been charged with accessory to murder and obstruction of justice."

"Wow!" Jay said. "Tell me how it all went down."

Aguilar said, "She's the keeper of the slush fund over at South Bay. We can prove that the slush fund was used to pay for criminal activities that originated from that organization."

"Love it!" Jay said. Then he dropped a bombshell of his own. "I've discovered in my research that Karl Brazelton was a partner with Mayor McGinnis. On top of that, the partners own just about all the land that surrounds Renaissance Estates. I can't print this yet, but we should be including

McGinnis on the list of people who are trying to get rid of Erica Knight as owner of the place."

"I'd like to see your proof of the partnership between Brazelton and McGinnis," Aguilar said. "It's an important piece in this investigation. Proving McGinnis's involvement won't be an easy job for us."

"Oh, I always cooperate with the local authorities, the upstanding citizen that I am!" Jay said laughing. "I'll email it to you."

CHAPTER THIRTY-TWO

Marsha Jackson knew that Willis Napier was a suspect in an unsolved federal extortion case involving Section 8 housing in the Chicago area. The MO of the Chicago extortionist was similar to what Jay and the auditors had discovered at Renaissance Estates. In an effort to use FBI resources to go after Napier, Jackson took two folders of evidence that she had accumulated into her supervisor's office.

"If you look at this, you can see that Willis Napier could be the person that the Chicago office is searching for," she said, presenting a report on her findings. "He also jumped bail here and left the state, making him a suspect for unlawful flight to avoid prosecution for murder."

The supervisor looked over the report and said, "You do have those accusations supported in those files, don't you?"

"Of course," Jackson said. "The problem is that Napier bought a plane ticket to Miami. He doesn't have his passport, but he nonetheless could hire a boat to take him to the Bahamas, where I think he is right now."

The supervisor continued to look at Jackson's report. Then he looked up and said, "I've got a friend in a certain place who might be able to help us apprehend him. We need to come up with a plan that will get him to travel from the Bahamas to Cancun. See what you can do."

Jackson went to work on this task. If it were true that Napier was hiding in the Bahamas, he had to be getting money somehow. The question was where, how, and when. If the FBI could interrupt this flow of money, he might be forced to go to Mexico for an emergency payment. To get help doing this, Jackson called Maria Carmen De La Rosa, an old friend who happened to be a CIA operative. It required permission from De La Rosa's boss, but she soon became available to help Jackson.

Maria Carmen De La Rosa would be the perfect foil to go to the Bahamas to link up with Napier. Jackson had known her since high school, where they both played on the women's basketball team. The two had remained good friends.

It took a few days in the Bahamas for De La Rosa to find her mark. She surveyed Napier's habitat and discovered that he enjoyed hanging out at an outdoor bar near the waterfront. She made her entrance into the bar at a time she knew he would be there. She casually brushed past him and sat on a bar stool just a few feet away. She was a tall, slim, attractive woman of Afro-Cuban extraction.

Napier couldn't resist what he was seeing. He slid over next to her and bought her a drink. Before long he struck up a conversation with her.

Skillfully, De La Rosa beguiled Napier into thinking that this might be his lucky day for a score. Napier fell for her charms like a chopped down pine tree and took her back to his place just outside of Nassau. Once there, De La Rosa kicked off her shoes and sat down in Napier's only easy chair. As Napier moved up for some play, she asked him to make them each a margarita. A few minutes later De La Rosa removed her jumpsuit. Napier brought out their drinks and set them down on an end table. Like something out of an espionage movie, she reached up behind his head with one hand and planted a huge kiss on his lips. While he was distracted, she discreetly inserted a pill into one of the drinks thereby creating a Mickey Finn. She reached behind her back to unfasten her bra. Then, with her breasts in full view, she picked up the drink without the drug in it. Napier picked up the other drink and quaffed it without losing his focus on De La Rosa's bosom. Within a short time, he passed out on the floor.

Once Napier was unconscious, De La Rosa got dressed and went around his apartment checking all the desk drawers, cabinets, and even trash receptacles for information as to how he got his money. She didn't find anything in the way of a record that pointed to a trail that the money went through. Luck was with her when the postman made a timely mail delivery. The mail included an envelope from Los Angeles. Holding it up to a light she observed that there was a check inside for a substantial amount of money. But she could not see all the details. She gingerly opened the envelope and confirmed that the check was payable to Napier from the bank account of a real estate company in Los Angeles.

With the check safely inside her handbag, she lifted Napier's car keys from his pocket and went to make photocopies. Then she destroyed the originals, thinking that the FBI would not be able to act on information that had been stolen from the official mail of another country. Before Napier woke up, the copies of the check and the envelope were on their way via Federal Express to Jackson, and De La Rosa was on her way back to Miami for her next job for the CIA.

Jackson traced the account number at the bank the check was drawn on to one of the holding companies owned by McGinnis, Brazelton, and other partners. With federal warrants, they seized the bank account and put a freeze on all transactions. The result was that not only did Napier never get the check that was delivered to his home, but he was also permanently cut off of all future funds.

Playing a hunch, Jackson went to Western Union to see if that was how the real estate company communicated with Napier. She hit the bullseye, as the clerk showed her several messages sent recently from Brazelton to Napier. These messages were written in such a way that they used a hidden code only the sender and recipient could understand. However, after a couple of days, Jackson figured out enough of the code to craft a telegram to Napier making it appear to come from the real estate company. The telegram told Napier that the bank had frozen the corporate account, and that he needed to travel to Cancun, where he would meet up with a representative from the company and be paid in cash.

Although the telegram appeared odd to Napier, he needed the money right away. He did not have his United States passport. But he did have a Bahamian one, that he had purchased on the black market. With just barely enough money for an airplane ticket, he flew to Cancun from Nassau.

Jackson's telegram had told Napier the representative would meet him at the airport in Mexico with his money after he called a telephone number. The representative turned out to be the chief of police for Cancun, who promptly arrested him. He didn't know at the time that the Cancun police chief was a friend of Jackson's boss. It took a few days to complete extradition. Napier waived any rights he might have had in Mexico, and was promptly returned to Los Angeles.

CHAPTER THIRTY-THREE

Following up on Captain Kreider's tip about Anita Martinez's imminent release, Aguilar and Lee went to court the day of her appearance. In a plea agreement that had been worked out with the district attorney's office, she pled guilty to a single charge of simple assault. In return, the judge suspended any jail time beyond time already served, that turned out to be three and a half weeks. She left the courtroom accompanied by a female friend, who would take her home. The detectives followed them out and then got into their unmarked car. They followed Martinez all the way to her home in Lynnwood where they observed her going up to her second-floor apartment alone. After her friend drove away, they set up a stakeout by parking on the street in an inconspicuous spot with a full view of her apartment.

Martinez stayed in her apartment all afternoon and evening, and the stakeout continued into the night. Finally, at ten o'clock, Fernando Suarez showed up just as Aguilar suspected. Suarez exited his car and began walking slowly toward the entrance of the apartment building. The two detectives leaped into action. Harry ran over to the apartment building to block the entrance, while Aguilar moved up behind Suarez to prevent his escape.

Startled, Suarez swung around to confront Aguilar.

"What do you think you're doing here, motherfucker?" Suarez said. At first, he did not seem to recognize Aguilar from their previous confrontation in the parking lot of the public park.

"I'm placing you under arrest," Aguilar said calmly. He displayed his badge that dangled around his neck on a chain.

Suarez took a step backward. "I remember you!" he said.

With his pistol drawn, Harry moved closer to back up Aguilar. Suarez began to cooperate as Aguilar turned him around and told him to put his hands on the trunk of a nearby tree. Harry then searched him but found no weapons of any kind. Aguilar checked Suarez's wallet and removed his driver's license.

"Luis Fernando Suarez Medina, Aguilar said, "you are under arrest for…"

Suddenly, a shot was fired from the upstairs window of Martinez's apartment. It whizzed past the two detectives and hit the trunk of the tree where they were standing. As they both looked up toward the window, Suarez turned around and punched Aguilar in the side of the head, knocking him backward. Then he made a break for his car.

Harry turned and aimed at Suarez before shouting, "Stop right there!" At that moment, another shot rang out. The bullet just missed Harry and ricocheted off a street light stand. Harry spun around to see who was shooting. Suarez continued running toward his car.

Aguilar quickly regained his composure, just as another shot came out of the window and hit a truck that was parked nearby. He shoved Harry toward the apartments, yelling, "Get the shooter!" He then raced after Suarez catching up to him at his car and shoving him against the driver's side door. Suarez turned around and swung his fist at the shorter Aguilar. But the former middleweight boxer ducked and provided a one-two combination of his own. Suarez then attempted to grab Aguilar, but the police detective slipped the grip and powered another one-two combination into Suarez's mid-section, doubling him over. Aguilar then grabbed Suarez by the shoulders and slammed him facedown onto the hood of the car. Suarez swung his elbow and hit Aguilar on the forehead, knocking him back a step. While Aguilar was temporarily dazed, Suarez gave him a hard shove, pushing him out of the way of the car door. Aguilar recovered, but Suarez opened the door and was able to get inside the car first. He then swung the door open again hitting Aguilar and knocking him backward off his feet.

Suarez started the car up. As he shifted gears to drive away, Aguilar pulled out his pistol and fired a single shot hitting Suarez's left rear tire. Suarez nonetheless raced off, the flat tire flapping and hampering his escape.

Aguilar knew he had to take Suarez alive to find "El Puma." He kept his pistol drawn and chased Suarez down the street on foot. Suarez reached the next corner but had to wait momentarily for some cross traffic before crossing. This gave Aguilar the chance to take another shot from ten yards away. Taking careful aim, he hit the other rear tire now flattening them both. He continued running after Suarez's car, now headed across the intersection. Throwing caution to the wind, he raced through the intersection himself—safely, as it turned out—and continued running after Suarez.

With both rear tires flat and nearly ripped off their rims, Suarez's rear wheels became so hot that they caught fire. He then pulled over and drew his own revolver from the glove compartment. He exited the car only to see that Aguilar was closing in on him. Suarez fired a shot at Aguilar from nearly fifty yards away, missing badly. He fired again as Aguilar got closer. Aguilar found some cover behind the trees along the other side of the street. When Aguilar was just across the street from him, Suarez opened up with a series of four shots that mostly hit the tree that Aguilar was standing behind. Then Aguilar fired a single shot grazing Suarez above the right knee.

Suarez was now out of ammunition. He shoved his pistol into his belt and started limping down the street away from Aguilar, who was still in hot pursuit. Seeing that Aguilar was about to catch him, Suarez changed course and hustled through the yard of one of the houses on the street. A light came on in the living room of the house, and Aguilar hollered as loudly as he could, "Call the police!" The yelling alerted others in the neighborhood and someone must have complied. A few minutes later, Aguilar could hear the sound of police sirens.

The foot chase went into the house's backyard. Suarez was climbing up a fence into the neighbor's yard when Aguilar got ahold of him. The two fell to the ground and began to wrestle.

Meanwhile, in front of the apartment building, Martinez continued to shoot at Harry from the second-story window. While the gunshots zipped all around Harry, he dodged back and forth until he found cover behind another tree near the street. Then he squeezed off several shots back at the window that crashed through the glass and forced Martinez to back away. He sprang from behind the tree and rushed to the building's entrance. He hurried up the steps two at a time to Martinez's second floor apartment and started banging on the front door with the handle of his pistol. Then he suddenly stopped and adeptly slipped to the side, just as Martinez fired several shots through the door. When the shooting stopped, Harry kicked the door just below the handle. Again, he stepped to the side expecting Martinez to once again shoot through the door. When she did not shoot, he finished kicking the door in and opened it from a squatting position.

He didn't see Martinez anywhere in the living room. He carefully made his way inside with his pistol drawn to check the remainder of the apartment. He quickly looked right and left, behind furniture and underneath the nearby dining room table. There he found a semi-automatic military style rifle lying on the floor as well as scattered empty shell casings. By the window, he could see more spent shell casings on the floor. Then he noticed that the hall closet door was closed. He approached it swiftly standing just to the side. With his pistol in his right hand, he reached with his left hand for the doorknob and swung the door open. But nobody was hiding inside.

Next, he turned his attention to the bedroom. Suddenly, he heard a door slam in the kitchen. He proceeded through the opening from the living room into the kitchen and quickly swung around to confront Martinez, but she was not there. He heard some commotion from outside the kitchen window and observed that there was another door in the kitchen that lead down the back stairs. He raced over to look out the doorway and saw Martinez running down the footpath away from the building. She was headed toward the other apartment buildings in the complex.

In a flash, Harry gave chase. He bolted down the back stairs and ran after Martinez. As he closed in on her, he saw Martinez run into a doorway at the far end of one of the buildings.

Harry raced over to the doorway. A light was on inside. He carefully poked his head into the doorway behind his drawn pistol and saw that he had cornered Martinez in the laundry room. Further, she had grabbed an African American woman resident who had been folding laundry. Martinez was now behind her, twisting her arm. She was pointing a pistol directly at the woman's head using her as a human shield.

"Drop your gun you chink sonofabitch!" Martinez told Harry.

Quickly Harry dropped down behind a row of washing machines laying his arms across the top with his pistol pointing directly at Martinez. "Drop your gun, now!" he said. "Let that woman go!"

"Go fuck yourself, chino mono!" Martinez said.

"Give yourself up now!" Harry said. "Don't make it any worse for you. You're already in a lot of trouble."

"Eat shit, dink!"

It seemed to Harry that the hostage had figured out what was taking place—that a police officer, and not a gang member, was confronting the person who was holding her captive. The hostage watched as Martinez took aim at Harry. At that moment, she yanked her arm free and punched Martinez in the face, knocking her backward and causing her to drop her pistol.

Martinez recovered and reached down to pick up her gun when Harry shouted, "Don't touch that!" She grabbed her gun anyway and pointed it again at the resident.

Harry then shot her in the leg, causing her to fall over and again drop her pistol. He rushed over and picked it up disarming Martinez. Then he cuffed her saying, "Anita Martinez, you are under arrest!"

With Martinez safely cuffed, Harry asked the woman, "Are you injured?"

Without answering she collapsed into a nearby chair. After a moment, she told Harry she was unhurt. But it was clear to Harry that she had been traumatized by having a gun pointed directly at her head.

A few blocks away, Aguilar had finally subdued Suarez in the backyard of a local home and cuffed him while on top of him on the ground. At that moment, a bright light shown down on him from the side of the house. "Police!" a loud voice said. "Put your hands where I can see them." As Aguilar complied, the officer said, "Put your gun on the ground." Aguilar again complied and continued kneeling next to Suarez. Two sheriff's deputies then approached him with their pistols drawn.

Aguilar said nothing, as the two deputies came closer and sized up the situation. Another patrol car screeched to a halt in front of the house and two more deputies came running also with weapons drawn. Finally, the first deputy said, "Who are you?" while looking directly at Aguilar.

"I'm Sergeant Carlos Aguilar of the LAPD. I'm arresting this suspect here on the ground next to me."

The deputy switched the flashlight onto Suarez and notice that he was cuffed. "OK, but I need you to stand up slowly so I can frisk you," he said to Aguilar.

"I'm in a hurry, gentlemen," Aguilar said as he rose to his feet with his hands still raised. "My partner was chasing an active shooter a few blocks down. Can we get this man into custody, so I can get back and help him?"

The officer shone his light on Aguilar's badge. "Roberts," he called out. "This guy's an LAPD officer. Take him back to find his partner. Call for more backup when you get there." To Aguilar he then said, "We'll take this other guy to the La Mirada sheriff's substation and hold him there but only for one day. What's his name?"

"Fernando Suarez," Aguilar said as he handed Suarez's wallet to the sheriff's deputy. Then he picked up his pistol and ran with Deputy Roberts back to the deputy's patrol car to go check on Harry.

Roberts drove back to Martinez's apartment building under Aguilar's direction. "He should be inside that building upstairs somewhere," Aguilar said.

"Just wait here for a moment," Roberts said, as he picked up the handset to call for backup. Instead, Aguilar jumped out of the patrol car and ran towards the entrance to the apartment building. He raced up to the top of the stairs and noticed the badly shot up front door that was still open. In the same manner that Harry had done earlier, he carefully entered the apartment expecting to find Martinez there in hiding, and Harry lying injured on the floor. He cleared the apartment room by room until he found on the floor what he feared the most—drops of blood. He maneuvered carefully around it and continued looking for either his partner or his suspect until he arrived in the kitchen. He did not find anyone but he saw that the back door was open, and there was a blood trail leading to it. He hurried down the back stairs looking right and left for any sign of either Harry or Martinez. A few curiosity seekers were milling about in the space between buildings.

"Police!" Aguilar said. Recognizing that neither Harry nor Martinez were in the crowd, he said, "Did any of you see a police officer chasing a suspect through here?"

One of the residents said, "There's something going on down in the laundry. I heard some shots." He pointed to the end of the apartment building where the laundry room was located.

Aguilar said, "All of you, stay back behind me." He went down to the end of the building where the resident had pointed. He saw the open door, and he cautiously made his way into the laundry room. There he saw Harry treating a cuffed Anita Martinez's leg wound with paper towels, and the resident who was still collapsed in the chair.

"I found blood on the floor of the apartment," Aguilar said. "Is it yours or hers?"

Harry showed him where a bullet from Martinez's assault rifle had hit him in the left shoulder while he was dodging back and forth behind the trees. His left sleeve was soaked.

An ambulance and sheriff's deputies soon arrived on the scene. The paramedics dressed both Harry's and Martinez's wounds, and then took an escorted Martinez to the hospital under guard.

Aguilar and Lee then got into their car to go to La Mirada to pick up Suarez. As they started to drive away Harry asked Aguilar, "Martinez called me a 'chino mono.' What did she mean by that?"

Aguilar let out a short laugh, that helped release the stress of the ordeal. "Welcome to the world of racial slurs," he said. "Chino mono means Chinese monkey."

Three days later at police headquarters in downtown Los Angeles, Suarez was put into an interrogation room with his attorney. When Aguilar arrived for questioning, Suarez was not interested in cooperating.

"Mr. Suarez," Aguilar said, "Witnesses place you at the scene of two murders, one at Paradise Cove nightclub in Torrance and another at Renaissance Estates on Sultan Road. Do you want to tell me what your activities were at those locations while the two victims were being killed?"

Suarez and his attorney sat silently.

"You had an accomplice with you both times. What is this man's name?"

More silence.

"You and this same accomplice picked up a brief case filled with cash in a public park from an employee of the South Bay Neighborhood Association. Why was that money being paid to you?"

Still silence. Both men sat motionless.

"All right, I'll tell it like it is. You're being charged with two counts of murder one. It's guaranteed life for you. That is, unless you feel like cooperating with us."

Suarez's attorney said, "You can't put a gun in his hands for the second murder, and you don't know if it was him who killed the woman in the first."

"Oh, I think you're wrong, counselor," Aguilar said. "We've got witnesses to both." He was stretching it a little, as Mrs. Robinson, who witnessed Ben Williams's murder, didn't see his face, and they couldn't confirm if Lisa Nguyen was killed in the parking lot or afterward.

"Fine, I'll rip them to shreds in court," the attorney said.

While Suarez was in custody, Harry was executing a search warrant at Suarez's apartment in Hawthorne. Finding what he was searching for, he took a yellow shirt from Suarez's closet and went back to the lab with the evidence recently furnished by CSI on the nightclub murder. The evidence was a tiny fiber that had gotten stuck in Lisa Nguyen's pants zipper. The fiber matched exactly some loose threads on the yellow shirt where it had been torn below the bottom button. Harry brought the results into the interrogation room and presented them to Aguilar.

"Well, what do we have here," Aguilar remarked. He took a moment to review the evidence and then showed it to Suarez. "It looks like a fiber from your shirt was caught in the pants zipper of victim number one," he said.

The attorney looked at the report along with the two pieces of fiber in plastic evidence bags. Neither he nor Suarez said anything.

Aguilar had another surprise for the accused. He reached over toward Suarez's shirt pocket for his pack of cigarettes. "May I?' he said. Suarez didn't answer, but Aguilar nonetheless lifted the pack and shook a cigarette partially out through the opened end.

"Want one?" Aguilar said, offering Suarez one of his own cigarettes.

"He most certainly does not!" the attorney said, clearly suspecting a DNA trap.

Aguilar compared the cigarette that he'd shaken loose from Suarez's pack to the cigarette butt found near Ben Williams's car that was also in a plastic evidence bag. "Same brand—Marlboro," he said. "How many Marlboros do you smoke a day?"

Suarez started to answer, but his attorney stopped him.

After a pause, Aguilar said, "Well, you may have smoked one too many. We tested this cigarette butt for DNA, and it matches the DNA from the coffee cup you drank out of the other night in La Mirada." He showed them a paper cup that was in a different evidence bag. "A witness saw you throw this cigarette butt onto the ground just after the Ben Williams shooting. Would you like to tell me about it?"

The attorney bore a look of disgust. It was clear that he understood that this forensic evidence had just placed his client at the scene of both crimes corroborating Aguilar's witnesses.

"Mr. Suarez," Aguilar continued, "your friend Anita Martinez is being charged with assault with a deadly weapon and the attempted murder of a peace officer. She should be inside for a minimum of twenty years and maybe longer," Aguilar said.

"Bullshit!" Suarez retorted.

"Oh, I'm sorry, it's no bullshit. She fired over twenty-five rounds at my partner, hitting him in the shoulder. She was trying to kill him. You better tell him, counselor."

Harry rolled up the sleeve of his shirt to display a heavy bandage.

The attorney whispered something into Suarez's ear. "So what about it?" Suarez finally said.

"If you ever want to cuddle up with her again, you need to tell me where I can find 'El Puma'."

Are you offering him something, sergeant?" the attorney said.

"I'm not allowed to offer him anything at this point. But the DA can. We know you've been handling 'El Puma' since he came up from Mexico. You can choose to cooperate right here and now. If you do, the DA will hear about it and there will be some consideration for it."

Suarez discussed the matter with his attorney in an exchange of whispers. This discussion went on for a minute before Suarez finally told Aguilar, "You can find 'El Puma' in the Inglewood-Crenshaw District. He lives as a refugee at the St. John the Baptist Catholic Refugee Support Center."

"Has he got a real name?" Aguilar said.

"Asdrubal Mendoza," Suarez said.

"We have some loose ends that need to be tied up," Aguilar said. "The first one involves the parking lot fight. Was the victim dead when you picked her up and put her into the back of the truck?"

Suarez consulted his attorney momentarily. Then he said, "She was unconscious but still breathing."

"Where did the fatal blow take place?"

"We drove from the nightclub to a vacant parking lot behind an office building. Mendoza took a large rock and bashed her in the chest and head with it. Then we put her body behind some bushes."

"There was practically no forensic evidence at the site. How did you move the body? She was bleeding badly."

"We had a plastic tarp."

"After Napier was arrested, who passed down the hit information?"

"Karl Brazelton."

"And that was for Williams, the Sirianni woman, and Millwood?"

"That's right."

"Who provided Mendoza with a maintenance uniform and condo key for the Sirianni murder?"

Once again, Suarez looked at his attorney, who nodded his head. "His name is Tomas Vicario Sanchez."

"How did he get inside the building after hours?"

"He got there before five o'clock and hid in a bathroom.

"Thank you, counselor," Aguilar said. "We have to hold him on a murder two warrant. But the DA will decide what to charge Mr. Suarez with, and I'll weigh in when that happens."

As he got up to leave, Aguilar said, "Oh, uh, one more question, if you don't mind. How did your shirttail get caught into the pants zipper of the parking lot victim?

Suarez spoke with this attorney and then said, "The woman was still breathing when we took her to the office parking lot. Mendoza wanted to fuck her before killing her. He unzipped her pants and started to pull them off. I told him not to waste time doing that and then I pulled the zipper back up."

CHAPTER THIRTY-FOUR

Jay was busy banging out the next installment of his story, when Dylan dropped by his workstation and asked if he wanted to get some coffee. They went down the street to their favorite coffee shop and got the usual—medium black coffee for Dylan, and a double latte for Jay.

"What's new with your story?" Dylan said.

"Did you read the piece I wrote after I talked to Millwood?" Jay said.

"Yes, and I admit I'm impressed. I saw your brief article about his death. What happened to Millwood anyway?" Dylan said.

"I don't know that part yet," Jay said.

"Do your LAPD contacts know what happened?"

"I haven't asked them about it. Millwood was found by a sheriff's deputy somewhere just west of Blythe."

"Christ! That's over one hundred fifty miles away."

"He was burned beyond recognition. They were only able to identify him after they determined that the car was his."

"That's gruesome."

"It's pretty hardcore, that's for sure."

"What are your next steps?"

"Since Millwood gave me the names of the silent partners that Mayor McGinnis was working with, I guess I should talk to them next."

"Have you found out where these people live yet?"

"Well, there's one in South Central, and another one in Long Beach. The third one lives somewhere between Inglewood and Hawthorne."

"When you approach these guys, take my advice and don't go alone," Dylan said. "Take somebody with you—anybody. The heat is being turned way up by the mayor's office. You've done so much research into Renaissance Estates. I'm afraid whoever is killing these people might get to you next."

Jay stopped for a moment to consider this. "Well, I'm not afraid," he finally said. "But I was, like, hoping that you would come along."

"I'd like to, but I'm taking my wife and kids to visit Grandma in Sacramento and then to Yosemite. We'll be gone for ten days."

Jay generally heeded Dylan's advice. But this time he reckoned that he needed to get to these people as soon as he could and get the story out before another tragedy took place. When he got back to his workstation, he was called into Meredith's office.

"I noticed from your article that another one of your sources is dead, a Mr. Brendan Millwood," Meredith said. "Is that going to shut you down, or do you have another direction to go?"

"Millwood gave me the names of Andrew McGinnis's silent partners," Jay said.

"I see. That should lead you right to the mayor's doorstep. Is there anything in all this mess at Renaissance Estates that points to who was behind the murders?"

"I don't quite have that yet. The police can't help me because they're still trying to catch the killers. Somebody else is calling the shots, and we haven't got him yet."

"What are you going to do about the silent partners?"

"I'm going to interview them, of course."

"Before you do that, I need something more thorough about Millwood. I'm sending your blip back to you." Meredith said. "Can you get to that right away? I don't want to be scooped again by somebody else. Even the local TV stations are jumping on this, so we've got to keep moving, too."

"There's not much known about what happened to Millwood, or why," Jay said. "The Riverside County Sheriff's Department found him out near Blythe. My guys in the LAPD haven't had time to weigh in on the murder yet."

"Do you have a copy of the police report?"

"No."

"Well, damn it, get one! Get me something on what happened to this man. We can't lose this story, Jay. You've taken over the front-page with it. Now get moving. And I need it by 3PM."

Jay looked up the police report that was on file and changed his blip about Brendan Millwood's demise into a more formal and informative piece. It was still early afternoon when he finished it and forwarded it to Meredith. Then he set out to talk to McGinnis's silent partners.

Jay found the home of the first partner in a place that he would never have expected. It was a modest, midcentury house on 51st Street in South Central LA. Jay knocked on the door, and an elderly African American woman answered.

"Good afternoon. My name is Jay Phillips and I'm a reporter for the *LA Daily Journal*. I was hoping to have a short talk with a Mr. Roger Blackstone. I was told that he lives here."

"Yeah, he's here. Wait just a moment, please," the woman said, and she went back inside the house.

A few minutes later a short African American man came to the door.

"Oh, hi," Jay said. "Are you Mr. Roger Blackstone?"

The man looked at Jay for a moment and then checked the street behind him. Then he said, "Yes, and you are…?"

"My name is Jay Phillips. I'm a reporter for the *LA Daily Journal*. I'm working on a story that involves the disposition of some land in the Harbor Gateway area. Your name turned up in my research as being a partner in a group that was attempting to acquire this land."

"Wait a minute, now," Blackstone said interrupting. "I don't know anything about being in any partnership over some land in Harbor Gateway."

"Well, I just wondered if I could ask you a couple of questions about…"

"No, I don't have anything to say. I'm sorry. Please, just go away and leave me alone."

"Were you connected to the mayor with this partnership?"

Blackstone slammed the door shut.

Jay shrugged that encounter off and set out to locate silent partner number two, Gary Smithfield, who lived in the Naples section of Long Beach. Smithfield was an attorney who owned a two-story house that overlooked Alamitos Bay. He agreed to talk to Jay, but would not allow him to use his recorder. They sat down on a park bench that overlooked the marina, and Jay began his second interview.

"Would you explain to me how three partnerships—Harbor Gateway Partners, Long Beach Property Connections, and Sultan Road Group—got control of a string of properties along Sultan Road that surround an apartment complex called Renaissance Estates?" Jay said.

"Without telling you the details, I can say that they were all acquired legally," Smithfield said.

"Was the land sold by Regal Management Associates to Harbor Gateway Partners?"

"No. Regal Management Associates is a front for the partnerships. The partnerships own the title to the different parcels of land."

"Was there a specific reason for getting title to those properties? I mean, was it for some big development?"

"It was. I'm sorry that I can't elaborate, since not all the requisite land has been acquired yet."

"Was it for a new NFL football stadium?"

"I'm not a source for any of that."

"How did you get involved with the silent partnership?"

"An attorney friend of mine, Roger Blackstone, told me about the project. He explained that it was the type of project that would set us up for life. It sounded like the kind of lucrative opportunity that I just couldn't pass up."

"I had a visit with Roger Blackstone," Jay said. "He didn't want to talk with me at all about this."

"That's understandable," Smithfield said. "He was the victim of a shakedown in the mayor's office over some leaks to the media. It was never clear if he himself was the source of the leaks, but he fell out of favor with Mayor McGinnis. As a result, he lost out on a bunch of other lucrative opportunities that otherwise might have been directed his way."

"Is the mayor the driving force behind the Regal Management Associates land acquisitions?" Jay said.

"Without answering that, I can tell you that he's the managing partner of the group."

"Was he the founder of the group?"

"No. Actually, that was another partner, Karl Brazelton," Smithfield said.

"What was Mr. Brazelton's relationship with the mayor before the partnership?"

"All I know about that is they've known each other for a long, long time. Brazelton has been dabbling in real estate with McGinnis since the mid 1980's. He was seriously injured in an auto accident about twenty years ago that he was found to be culpable for since he was drunk at the time. It left him confined to a wheelchair. Regardless, McGinnis didn't give up on the connection since Brazelton knew a hell of a lot about real estate in the area. He also was an expert in real estate law. He came up with the idea of using a silent partnership arrangement to provide cover for McGinnis, who had his own political ambitions."

"I noticed from public records that at least three separate companies own most of the land along Sultan Road. Was McGinnis a partner in all those firms?"

"Yes, he was the managing partner in all of them."

"How many companies in total were actually involved?"

"I can't tell you that."

"But what we know for sure is that Regal Management Associates is owned by, or is one and the same as, Harbor Gateway Partners, Long Beach Property Connections, and Sultan Road Group. Am I correct?"

Without answering, Smithfield nodded his head.

"There's an apartment complex on Sultan Road that may be standing in the way of a large development," Jay said. "The owner is under pressure to sell it for some reason. Is anyone in any of the partnerships pressuring this owner to sell?"

"No. That's not the way we do business. And, it's not the way that anybody in real estate should be doing business, either."

"Have you ever heard of Jefferson Square?"

"Yes, I have heard of Jefferson Square."

"When the Jefferson Square Company migrated the houses from near the airport to Sultan Road, they promised their residents that their terms of occupation included a path to ownership," Jay said, leading up to his next question. "This promise was broken by Regal Management Associates, who forced the occupants out. Was the partnership involved with forcing people out of their homes?"

"No, it wasn't. I told you already that all the land was acquired through legal and ethical transactions. The company that managed—or should I say mismanaged—those properties is to blame for the people being forced out. We were just there to take advantage of the situation, that's all."

"And that company would be Jefferson Square."

Smithfield looked at Jay without answering, but his smug smile told Jay what his answer really was.

"There have been four people murdered in connection with Renaissance Estates," Jay told him. "The police think it's the work of a professional killer and not some random maniac. Do you know if the mayor is involved with these murders?"

"Absolutely not. I repeat, that's not the way to do business in real estate."

"Can I use you as a source for this part of the story?" Jay said.

"No! I'm not a source at all. We never spoke. And if you quote me, I'll need to make a public denial and perhaps take legal action against the newspaper. I'm sure you understand why I need to remain anonymous."

Jay pondered that for a moment. He broke eye contact momentarily and said, "It must be the serial killer then."

Again, Smithfield did not say a word.

"I want to thank you for your time, Mr. Smithfield," Jay said. Then he got up and left Smithfield sitting alone on the bench.

Karl Brazelton lived in a small, unincorporated part of Los Angeles County, just east of Inglewood. By the time Jay got there, it was after seven-thirty in the evening, and daylight was fading. Further, Jay was completely unfamiliar with the area. He walked up to Brazelton's house and knocked on the door. No one answered. He peered through the window but couldn't see anything since no lights inside were on.

After waiting a few minutes, he decided to walk around to the back of the house to see if there was another door. Indeed, there was, and Jay knocked on the back door to no avail. He looked inside the window for some sign of Brazelton. He noticed a wheelchair ramp that led from the driveway up to the back door that made him certain that he had the right house.

He looked through the window again trying to find Brazelton. Then he saw a man in the living room lying motionless on the floor facedown. He could see an overturned wheelchair behind this person. Stunned, Jay tried to see if the person was still alive. After a few minutes, he pulled out his cell phone and tried to call Aguilar but couldn't reach him at his office. He then called Aguilar's cell phone and left a message when Aguilar did not pick up. Calmly, he left the address in the message and explained that he had been intending to interview Brazelton about Renaissance Estates but had seen him lying motionless on the floor of his living room. When he finished leaving the message, he decided he should call 911. As he turned around, he looked directly at a man with a jet-black shock of hair and droopy eyes, who was standing fifteen feet away.

"Whoa!" Jay said. "You startled me."

The man stood there silently. Something about his appearance and silence alarmed Jay.

"My name is Jay Phillips, and I'm a reporter for the *Daily Journal*," Jay said regaining his composure. "Did you know the man who lived here?"

Without breaking eye contact, the man pulled a switchblade out of his pants pocket and clicked it open.

Jay's eyes widened. He backed away from the house watching the man's every movement. Still backing up, he reached over his shoulder and pulled his skateboard out of his backpack.

The man with the black hair and droopy eyes continued to close in on Jay cornering him against a fence. Jay could not take his eyes off the switchblade. When the man was within striking distance, Jay swung the skateboard with both hands and hit him on the side of the head. With his assailant temporarily dazed, Jay scaled the fence and ran around to the front of the house only to find the man waiting for him by his van. Jay then took off on his skateboard in the other direction.

Jay knew could easily outdistance the assailant on his skateboard if he was following Jay on foot. When he turned the corner at the end of the block, Jay noticed the man with black hair getting into a gray truck and coming after him. Some sharp turns on the skateboard and some hustling through narrow passageways between buildings on foot, briefly helped Jay. He reached Century Boulevard and thought it appeared commercial enough to give him a place to hide. He sped along past the Hollywood Park Casino, trying not to alarm any of the passersby. Then he came upon a mini market in the ground floor of an old building. He ducked inside and slipped down one of the aisles toward the refrigeration units in the rear.

An African American teenager noticed Jay's obvious anxiety and said, "Man, are you OK?"

Jay nodded, but kept a close eye on the door. Sweat was pouring down his face.

The teenager then said, "Pardon my askin', but what's a white boy like you doing down here in my neighborhood?"

Still breathing hard, Jay turned around and said between breaths, "I'm a reporter for the *Daily Journal*. I'm working on a story about four murders. And the guy that did it just chased me in here."

"Four murders?" the teenager said, surprised. "And the guy that did it chased you in here?"

"Yeah, man," Jay said. "I'm really scared."

At that moment "El Puma" came rushing through the front door. He stopped to case the store looking for Jay. When he saw Jay down one of the aisles, he made a mad dash for him. Jay raced around the end of the shelves and started to run up the next aisle trying to get to the exit.

The teenager stepped directly in front of "El Puma's" path. "What the fuck you doin', man?" the teenager said. He was promptly shoved into the shelves behind him, knocking cans and other merchandise onto the floor.

"El Puma" stopped momentarily at the end of the aisle to check which way Jay had gone. He was then knocked on the side of the head by the teenager, who had a can in his hand. He punched the teenager, who dropped the can, but stepped back and put up his fists. Then, "El Puma" saw Jay running toward the exit and raced down the other aisle after him.

Jay ran around the building into the parking lot behind it looking for somewhere to hide. He quickly saw that he was cornered again and out of luck. But "El Puma" didn't come rushing around the corner of the building after him. An eerie quiet set in as he waited. Jay couldn't decide what had happened, and was too terrified to move. He held his breath as he watched the corner of the building. At that moment, he was jumped from behind by "El Puma," who had gone around the building and climbed over the fence from the other side. Jay was knocked to the ground and separated from his only weapon and shield—his skateboard.

"El Puma" clicked open his switchblade again. Holding Jay on the ground, he lifted the blade high into the air to bring it down onto Jay's chest. Jay managed to swiftly kick him in the groin. Momentarily free, Jay rolled over and picked up his skateboard. He got to his knees as "El Puma" leaped at him with his knife raised. Just in time, Jay raised his skateboard and parried "El Puma's" thrust. Swinging the skateboard furiously, he bashed "El Puma" in the head again, this time with the wheels protruding. "El Puma" dropped his knife out of reach a few feet away. He and Jay wrestled for a moment, until "El Puma" recovered the knife and pounced on top Jay with his knee on Jay's chest. He had swung the knife up again, when he was grabbed around the neck from behind and thrown over by the teenager from inside the mini market.

Jay then swatted "El Puma" again with his skateboard making a bloody gash across his forehead. At that moment, a car came screeching around the corner and halted a few yards away. Out jumped Aguilar and Lee.

Surprised, "El Puma" whirled around. Then like the big cat he was named after, he leaped to his feet and bounded on top of a dumpster. From there he clambered back over the fence.

Aguilar had his pistol drawn, and shouted "Détente o dispare!" *Halt or I'll shoot.* But, within seconds, "El Puma" was over to the other side.

Aguilar said to Harry, "Scale the fence. I'm going around the other side of the building." As he ran past Jay, he shouted, "Newsboy, watch the car!"

Harry bounded over the fence just as quickly as "El Puma" had done a few seconds earlier. With his pistol drawn, he looked right and left for him. He saw him running down the street in the other direction, and then saw that Aguilar had blocked his escape. Surrounded by Harry behind him and Aguilar in front, "El Puma" had nowhere to go except across the busy boulevard. Without hesitating he leaped into Century Boulevard trying to cross it. Within a split second, he was hit by a transfer truck that knocked him back onto the sidewalk killing him instantly.

Jay drove the undercover car around the convenience store and joined the detectives for the aftermath of the chase.

"Are you all right Newsboy?" Aguilar said.

"Sergeant Aguilar, I am so totally happy to see you here!" Jay said. "I was scared shitless that I was going to be killed. How'd you find me?"

"We weren't that far away to begin with," Aguilar said. "I got your message and we went to the address you gave me. Then we picked up on a 911 call from a store clerk through the police band that a Mexican was chasing a blond haired, white boy through a convenience store in a predominantly black neighborhood."

Jay took a look at "El Puma" and said, "Well, here's your killer." He then pulled out his cell phone and took a few pictures of the dead body for the next installment of his story.

"Where did he find you?" Aguilar said.

"He was at Brazelton's house. He must have killed him, also," Jay said.

The detectives took Jay's statement about being chased by "El Puma," and also about him finding Brazelton dead. After an ambulance took "El Puma's" body away, Aguilar said, "Come on, Newsboy, I'll buy you a beer."

The two detectives dropped Jay off at his van, and he followed them back to a bar in Harbor City. The drinks were on Aguilar.

After the first round, Jay said, "You know, it's been sometime since I've interviewed you guys for this story. Would you be willing to answer a few of my questions about 'El Puma'? I've got to get another segment out."

Aguilar and Lee looked at each other and then back at Jay. Aguilar said, "Sure, Newsboy, we'll answer some of your questions. We have our limits though, as you know."

"Oh, totally," Jay said. "I'd appreciate hearing any secrets you want to tell me, but I'm not counting on it," he added with a laugh. He set up his recorder.

Jay started by asking about the details surrounding the arrest of Suarez. Aguilar obliged, explaining that Suarez had turned state's evidence and was the reason that they were in the area in the first place. Suarez told them that "El Puma" was headquartered at a nearby refugee center and operated out of the Inglewood/Crenshaw District. Aguilar went on to explain the forensic evidence that implicated Suarez by putting him at the scene of both the nightclub murder and Ben Williams's murder. He also said that Suarez's girlfriend had been arrested again and charged with assault with a deadly weapon on a police officer. Harry even rolled up his sleeve to show Jay where he had been shot by Martinez. Aguilar said that she would also likely be charged with stealing the twenty thousand from Renaissance Estates, based upon the evidence provided by Rudi on the flash drive that Jay had given them.

The interview went on for over half an hour. When Jay ran out of questions, he provided another bombshell for the two detectives.

"I interviewed one of the partners from Regal Management Associates," Jay said, "or actually the Harbor City Partners which is the real name. He refused to be quoted, but he confirmed to me that McGinnis is the managing partner of that firm. That tells me that McGinnis was not only a party to the process of acquiring the land surrounding Sultan Road, but that he was also the driving force behind it. That means he must have been one of the people trying to push Erica Knight into selling Renaissance Estates, although my source wouldn't confirm that. I can tell you that McGinnis had a close relationship with Millwood, probably to the extent that he convinced Millwood to make Renaissance Estates look like it was badly managed. They would need Renaissance Estates to have that appearance in order to persuade HUD to complete the sale of the property.

"I also discovered that Karl Brazelton was one of the key partners, that brings up an interesting question," Jay continued. "Rudi told me that the phone call where she overheard Millwood say, '...kill the bastard!' was with somebody named 'KB.' Do you suppose that person was Karl Brazelton?"

"It has to be. We can find out for sure by checking the phone records," Aguilar said.

"If so, that would mean that Brazelton was the driving force behind having 'El Puma' make the hits on each of the victims."

"We've thought that for some time, Newsboy," Aguilar said. "We just couldn't connect Brazelton to 'El Puma.' We can now, thanks to your research."

"But can you connect McGinnis to Brazelton? I mean, if Brazelton was protecting McGinnis, how do we prove that McGinnis was the kingpin of it all? Jay said.

"We think we've got that covered, but I can't tell you about it just yet," Aguilar said.

After a moment's recollection Jay said, "I'm really grateful I don't have to see that wiry sonofabitch with the droopy eyes again. I might be wrestling with him in my dreams for some time to come.

CHAPTER THIRTY-FIVE

Thanks to the FBI's involvement, Willis Napier now faced a series of federal charges in connection with an extortion case involving a Chicago area Section 8 housing project. He was also charged with unlawful flight to avoid prosecution for murder, to provide leverage for the local DA. Owing to his role as the facilitator of the Renaissance Estates crimes, he was charged with conspiracy to commit murder in the Lisa Nguyen case. After discussing the situation with Richard Frederick, federal prosecutors agreed to give priority to the state and local cases and deal with the federal charges once the more serious murder related charges were settled. Since it was apparent that McGinnis had made an attempt on Napier's life, Frederick worked out a plea deal that turned Napier into state's evidence. He pled guilty to one count of conspiracy to commit murder. But if he would agree to testify against McGinnis, Suarez, and Anita Martinez, he would receive a recommendation of leniency in sentencing, and also imprisonment at a medium security facility.

After a court appearance where his sentence was handed down, Napier was interviewed by Frederick with Carlos Aguilar, Marsha Jackson, David Chen from the California Attorney General's office, and his own attorney. His testimony began with Mayor Andrew McGinnis.

"The whole thing began a long time ago when the Raiders and the Rams both left LA, and there was no NFL team in town," Napier began. "McGinnis thought that for sure a team would return here someday, and he wanted to be the one who owned the land the stadium was built on. He put some real estate people, who had formerly worked for him, on the job of finding the best place for a new football stadium. They came up with a short list, but the one he liked the best was on Sultan Road, north of Harbor City between the 110 and 405 freeways."

"How did he go about acquiring the land on Sultan Road?" Frederick said.

"He formed a group of real estate lawyers into a partnership by the name of Regal Management Associates. He got them to do all the legal filings and manage all the titles and everything, thereby keeping him out of view. He even had the city council push through a law that made it easier to force the former owner into bankruptcy. Then they swooped in and bought up much of the land cheap."

"But he couldn't get his hands around Renaissance Estates," Frederick said.

"That's right. And it was right in the middle of the land he wanted," Napier said.

"How did you get connected with McGinnis?"

"He found out about the Chicago job I worked on. He brought me out here and spent some time feeling me out to see if I was willing to do the same thing again here in LA. After a while, he told me what he wanted from me and sent me over to meet Karl Brazelton, who owned the South Bay

Neighborhood Association. Brazelton would be furnishing the support and resources for all the activities."

"And you agreed to do it for a certain amount of money."

"That's right."

"Did you receive help from any other source?"

"They had a guy on location working in the office at Renaissance Estates."

"What was his name?"

"Brendan Millwood. The company was called Millwood Properties."

"You know that Millwood is dead, don't you?"

"Yeah, but I don't know much about it. I was out of the country when that happened."

"What support did Millwood provide you?"

"Millwood was sort of a facilitator. He worked inside the housing project and provided some help and logistical information. His job was to drive the place into the ground so that the woman who owned it would have to sell it. He told us the best time for…"

Frederick cut Napier off at that remark. "Wait a minute. When you say 'us,' who else do you mean?" he said.

"Brazelton and sometimes Fernando Suarez."

"Your primary role was as the moneyman. How did that work?"

"The scheme was to get money out of the project over to South Bay Neighborhood Association to pay for what McGinnis wanted us to do."

"How did you manage to take money out of the project?"

"Millwood called up Brazelton and said that the receptionist was taking a vacation, and a temporary replacement was needed. This was happening at the beginning of the month, when all the rent money got paid. It provided a great opportunity for us since the receptionist collected most of the rent money. We decided to send in Suarez's girlfriend, and we told her to look for a way to steal as much cash as she could get without getting noticed. She had worked in accounting offices before and knew how records were kept. In the two weeks she worked there, she came away with, I think, about twenty thousand or thereabouts. We kept that in the safe at South Bay," Napier said.

"Suarez's girlfriend is named Anita Martinez, correct?"

"That's right."

"And that was the beginning of a slush fund that provided the money needed to conduct your other activities," Frederick said.

"Yeah, that's right."

"Were there other sources of money for the slush fund?" Frederick said.

"I explained to Millwood that we could pull money out of Renaissance Estates by having South Bay overcharge for their security services. When the check came in to South Bay, I would take it over to the bank and get it cashed. The people at South Bay knew how much was owed to them, and the extra amount went into the safe."

"How did McGinnis contact you to tell you that he wanted someone killed?" Frederick said.

"He would call me and tell me to meet him at the club—that was the Long Beach Athletic Club. We would sit in the sauna or steam room when nobody else was in there, and he would tell me what he wanted."

"What did you do to carry out the hits?" Frederick said.

"I would meet with Brazelton in his office and relay the plan to him and to Suarez, who would sometimes be there."

"Did you figure out the plan? Or did Brazelton?"

"Usually Brazelton, but sometimes Suarez. I had to know about the plan because the victim needed to be maneuvered into the right place," Napier said.

"What caused the hit to be made on Lisa Nguyen?" Frederick said.

"Wasn't she the bookkeeper?"

"Yes."

"The bookkeeper figured out that they were overpaying for the security services. I think she also knew who had stolen the money. She confronted Millwood, who told McGinnis. That put us to work."

"How did she wind up at the specific nightclub that you wanted?"

"She didn't have a boyfriend, but we knew this Vietnamese guy who was about her age. We paid him to get her to go out to the nightclub on a certain night."

"Was his name Randy Vo?"

"I don't know. Suarez dug him up from somewhere."

"What else did Suarez do to manage the hits?"

"Suarez's main job was to handle our man, 'El Puma'. We didn't want him exposed, so Suarez found a way to keep him covered and brought him out when we needed him."

"What was 'El Puma's' real name?"

"Asdrubal Mendoza."

"And you said Suarez kept him covered?"

"Yeah, he kept him in some kind of halfway house for refugees and immigrants. I don't know where it is. I wasn't supposed to know."

"Why was the hit made on Rudi Sirianni?"

"Who's that?"

"She was the person killed in the high-rise condo."

"I didn't know her name. But I found out later that the person there was killed by mistake. The target was the woman who owned Renaissance Estates, only she wasn't there at the time."

"That would be Erica Knight. Why was Ms. Knight a target?"

"I wasn't here when it happened, but I know that McGinnis was getting desperate. He believed that he needed to have all that land before the NFL announced when and where it would return to Los Angeles. If he didn't have the land and they decided to come to Sultan Road, it would cost him an impossible amount of money to get Renaissance Estates. As time went by, he became more and more obsessed with it. He finally thought he would be better off dealing with her estate after her death rather than try to get her to sell."

"What about Brazelton? Suarez was in custody at the time of his murder, and you were still out of the country. How did the hit go down for him?" Frederick said.

Napier thought for a moment. Finally, he said, "I can't finger anybody for that one, but I can tell you that McGinnis had a clerk in his office that he trusted completely. He might have used him for it."

"What is the clerk's name?"

"I don't know what it is. Sorry."

"Did Suarez take an active role in killing any of the victims?" Frederick said.

"No, at least, he was not supposed to," Napier said. "He's a former cop so he knew how to sanitize a murder scene. That's what Brazelton used him for. He wanted Mendoza to do all the killing. That way, Suarez would never face murder charges himself."

"When Ben Williams was murdered, how was that orchestrated?" Frederick said.

"Before I left, Millwood told us that Ben Williams went to visit his daughter at about 4 o'clock most afternoons. We set up the hit to look like a carjacking gone bad."

At that point Frederick turned to Aguilar and said, "Did you tie Mendoza to the murder weapon used on Ben Williams?"

"Yes, forensics did," Aguilar said.

Turning back to Napier, Frederick said, "For the first victim, you hired Maria Maldonado to assault and beat her senseless. Tell us how that worked."

"We wanted the first victim to be killed in what appeared to be a barroom fight. I found this big woman, who was in a car accident and didn't have the money to get her car fixed. I paid her five thousand to start the fight."

"That was just to start the fight and not to beat her to death. Correct?" Frederick said.

"Just start the fight and help push it out into the parking lot. That's all."

"Who else was there on your payroll to help push the fight out into the parking lot?"

"Anita Martinez."

"What was Anita Martinez's job?"

"She was there to make sure that the fight got started. We thought we could frame the big woman for murder if the victim died in the parking lot. Martinez would have been useful if that would have happened."

Frederick then addressed the entire meeting. "I've finished with all the questions I have for today. Does anyone else have a question for Mr. Napier?" he said.

Marsha Jackson had a question for Napier. "Was DeShawn Walker from HUD in any way involved in the scam to take money from Renaissance Estates, or in any of the murders themselves?"

"HUD? Oh, not a chance," Napier said. "McGinnis said specifically to keep HUD out of the way. He was so afraid of the feds he didn't even want to hear the word 'HUD' mentioned."

"Was Walker ever bribed from the slush fund?" Jackson said.

"No way. Something like that would have brought the FBI right down on our asses, since it was a federally backed housing project."

Aguilar asked the next question. "Was there ever a hit on the reporter for the *Daily Journal* that broke the story?"

"Not while I was around," Napier said.

"Wasn't there a hit on *you* when you left the country?" Aguilar said.

"Suarez and Mendoza tried to kill me when I made bail and left for the airport."

"Was McGinnis behind that also? Aguilar said.

"It had to be McGinnis," Napier said.

"If it was McGinnis, who was sending you money while you were in the Bahamas? Aguilar said.

"It was Karl," Napier said.

"You mean, Karl Brazelton," Aguilar said.

"That's right," Napier said.

The interview concluded, and Napier was returned to custody to await his next court appearance. Frederick, Aguilar, Jackson, and Chen remained in the conference room to discuss what evidence they had gathered against McGinnis."

"Well, we've got McGinnis calling out three hits that resulted in murder," Frederick said. "There are two more hits that we can't pin on him, plus an attempted murder of our star witness. I believe our chances of convicting him on those other two are very slim, unless Suarez decides to help us. Turning to Aguilar, he said, "What have we gotten from Suarez so far?"

"He can explain Mendoza's and Brazelton's involvement," Aguilar said. "I think we can get him to give up the guy that got Mendoza into the high rise for the Sirianni killing."

"Did he tie McGinnis into Brazelton's or Millwood's murders?"

"He hasn't yet," Aguilar said. "He was in custody when Brazelton was killed, and he likely won't talk about Millwood's murder, as it could result in another count against him.

"Did you promise him anything?" Frederick said.

"I told him that you'd be the one that who would do that for me."

"He sounds like a tough piece of work," Frederick said. "What made him knuckle under?"

"It helped that we had forensic evidence to show him when we talked to him," Aguilar said. "He did give up Mendoza's whereabouts after I told him that Anita Martinez could be in jail for a long time. We continued talking and he tied up some other loose ends."

"What loose ends, exactly?" Frederick said.

"He told me that the nightclub victim was still alive when they took her away in the truck," Aguilar said. "He said she was unconscious, but he could see that she was still breathing."

"She still might have been fatally wounded at that point, though," Frederick said.

"He also said that Mendoza took a large rock and smashed it into her upper body and head," Aguilar went on to say.

"Well, that's likely to keep Suarez away from a murder two charge, as well. Did Anita Martinez cooperate?" Frederick said.

"No. She wouldn't cooperate the first time we interrogated her, either," Aguilar said.

"What about Maria Maldonado?"

"I'm satisfied that she didn't kill Lisa Nguyen—only beat her senseless, that's all," Aguilar said. "And without her help, we wouldn't have gotten to Napier. If there is anything you can do for her, we would be willing to support it."

"I can go back to court and ask for her release based on time served. We'll still need her for the main event, though." Frederick said.

Then David Chen asked Frederick a question. "Speaking of the main event, how do we proceed against McGinnis?"

"Let me ask you first, Mr. Chen, to explain to this group what the State Attorney General's position is in this inquiry," Frederick said.

"We've been privy to copies of a large body of evidence furnished by the FBI that paints a picture of corruption at Renaissance Estates pretty well," Chen said. "We are interested in finding out why the LAPD believes that it cannot conduct a totally impartial investigation of the mayor. Perhaps Sergeant Aguilar could answer that one for us?"

As the focus of the meeting turned to Aguilar, he said, "On several occasions I explained to my boss, Captain

Kreider, that this case involved other persons than just the killers, meaning somebody was orchestrating it. He refused to believe that any of the evidence I showed him pointed to a wider plot. He wouldn't discuss any part of the investigation that didn't involve only the killers. I made sure he saw the connection to South Bay Neighborhood Association and the slush fund. But he attempted to tie my hands when it came to pursuing them.

"Another time when I explained to Kreider that we had circumstantial evidence that pointed to the mayor, he told me specifically to stick with finding the killer and leave anything that might lead to city hall with him. As a result, we had to rely on the investigative reporting of Jason Phillips of the *LA Daily Journal*. He was able to put together that body of evidence that pointed to the mayor."

"I see," Frederick said. "OK, Mr. Chen, we'll copy you in on everything that goes on. Sergeant Aguilar, I'm going to ask you to bring any further evidence you might find that does implicate the mayor directly to me first, and only to inform Captain Kreider afterwards. I'll explain to Chief Gutierrez that we'll need to work around Kreider in this case."

Frederick then turned to Marsha Jackson and said, "Ms. Jackson, what does the federal government want from our star witness?"

"We're interested in cleaning up the case in Chicago that Napier mentioned," Jackson said. "We want him to explain in more detail how he embezzled money from a Section 8 property up there, and also more details about the extortion scam here."

"I spoke recently with two federal prosecutors who said that they were willing to wait with the Chicago case until the murder charges out here in Los Angeles were settled," Frederick said. "Do you see any other charges that we would expect the federal government to file against Napier?"

"Not unless he decides not to cooperate with us," Jackson said. "If that is the case, we will add the unlawful flight charges. We're basically interested in tightening our internal controls with HUD operations, and we're looking for his help in this matter."

"All right, we're keeping you in the loop as well," Frederick said.

As this inquiry started to wind down, Frederick said, "Does anyone have any other questions at this time?"

"What's to become of the South Bay Neighborhood Association?" Aguilar said. "I don't think the LAPD will move on them now that this case is resolving, and the owner of the association is dead."

Frederick thought about that for a moment and said, "We could get the city auditor's office to see if there are any tax-related discrepancies. An audit, might discover other criminal activities with the association's finances. With the death of the owner, it isn't clear if they will continue to be an ongoing business enterprise or not."

"What will our next steps be, Mr. Frederick?" Chen said.

"First let me run down what we have against McGinnis," Frederick said.

He then proceeded to go over the entire case point by point against the mayor, showing how McGinnis arranged at least three murders and one attempted murder. The motive was tied to an effort to cover up how he was trying to acquire the entire parcel of land that surrounded Sultan Road. The evidence was in the form of paperwork that showed the existence of shell companies that had been set up to disguise the unethical, and often illegal, actions taken to remove homeowners from their homes, and then clear those houses from the property. He further went on to explain how McGinnis had hired henchmen to carry out his plans including defrauding a federal housing sponsored project by using a criminal organization that was operating as a legitimate business to extort funds for illegal use.

In conclusion Frederick said, “We’re going to sidestep a grand jury in favor of a pretrial hearing in front of a judge. We’ll bring our evidence and our star witnesses into court and take it from there.”

To those gathered for the meeting Frederick said, “Thank you all for coming.”

CHAPTER THIRTY-SIX

Rudi's murder hit Erica especially hard. It was not only an ever more sensual romantic relationship that was suddenly destroyed, but Rudi was also Erica's last friend and ally at Renaissance Estates. She was now effectively cut off from her life's work and left with virtually no means to survive. She went to her doctor for some pills to keep her from coming apart. Her doctor persuaded her to stop drinking immediately before taking any strong anti-depressant treatment. She also required Erica to visit her twice per month to get the prescriptions renewed. In time, Erica began to heal, but her biggest boost came from an unlikely source. DeShawn Walker called Erica and asked her to come to his office as soon as possible.

Erica contacted Joyce Mitchell, her attorney, for advice on how to proceed with Walker. Joyce told her that this might mean that a settlement to HUD's lawsuit against her was in the works. Erica pondered that for a moment and then decided that she had nothing to lose by talking, so she agreed to a meeting with Walker.

It was two days later when Erica and Joyce sat down in front of Walker's desk without anyone else present.

"I'm glad you could make it here as soon as you did," Walker began. "This meeting will be a lot more hospitable than the last one, because I have some important news to tell you. But before we get into that, I want to apologize for what has transpired between us over the last several months."

Erica and Joyce took a look at each other and then sat forward to listen intently.

"I thought that the problems taking place at Renaissance Estates were created by you during your tenure as property manager," Walker said. "But after reading the police reports and newspaper accounts of events, I see that it was Millwood who was responsible all along. It also appears that he was working the other side of the street to enrich himself. What's more, it was my fault for being duped by him into thinking exactly what he wanted me to think. I now believe that he only wanted to ensure that I would approve any sale of the property that would enrich him further.

"My goal has only been to make Renaissance Estates run more smoothly so that it would continue to make money like it did before. It's my fault for not getting out to visit Renaissance Estates more often than I did. I wound up being fooled by someone I trusted who had done good things for me in the past. Millwood was a terrific help in turning around other Section 8 housing projects that had managerial problems. I am most surprised that he didn't work out the same way for Renaissance Estates. I'm hoping that you'll accept my apology. And I also want to give you these documents that conclude the government's legal action in your favor."

Walker handed a folder of legal papers to Erica and said, "Please take a moment to look through the documents and ask any questions you may have."

Erica handed the folder to Joyce, who spent a few minutes looking through Walker's paperwork. "Then you're dropping the lawsuit with prejudice?" Joyce finally said.

"That's correct. Or perhaps we should say that the government is dropping the lawsuit. That's actually the case."

"What does 'with prejudice' mean?" Erica said.

Joyce provided the answer. "It means that the lawsuit cannot be opened again," she said. "It's forever dead—there's no more issue for the courts to decide."

Then Walker said, "I would like to add that Millwood Property Management has been fired from Renaissance Estates. This may seem to be moot since Millwood himself is now deceased. I wanted to make an official separation a part of the healing process between you and me."

"I see," Erica said.

"At the moment, there is no manager at Renaissance Estates," Walker said. "I had to take someone from this office and send him there to run the place until I can get the right management to take it over."

Erica continued to listen intently.

"I want to ask you to reapply to be property manager," he said.

"You what?" Erica said, her jawed dropping.

"That's right," Walker said. "I want you to apply for the job. There's nobody more qualified than you to do it. If you agree to apply, I will personally walk your application through the approval process so I can get you reinstated as soon as possible."

"I don't know what to say," Erica said. This was the last thing she thought she would ever hear from Walker.

Walker smiled and said, "Well, why don't you say you'll take it? I'm personally happy to have you back, and I'm looking forward to renewing our formerly good working relationship."

Erica was still astonished. She turned toward Joyce and gave her a confused look.

"You're in the clear, as far as this legal paperwork is concerned," Joyce said.

Erica was about to answer when Walker spoke again. "I will also put together a refinancing package, backed by HUD, to provide you with some capital to upgrade the place. You might even consider adding more units on the spare strip of land behind it.

Astonished, Erica replied, "All right, I'll take it. When do we get started?"

"Here's some more paperwork," Walker said as he handed her a large manila envelope.

"Yes, I know," Erica said, with a laugh. "It wouldn't be the government if there weren't lots of paperwork. And to think that I believed that all this mess was due to my breaking off our relationship a few years ago."

Walker let out a chuckle and said, "Oh, that's long over. I'm married now with two kids. Besides, I would never hold something like that against you in a business matter like this.

I just don't think that we could ever have been happily married anyway."

"Well, why is that?" Erica said smiling, although she was genuinely interested to hear the answer.

"We'd fight too much!" he replied.

CHAPTER THIRTY-SEVEN

Before Richard Frederick took his case against Mayor McGinnis into a courtroom, He turned what he had over to Raphael Gutierrez, the LAPD chief of police. Gutierrez made a thorough review of both the case as it was set down in the arrest warrant and the notes of the meeting Frederick had held with Napier. He also conferenced with David Chen from the California Attorney General's office, his own attorney, and other law enforcement personnel connected to the case. The conference became a symposium about the conduct of Captain William Kreider, Sergeant Aguilar's boss.

Gutierrez's attention was particularly piqued when Chen said that the LAPD might not be able to conduct an independent investigation of the mayor owing to the fact that Captain Kreider was in the way.

Gutierrez was further upset when the meeting notes mentioned that Kreider would not pursue South Bay Neighborhood Association or any of its employees. He considered it an embarrassment that two of his detectives had to rely upon a news reporter in order to gain insight into the source of the malfeasance. It was no secret to him that Kreider also had been a personal friend of McGinnis's for many years, and that his being appointed to the rank of captain was likely due to this friendship. He did not see any concrete evidence that would point to the need to investigate Kreider. Instead he decided to order Kreider to be the one who would personally execute the arrest warrant on McGinnis. Once that was done, he would push Kreider into retirement.

Frederick prevailed in the preliminary hearing, even though two of the main henchmen, Brazelton and Mendoza, were dead. McGinnis was charged with three counts of murder for hire and one count of attempted murder. In a trial that was televised locally and covered by the media across the nation, McGinnis was found guilty on all counts and was subsequently sentenced to life in prison. Fernando Suarez and Anita Martinez were found guilty of conspiracy to commit murder and attempted murder of a police officer respectively.

In an ironic twist of fate, the NFL decided that the St. Louis Rams would be the team permitted to relocate to Los Angeles. The site chosen for the new stadium would be the old racetrack in Inglewood. The owner of the Rams would use his own copious resources to build a new stadium and to develop the surrounding land (that he already owned) into retail stores and restaurants, parking structures, office buildings, and housing.

Jay was forever grateful for Dylan's help and mentoring while writing the story. Dylan was happy just to be doing his "summer" job while the Lakers were in their off season. His research about the NFL's stadium requirements, and his help in tying the vacant land along Sultan Road to the mayor, proved to be invaluable to Jay's story.

Jay saved all his notes and transcribed all his recorded interviews. Working together, he and Dylan put the events down into a book that chronicled how the situation began, how it unfolded, and how it brought down the mayor of Los Angeles. Even before the book was published, the subject matter drew substantial attention in Hollywood, where offers of movie rights began to materialize.

Sergeant Carlos Aguilar was decorated for tracking and killing the serial killer known as "El Puma." He was further promoted to lieutenant and given an office downtown, where a special detail of detectives worked under him. Officer Harry Lee was promoted to sergeant and became the lead of a team of detectives working the Koreatown area of Los Angeles.

With Erica Knight back as manager, Renaissance Estates returned quickly to profitability and became the poster child for all other Section 8 housing projects in Southern California. In time, the barren land along Sultan Road surrounding Renaissance Estates began to flourish as office buildings, industrial complexes, and residential communities sprouted up in the area.

Millwood Property Management, had provided Rudi Sirianni with a generous life insurance policy as a perk for working with them. Upon her death, two hundred thousand dollars was sent to her parents in Mosul, Iraq, that enabled them, along with her younger sister, to evacuate the terrorist-controlled area and immigrate to Los Angeles.

On a warm, breezy Sunday afternoon at the pier in Huntington Beach, Carlos Aguilar and his family were enjoying a day trip to the coastline. While the kids splashed in the waves, Aguilar went up onto the pier to meet a friend he hadn't seen in a while. A short time later author Jason Phillips got out of his new SUV and walked up to the pier to meet him.

"Lieutenant Aguilar!" Jay said.

"Newsboy!" Aguilar said with a huge smile on his face and his hand extended for a handshake.

"Man, it's good to see you," Jay said pumping Aguilar's hand. "I want to congratulate you on your promotion. Here, this is for you." He handed Aguilar a copy of his and Dylan's newly published book entitled, *'Lethal Office: One Mayor's Twisted Dream.'*

"Well, what's this?" Aguilar asked as he looked the book over. He opened it to the dedication page where his name prominently stood out.

"That book is the whole saga written up. Everything. From my notes to your police reports and other legal documents."

"Terrific," Aguilar said. He thumbed through the pages briefly and then said, "It looks like a tremendous piece of work."

"I want to wish you the best of luck, lieutenant, with your new position," Jay said. His posture, stylish casual dress, and dignified demeanor all told Aguilar that Jay had finally grown up. "I hope this book explains what you had to go through to catch that serial killer and break up that criminal organization."

"Did you make me into a star?" Aguilar said with a grin.

"I didn't need to," Jay said. "You were a star all along. I don't know how anybody else could have done what you did. I don't think I'll ever be able to thank you enough for saving my life."

"Hey, it's just a part of my job. I'm only sorry that I couldn't save a few more of those other people who were killed. I hope, by the way, that you understood your efforts in investigative reporting helped us break the case open."

"I wouldn't have had it any other way."

"Say, ah, how come you didn't come here on your skateboard?" Aguilar said, still grinning.

"We all have to grow up at some time or another, lieutenant," Jay said with a modest smile.

"Well, if you look behind you, I think you could use it right now," Aguilar said.

Jay turned around and looked down the pier. Walking directly at him was an attractive, young woman wearing a brightly colored dress that fluttered back and forth in the breeze. With her long golden hair tossed back behind her head, she walked in high heels toward Jay staring directly into his eyes, just as a leopardess would stalk her prey.

Jay looked back at Aguilar and said, "It's been good to see you, lieutenant. But I think I'm going to be busy for a while. Another 'Puma' just showed up! But this one's my better half."

"Good luck to you, Jason," Aguilar said using his correct name for the first time in their business relationship since the day they had met in the morgue.

"You can call me 'Jay'," Jay said, as they shook hands firmly for a long time.

The woman walked up to Jay and wrapped her left arm around his upper back. She cradled his cheek with her right hand and then kissed him on the lips. Arm in arm they walked together back down the pier toward a life of happiness.

CPSIA information can be obtained
at www.ICGtesting.com
Printed in the USA
LVHW022000260323
742648LV00007B/202

9 781647 186951